The CHERRYWOOD Murders

PENNY BLACKWELL

ACCENT

First published in 2023 by Headline Accent
An imprint of HEADLINE PUBLISHING GROUP

1

Cataloguing in Publication Data is available from the British Library

ISBN 978 1 0354 0008 9

Typeset in 11.75/15.75pt Dante MT Std by Jouve (UK), Milton Keynes

Printed and bound in Great Britain by Clays Ltd, Elcograf S.p.A.

HEADLINE PUBLISHING GROUP
An Hachette UK Company
Carmelite House
50 Victoria Embankment
London EC4Y 0DZ

www.headline.co.uk
www.hachette.co.uk

For the Horan twins, Mary and Tessie.

Prologue

Nosy cow.

Clemmie was terrified for a moment that she might actually have uttered the words aloud. Her hand flew to her mouth and a brief, high-pitched giggle bubbled from her.

She shouldn't say that. Shouldn't even think it, no matter what state she'd just found her drawer in. If you can't say something nice then don't say anything at all, Mother used to tell them when they were children. Clemmie may not be good – sometimes, when she lay awake at night, she worried she might actually be downright wicked – but she did try to live her life in a spirit of Christian charity.

She shivered, pulling her cardigan tighter. The sun was going down.

Not that Mother had said or done many nice things herself, when she'd been alive. But that hadn't been her fault. She was like Prue – she couldn't help what life had made her, any more than Clemmie could suddenly stop being the person it had made her.

And Prue had really been very good to her since Mother had been gone. Yes, very good. If she'd pressed to sell Ling

Cottage, Clemmie could be in some poky flat now – in a grim concrete high-rise, perhaps; the sort of place the lonely went to die. She had no savings of her own to offer to buy Prue's half of the house.

But Prue had been kind, as far as someone like Prue was capable of showing kindness. It was ungrateful of Clemmie to feel otherwise. Although perhaps kind wasn't quite the right word for Prue. It was too warm a word for someone like her, someone who was practical to the point of austerity and unemotional to the point of—

Heck, and she was doing it again. What on earth was wrong with her this evening?

'You're becoming bitter, Clemency Ackroyd,' she muttered. 'Just a bitter, sour old lady. Aren't you, my girl?'

Clemmie reached up to grasp her St Christopher medal, fumbling in the folds of the thick knitted muffler she'd slung around her neck in a futile attempt to keep out the chill. Finally she caught hold of it, pressing it between her fingers until the little figure and his child burden were printed on the tips. She felt jittery, for some reason. Like something was coming.

It was always chilly in Ling Cottage, no matter the weather outside. Tonight was a mild, moonless evening in late March, yet Clemmie was shrouded in woollen layers as if it was winter. The house harboured a damp sort of cold that seemed to get into your very essence – into your bones, your blood, your soul.

Clemmie frowned and looked round, convinced she'd heard something. Prue had left a short while ago to drive the last of the Women's Guild ladies into the village, no doubt then being persuaded inside for tea, since she still hadn't returned home. Although the village was little more than a mile away, on nights like tonight, when the moors that surrounded the house were swallowed up by the darkness, Ling Cottage could feel very far from civilisation indeed.

'Hello?' she called. 'Is somebody th—'

A feline figure slunk from the darkness and wove itself around her feet, purring.

'Oh. It's you, puss.' Clemmie bent painfully to tickle her old tom Nelson between the ears and he rewarded her with a cold nose pressed against her calf.

It felt comforting, that bulk of warm fur against her skin, but Nelson was soon bored and off to search for new adventures. Clemmie watched him pad away and went back to rearranging the contents of her little drawer in the sideboard.

Her coin collection on the left, nestled into layers of filmy tissue paper inside an old tea tin. Her papers beside it, carefully arranged into piles of letters, bills, receipts. Old notepads and memorandum books she ought to have thrown away years ago. But then you never knew, did you, if you might need them again?

Now, what had she been thinking about? Something to do with . . . oh, Prue, yes.

Clemmie remembered what her sister had said to her, the day they'd buried Mother. 'We're two old maids now, Clem. We need to take care of one another.'

How Clemmie hated that term, *old maid*! So old-fashioned

and judgemental. She wished Prue wouldn't describe them that way.

Except, whispered the spiteful little girl who would insist upon talking in her ear, *Prue is such a very old-maidy sort of person, isn't she?*

So the decision had been made. With Mother gone, Prue had installed herself back at Ling Cottage, and life had carried on.

And Prue was right, Clemmie told herself as she moved a stack of letters – all opened once and carefully resealed – back into their correct place. It was good that they should keep each other company. They were in their mid-seventies now. The age of love affairs had long passed and they were all the family each had. Loneliness in old age was a terrible thing.

But oh, it drove her *mad*, the constant fiddling and prying! Prue could be such a busybody; she'd been so from a child. So many times, Clemmie had had to rescue some precious possession from the bin after Prue had decided it needed to go, and she knew her sister went through her private things. Her drawers were never in quite the same order when she returned from shopping. Clemmie could tell Prue had treated herself to a good rummage earlier, while she'd been out buying fairy cakes for the Women's Guild meeting they'd hosted this evening.

She lifted a yellowing letter from her pile and frowned. It looked as though . . . could it have been? The colouring on the lip of the upper flap looked different. As though the seal had been broken, then regummed and stuck back down.

No. She wouldn't, surely. Clemmie knew Prue was ruthless in her drive to clear the cottage of what she snippily referred to as 'tat' and 'clutter', but to open Clemmie's letters . . .

Well, that was crossing the line. Going through her letters – her private papers! Clemmie slammed the drawer of the mahogany cabinet shut, relishing the satisfying *thunk* it made as it slid back into place.

Thunk . . .

White pain blossomed in Clemmie's brain, casting its roots far down into her body, and she heard herself scream.

That one, she thought as she stumbled on to her hands and knees, had been a lot less satisfying.

With an effort she pulled her fogged vision upwards to her attacker, standing over her with weapon poised to strike again. But the numbing pain was too great for surprise as she stared into familiar eyes.

The next blow came. And then another, darkness dogging its heels, and . . . oh dear. Such a lot of red, red blood, soaking into Mother's Turkish rug.

Prue did so hate mess.

Chapter 1

'It's a bad business, this,' Neil Hobson said soberly as Tess poured his pint. He nodded to the local paper on the bar, bearing the latest report on the police investigation into Clemmie Ackroyd's murder. 'Never thought I'd see the like.'

Tess left his pint to settle. 'I know. A murder, in Cherrywood! The worst crime I can remember happening around here was when Rita Sullivan was caught cycling without lights. Who on earth could have it in them to hurt Aunty Clemmie?'

The murder of the softly spoken former nursery teacher, affectionately known to those she had taught as 'Aunty', had shaken Cherrywood to its core. Clemmie had been a sweet old lady with a kind word for everyone, and it made no sense at all that someone could have wanted her dead.

'You've not heard then?' Neil asked, one eye on his pint as Tess topped it up.

'Heard what? There's not been an arrest?'

'Yes, this morning. Not only that, he's been charged – Terry Braithwaite, Fred's youngest. Robbery gone wrong, or that's what police are giving out.'

Tess frowned. 'They've solved the case that quickly? It can't be right, surely.'

'Why not? You know better than anyone that he was always a wrong 'un, Terry Braithwaite. Won't be his first time inside.'

'I know, but . . . murder?' Tess said. 'Police can't have investigated thoroughly in a month.'

Neil shrugged. 'All that means is it must've been an open and shut case. Nice to be able to sleep easy again, eh?'

'Yes,' Tess said vaguely, putting his pint down on the bar. 'I suppose so.'

Neil paid for his drink and went back to his table while Tess lapsed into a thoughtful silence – until a moment later, when the door to the Star and Garter opened and Raven walked in. Tess groaned as her best friend joined her at the bar.

'I was hoping you'd forget,' she said.

'Of course I didn't forget, darling. Gin. Double.'

Tess sighed and did as she was told, pouring a double measure from one of the optics before throwing in some ice and a slice of lemon. No tonic. Raven didn't approve of watering down perfectly good spirits with anything as vulgar as mixers.

'You're not really going to make me do this dreadful thing, are you, Rave?'

'Trust me, you'll be thanking me later.' Raven gave her gin a suspicious sniff. 'Hang on. What brand is this?'

Tess cast a look behind her at the spirit optic. 'Tanqueray. That's all right for her ladyship's refined palette, isn't it?'

Raven sniffed it again. 'It bloody isn't Tanqueray, it's Morrison's own. Ian and Bev must've been refilling the bottle with a cheaper brand.'

Tess shook her head. 'How do you *do* that? I've never known anyone else who could identify gin brands just from the smell.'

'Years of practice, darling.' She swallowed a mouthful of her drink. 'Anyway, never mind what brand it is right now. I'm just grateful for some Dutch courage before I have to make polite chitchat with Grandmother in an hour.'

'You know, Rave, we could just not go.'

Raven sighed besottedly. 'You wouldn't say that if you'd seen Sam.'

'I can't believe I'm joining the Cherrywood Women's Guild to help you pull,' Tess muttered. 'Of all the places to pick up men.'

'We're not joining. We'll just go to this one meeting.'

'Hmm. If they let us off that easily.'

Tess had a very specific idea of what Cherrywood Women's Guild meetings must be like. There was barely a member under sixty, with the group consisting largely of the more terrifying variety of older village lady. In Tess's mind the meetings resembled a scene from *The Night of the Living Dead*, only with knitting. Her general feeling was that if she ended up joining the Guild at thirty and committing herself to jam-making and cat-collecting for the rest of her time on earth, then she might as well go straight to the churchyard and start digging herself a spot.

'Sam's worth it, Tessie, honestly,' Raven said, flicking out her black bob. 'I defy you not to melt in a puddle at the man's feet. Hiring him might be the best thing my gran ever did for me.' She lifted an eyebrow. 'Except I forgot, sorry. You've sworn off men for life.'

'Not life. I might think about getting out on the dating scene again when I hit seventyish.'

'Seriously, it's been a year. You can't write yourself off just because some greasy London sort did you wrong.'

'I bloody can,' Tess said, scowling. 'This time eighteen months ago, I had a boyfriend, a job with great pay and prospects, an exciting life in the big city . . .' She lifted the split ends of her brown hair, which she'd accidentally spilt a bit of someone's pint on earlier. 'Now look at me. I'm stuck doing minimum-wage work in the same dull Yorkshire village I grew up in, I'm sharing a place with you that only barely crosses the line from "closet" to "flat", I stink of John Smith's and the highlight of my social calendar is going to a Women's Guild meeting.'

'Come on, admit it. For all your whinging, there's a part of you that's glad to be home. Me and Oliver are here, aren't we?'

Tess summoned a smile. 'I did miss you guys when I was down south.'

'I don't see what's so great about London,' Raven said. 'People selling sheds they've sloshed a bit of Farrow and Ball over for a million quid plus and calling them des res maisonettes. Over a tenner a pint in every bar. Cherrywood isn't so bad – at least you can afford to live in it.'

Tess glanced behind her at the brass plaque mounted

above the bar, engraved with the pub name over the slogan 'Ye Olde Traditionale Englishe Pube'. She grimaced. It was hard to take yourself seriously when you worked in a Traditionale Englishe Pube.

'It's just such a big step down, going from PA at a London insurance firm to pulling pints in a backwater country pub,' she said, propping her chin on her fist. 'I mean, career-trajectory-wise I feel like a total failure.'

'You're not a failure. You're just . . . regrouping.'

'More like I'm stuck in a rut. Let's face it, I've been here a year and I've had zero luck finding anything else. I'm unemployable anywhere but behind the bar in an Englishe pube.'

'Oh, rubbish. You need to cut out this "poor me" stuff and give yourself a kick up the bum.' Raven frowned as the strains of something that might loosely be described as music drifted through from the function room. 'Darling, what is that godawful noise?'

'"Dancing Queen", I think.'

'It sounds like a moose being waterboarded.'

'It's Beverley and the am-dram gang,' Tess said. 'They're using the function room to rehearse their summer production of *Mamma Mia*. Coming soon to a village hall near you.'

'You mean after the Shakespeare in the Park travesty last year, Bouncing Bev's still soldiering on? Sweet Baby Jesus.'

Tess nodded to the door of the pub. 'Speaking of which . . .'

A lanky, fair-haired young man in a clerical shirt and dog

collar had just come in. He made a beeline for where Tess was serving, pulled up a stool and slumped face-first against the bar.

'Pint of Prozac and a gun please, Tessie.'

'What's up, Oliver?' Raven asked, giving the vicar's head a sympathetic pat. 'You didn't catch Peggy Bristow helping herself to the communion wine again?'

'Miss Ackroyd,' he muttered. 'She's home. And she's worse than ever.'

Raven shot a look at Tess. 'Prue Ackroyd's back in Ling Cottage?'

'She can't stay away for ever,' Tess said.

'Yes, but it's only been a month. There are some pretty horrific memories waiting there for her. I don't know why she doesn't put the place up for sale.'

'After Aunty Clemmie had her head bashed in in the study? Would you buy it?'

'Good point,' Raven said.

Tess grabbed a glass and started pumping Oliver a pint of best. 'Did you two hear about Terry Braithwaite?'

'That they've charged him for the murder?' Raven nodded. 'It's all over the village.'

'What do you think of that?'

'It's good, isn't it? People can feel safe again now they know the person who did it is locked away. And I suppose there's a sort of closure for us, as a community.'

'I don't know, guys. It doesn't sit right with me.'

'Why not?' Oliver asked, still facedown against the bar.

'It just feels too . . . neat, I suppose. Too easy.'

'Tessie, you need to stop watching repeats of *Murder, She Wrote*,' Raven said as she finished her gin.

'I just want to be sure justice is being done, that's all. Aunty Clemmie might be not much more than a statistic to the police – just an insignificant old lady who was in the wrong place at the wrong time – but she meant a lot to this village, didn't she? She taught half of Cherrywood when we were nursery tots, the three of us included. I want to know whoever did this to her is going to be punished for it.'

'I'm sure the police know what they're doing,' Oliver said. 'They must have plenty of evidence against Terry to charge him.'

'I suppose.' But there was something still niggling Tess. Some sixth sense that said things weren't quite right.

'I wonder if she'll be there tonight,' Raven said. 'Prue Ackroyd, I mean.'

'Why, what's tonight?' Oliver asked.

Tess pulled a face. 'Raven's forcing me to go to a Women's Guild meeting. This sexy new gardener her gran hired is giving a talk and I've been recruited for wingman duties.'

'You should see him, Ol. He's an angel,' Raven said in a voice that was more than half sigh. 'I think he's The One, you guys. Baby-making genes if I ever saw them. I knew it the minute I spotted him raking leaves with his shirt off.'

'You know, as a metaphor, angels aren't all they're cracked up to be,' Oliver said. 'The cherubim are ugly buggers. Bodies covered in eyes, according to Ezekiel.'

Tess grimaced. 'Covered in *eyes*? Well that's the stuff of nightmares. Cheers, Ol.'

'All right, smartarse, then he's got abs like a Chippendale and a fully biteable pair of buttocks,' Raven told Oliver. 'Are you and Ezekiel happy with that description?'

'Ecstatic,' Oliver mumbled to the bar. 'The image of you biting some poor lad on the backside is the only thing that gets me through evensong.'

Tess sighed. 'Depressed vicars and sex-crazed heiresses. Another day, another dollar.' She tugged at the back of Oliver's collar to make him lift his head and slid his pint to him. 'Here you go, Ol. Get that down you and tell us what Miss Ackroyd's been doing to make life at the vicarage a living hell.'

Oliver took a pull on his beer to fortify himself.

'Well, she turned up at church this morning, sitting in her and Aunty Clemmie's usual pew like nothing had happened,' he said. 'Paler, but as frosty as ever. Then after the service, she asked if she could come see me at the vicarage this afternoon.'

'And?' Raven said, leaning towards him.

'I thought she'd want to talk about her sister. I was flattered, to be honest. I mean, I know that's the last thing I should be thinking when I've got a bereaved parishioner in need of spiritual guidance,' he said, flushing. 'But ever since I was given this parish, it's felt like the old guard at St Stephen's haven't taken me seriously. Everyone still sees me as little Oliver, who was our paperboy, and his old man used to repair the telly when it went on the blink and his mum worked down the bakery. Miss Ackroyd's the worst of the lot.'

Raven shuddered. 'She always was. The Beast of Cherrywood Primary.'

'Exactly. To her I'm the same snot-nosed eight-year-old who doodled willies in his exercise books.' He took another deep swallow of his pint and stifled a burp. 'She's just got this look on her, you know? Like it's a wonder an idiot like me can tell one end of a baby from the other and doesn't dunk them in the font arse-first.'

'She looks at everyone like that, Ol,' Tess pointed out.

'It's just a lot to live up to,' Oliver muttered, half unconsciously zipping up his fleece to cover his dog collar. 'Being a young vicar's hard enough without working in the village you grew up in. This is exactly why vicars never apply for their home parishes. A prophet's never respected in his hometown and all that.'

'So why did you?'

He shrugged. 'Suppose I got attached to the place.'

'Miss Ackroyd must respect you a bit if she came to you for bereavement advice,' Raven said.

'Except she didn't. I just assumed. What she actually wanted was to tell me off about the bloody KJV.' He glanced upwards. 'Sorry.'

'The what?' Tess said.

'The KJV. King James Version of the Bible. We've dropped it from the ladies' Bible study group in favour of a newer translation and she's not happy.' He winced. 'She's *really* not happy.'

'Gave you a bollocking, did she?'

'I thought she was going to yank me back to school by the

ear and put me in Naughty Boy Corner.' Oliver's eyes had fixed on the doorway to the bar storeroom, just behind Tess. 'Um, who's that, by the way?'

Tess glanced over her shoulder at the pretty, tawny-haired girl refilling the peanut dispensers. 'New barmaid – Tammy McDermot. She's taken Emma's old job.'

'Has she?' Oliver said, not removing his gaze.

'Oh God, is it that time of year already?' Raven muttered.

'What time of year?'

'The time of year when you develop a graphically unrequited crush on some girl, spend weeks getting up the nerve to talk to her, only to wimp out and end up crying into a bottle of wine at our place.'

'Well. I like to fall in love over the summer. It gives me something to be miserable about come autumn.'

'You've got no excuse to avoid talking to her this time,' Tess said. 'She's about to relieve my shift. You can fill her in on your VKJ woes while you finish your pint.'

'KJV.'

'Whatever.' She raised her voice. 'Tam! I'm going to get off now. Will you be OK on your own?'

Tammy came through and smiled at her. 'I'll be fine, Tess. You go have a good time.'

'I'm not sure a good time is really going to be on the cards, are you?' Tess said, pulling a face.

'You never know, it might be a laugh. Women's Guilds are supposed to be dead edgy nowadays. I bet it's all nude calendars and Class A drugs.'

Tess laughed. 'I hope not. Left my crack pipe in my other jeans.'

'Hi, Raven.' Tammy turned to smile at Oliver. 'And hi, stranger.'

'Hi.' He cleared his throat, deepening his voice slightly. 'Er, hi. Good to . . . hi.'

'Now I know I've seen you around,' she said, tilting her head. 'You'll have to give me a clue. Mr . . .?'

'Actually, it's –' Tess began.

'Maynard! Oliver Maynard,' he butted in. 'But call me Oliver, please. Mr Maynard's my dad.' He let out a high-pitched laugh, then stopped abruptly, staring at her in socially mortified horror.

'Right,' Tammy said, looking amused. 'Well, in that case I'm Tammy. Nice to meet you, Oliver Maynard.' She held out a hand and he shook it limply, love hearts in both eyes and chirruping tweety birds circling his head.

'OK, Rave, come on,' Tess said, coming out from behind the bar. 'The sooner we get to the meeting, the sooner we can get this hellish ordeal over with.'

Oliver was looking increasingly anxious at the prospect of being left alone with Tammy, who was regarding him with an expression of detached curiosity. The two women walked to the door and stopped.

'One. Two. Three,' Raven muttered under her breath.

'Wait!' came Oliver's voice. 'I'll walk you to the meeting.'

Chapter 2

'OK, what was that all about?' Tess asked Oliver as they made their way through the lovingly tended gardens of Cherrywood Hall towards the manor house. There was a fresh, earthy, delicious smell hanging in the air after a recent shower of rain, and the village was glowing with the tender pastels of spring.

Raven nudged him. 'Not ashamed of our calling, are we, darling?'

He flushed. 'Of course not. I'd never be ashamed of what I do.'

'Then what was with the abrupt change of subject?' Tess said. 'You knew I was about to tell her it was Reverend, not Mr.'

'Wanted to make a good first impression, didn't I?' He sighed. 'Let's face it, guys. People think vicars are weird.'

'No, they don't.'

'Come on, you know they do.'

'Well . . . OK, some people might,' Tess conceded as they took a shortcut through the Japanese garden and turned their steps towards the large, gabled building in the distance. 'Unusual, not weird. But that's not everyone.'

'Faith at that level is scary, Tess. It makes people nervous.'

'You don't make us nervous,' Raven said. 'And we're just a pair of cynical heathens.'

'You knew me before though.' He absently plucked a cherry blossom from one of the candyfloss-pink trees that lined the path, sniffed it, then tossed it away. 'When I meet people now, all they see is the collar.'

'It's not weird to people who have that same faith, is it?' Tess said. 'Maybe Tam's a Christian too.'

'I've never seen her at church.'

'She doesn't live in Cherrywood; she just works here. Besides, not being a churchgoer doesn't mean she isn't a Christian.'

'Even Christians think vicars are weird,' Oliver said gloomily. 'I mean, maybe not when we're giving sermons or selling iced fingers at the vicarage garden party or having tea with your nana. But we rarely fall into the category of potential boyfriends.'

'Tammy's very sweet though. Perfect vicar's wife material.'

'This is exactly what I'm talking about,' Oliver said, scowling at a pagoda-shaped summerhouse as if it was personally responsible for his love-life woes. 'I meet a girl and straight away everyone's piling in with the vicar's wife cracks. I wouldn't mind getting her out on a date before you send her running.'

'OK,' Tess said gently. 'You know I'm only teasing, Ol.'

'I know.' He summoned a smile. 'Sorry, Tessie. Didn't mean to snap.'

'I don't know what you've got to gain from lying to the

girl,' Raven said. 'She'll find out sooner or later. And when she does, she's likely to be rather hacked off that you weren't up front with her.'

Tess nodded. 'Honesty from the get-go's the best policy when it comes to fledgling relationships. Trust me, I've got that T-shirt.'

'I think we've all got that T-shirt,' Raven said.

'All right,' Oliver said with a sigh. 'I just thought I could test the water a bit. Actually have a conversation where she looks at me like a normal, perhaps even shaggable, human male before she gets Vicar Face. You know, the one filled with dread that at any moment I might produce a collecting tin and tambourine.'

'If it means that much to you, your secret's safe with us,' Tess said, patting his arm.

'You could be having a highly shaggable conversation with her right now if you'd put your big boy pants on instead of running away,' Raven told him with a stern look.

'Well, you'd better get used to it because I'm about to do it again.' They'd reached Cherrywood Hall now, and Oliver nodded to an elderly woman in tweed who was about to enter the building. 'There's Miss Ackroyd, which means I need to make myself scarce before I get another lecture on the deathless poetry of the KJV. See you later, girls.' He gave them a hasty peck on the cheek each and scurried off.

'Poor Oliver,' Tess said when he'd gone. 'The dating scene's tough when you're God's representative on earth.'

'He's not the Pope, Tess. Anyway, never mind poor Oliver. What about poor Raven?'

'Oh right, you've got problems.'

'Yes, I jolly well have. I guarantee I'll have my gran on my case as soon as I get through that door,' Raven said, nodding to the manor house. 'She's worried Cherrywood Hall's going to end up with English Heritage in fifty years if I don't squeeze an heir out soon. All her nightmares now involve gangs of thuggish schoolkids wiping snot on the tapestries and feeling each other up on the Queen Anne bedsteads.'

'Has she noticed you making eyes at Mellors?'

'Darling, not only that – she actually seems to approve.'

Tess raised an eyebrow. 'You're kidding.'

'I'm not. I caught her smiling maternally at me the other day when she found me trying to make sultry conversation about bedding plants with him.'

'I thought she'd have you disinherited and scrubbed out of the family Bible for flirting with the help.' Tess shook her head. '*Downton Abbey* lied to me.'

'Those bastards.'

'Right?'

Raven laughed. 'To be honest, I think at this stage she'd be happy if I got knocked up by the chap in the tinfoil hat who wanders around outside Morrison's screaming about government brain implants. She's desperate to see me produce the next in the Walton-Lord line before she pops off.'

Tess looked up at the old mansion, home to the Walton-Lords for seven generations. Raven was the last of them, and her grandmother was becoming increasingly panicked that at thirty, the family's sole heir was still boyfriendless, childless, and apparently in no hurry to rectify the situation.

'I can't believe you'll own all that one day,' Tess said. 'I mean, you, who used to eat crayons at nursery. Where's my manor house?'

'You can have mine if you want. I hated growing up in this pile. So rude of my father to drop dead like that.' She tugged at Tess's arm. 'Come on. We don't want to miss Sam.'

They entered through the double doors and made their way down an oak-panelled passage to the library.

'So do the ladies all take turns to host?' Tess whispered.

'That seems to be how it works.' Raven grinned. 'Looking forward to our turn? You'd better remember not to leave your knickers drying over the mantelpiece.'

'Oh no. Just tonight, Rave, you promised me. I am not joining the bloody Women's Guild.'

'Relax, darling, I'm kidding. We'll tell them we're just trying it on for size. Then you can help me chat Sam up, we'll get him to sort you out with one of his sexy friends—'

'Has he got any?'

'Of course he has. Hot gardeners always have hot gardener friends. And once that's all arranged, we'll just tell Gracie it's not for us.'

'Gracie Lister?'

'Yes, she's the president.'

'Might've guessed.'

When they reached the library where the meeting was due to take place, the chat was in full flow. Women were milling around, drinking tea and chatting. The meeting looked exactly the way Tess had imagined it.

'Night of the Living Dead,' she muttered to herself.

22

'What?' Raven said.

'Oh, nothing. I think I just had my feminist card revoked, that's all. It's like stepping into the 1950s in here.'

Tess looked around the room, picking out familiar faces. She soon spotted Candice Walton-Lord, Raven's grandmother – tiny, a little hunched, but with a steel in her blue eyes that suggested she wasn't someone to cross, even at seventy-nine. She was talking to Beverley Stringer, Tess's boss at the pub, who ran Cherrywood's famously awful amateur dramatics group. The peroxide-blonde landlady was buxom in leopard-skin as always, and Tess could see Candice casting the occasional disapproving glance in the direction of Bev's over-exposed cleavage.

Not far from them, under a bouncing champagne perm, was Gracie Lister. One of life's chairmen, she had her chubby finger in a lot of village pies – as well as president of the Women's Guild, she was parish council chair, a trustee of the village hall, and she ran a friendship group for dementia patients at the church. She was gesticulating enthusiastically as she chatted to Peggy Bristow, cleaner at St Stephen's Church and self-proclaimed psychic. Several other women were seated on the uncomfortable-looking wooden chairs that had been laid out in rows in front of a projector and screen.

'Oh great,' Tess whispered to Raven. 'There's going to be a sodding PowerPoint. Gosh, it's like all my Christmases have come at once.'

'Don't be such a grump. You never know, you might learn something.'

'About gardening.'

'Exactly.'

'Raven, we live in a flat that's barely six-foot square. We don't even have a window box.'

Raven shrugged. 'Well, maybe this'll inspire us to get one.'

Tess skimmed the room again. Apart from the animated chatter of a little group of younger women who were standing near the table where teas were being served, there was a sober vibe. It was the first Guild meeting since Clemmie's death, of course. Cherrywood had been doing its best to keep calm and carry on, ignoring the unfamiliar sight of police officers and yellow-and-black tape that had invaded the village in the wake of the first murder there in living memory, but as a community they were still grieving. Tess noted the hushed tones of Clemmie's old friends as they no doubt discussed the latest development in the murder case: the arrest of Terry Braithwaite.

She scanned the crowd until she spotted the face she was really looking for. Prue Ackroyd. Clemmie's sister was standing a little distance from the other women, talking in an earnest manner to Raven's old nanny, Marianne Priestley.

And Tess wasn't the only one trying to sneak a peek at the woman who was currently Cherrywood's most notorious resident. She could see other eyes darting furtively in Prue's direction.

It was funny how people could become starstruck by someone they'd known all their lives, just because that person had been in the papers. Even when it was for something as horrific as discovering the brutal murder of a family member.

Tess wondered what had prompted Miss Ackroyd to turn up tonight. Her sister had been killed the night of the last Women's Guild meeting. Seeing those faces again, having all the memories stirred afresh, must surely be the last thing she wanted.

One month ago, Prue Ackroyd had come back from giving Peggy Bristow a lift home and found her sister lifeless on the floor, her head caved in with – of all the unlikely weapons – their mother's brass carriage clock. The back door, it transpired, had been left unlocked, and it seemed that Clemmie, having disturbed the culprit burgling what he believed was an empty house, had paid the ultimate price. Terry Braithwaite was the son of a nearby farmer: a veteran felon who had done time on multiple occasions for theft and housebreaking. And yet . . .

It was all very odd. The place was so isolated, a mile's walk from the village in the midst of rolling moorland. That meant it was likely to have been deliberately targeted – but why? The Ackroyd sisters weren't rich. The only items reported missing had been old Mr Ackroyd's fob watch, a couple of antique silver candlesticks and about a hundred quid in pound coins that Clemmie had been saving up in an old Bell's whisky bottle. Nothing worth killing for. Terry was a thief, but did he really have it in him to kill a neighbour, his own former nursery teacher – and for so little? In all of Terry's criminal past, he'd never been such a fool as to target houses in his own community. Something about it just didn't add up for Tess.

If Clemmie was well liked in the village, then her stern, acerbic sister Prue definitely wasn't. Her unpopularity, plus the fact she'd been the one to find her sister's body, had soon set village tongues wagging.

'Terry Braithwaite my backside,' Tess heard Peggy Bristow whisper to Gracie. 'I still say it was Prue who grabbed that carriage clock and planted it in Clemmie's head. There never was any love lost between them. She's only lucky she had an ex-con living nearby to pin it on.'

Tess could hear other snatches of conversation as she and Raven wove through the crowd.

'. . . and I said, "For God's sake, Ian, if you can't reheat a steak and kidney pie without all hell breaking loose" . . .'

'. . . yes, but it was only her fingerprints found on the thing . . .'

'. . . practically melted the oven by the time I got home . . .'

'. . . you know we're not so innocent in this, Prue.'

Tess stopped short. The last comment had been made in a hushed, determined tone and it definitely didn't sound like idle gossip. It had come from Marianne Priestley, who was still deep in conversation with Miss Ackroyd.

Tess's eavesdropping was interrupted by Gracie Lister, the Guild president, coming over to welcome them.

'Raven,' she said when she reached them, beaming. 'And Tess too. Surely you two young people aren't joining us?'

'Hi Gracie,' Tess said. 'Er, yes. That is to say, we're just trying it on for size.'

Gracie smiled knowingly. 'You know, you're the fifth one tonight who's turned up to "try it on for size".' She nodded to the group of lively younger women Tess had observed earlier. 'Whatever could be behind our newfound popularity, do you think?'

'Oh, it's very now, the Women's Guild,' Raven said innocently. 'All the cool kids are getting into it.'

'It's funny, but as soon as your grandmother announced that her new gardener was due to be tonight's speaker, we had a sudden surge in membership enquiries.'

'Like I said. Very now.' In order to change the subject, Raven pointed to the table of vegetables from which people were helping themselves. 'These look good. Some of yours?'

Gracie swelled a little. 'The squashes are mine, and some of the carrots.'

'What about the marrow?' Tess asked. 'I don't think I've ever seen one that big.'

'That one is Beverley's.' Gracie cast a distrustful glance at the pub landlady in her leopard-skin dress. 'I heard a rumour she's been using imported stuff on her veg this year. Bound to be illegal, of course, but you know the judges won't do a thing about it. And as for Peggy Bristow and her carrots, well . . .'

Tess stifled a smile. The competitive spirit that arose among the village's vegetable-growers in the run-up to the Cherrywood Spring Show in May was the stuff of legend, and despite winning in all her categories for the past five years, Gracie was by far the worst culprit.

'You know you'll sweep the board as per usual, Gracie,' Raven said. 'It doesn't matter what Bev uses on her marrows: they won't stand a chance against yours.'

'Well, Raven, that's very sweet of you to say.' Gracie pursed her lips, casting a look at the table of fruit and veg. 'I suppose my record is the reason *some* people around here have felt it necessary to bring in outside help.'

Raven frowned. 'Have they?'

'Oh, I imagine your grandmother's found a semi-plausible excuse to replace her old gardener . . .'

'John? She didn't replace him, he retired.'

'Mmm, and just a month before the show; how very convenient. All I can say is, she never brought onions that size along for the vegetable swap table before Sam Mitchell went to work for her.' Clemmie patted Raven's arm. 'But it's not your fault, dear. I'd never dream of holding it against you. Now excuse me, I must go make sure Mr Mitchell has everything he needs.'

'Now how can you say this place is duller than London?' Raven whispered to Tess. 'Dirty dealings at the village show. Mutant mega-marrows and colossal carrots. It's a cut-throat world, competitive vegetable growing.'

Tess wasn't listening. Her gaze had fixed on Marianne and Miss Ackroyd, who were still talking in furtive whispers a little way from the rest of the gathering.

'Let's go say hello to Marianne,' she said.

Raven shrugged. 'If you like.'

'It wasn't us who—' Miss Ackroyd was saying, but she stopped abruptly when she caught sight of Tess and Raven.

She jerked her head to indicate that Marianne should turn around.

Marianne looked taken aback for a moment, but quickly broke into a smile.

'Raven,' she said as she came forward to embrace her. 'And Tess too, how wonderful. Your grandmother and I thought you were teasing us when you said you wanted to join.'

'When do I ever tease you, Mari?' Raven said, kissing her on both cheeks.

'Do you really want me to answer that? Because I have been keeping a list.'

Tess glanced at Miss Ackroyd. She was a hard person to read – certainly her expression never gave anything away. But she'd recently lost her only living relative, and it seemed to Tess that the village ought to be doing a little more rallying round and a little less behind-hand gossiping. Miss Ackroyd could be hard work, but the idea she might be a killer was ridiculous. Spreading wild, unfounded rumours was Cherrywood's favourite hobby, and this time there was more than the reputation of Beverley's marrows at stake.

'How are you doing, Miss Ackroyd?' Tess asked kindly.

Tess had been afraid of Miss Ackroyd at primary school – all the children had – but for some reason the stern teacher had taken rather a shine to her. Tess Feather was one of the few people in the village she'd condescend to crack a smile for.

But there was no smile for Tess today.

'I'm doing perfectly well, thank you, Teresa,' Miss Ackroyd

answered stiffly. 'Although I might be doing rather better if people would stop asking how I'm doing every five minutes.'

'Oh. Right.'

Miss Ackroyd's expression softened slightly. 'I'm sorry, I didn't mean to be sharp. Things are rather unpleasant, as you can imagine. Dealing with the police this past month has been exhausting, and then being back at home without . . . they returned her things today.'

'Her things?'

'Yes, the items that were taken. Not the money, of course – I suppose Braithwaite had already spent it – but the candlesticks and Father's watch were found under a loose floorboard in his room at Black Moor Farm.' She shuddered. 'I wish the police hadn't bothered. I hate to have them in the house now.'

'Of course you do. If there's anything I can do, just ask.'

Miss Ackroyd summoned a tight-lipped smile. 'Oh, let's not talk of it. I'm thoroughly sick of the subject. So, you young ladies are joining us, are you?'

Before Tess could answer, Gracie Lister bounced over, hugging a Tupperware tub to her jiggling chest.

'Prue, it's so good of you to come tonight,' she said. 'I know it must be . . . well, poor Clemmie and all. Anyway, I wanted to do something, only I didn't know . . .' Gracie laughed, fanning herself. 'Listen to me, old motormouth. I never do manage to open my cakehole without ending up with a foot sticking out of it, do I?'

'Do you intend to make a point any time this evening, Gracie?' Miss Ackroyd asked coldly.

'Yes. Well, no, not a point so much as a . . . casserole.'
Gracie held out the tub. 'Chicken. I knew you probably
wouldn't be in the mood to cook, and I wanted to, you
know . . .'

'What you know could be written on the back of a six-
penny stamp, Gracie Lister,' she snapped. 'For God's sake, do
leave me alone.'

Gracie blinked. 'Me?'

'All of you. I didn't come here to fuel the gossip of a bunch
of frustrated curtain-twitchers.' Miss Ackroyd swatted the
casserole away. 'Yes, I know what you're all whispering
about. I may be in mourning but I'm not, as it turns out,
deaf.' She stomped off.

Chapter 3

Gracie stared after Miss Ackroyd in dismay, still clutching her Tupperware tub.

'Oh dear,' she whispered. 'Now I've offended her. Story of my life.' She turned to Marianne. 'I honestly wasn't whispering about her. I wouldn't dare.'

'Don't take it hard, Gracie,' Marianne said, patting her arm. 'Prue doesn't mean anything by it. She snapped at Tess too; it's not just you.'

'Yes.' Gracie summoned a smile. 'Grief can make people behave that way, I suppose. I didn't mean to annoy her, I just wanted to help.'

'That was very kind of you. And I'm sure your chicken casserole is delicious. You know, it's Candice's favourite.'

Gracie brightened at once. 'Oh, would she like it?'

'She'd love it,' Marianne said. 'Thank you. Now, why don't you get everyone organised? We'll be starting soon.'

When Gracie had bounced away, Tess smiled at Marianne. 'Well handled.'

'What is Miss Ackroyd's problem?' Raven demanded. 'There was no need for that.'

'She did just lose her sister,' Tess said. 'And she's not wrong, is she? Everyone is whispering about her.'

'Prue's lonely. Lonely and afraid.' Marianne watched Miss Ackroyd as she took a seat at the back by herself. 'Now Clemmie's gone, she's got no one left. Everyone needs someone to love.'

'Is that a hint?' Raven said. 'I didn't come for you and Grandmother to start trying to marry me off again.'

Marianne turned to look at her. 'Why did you come?'

Raven shrugged. 'Idle curiosity.'

'Mmm. And I know what about.'

Tess swept in with another diplomatic subject-change in the direction of vegetables. 'It sounds like competition's already very healthy for this year's spring show.'

Marianne laughed. 'You've been talking to Gracie.'

'So, is it true?' Raven asked. 'Did you and Grandmother bring Sam in as a ringer?'

'Darling, I'm shocked,' Marianne said, holding a hand to her heart. 'Your grandmother is a Walton-Lord. She would never stoop so low.' She lowered her voice. 'But that doesn't stop the two of us having a little fun with the other growers. What they don't know is, I've been bringing along some of the big organic onions from the farm shop to donate to the produce table. Just to see the look on their faces.'

'Where's Sam?' Raven asked, in her best attempt at nonchalance.

'In the study, hiding,' Marianne said, grinning. 'Gracie's going to fetch him once we're ready. Raven, you'd better go say hello to your grandmother before you find yourselves a seat. There isn't long.'

Raven groaned. 'Do I have to?'

'Now come on, don't be like that. She's been looking forward to seeing you.'

'Fine. Fine, I'm going.'

Tess and Raven headed for Candice, who was examining the refreshments.

'Can you believe that?' she said when they reached her, shaking her grey curls. 'Finger foods, I said. What do the caterers bring? Bloody rice pudding! Of course, no one's touched it. We'll be eating the stuff for a month.'

'I think that's couscous,' Tess said.

'I'll tell you what it isn't: canapés. I definitely told them canapés on the telephone. The idiot stuttered at me like I'd started speaking another language.'

Tess bit her tongue to stop herself pointing out that this was literally true.

'We'll take some back to the flat with us if you like,' Raven said. 'Hello, Grandmother.'

Candice turned round and her face softened a little. 'Raven. Well, dear, I'm glad to see you.' She held out her hand and Raven gave it a shake. Tess averted her eyes, embarrassed by the formal way they always greeted each other.

'How's work?' Candice asked Raven.

'Same as usual.' Raven worked as a copywriter for a wall-art company, coming up with trite slogans for a range of dreadful motivational posters. She often claimed to be the brains behind 'Live, Laugh, Love', with her usual creative approach to the truth.

'Courting at all?' Candice enquired.

'Nope.'

'And have you decided to give up that horrid poky flat and come back to Marianne and me?'

'Certainly not. It's a wonderful poky flat. It's got Tess in it, for a start.'

Candice smiled at Tess. 'That is one positive feature. So, you're joining us, are you, girls?'

'We're just trying it on for size,' Tess said. 'Um, Raven said your new gardener's speaking tonight?'

'Yes, it was rather a mess actually,' Candice said. 'We had planned to cancel tonight's meeting. Well, it didn't seem appropriate, so soon after Clemmie's death – especially when it happened right after our last meeting. Gracie went ahead and cancelled the scheduled speaker, only for Prue to telephone and insist we went ahead as usual. She was very anxious about it – quite upset, Gracie said, and adamant it was what Clemmie would want. We were very lucky Sam was able to step in at the last moment.'

Gracie approached them, bringing the conversation to a halt.

'Now, Candice,' she said, looking stern. 'What have we forgotten?'

Candice was dumb.

'The friendship horseshoe!' Gracie said in an exasperated tone. She gestured to the chairs that had been laid out for them. 'How are we supposed to build a sisterhood sitting in these nasty little rows?'

'I thought they were rather sweet little rows.'

'No, you didn't. You forgot. Everyone always forgets the friendship horseshoe.' Gracie prodded Peggy Bristow nearby, who nearly choked on the eclair she was eating. 'Peggy, you'll be hosting next time. Just remember, chairs arranged in a lovely lucky horseshoe, OK? That way we can all see each other.' She clapped her hands and raised her voice over the babble. 'Now, ladies, I'm going to ask you to fill your teacups, empty your bladders if you need to and take your seats. Five-minute warning before I introduce our guest speaker.'

'That woman and her hippy-drippy horseshoe nonsense,' Candice muttered as Gracie made her way to the front.

Raven grabbed Tess's arm and led her to the back row.

'Don't you want to sit at the front, be closer to Sex-on-legs Sam?' Tess asked.

'No, I want to be where I can have a jolly good perve without him seeing. We can talk to him after. You're going to help me lure him to the pub.'

Tess glanced around the newly swelled ranks of Cherrywood Women's Guild. 'Looks like you've got a bit of competition.'

'Are any of them heirs to a country estate?'

'Touché.' Tess grinned. 'Hey, what if it's me he fancies? You never know, he might have a kink for short-arse barmaids with unbrushed hair who reek of beer.'

Raven shrugged. 'I can always use the family fortune to have you bumped off.'

Tess watched Candice take a seat next to Marianne a couple of rows ahead of them.

Marianne had worked for the Walton-Lords for nearly thirty years, ever since Raven had been a baby. Raven's mother, who'd reportedly been a great beauty, had quickly grown bored of being mum to a demanding infant. After Raven's father died, she'd left her tiny daughter at Cherry-wood Hall to be raised by her paternal grandmother – and pocketed a tidy sum for agreeing never to contact the child again, according to rumour.

Candice was a kind woman but undemonstrative, puzzled by the ways of children, and little Raven had naturally come to look on her cuddly, affectionate nanny as the closest thing she had to a mother. Marianne had grown close to her employer too, and when Raven had grown up she'd stayed on as Candice's companion.

'So are they a couple?' Tess whispered to Raven. It had been a favourite piece of gossip in the village for decades.

Raven shrugged. 'No idea.'

'Didn't you notice? You grew up here.'

'They've never shared a bedroom. I've never seen them kiss or hug, or hold hands even.' She smiled. 'But they adore one another. Marianne's the only person Grandmother's eyes light up for.'

'Aww. They are then.'

'I told you, I don't know. They love each other, but I don't know if it's a romantic kind of love. Then again, it might be – it would've been a big taboo when they were young; that's not something you just shake off.' Raven shrugged. 'I don't know that it matters either way, if they're happy with each other. It's really nobody's business but theirs.'

Tess watched the two of them, sitting shoulder to shoulder. Candice was saying something, and Marianne inclined her white head towards her as she listened. They looked very comfortable sharing each other's personal space.

'No,' Tess said. 'I don't suppose it is.'

Gracie clapped her hands again. 'Let's get things started. It's lovely to see so many new people here tonight.' Her face took on a sober expression. 'But of course, there's one member who can't be with us. Before we begin, I'd like to ask everyone to observe a minute's silence for our friend Clemmie Ackroyd, who as you all know passed away last month. Several members have asked that tonight's meeting be dedicated to her memory. So tonight is for our Clemmie, honorary aunty to three generations of Cherrywooders. To Clemmie, who loved this village, and was loved in return by all who knew her.'

'To Clemmie,' everyone muttered in unison.

Hands were clasped and eyes lowered. Tess couldn't help sneaking a look at Miss Ackroyd, seated alone at the other end of their row. She was sitting rigidly upright, staring straight ahead.

'Thank you, ladies,' Gracie said when the moment's observation was over. 'Now, a few bits of admin before we welcome our speaker. Firstly, I'd like to draw the attention of our new members to the book swap table – yes, the Jackie Collins are all mine,' she said with a little laugh. 'If you have any to exchange, please do help yourself. The honesty system, of course. We also have our produce table, with all money raised going towards the spring show.' She squinted at it. 'An excess of Peggy's cabbage chutney, it seems.'

'Yum,' Raven muttered to Tess.

'And my girls have been very busy, so plenty of honey for those with a sweet tooth,' Gracie said, nodding to a row of amber jars. Her 'girls' were her pride and joy – the colony of honey bees she tended with loving care throughout the year.

'And finally, the shoebox campaign.' Gracie waved a sad-looking knitted bear in the air. He had mismatched eyes, was wearing a dull blue waistcoat and had the two-dimensional look of woollen roadkill. 'Now, I won't name names. But this . . .' She indicated a large button that had been sewn on to the bear's front. 'Ladies, you know adornments of any kind are against the rules. It might produce jealousy among the children; it might choke them. Stick to the pattern provided and no more flashes of inspiration, please.'

'Um, what are the bear things for?' one of the other new members asked. Tess recognised her – Audrey Felcher, a pretty girl who worked in the village tearoom. She'd been in the year below her, Raven and Oliver at school.

'For our annual Christmas shoebox campaign.' Gracie indicated a pile of boxes under the buffet table. 'Each box contains a knitted bear, plus toothpaste, toothbrush, pencils and a book. They're giftwrapped and sent to displaced children living in refugee camps. All for charity.'

Prue Ackroyd's head, which had been drooping against her chest, shot up.

'Pardon?' she said sharply.

Gracie blinked. 'For the refugee charity, dear. The bears, you know?'

'Oh. Yes.' Miss Ackroyd looked relieved. 'Of course.'

'Right. So now we begin the meeting proper,' Gracie said. 'And we all know what comes first. Up, up, up!'

Tess turned a look of horror on Raven. 'Women's Guilds still do this?'

'Ours does, apparently.' Raven grimaced apologetically as she got to her feet. 'Sorry.'

'You deliberately didn't tell me. You withheld the fact of . . . of *singing* from me.'

'Come on, you sing. You're always bloody singing.'

'Not when I don't know the words!'

'I don't know them either,' Raven whispered. 'Just mime it.'

Tess noticed Audrey rolling her eyes as the group launched into the dreary, tuneless notes of 'Jerusalem'.

'And did those . . . mmms in ancient mmm . . . walk upon England's mmm-mmm mmm,' Tess mumbled, avoiding the glare Gracie fixed on her.

'Well, ladies, I think I've teased you long enough,' Gracie said when they'd all resumed their seats. 'Without further ado, I'd like to introduce our guest speaker, Sam Mitchell. Sam is the new gardener at Cherrywood Hall, which I'm sure those of you familiar with the beautiful gardens here will appreciate is no small job. Already he seems to be making a big difference to the vegetable patches.' Gracie cast another resentful glance at Marianne's shop-bought onions before continuing. 'Sam is going to share his expert knowledge with us and explain how to get the most out of our gardens. A big hand for him, please.'

Raven hadn't been exaggerating, Tess thought as Sam

entered the room to vigorous applause. He was really very good-looking. Muscular arms, check. Deep brown eyes set in deep brown face, check. Dusting of stubble, check. Unruly black hair flopping into his eyes, check. He'd obviously come straight from work, dressed in a pair of dirty stonewashed jeans and a tight-fitting T-shirt.

All eyes had fixed on him, and it looked like there was imminent risk of some collective swooning. But the man didn't seem fazed by the sea of dilated pupils and flushed cheeks. He strode to the front like someone who was not only used to being the centre of attention but expected to be, and smiled with one side of his mouth.

The thing was, the arms, the eyes, the smile, the charm – Tess had seen them all before, and they hadn't been attached to anyone who went by the name of Sam Mitchell.

They'd been attached to a man called Liam Hanley. And Liam Hanley wasn't a gardener. He was a private investigator.

He was also the man who'd ruined her life.

Chapter 4

'Shit!' Tess muttered.

'Oi. Watch the mouth, darling,' Raven whispered. 'He does rather have that effect though, doesn't he?'

'Rave, I need to get out of here.'

Raven turned to look at her. 'Are you feeling OK?'

'Yeah, just . . . need the loo.'

'Can't you wait until after the talk?'

'Not really.'

Tess started to rise, hoping she could get out of the room before he spotted her. But in front of her, Audrey's hand had shot up to ask a question. Tess dropped back into her seat as Liam looked in their direction, dipping her head.

'Honestly, what is wrong with you?' Raven hissed.

'Nothing. Hush now.' She didn't want to attract Liam's attention if she could get away with it.

'Good evening, everyone,' he said, smiling around the room. He nodded to Audrey. 'If we could save specific questions till the end, I'm happy to hang around and talk about any personal issues you ladies might have with your gardens.'

Audrey blushed and dropped her hand again. The friend she'd come with nudged her and giggled.

'So. Mrs Lister has asked if I can give some tips on caring for your gardens this spring and summer. First of all, in terms of planning you should already be well ahead and into the autumn . . .'

Tess barely heard any of Liam's gardening talk. He'd obviously done his research, but all she could think about was not being seen. She kept her head bent all through his PowerPoint presentation, pretending she was making notes on her phone.

When she thought she could get away with it, she glanced up to take a sly look at the man.

The night they'd met he'd been in black tie, attending a charity fundraiser hosted by Porter, the insurance firm she'd been working for in London. Not that any of the money had made it to the charity, Tess later discovered. Her boss Jackie had skimmed most of it off in an embezzlement scam that had been going on for a decade – since long before Tess had got the job as Jackie's PA.

Liam had been suave and well-groomed in his dinner suit that evening, very different from the scruffy denims and lumberjack stubble he was sporting in gardener mode. But his face hadn't changed. It was still the same old Liam: that wry humour, the glint that suggested he was secretly laughing at everyone. All this time she'd spent trying to forget him, and now he'd turned up in Cherrywood – with a fake name and a fake job. Why? Was he investigating Aunty Clemmie's murder? Beneath her anger at seeing his stupid, treacherous, handsome face again, the mystery-loving part of Tess's brain was forced to confess itself intrigued.

Tess was peeping up at him, examining the familiar contours of his cheekbones, when too late she realised Raven's arm was waving in the air. The talk was over and they'd moved on to questions.

'Rave, no!' she whispered. But it was no good; Liam had turned in their direction. Tess bent her head still further, staring intently at her phone.

'Miss Walton-Lord,' Liam said with a nod. 'I didn't expect to see you here.'

'Oh, yes. I love gardening,' Raven purred, deepening her voice in the way she thought made her sound sultry. 'I mean, I live in a flat – with my friend Tess here – but I would love it. You know, if we had the space.'

Tess winced. She tipped her head up ever so slightly to acknowledge her name but managed to avoid lifting her face.

'Anyway,' Raven went on in merry oblivion, 'I just wondered if you had any tips for us. We'd love to introduce some greenery, but we only have a little balcony. I'd adore some flowers and Tess is always talking about creating a herb garden for cooking. Aren't you, darling?'

'Yes,' Tess muttered.

'I'm sorry?' Liam said.

OK. She couldn't avoid it any longer.

'Yes,' she said, lifting her head. She stuck out her chin and met his eyes. 'Yes.'

For a split second he looked shocked. But only for a split second. Then his face broke into a smile.

Oh, he was good . . .

'Well . . . Tess, was it? I could certainly recommend some hardy herbs that ought to thrive in shallower soil.'

'What about flowers?' Raven asked, keen to keep his attention away from Audrey, who was waving her hand in front of them. 'Something colourful would be so sweet: azaleas or dog roses perhaps. We could get cuttings from you.'

Liam laughed. 'I wouldn't recommend growing your azaleas too close to this kitchen garden of your flatmate's. They're poisonous, you know.'

Raven blinked. 'Azaleas can kill you?'

'Nothing that serious. They'd leave you with one hell of a tummy ache if you got them muddled with your rosemary though.' Liam glanced around the sea of eager hands waiting for his attention. 'We should move on. Perhaps you and your friend would like to discuss it with me afterwards.'

'We'll have to rush off,' Tess said.

Raven glared at her. 'No, we won't.' She nodded to Liam. 'Thanks, that'll be great. Er, maybe we could chat at the pub. A pint's the least we owe you after such an informative talk.' She ignored the dirty look Audrey turned to give her.

'Maybe a quick one. Thanks.'

Raven beamed.

'What did you go and say that for?' she hissed to Tess when he'd turned his attention to one of the other ladies.

'I just . . . I'm not sure I fancy the pub. I've been there all afternoon.'

'Oh come *on*. You are the worst wingman tonight.'

'You want to treat him mean and keep him keen, don't you?'

'If I treat him mean, Audrey'll go marching in with her push-up bra before I get my chance.'

'Do you even know if he's single?' Tess demanded. 'Maybe's he's got a girlfriend. Maybe he's married. Maybe he's a bigamist with fourteen wives.' She wouldn't put it past him either.

'No ring, though. And he's been flirting with me, I'm sure of it.'

Tess felt a pang she immediately stifled.

Why should she care if Liam had been flirting? He was a free agent. As free as the air, as far as she was concerned. She certainly never wanted to see him again.

She was worried about Raven, though. Her friend already seemed pretty far gone on 'Sam', and she said he'd shown interest in her. Was Liam using Raven to get information for a case, just as he'd used Tess? Well, messing with Tess's emotions was one thing. Messing with her best friend's was entirely another.

Rave's crushes were invariably short-lived, but Tess knew from first-hand experience that Liam Hanley was a natural when it came to charming the birds from the trees and the pants from any attractive women he happened to encounter. If her friend got in too deep, she could end up . . . well, she could end up feeling just as much of a sucker as Tess had. Above all else, Tess needed to protect her.

Once the Q&A session was done with, Gracie thanked Liam or Sam or whatever his name was for the talk. Then he handed out business cards to everyone present – Candice wasn't averse to letting him do a bit of moonlighting when he wasn't trimming her topiary, apparently – and disappeared off. Raven watched him go, looking worried.

'He said he'd come for a drink,' she whispered to Tess.

'Maybe he's planning to meet you at the pub.'

'Us, you mean. You're not getting out of it, darling.'

'Wouldn't you rather be alone with him?'

'No, I need you there. I don't want Sam to think it's a date until . . . well, it turns into a date.'

Gracie clapped her hands for quiet.

'Well, ladies, wasn't that fascinating? We've got a packed programme for you in the year ahead too.' She gestured to the book swap table, where there were a couple of clipboards with A4 sheets attached. 'Do take a look at what we've got coming up, and we've also got some super activities organised by the regional federation that you're welcome to sign up for.'

'We'd better go look,' Raven murmured to Tess. 'Grandmother and Marianne are right by the clipboards. We need to at least pretend we considered joining.'

They headed to the table. Tess picked up one of the clipboards listing the activities coming up in the months that followed.

'You know, some of those actually sound pretty good,' Raven said, peering over her shoulder. 'Look, they're having a gin-tasting night. How me is that? I thought it'd be all scone-baking and raffia mat-weaving.'

'A spa afternoon here at Cherrywood Hall,' Tess read. 'I didn't know your gran ran spa days as well as those writers' retreat weekends.'

Candice looked up from the books table. 'Yes, it's a new venture. Anything to help keep the roof on the old place for another few years. I've booked a couple of masseuses, got the pool refilled and had a pair of hot tubs installed in the summerhouse. The Guild ladies are going to be trialling it for me before I start advertising.'

'That sounds great.' Tess glanced at Raven. 'I'm liking the sound of a hot tub massage.'

Audrey had approached them. She curled her lip as she picked up the second clipboard.

'Creating a garden at a women's refuge, wildlife conservation walk, glass-staining, cake-decorating, jam-making . . .' she read. 'It's a bit old-fashioned, all this, isn't it?'

'I reckon it might be a laugh,' Tess said. 'There's nothing wrong with old-fashioned if it's fun. Besides, vintage is in.'

'Mmm. Must remember to dig out my flowery pinny and curlers.'

Tess frowned. All right, so it hadn't been so long ago she'd been expressing a similar sentiment herself, but the girl's above-it-all tone irritated her.

'You didn't have to come,' she said.

'I came because I'd heard Women's Guilds were dead modern now,' Audrey told her sniffily. 'I thought they'd moved on from the trad wife stuff.'

'You came because you were thinking with your ovaries,' Raven said.

'Like you weren't,' Audrey said with a shrug. 'I just thought it'd be a bit less . . . twee. Like, I read about this one in London where all the members are goths. In Cherrywood it's still old ladies and jam.'

Candice looked up to glare at her. 'And just what do you mean by that, Audrey Felcher?'

'Well, I . . .' The girl took a step backwards, faltering in the face of Candice's withering stare. 'It's just, some of them now do all sorts of cool stuff. Pole dancing and things.'

Candice scoffed. 'What nonsense. I can't stand all this ironic, post-modern rubbish. Pole dancing, striptease, foul-mouthed cross-stitch. Oh yes, I've read about it and I don't doubt it's good for grabbing headlines, but honestly, if that's the way we're expected to entice new members then God help us.'

'I just thought it was a bit more feminist these days,' Audrey mumbled, looking immensely sorry she'd opened her mouth.

'Feminist?' Candice drew herself up to her full height, all five foot two of it. 'Young lady, I was a member of this organisation when we marched for single mothers' rights – many, many moons before you were even thought of. I strong-armed our politicians into campaigning for sexual health education for women and girls. In the early nineties I was on the streets to protest the legality of marital rape, along with many thousands of other Guild members. So don't you dare turn up here and presume to start lecturing me on what it means to be a feminist just because I've never gyrated my aged backside round a greased bloody pole. Who do you think earned you that right?'

'Wow,' Raven muttered to Tess. 'Go, Grandmother!'

'Sorry,' Audrey said in a hushed voice. 'Sorry, Mrs Walton-Lord. I didn't know . . . didn't think.'

Candice relented a little. 'Well, you're young. But perhaps you might like to consider that not everything we do or say as women has to be a feminist statement. Sometimes, jam is just jam.'

Raven nodded. 'And who doesn't like jam?'

'No one,' Tess said. 'Everyone likes jam, it's delicious.' Impulsively, she grabbed the clipboard and scribbled her name next to the jam-making session. 'In fact, sign me up. I've always wanted to learn how to make it.'

'You don't have to sign up for that one,' Candice said. 'That's part of the regular programme, we all attend those.' She raised an eyebrow. 'That is, assuming you girls are joining us permanently?'

Raven turned to look at Tess. 'Apparently we are.'

*

'I can't believe he didn't show up,' Raven grumbled, unlocking the flat they shared over the old apothecary's on Cherrywood's main street. 'Men. They're all the same.'

'No, they're not,' Tess said as she followed her in. 'Only some of them are the same.'

'If you mean Oliver, he doesn't count.'

'Vicarist. Ol's got just as much right to be a bastard as the next lad his age.'

'He wouldn't, though. He's too nice.'

'Do you know if Oliver even believes in doing sex stuff outside marriage?' Tess asked as she threw herself down on the sofa. 'I mean, is he allowed to? I know when we were teens he got up to the same sort of stuff as we all did, but that was . . . well, you know. Before.'

'He once told me he believes in sex before marriage the same way he believes in grizzly bears,' Raven said. 'He knows they exist. He's been told that in some areas, they're even quite common. But he never seems to see any.'

Tess laughed. 'Poor old Ol. Let's hope things go well for him with Tammy. They'd suit each other, if she doesn't have an issue with his job and he doesn't cock it up with his incurable awkwardness around girls he likes.' She squirmed. 'What's under me?'

She fished under her bum, wriggling out the paperback that had been lying face down on the cushion.

'Rave, can you stop leaving your mucky books on the sofa?' Tess glanced at the book's cover, which bore a photo of a uniformed man's torso and the title *Her Ruthless Bodyguard*. 'See, I blame this stuff for you.'

'And I blame dodgy birth control for you,' Raven said, chucking herself down next to Tess.

'Seriously. You fall in love at the drop of a hat, then three months in you're bored of him.' Tess waved the book. 'It's this stuff – it creates unrealistic expectations. As soon as you find out he scratches his bits and farts in bed the same as every other bloke, you can't get him out of the door fast enough.'

'That's a great read, that is. Diana Skye's a genius,' Raven said, snatching the book away. She let out a nauseatingly smitten sigh. 'And I bet Sam doesn't fart in bed.'

'How much?' Tess muttered.

'What?'

'Nothing.'

'So what was with you tonight then?' Raven demanded, shuffling to face her. 'You were being dead weird. And after all my efforts to drag you there so you could give him your seal of approval, you barely looked at Sam.'

Tess shrugged. 'I'm just not that into gardening.'

'There was no need to be rude. What did you tell him we had to hurry off for? I bet it was you who scared him away from the pub.'

'I just . . .' Tess sighed. 'I worry about you, Rave. You always rush into these things. For once why not take it slow, eh?'

'I need the chance to take it slow first.' Raven shook her head. 'I can't believe he didn't come to the pub. I hope Audrey didn't get her claws into him while I wasn't looking.'

Tess put an arm around her. 'Really, love, you're well out of it. Guys like that are ten a penny. Dripping charm, off as soon as they've seen what colour your knickers are.'

'Suits me.'

'Come on, you know you'd fall for him. You always fall for them. For a bit, anyway.'

'So what if I do? I'm a big girl.' Raven smiled dreamily. 'He is gorgeous though, isn't he?'

'Too gorgeous for his own good. Never trust the ones who know it.'

'But you wouldn't kick him out of bed, right?'

'I bloody would. I've been burned one too many times.'

'You're not seriously off men for life thanks to this Liam Bradley, are you?'

'Hanley,' Tess muttered. 'Liam Hanley. Sexy, charming, great in bed and an absolute grade-A shitbadger. I'd still be in London if it wasn't for him.'

Raven shook her head. 'I've never understood how this grade-A shitbadger was responsible for you losing your job. Was he involved in your company going out of business?'

'Yeah. Something like that.'

'Oh well, sod him,' Raven said, waving a hand dismissively. 'There are plenty of less shit badgers in the sea. You just need to get out there and look for them.'

'Not right now, Rave. Besides, I'm busy. It's not like I work the most sociable hours, is it?'

'Are you with Ian tomorrow?'

Tess grimaced. 'Yep. Better remember to brush my wig before bed.'

Raven laughed. 'No time for boyfriends, but time to brush your fake hair. And time to join the Women's Guild. Why the sudden change of heart? I practically had to drag you there tonight, and now apparently we're getting up to our elbows in homemade jam.'

Tess shrugged. 'When your nan told Audrey off . . . I couldn't help being impressed. Did you know she'd done all that stuff?'

'I remember her making the trip to London sometimes when I was little. I had no idea she was setting her bra alight outside Westminster for single mothers' rights.'

'I didn't know the Women's Guild did things like that.

And the other activities look kind of fun, even the old-school ones.' Tess smiled. 'I'm quite looking forward to the jam, actually.'

'I mainly agreed for the gin-tasting.' Raven got to her feet. 'Speaking of which, I need a drink.'

'Put some tonic in it, Rave, for God's sake. You already had a couple of doubles in the pub. Do it for me and your liver.'

'All right, Mum, no need to lecture. You having one?'

'A little one. Cheers.'

Raven headed into the kitchen. Tess kicked off her shoes and stretched her feet out on to the coffee table, relishing the sensation of having someone bring her a drink for a change. She picked up Raven's copy of *Her Ruthless Bodyguard* and flicked to a random page.

Aurelia had always had all that she desired – wealth, possessions, grand homes. Everything except love. But could she really trust rakish lawman Blaze with her heart?

Shaking her head, Tess put the book back down. If Aurelia had a jot of sense, she'd flee for the hills while she still could.

Chapter 5

In his bedroom at the vicarage the following evening, the Reverend Oliver Maynard's thoughts were far from divine. A more earthbound drive was in play as he looked through his wardrobe, trying to find something to wear that would give him the confidence he needed to ask Tammy out at the pub later.

'Come on, boss, don't look at me like that,' he said, catching the eye of Christ suffering the little children to come unto him in the painting hanging on his wall. 'I'm going to tell her, all right?'

Jesus didn't answer, but Oliver was sure he had a disapproving look in his eye that hadn't been there before.

'One date, is that too much to ask?' he said in a pleading tone. 'Look, it's not you, it's . . . people. They don't always get it.'

His boss didn't look convinced. Oliver turned away from his guilt-inducing gaze and back to the cupboard.

He was just about to select a pair of black jeans and a polo shirt his mum had given him for Christmas – Raven had once told him it made him look like a young Edward Norton, and he'd immediately upgraded it to his official sexiest item of clothing – when there was a sharp rap at the door.

'Oh great,' he muttered. 'That better not be who I think it is.'

One glance through the peephole confirmed his worst fears. The tweed-clad figure of Prudence Ackroyd was standing on the vicarage's front doorstep, looking scarier than ever and with a copy of the King James Bible under her arm. Sighing, he opened the door.

'Miss Ackroyd. How nice to see you again so very, very soon.' He glanced at the Bible. 'Er, did you have a scripture question for me?'

'In a way, yes.' She stood, frowning at him expectantly.

'Oh. Perhaps you'd like to come in.'

'Thank you,' she said, in a tone that suggested it wasn't before time. She pushed past him and marched down the passage to the front room like she owned the place, Oliver trailing behind.

He was thirty-one years old, but there was something about Prue Ackroyd that sapped every ounce of grown-up out of him and turned him back into the snivelling little boy she'd terrified the life out of back at Cherrywood Primary. Typical she'd turn up now, when he'd just about managed to build his confidence levels up ready for the pub.

But Miss Ackroyd was grieving, and he was her parish priest. Now was no time to shirk his duty so he could flirt with pretty girls. He fixed his face into an understanding smile as he gestured for her to take a seat on the sofa.

'Such a ridiculous house for a bachelor,' she said when she

was sitting down, pursing her lips as she cast a disapproving gaze around the large, old-fashioned room.

'Well, it kind of came with the job.'

'Why on earth don't you get married, Oliver?'

Oliver turned his smile up a notch. 'Can I get you some tea, Miss Ackroyd?'

She stared at him for a moment.

'Reverend Springer always had French fancies,' she said at last.

'Um, I've got some digestives?'

'That will do, I suppose.'

' "That will do, I suppose," ' Oliver muttered to himself as he made their tea in the kitchen. ' "Oh, when dear Reverend Springer was alive, he always offered me a foot massage and a line of cocaine before Bible study . . ." '

He'd managed to fix his face back into a reassuring expression by the time he entered the front room again, bearing a tray with two mugs of tea and a plate of digestives. Miss Ackroyd subjected them to a critical gaze.

'They're chocolate,' Oliver pointed out hopefully.

'Mmm. So I see.' She deigned to take one and dunked it in her tea.

'So, er . . . this isn't about the ladies' Bible study group again, is it?' Oliver asked, warily eyeing the book she'd placed on the table. He couldn't help noticing a number of Post-its sticking out of the pages.

'It is not. I've resigned myself to your inflexibility on that point.' She flicked a crumb from her mouth. 'Although my misgivings on the Good News translation remain, of course.'

'Right. So . . . your sister, perhaps?'

Miss Ackroyd shuddered. 'Yes. Clemmie's the reason I came.'

Oliver flashed her a genuine smile, pleased to think he could finally do what he'd entered the Church for and give comfort to a soul in pain. 'Of course. I know how difficult this must be for you. In fact, I took the liberty of bookmarking some passages that might be helpful in working through your grief. We can talk them over together.' He made a move to stand up, but Miss Ackroyd waved him down.

'Sit, please. You're misunderstanding me. That's not why I'm here.'

'Oh.'

'Oliver . . .' She leaned towards him. 'Now, I've known you and your family a long time – your mother and father, and young Archie while we had him. Isn't that so?'

'Well, yes.' Everyone knew everyone else in Cherrywood, pretty much, so it wasn't the world's most groundbreaking observation.

'And as hard as it is to – but nevertheless, you're no longer a child. You're a man of God.' She cast a withering look at the plate of biscuits. 'And French fancies or not, you're the only one who can help me.'

Oliver was puzzled now. If she wasn't here for grief counselling, what sort of help had she come for?

'Miss Ackroyd. Prue.'

'Miss Ackroyd.'

'Miss Ackroyd. I'll do whatever I can to ease your mind. Tell me what's troubling you.'

'Like I said, it's Clemmie.' She lowered her voice. 'Oliver, you may find this hard to believe, but . . . I know who killed my sister, and it wasn't Terry Braithwaite.'

Oliver nearly dropped his digestive into his tea. 'Oh my God! Have you told the police?'

'Don't be ridiculous, boy, of course I haven't.'

Oliver blinked. 'But you're telling me?'

'I told you, you're the only one who can help.' She glanced around, as if afraid the walls might have ears. 'There's something in Ling Cottage,' she whispered.

'Something?'

'A presence. A malevolent presence.'

'You can't mean, like . . . a poltergeist?'

'Something supernatural. It killed Clemmie and now it's trying to kill me.'

Oliver wondered how to proceed. Nothing in his training had prepared him for this. He cast a helpless look at a crucifix on his wall, but it didn't offer any inspiration. Nor did anything plausible present itself when he tried to think of an excuse to leave the room so that he could place a quick call to his bishop.

Miss Ackroyd's eyes were fixed on him. As steely as they were, there was an undercurrent of need there too. She needed him to believe her.

'OK,' he said, keeping his voice even. 'Could you tell me what's led to the discovery of this . . . this spirit, or whatever it might be?'

'There's no whatever about it: it is a spirit. A thing *not of this world.*' She mouthed the words, as if merely saying them aloud could summon the phantom to them. 'And I'm positive it's responsible for my sister's death.'

'Why should you suspect that had a supernatural cause?'

'Because of this.' Miss Ackroyd withdrew a small gold medallion from her handbag and handed it to Oliver.

He dangled it in front of his eyes. 'A Madonna and child. What of it?'

'Clemmie was wearing it when she . . . that is to say, the police found it on her body.'

'Well?'

'It isn't hers,' Miss Ackroyd said quietly, taking it from him and gazing at the mother and baby. 'She didn't own any such item of jewellery. The only medallion she wore was a St Christopher.'

'Oh, I'm sure she must have –'

Miss Ackroyd raised a hand to silence him. 'If you dare to tell me I'm a potty old lady, Oliver Maynard, I shall march right out of here and telephone your mother.'

Oliver drew himself up. 'Now let's get one thing straight. I'm the vicar of this parish, not a little boy in class. You've come to me for my professional advice and I want to help you, but I'll do so only on the basis of mutual respect. I'll thank you to leave my mum out of things.'

Miss Ackroyd held his gaze for a moment. Then she broke into a rare smile. 'I've been waiting a long time for you to say that to me.'

He blinked. 'Have you?'

'Certainly. It's high time you learnt to stand up for yourself, young man.' She raised an eyebrow. 'So now we understand one another, will you believe me?'

'I want to, but I just can't see how your sister's medallion is evidence of a haunting. The most likely explanation is she bought it for herself.'

'Then where's her St Christopher?'

'In the house somewhere, I expect.'

Miss Ackroyd shook her head. 'I've searched everywhere: her jewel box; the drawer in the sideboard where she kept her most precious things. It's gone. Vanished.'

'Perhaps Terry took it.'

'The police recovered everything that was stolen. The watch and the candlesticks were there, but not Clemmie's St Christopher.'

'So you think the spirit took it?'

'I think it was transformed,' she said in a hushed voice.

'But why?'

'I don't know why. All I know are the facts,' she told him stiffly. 'And that's not the only thing.' She shuddered. 'There have been . . . incidents. Things moved from their right places. Sounds, movements. And . . . other things.'

'Nelson, surely.'

She looked at him sharply. 'It certainly was not Nelson. Don't you think I know the difference between an incontinent old tom and an evil spirit, boy?'

'So you want me . . .'

'To perform an exorcism. Yes,' she told him matter-of-factly, as if he banished evil spirits from little old ladies' homes on a daily basis.

'Um, I'm not sure the diocese would allow me—'

'Pooh. Nonsense,' she said, waving away his objection. 'It's all above board; I got Beverley Stringer to look it up on the Google. Preachers do it all the time in America.'

'Maybe they do, but in the Church of England we don't tend—'

'And the apostles were always exorcising.' Miss Ackroyd picked up her Bible and flicked to one of the Post-its. ' "But Paul, being grieved, turned and said to the spirit, I command thee in the name of Jesus Christ to come out of her. And he came out the same hour." Acts 16:18.' She looked at him expectantly.

'Well, that was—'

' "And He preached in their synagogues throughout all Galilee, and cast out devils." Mark 1:39. And that was Jesus himself.'

'Yes, but—'

'I've got at least another ten bookmarked. If it was good enough for the early apostles, I don't see why it shouldn't be good enough for the modern Church.' She put down the Bible and glared at him. 'Will you do my exorcism or not? I can't share my home with this . . . this *thing* another minute.' She leaned towards him. 'This is not some monster under the bed, Oliver. This is real.'

Beneath the habitually stern expression Miss Ackroyd did look genuinely afraid, and Oliver felt his heart go out to her. He reached out to pat her papery hand.

'Let me speak to my bishop,' he said. 'I'll see what I can do.'

Chapter 6

Tess shook her head as she served Oliver his pint.

'She's gone dotty.'

'Grief. It can make people do strange things.' He sipped his beer. 'You should've seen her, though, Tessie. She was trying to hide it, but she genuinely looked terrified when she told me about the medallion.'

Beverley Stringer, who was crouching next to Tess unloading the glass washer, looked up. 'Not surprised she's gone funny, up in that creepy old house all on her own. Blood stains still in the rug and everyone in the village gabbing about her.'

'Come on, Bev, you're the worst one for gabbing,' Tess said.

'I never suggested she did it though, did I? Prue's a tough old cow but she's no killer, no matter what that Peggy Bristow's been putting about.' Bev sighed. 'Poor sausage, it's no life. I'll walk up tomorrow with some buns for her.'

'Be careful. Gracie tried to give her a casserole at the Women's Guild meeting and Miss Ackroyd practically inserted it into her.'

'No one says no to Bev's buns though,' Oliver said, smiling.

'So what was the thing with the medallion?' Tess asked him.

'Something about it being the wrong one. Aunty Clemmie's St Christopher had been transformed into a Madonna and child. At least, that's what Miss Ackroyd thinks.'

'Right. Through ghostly powers.'

'Apparently.'

'But why?' Tess asked. 'Why would this fashion-conscious ghost want to turn one bit of jewellery into another? And why's that the first explanation Miss Ackroyd thought of? It doesn't make sense.'

'Nor does losing someone, does it?' He sipped his drink thoughtfully. 'She's confused, poor soul. I wish I could do more to help settle her mind.'

'Did you talk to your bishop about this exorcism?'

'Not yet. I'm not quite sure how to broach it, to be honest. "Hi Michael, how's the wife? Oh and by the way, any idea how to get rid of a ghost?"'

'Maybe it's Clemmie's ghost,' Bev said.

'Miss Ackroyd didn't seem to think so. She was convinced it was the ghost that had done Clemmie in.'

'For God's sake, listen to the pair of you,' Tess said, rolling her eyes. 'There's no such thing as bloody ghosts.'

Bev shrugged. 'More things in heaven and earth, I always say.'

'And me, obviously,' Oliver said.

Tess pondered a moment. 'It's funny though, isn't it?'

'What is?' Oliver asked.

'Aunty Clemmie wearing a St Christopher. That's to protect travellers, right? It's not like she got out much.'

'Well, she had health issues. She might've been all over the place when she was young.'

Bev shook her head. 'Yearly coach trip to Blackpool with her awful mother and that was it, as far as I know.'

'Was St Christopher the patron of anything else?' Tess asked Oliver.

'How should I know?'

'Didn't you learn about him when you were training?'

'Sorry. I left my *Boy's Own Book of Martyrs* back at the vicarage.'

'You never know, it might be important. To the murder investigation, I mean,' Tess said, thinking of Liam.

'The investigation's closed, Tess. Terry's been charged and that's an end of it, as far as police are concerned.'

'Yes, but they'll open it again if new evidence comes to light, surely. It seems pretty odd to me, a woman who never went further than the shops wearing a medallion to protect travellers.'

'Hang on, I'll look on Wikipedia.' Oliver pulled out his phone. 'OK, St Christopher . . .' He scrolled down the entry. 'Patron saint of travellers. Also offers patronage to mariners, soldiers, archers, gardeners, bookbinders . . . and protects against toothache.'

'Hmm.' Tess turned to put away Bev's clean glasses on the shelves above the spirit optics. 'Aunty Clemmie wasn't into archery, was she, Bev?'

'With her arthritis?'

Oliver pushed back his barstool. 'Right. The little boys' room calls. Mind my pint for us, Tess.'

When he'd gone, Bev glanced around to check they weren't being overheard, then leaned in to Tess, enveloping her in a fog of stale fags and Chanel Number Five.

'I'll tell you summat, though – it isn't the first time things have gone missing from Ling Cottage,' she murmured. 'And it doesn't take ghostly intervention to work out where they went, neither.'

'How do you mean?'

'Well, you know me, I'm not one to gossip,' Bev said, her nose spontaneously growing at least three inches. 'But why do you think Prue Ackroyd moved into that cottage in the first place?'

'To keep from being lonely, I suppose.'

Bev snorted. 'Like hell. She was skint, love. Her mum dying happened right in the nick of time.'

Tess blinked. 'Miss Ackroyd was hard up? How come?'

'Not for me to say, I'm sure. I'd just like to know what became of that money she claimed was taken.'

'You can't mean she stole it? She wouldn't lie to the police.'

'Hmm. Wouldn't she, though? She's no killer, but she's a sly one. I wouldn't put a bit of petty theft past her if she thought there was no chance of getting caught.'

Bev stopped when Oliver plonked himself back on his stool and waggled her eyebrows at Tess to keep schtum.

'So are you on the bar after Tess, Bev?' Oliver asked her in a casual tone.

'No, young Tammy is.'

'Oh. Good.'

Tess smiled. 'So that explains the two pub nights in a row. I thought you were looking smart, Ol.'

'Don't know what you mean.'

Bev grinned at Tess. 'That time of year again, is it?'

'Yep,' she said. 'But it's ix-nay on the ogcollar-day, Bev. We've all been sworn to secrecy.'

'Only temporary,' Oliver muttered. 'How was your Women's Guild meeting, Tessie?'

'Yeah, not bad. Me and Rave have decided we're going to keep up with it, actually.' Tess stood on tiptoes to place a pint glass on the top shelf. 'Which reminds me, I need you to teach me the words to "Jerusalem".'

Oliver helped himself to some peanuts from a bowl on the bar. 'How about this gardener? Is he all Rave made him out to be?'

'God, it was oestrogen on acid in there.' Tess put on a high-pitched voice. ' "Ooh, Sam, I'm having dreadful trouble with me begonias, could you come and have a fiddle with them? Ooh, Sam, what a lovely big hose you've got. Do you fancy a stroke of my clematis?" '

'And ooh, Sam is right behind you,' Bev said, tapping Tess's shoulder to indicate she should look around.

'Well, of course he is. Where else would he be?' Tess sighed and turned round. Liam had materialised next to Oliver's barstool.

'Er, hi,' he said.

'Hi.' She tried not to glare at him too obviously.

'Tess, right? We spoke briefly at the meeting last night.'

'I know, I was there. What can I get you?'

'Actually, I just wondered if I could have a quick word with you about . . . a thing.'

'I'm working. What is it?'

'The, er . . . the window boxes, out in the beer garden. They're looking a bit sad and I think I know what to recommend. Could you come take a look?'

Tess nodded to Bev. 'This is the landlady. Talk to her.'

'I'm not sure I quite fit the bill for this job,' Bev said with a knowing smile. 'Go on, Tess. I'll keep an eye on the bar till Tam arrives.'

Tess hesitated. She knew she needed to have things out with Liam, but she could really do without it being tonight.

Bev nudged her. 'You don't want to be playing too hard to get,' she whispered. 'Not with a man who looks like that.'

'Fine,' Tess said, wincing. Her boss was an incurable gossip but the art of being subtle still eluded her. 'Make it quick then, mate.'

Bev grinned at Oliver. 'What is the Church's position on clematis-stroking before marriage, Reverend?'

'Oh, very strict,' he said, nodding soberly. 'We tend to be pretty liberal nowadays, but I'm afraid it's still the full hell-fire and brimstone job for anything involving climbing plants.'

Tess shot them a dirty look before coming out from behind the bar and beckoning to Liam – Sam, damn it – to follow her. She guided him down the passageway that led to the beer garden, and, when she was certain no one was look-ing, pulled him into a convenient cleaning cupboard.

'Hey,' he said as she shut the door behind them. 'My night's looking up.'

'Seriously, window boxes?' she hissed. 'That's the best your detective brain could come up with?'

'Sorry. Couldn't think of anything else.'

'I won't ask what the hell you're doing here, since with the fake name and the fake gardening expertise you're clearly on a case. Just tell me what's going on so I can decide what to do about you.'

'The gardening expertise is a hundred per cent bona fide. I'm a trained horticulturist.'

She frowned. 'What, really?'

'Yeah. Two years of college before I decided on a career change and joined the force.'

'So come on, what do you think you're doing here?' Tess demanded. 'Not content with ruining my life down in Lon-don, you thought you'd have a crack at destroying this one too, did you?'

'Look, I never meant for that to happen,' Liam said in a low voice. 'And I didn't know you were here, OK? If I had, I'd never have taken the case.'

'Yeah, right. Of all the crumbling country pubs in all the dull backwater villages in all the world, you just happened to walk into mine.' She glared at him. 'And perhaps you might like to explain what you think you're playing at flirting with my best mate.'

'What, the Walton-Lord kid? I wasn't flirting with her.'

She snorted. 'OK, sure. Like you didn't date me for four months to get information on Jackie.'

'I didn't. Honestly, I didn't.' He put a hand on her shoulder. 'Tessie, you have to believe that when I was on the Porter case, I never meant for you to get dragged in.'

'So you're saying you didn't ask me out that night at the fundraising gala because you wanted inside info on Jackie, are you?'

Liam flushed – ashamed, Tess sincerely hoped. 'All right, maybe that first time . . . you were the only one who could get me access to her.'

She shook her head. 'Don't you freelancers have any code of ethics? If you were still with the Met, you'd be struck off for something like that, I'm sure.'

'Look, I never meant for you to get hurt.' He met her eyes. 'Just because it was work-motivated the first time I asked you out doesn't mean it wasn't real after that. I asked you out a second time, greatly against my better judgement, because I couldn't stand the idea of not seeing you again.'

'You know that I not only lost my job thanks to you, but that I couldn't get another?' Tess said, folding her arms. 'That after the Porter scandal broke, I couldn't get PA work for love nor money?'

He frowned. 'Why not?'

She gave a hard laugh. 'Why do you think, Liam? Aside from the fact that my former boss is unable to give me a reference on account of being banged up, businesspeople don't tend to want assistants who they know are indiscreet enough to spill company details to any pretty undercover investigator who bats his eyes at them. Hence why I'm now back in this place, pulling pints for minimum wage just so I can afford the rent on my crappy shared flat.'

'Tessie, I'm sorry. I'm genuinely sorry.' He took her hand. 'If it makes any difference to you, I wouldn't do anything like that again. I don't ever want to hurt anyone the way I hurt you.'

She snatched her hand away. 'Mmm. Funny how I don't believe you. Just leave Raven out of it, that's all.'

'Look, I don't know what she's told you, but any flirting is entirely in her own head. I've been polite and that's it.'

'Huh,' Tess muttered. 'That's the problem with you – it's impossible to tell the difference. Just try not to politely go to bed with her, will you?'

'There's not going to be anything like that. Just don't tell her who I am, please.'

Tess frowned. 'Why not? She's not a suspect, is she?'

'She could be. I haven't worked it out yet.'

'Seriously, you're investigating Raven? I can tell you the sum total of her law-breaking activities, Liam: one joint behind the bandstand in the park when she was sixteen, which gave her a nosebleed, and illegally downloading a Coldplay album in 2006. If you've been hired to investigate either of those, you really must have fallen on hard times.'

'Tess, seriously, you can't blow my cover on this,' he said in a low voice. 'I'm too far in now.'

'What's the case then? Is Jim the butcher putting horse-meat in his premium sausages? Or are you here investigating illegal growing methods at the village show? Because if so,

I'm reliably informed you ought to give Bev's marrows a look over.'

'Well . . . I can't tell you.'

'All right, then you won't mind if I just march out into the pub and let everyone know who Sam Mitchell really is.' She went to open the door.

'Wait.' Liam exhaled through his teeth. 'OK, if you promise to keep it quiet. It's the old lady, Clemency Ackroyd.'

Tess's interest rose. 'I thought it must be. So this is a murder investigation?'

'Threatening letters. But my client thinks the letters and the murder are connected.'

'I knew there must be more to it,' Tess murmured. 'Who's the client?'

'I really can't tell you.'

She went for the door again.

'Tess, come on,' he said, drawing her back. 'Honestly, I can't, not at this stage.'

'Why doesn't this client of yours go to the police?'

'They've got nothing solid, just gut feeling. They want me to investigate the sister.'

Tess frowned. 'Miss Ackroyd? You think she killed Clemmie?'

'Not necessarily, but I'm sure she's hiding something. I'm here to get to the bottom of it.'

'She has been acting strangely,' Tess murmured. 'She thinks her house is haunted. Mind you, she just lost her sister. In that horrible, violent way too – you know, she was the one who found her.'

'I know.' He dipped his head to look into her face. 'What else have you heard?'

She narrowed one eye. 'Why should I tell you?'

'Because I'm trying to solve this case. You want the killer caught, don't you?'

'Course I do. That's what the police are for though, isn't it?'

'The police round here can't tell their backsides from their elbows. You must know Terry Braithwaite didn't do it.'

'Hmm. Maybe.'

'Did you know her? The old lady?'

Tess bowed her head. 'She was my nursery teacher. Aunty Clemmie, those of us who were kids here knew her as. Everyone in Cherrywood loved her. It's rocked the whole village, knowing someone could do that to her.'

'I'm sorry.'

Tess sighed. 'I don't know, Liam. I want to see justice done for Clemmie, and there is some funny stuff going on, but I can't see how it relates to the murder.'

'What sort of funny stuff?'

'Prue Ackroyd. Like I said, she's got this theory her house is haunted – that Clemmie was killed by something supernatural. And then there's St Christopher.'

'St Christopher?'

'Clemmie wore a medallion. For some reason it wasn't on her body, although Miss Ackroyd says she never took it off. She was wearing a Madonna and child instead. No one knows where that came from.'

'Do you think that's significant?'

Tess raised an eyebrow. 'What, you want my opinion?'

'Sure I do.'

'Not as significant as the missing St Christopher – as in, why Clemmie was wearing one in the first place. She barely left the house, let alone travelled. Look into whether she had a passport. I'd bet my pint-pulling arm that she didn't.'

'I will. Thanks.' Liam took a notebook from his pocket and scribbled a few notes. 'Anything else?'

'Only that my boss thinks Miss Ackroyd's a petty thief, but I wouldn't pay that too much mind. She's a notorious gossip.' Tess examined his face as he wrote. 'So why were you hired? What is there in all this to suggest it wasn't just a robbery gone wrong, as the police believe?'

'I thought that at first. Then I discovered something that seemed to put a new complexion on things.'

'What was it?'

'Clemency Ackroyd had private savings of over two hundred thousand pounds.'

Chapter 7

'*What?*'

'Clemency had two hundred grand tucked away in a high-interest savings account,' Liam repeated. 'I've seen the documents.'

Tess shook her head. 'No, that can't be right. Clemmie wasn't rich. She had her state pension and that was it.'

'It's true. Never accessed; it's been collecting interest for decades. Clemency's possessions and her share of the cottage were left to her sister, but the money's going to someone called Nadia Harris. I had to tell the police what I'd found, since it might be relevant to the murder investigation, but they didn't seem to feel it was significant. Personally, I disagree.'

'Did you tell them about the threatening letters?' Tess asked.

'No. I've got no concrete evidence they're connected to either Clemency or the murder – not yet.'

'Who is this Nadia Harris? I've never heard of anyone by that name.'

'No one seems to have, in Cherrywood or anywhere else,' Liam said. 'We know from Clemency's will that Nadia's father was a Colonel Harris, but the last record I can find refers to them living in Turkey in the late Seventies. Then the old man passed away and that was the last anyone saw of her.'

'But what's her connection to Clemmie?'

He shrugged. 'Your guess is as good as mine. The family were living here in the mid-Sixties, when this Nadia was born, but I can't find any link to the Ackroyds.'

'So you've got no concrete leads at all?'

'One.'

'Go on, what?'

He looked at her keenly. 'I can trust you?'

She shook her head. 'Oh no. You don't get to ask that. I get to ask that. And it'd be strictly rhetorical because I know full well what the answer is.'

'I guess I deserved that.' He paused, looking into her face, then made his decision. 'OK. Colonel and Mrs Harris employed a domestic staff.'

'Servants?'

'Yes. A cook, long deceased, and a maid, still living. One Marianne Priestley.'

She stared at him. 'You mean, our Marianne – Raven's Marianne?'

'That Marianne.' He clasped her shoulder. 'Tess, I could really use your help with this. You're a friend of the family, and you're perfectly placed at the pub to hear any rumours that might be flying about. What do you say?'

'I'm a useful tool when you need me, eh?' She shook his

hand away. 'I'm not doing your job for you, Liam, and I'm certainly not spying on my nearest and dearest for you. They were the ones who picked me up and helped me dust myself off when you plonked me in this mess.'

'I'm not asking you to spy on anyone. Just pass on anything you hear that sounds like it might be relevant – for the old lady's sake.' He pressed a card into her hand. 'This is my number. I'm staying at the old groundskeeper's cottage on the estate if you need me.'

'I'm sorry, but no. I can't work with you. It'd be too . . . I just can't, that's all.' She gave the card back. 'I need to go.'

She turned to the door, but he rested a hand on her shoulder. 'You won't blow my cover, will you?'

She hesitated. 'I don't know, Liam.'

'Come on. I know you don't owe me anything—'

'Apart from a kick in the balls.'

'Fair enough, apart from a kick in the balls, but I need this case. If you can just keep it quiet for a few weeks, I promise I'll be out of your life for good.'

'Hmm. Well, that I like the sound of.'

He squeezed her hand. 'Thanks, Tessie. You won't regret it, I promise.'

The door opened and Bev's gravity-defying bosom appeared, followed by her smirking face. 'So there you two are. I should've guessed.'

Tess jumped away from Liam's hand. 'Um. Hiya.'

'I hate to interrupt while you two are in here inspecting the, er, window boxes, but Tess, Ian's ready to go.'

The colour rose in Tess's cheeks. 'We weren't doing anything.'

Bev held up her hands. 'No need to explain to me, love. We were all young once.'

'I'll go change,' Tess muttered.

'Leave, can you?' she whispered to Liam as she followed Bev out. 'You've got me into enough trouble.'

She darted upstairs to the staff bathroom to get into her costume – a pair of striped flared trousers, furry waistcoat and a long black wig – hoping that Liam would be gone by the time she got back to the bar.

But he wasn't. Private investigators never do leave when you tell them to, do they? They hang around to find out what piece of juicy info you were trying to cover up.

And oh, this piece was a doozy. Tess could feel her cheeks burning as she marched through the pub, bell-bottoms swinging around her ankles.

Liam was perched on a barstool next to Oliver, with whom he seemed to have struck up a conversation. Tess deliberately avoided eye contact as she passed.

'Took your time,' Ian said when she joined him on the small stage at the front of the pub. A couple of stools had been set up next to mike stands for them, with a sparkling foil backdrop behind.

'Sorry. Got held up.'

'Mmm, in the cupboard; my missus told me. You know, love, we don't pay you to enjoy yourself.'

Bloody Bev. She obviously hadn't wasted any time circulating the gossip. Given what she knew about Ian's own extra-curricular activities in the past, Tess couldn't help feeling this was a bit rich.

'Look, it was all innocent,' she muttered. 'Can we get on with it?'

At first glance the Star and Garter's landlord appeared to be in a matching costume to her own, but Tess knew better. If there was such a thing as a method tribute act, then Ian Stringer was it.

The long hair was no wig: it had been grown specially, as had the bushy moustache. The fringed suede suit with its wide, fur-trimmed lapels was genuine retro, sourced from a specialist supplier. The Cuban heels, Tess suspected, he'd already had in his wardrobe.

'Right,' he said. 'Let's give 'em a treat tonight, shall we? "I've Got You, Babe" to warm them up, then we'll do "Dark Lady", since Mystic Peg's in.'

'Don't tease her, Ian, it's cruel.'

'Oh, go on. Might put a smile on the old cow's face.'

Tess managed to get through their set, humiliation adding a tremulous note to her voice as she belted out song after song. She could see Liam in her peripheral vision, his initial surprise soon turning into an amused grin, but she did her best to ignore him.

When they'd finished, Bev fought her way through the crowds of screaming fans – or rather, sauntered through a smattering of polite applause – to join them. Ian pulled her on to his knee to kiss her neck.

She giggled. 'Get off, you randy sod.'

'Is it a crime to find my own wife irresistible?'

79

'Ah, give over. Your moustache is tickling me.' She extricated herself and turned to Tess. 'You OK, love? You sounded a bit off.'

'Sorry. Think I might be coming down with a sore throat.'

'Glandular fever,' she said, nodding knowledgeably. 'You get that from snogging, you know. In cupboards.'

Tess glared at her. 'It is not glandular fever and I have not been snogging in cupboards. Sam just wanted to ask me something in private.'

'I'm sure,' Bev said, grinning. 'Hey, are you really not going to join us for *Mamma Mia*? We could use someone with your pipes.'

'Nope,' Tess said firmly. 'I don't put myself through this sort of epic humiliation for my own amusement. If I don't get paid, I don't sing.'

'Not even one number with Ian? It'll be good publicity for the act.'

'Sorry.' Tess yanked off her wig and hung it on the microphone stand. 'Look, there's no one serving. I'd better go keep an eye on the bar till Tam gets back.'

She screwed her toes into her platform shoes as she approached the bar. Liam was leaning against it, waiting for her. He grinned as she took up her customary position behind the beer pumps.

'So,' he said.

'So.'

'You're a Cher impersonator.'

'Round here, we like to think Cher's more of a Tess impersonator,' Oliver said.

'We're only Sonny and Cher in spring and summer,' Tess told Liam. 'If you come back in autumn, we'll be Dolly Parton and Kenny Rogers.'

'How'd you get into that then?'

'Well I used to be a PA, until some tosspot lost me my job. Turns out the only other things I'm any good at are pulling pints and belting a tune.'

'You were good. I actually thought your version of "If I Could Turn Back Time" was definitive.'

Tess glared at him. 'Don't you have gardening to do?'

'Nope.' He downed the last of his pint. 'But I do have a social engagement. Old Fred Braithwaite's invited me over for a drink.'

'You're going to see Terry's dad?'

'Yes, he's pretty down at the moment. Poor old chap thought the lad really had gone straight this time.' Liam nodded to Oliver as he got to his feet. 'Good to meet you, Reverend. I'll catch you both later.'

'So was that flirty rudeness or rudeness rudeness?' Oliver asked when Liam had gone.

'It was rudeness rudeness.'

'And earlier, was that flirty caught in a cupboard with him or did he just ask you to show him where Bev keeps the Domestos?'

'That was completely innocent.' Tess lowered her voice. 'And please, don't say stuff like that around Rave. You know she's keen on him. She might get the wrong idea.'

'What was the rudeness in aid of then?' Oliver asked.

'He . . . I don't like him taking the piss out of my career.'

'As a Cher impersonator? We all take the piss out of that. And if you think you'll get any sympathy from me with the amount of vicar jokes I have to take off you and Raven, you can forget it.'

'Yeah, but I know you lot. That guy's not even local,' she muttered. 'And . . . I just don't like him, that's all. Seems like he fancies himself a bit to me.'

'Seems like he fancies you a bit to me.'

'Well it's not mutual, so he can knock that on the head quick as he likes.' She glanced over her shoulder into the bar storage room. 'Speaking of unrequited lust, where's Tam?'

'Changing a barrel.'

'Asked her out yet?'

'Nearly.'

Tess cocked an eyebrow. 'Nearly?'

'Well, I asked her if it had been busy tonight. That's a start, right?'

'What kind of question is that? You've been here longer than she has, you pillock.'

Oliver grimaced. 'Yeah. Panicked a bit.'

She leaned over the bar. 'Look. How about you bugger off for a while? Go talk to Peggy Bristow, she's all on her tod.'

'My conversation that dull, is it?'

'Go on. Then when Tam comes back, I can build you up a bit.'

He blinked. 'Would you do that?'

'Course.'

'Thanks, Tessie, you're a pal.' Oliver gave her arm a grateful squeeze, then went to join Peggy.

Tammy appeared beside her a few minutes later.

'Hi, Tess,' she said. 'Sorry, I thought Bev was minding the bar.'

'Mmm.' Tess glanced at Bev, who was perched on Ian's knee while he whispered not-so-sweet nothings into her ear, occasionally emitting a filthy laugh Sid James would've been proud of. 'I think Bev's busy minding something else.'

Tammy shook her head. 'Those two are terrible.'

'It's not like they can't get a room if they want. They bloody live here.'

'They do it to wind Peggy up, I'm sure.'

Tess looked at Peggy Bristow, Ian's first wife, who was supping her crème de menthe with Oliver while looking anywhere but at the pub's over-amorous proprietors. A small, dowdy woman with a librarianish air, she easily disappeared into the shade in Beverley's larger-than-life presence.

'Bev got her man,' Tess said. 'I don't know why she has to rub poor Peggy's face in it.'

'Why are they even still speaking?' Tammy said. 'If a mate of mine did that to me, buggered if I'd ever talk to her again.'

'Because this is Cherrywood, and in Cherrywood we're far too civilised to get upset when our best friend runs off with our hubby of twenty years. We channel our rage into cake-making and smiling like a Stepford Wife.' Tess thought of Raven. 'Still. Bad friend. I know Bev likes a flirt, but I'd never have expected her to do the dirty on Peggy the way she did.'

'It's nice of your mate Oliver to cheer her up.'

'Yeah, he's a considerate lad.'

'Sort of good-looking in an awkward kind of way,' Tammy said, smiling in Oliver's direction. 'You and him aren't a thing, are you?'

'Me and Ol?' Tess laughed. 'Oh, no. I'm not his type at all.'

'Ah, right. Gay. Just our luck, eh?'

'No, I didn't mean that. We're old friends, that's all. Feelings for each other strictly brother-and-sisterly.'

'Oh. OK.' Tammy looked at Oliver with renewed interest. 'So what does he do?'

'He's a . . .' Tess hesitated. '. . . um, a motivational speaker.'

'That's unusual. What type of thing?'

'Oh, sort of . . . life coaching and that. Chivvying people up, you know.'

'Really? He seems so quiet. Just goes to show, you never can tell.'

'You really can't.' Tess turned to her. 'So you think he's good-looking, do you?'

'I guess.'

'You think you might like to ask him out? I'm happy to vouch for the fact he's worth it.'

Tammy looked unsure. 'Dunno, Tess. I've never asked a boy out before.'

'Well you'll be hanging on till the End of Days if you wait for Ol to ask you. He tries, poor soul, but shyness always gets the better of him.' Tess nudged her. 'He likes you, you know. That's why he's here. He never normally comes in if there's the off-chance he'll be forced to hear me sing.'

Tammy blinked. 'Does he? He's barely said two words to me.'

'Like I said. Shy. He's probably psyching himself up to ask you for a date.' Tess lowered her voice. 'He's coming over. Go on, help the lad out.'

'Um, hi,' Oliver said, flushing to the roots of his blond hair. He put his empty pint glass on the bar. 'One more, I think, and same again for Peggy.'

'Right.' Tammy started pumping him a beer. 'Er, so . . .'

'Look, Tammy, I thought maybe . . .'

'Tess was saying . . . I mean, I wondered if you might like . . .'

'You fancy going out sometime?' a now bright-red Oliver asked, at almost exactly the same time as Tammy blurted out, 'You want to go for a drink with me?'

They both laughed.

'Sorry,' they said at the same time.

'So was that a yes?' Oliver asked.

'If it's a yes from you, it's a yes from me,' Tammy said, her cheeks now as pink as his.

Smiling, Tess went to hide in the bar storage room while they arranged their date.

Chapter 8

Over the next week, Tess did her best to put Liam Hanley out of her head so life could go back to normal – at least, as normal as it ever was when you pulled pints and impersonated Cher for a living at the village pub.

But the man was determined to make it difficult for her. Everywhere Tess went in Cherrywood, he seemed to be there.

She went out with Raven to pick up a few bits from the corner shop and there was Liam, doing some work in Peggy Bristow's garden. The next day, when they went for a walk on the moors, there he was again, taking Candice's Pomeranian Susie for a scamper. When they walked down to the allotments to buy some spring greens from Neil Hobson, lo and behold there was Liam, giving Neil advice on how to increase his yield of raspberries. Whenever Liam saw Tess he'd smile and wave, as if they were the best of friends rather than exes only reluctantly on speaking terms.

By Friday, Tess had accidentally bumped into Liam five times and was thoroughly sick of the sight of him. Raven, on the other hand, was delighted.

'Darling, I honestly think he must be doing it on purpose,' she said as she drove them to the Embassy, an independent theatre in a nearby town.

Tess started. 'What?'

'Sam. I think he's engineering these little rendezvous of ours.' She glanced at Tess in the rear-view mirror. 'What is wrong with you this week? You're so jumpy.'

'Sorry.'

'So, do you think I'm right?'

'What, that he took on gardening work at Peggy's place and helped Neil out with his raspberries just so he could catch a glimpse of your beautiful face? No.'

Raven frowned. 'All right. You don't need to piddle on my bonfire quite as thoroughly as all that.'

Tess sighed. 'Sorry, Rave. I'm just on edge today.'

'Well, tonight should take your mind off it. I'm really looking forward to this. I've always had a thing for the stage.'

'You mean you've always been a drama queen.'

'I prefer the term prima donna,' Raven said, flicking out her bob. 'Makes me sound exotic.'

They were on their way to one of the regional events they'd signed up for at their first Women's Guild meeting: a backstage tour of a working theatre.

Tess had been quite looking forward to it herself, until her talk with Liam. Now, the memory of what he'd told her was casting long shadows over any social engagements involving Prue Ackroyd and the Women's Guild ladies.

No matter how much she tried to put it out of her mind,

87

she couldn't help brooding on Aunty Clemmie's murder and the strange facts surrounding it. And the £200,000, sitting untouched until this mysterious woman, Nadia Harris, appeared to claim it. Who was she? A long-lost relative? Perhaps even an ex-lover?

Two hundred grand! Tess could still hardly believe it. Aunty Clemmie, who'd shivered in scarves and triple cardies come wintertime because she could barely afford coal for her fire. Aunty Clemmie, who paid for her port and lemon in coppers – coppers that Tess had got into the habit of deliberately miscounting, making up the difference herself when they fell short.

Why sit on that amount of money and never spend it? And more importantly, where the hell did she get it?

Did Miss Ackroyd know about the will? Did she know about Clemmie's money? Before, the idea that Prue Ackroyd could have killed her sister in cold blood had seemed ridiculous. But now . . . money like that could change people. Turn them into something ugly. Perhaps, after all, it was suppressed guilt that was responsible for Miss Ackroyd's sudden faith in the occult.

And then there was Marianne – kind, funny Marianne, the person Raven loved most in the world, who might be the key to finding this Nadia Harris. She couldn't be mixed up in this shady business, surely.

And yet . . . *we're not so innocent in this, Prue*. Marianne's muttered words to Miss Ackroyd at the first Women's Guild meeting. Just what did the pair of them have to hide?

Secrets. Secrets and lies, backstabbing and blood. It really wasn't what Tess had expected when she'd agreed to join the Women's Guild.

More fool you, whispered a cynical voice in the back of her head.

She'd been thinking, too, about Liam's invitation to help him with his investigation. On the one hand, seeing more of him was the last thing she wanted. Tess would rather die than admit it out loud, but Liam hadn't only humiliated her when she'd discovered the game he'd been playing in London – he'd broken her heart too. She'd been falling for him hard and fast, believing his feelings for her were equally deep, and then . . . the ultimate betrayal. Every time she saw him in the village it made her feel a little sick inside, remembering that awful day when it had all come out. Then the fallout as she'd found herself unemployed and unemployable in her adopted city, forced to admit defeat and return home to beg for support from her old friends in Cherrywood . . .

On the other hand, it had occurred to Tess that despite the pain constant contact with Liam would bring, there were advantages to taking him up on his offer. She was familiar with this community, these people, in a way he wasn't. People she knew well were apparently mixed up in this – Candice, Marianne and of course Raven were all people of interest, Liam had said – and Tess wanted to make damn sure no one she cared about was going to be unfairly accused of anything she knew them to be incapable of. Plus she might be able to help get justice for Aunty Clemmie, and for an innocent man. Scumbag he may be, but Tess couldn't believe

Terry Braithwaite was capable of murder, and certainly not of this murder – the facts just didn't add up.

And then there was the most compelling reason of all to get involved, which was that the faster Tess could help Liam solve his case, the faster he would be back in London and out of her life. She wouldn't have to see him everywhere she went, reminding her of a part of her past that brought unspeakable pain. She wouldn't have to worry that he was using his old tricks on her best friend, breaking Raven's heart as he'd once broken hers. Her world could go back to being safe, quiet and Liam-free, as it had been before.

'Penny for them?' Raven said.

'Hmm?' Tess roused herself. 'Sorry, miles away. Are we here?'

'Yes, this is it.' Raven parked up opposite a Renaissance-style building with white cupolas. 'And there's Gracie waiting for us.'

They got out and headed for Gracie, who was frowning as she scribbled in a notebook. She jumped when they hailed her, and stashed it hurriedly away.

'Writing your memoirs, Gracie?' Raven asked.

Gracie laughed. 'I'm writing my shopping list for the spring show in two weeks, but I imagine it would amount to much the same thing. Life feels like one big shopping list sometimes, I'm sure.'

'Are we the first?' Tess asked.

'No, the others are inside, mingling with the ladies from the other groups.' She shot them a censorious look. 'You're actually rather late, girls.'

'That's because someone drove us the long way round in the hope of catching Sam Mitchell working on Neil's allotment, isn't it?' Tess murmured to Raven.

Raven shrugged. 'It's warm today. Thought he might have his shirt off.'

They followed Gracie inside, down a plush, red-carpeted corridor that led into an opulent gilded foyer. A large group of women were enjoying canapés and fizz, their own little gang of Cherrywooders dispersed among them. Tess looked around for Miss Ackroyd and spotted her lurking alone in a corner, chewing thoughtfully on a plate of cheese and crackers.

'I'm not sure I dare speak to her after the last time,' Gracie whispered to Tess.

'We'll all go,' Tess said. 'Strength in numbers.'

But they didn't have time for much more than a preliminary hello before a woman draped in scarves clapped her hands for quiet.

'Sophie, the theatre director,' Gracie murmured to them.

The tour was really quite fascinating. They were shown the cubby hole at the front of the stage where the prompter hid, and how to work the trapdoor that allowed the villainous Wicked Stepmother or King Rat to do their disappearing act in a puff of smoke come panto season. They were introduced to the choreographer, who taught them how to do a shuffle ball change, and the lead actor from their current production of *The Crucible* – a reasonably well-known television star who made Gracie go quite giggly. Finally they were introduced to Gerard, the Embassy's make-up artist, who instructed them to get into pairs for a short masterclass in stage make-up.

'Do you want to buddy up?' Raven asked Tess.

'You go with Marianne. I'm going to ask Miss Ackroyd.'

It wasn't snooping, Tess told herself as she made a beeline for Prue Ackroyd. It certainly wasn't spying. Miss Ackroyd needed a partner, and it was unlikely any of the others would be queueing up to volunteer. And if they happened to talk a little bit about Aunty Clemmie, so what? It'd be good for Miss Ackroyd to have someone to confide in. Tess certainly wasn't doing it for Liam Hanley's benefit, that was for sure.

'Um, hi,' Tess said when she reached her. 'Do you want to go with me?'

Miss Ackroyd was staring at a fixed point in the distance, her lips moving silently.

'Miss Ackroyd?'

She jumped. 'Oh. Yes. Thank you, Teresa, that will be . . . very nice.'

Chairs had been set up in facing pairs on the stage, each with a box of make-up on a table between them.

Gerard clapped his hands. 'OK, ladies, if you'd like to decide between you who will be getting made over first, you can take your seats. Your mission should you choose to accept it is this.' He held up a photo of one of *The Crucible*'s cast members. Her hair was combed over her temples, puritan style, and dark-ringed eyes stood out from a pale face.

'But she isn't wearing any make-up, is she?' said Peggy, who'd seated herself opposite Gracie.

'Aha, but she is,' Gerard said. 'And I say so with some

professional pride. There is no harder job than to apply stage make-up to an actor who needs to look like she's not wearing any make-up at all.' He went to a large spotlight and flicked it on, then did the same to its partner at the other side of the stage. 'Now. Take a good look at one another in the cold light of synthetic day.'

Tess blinked at Miss Ackroyd in the glare of the stage lights. The effect was far from flattering. Frown lines that had seemed soft in the tender rays of the sun looked harsh and deep, the skin a malaria yellow. Tess dreaded to think how her own face must look.

'Not pretty, is it?' Gerard said, grinning. 'My first job is always to offset the effect of the lights. Once that's done and I have my canvas, I can start building my character. Off you go, ladies, and let's see what you can make of one another.'

'Do you want to go first or shall I?' Tess asked Miss Ackroyd.

'I'll go first. Goodness knows what awful thing he might have us turning each other into next. I think I can cope with being a puritan.'

Tess selected a sponge and base foundation from the make-up box and started dabbing at her face.

'So how's the singing going, young lady?' Miss Ackroyd asked.

'Oh, you know. Paying the bills.'

'You could be so much more, you know. You were always a clever girl.'

Tess smiled. 'And I was always grateful to you for finding it out.'

Miss Ackroyd shook her head. 'Growing up in that madhouse . . . How did you ever manage to read as much as you did?'

'I did my reading at the library.'

'You're better than that tacky pub, Teresa. You're better than Ian Stringer and his ridiculous dressing-up fetish. I don't know why you stay there.'

'Because I need to eat,' Tess said. 'And I do like working there. It'd be nice if the money was better, I admit, but you never get lonely when you're behind a bar.'

'But you're not making use of that brain of yours,' Miss Ackroyd said, tapping the side of her head. 'It was a terrible shame about your job in London. We all believed you were headed for great things. Was there no other work when your company went out of business?'

'Plenty. They just didn't want me,' Tess murmured as she dabbed at Miss Ackroyd's face with the sponge.

'Whyever not?'

Tess hesitated. She'd never told anyone back in Cherrywood the whole story of what had happened with Porter. Of course they knew the company had gone bankrupt following an embezzlement scandal, and that she'd struggled to find another job and ended up moving back home, but they didn't know it was her involvement with an undercover detective that had led to Porter's downfall – and her inability to find further work as a PA.

But sometimes you needed to give a little to get a little. If she wanted Miss Ackroyd to take her into her confidence, then she needed to make an offering of her own.

'Well, because . . . because employers don't tend to like the idea of a PA who shoots her mouth off to private investigators,' she said quietly.

Miss Ackroyd frowned. 'Was that what happened?'

'I'm afraid so.'

'But if the company was breaking the law, of course you were going to cooperate with the people investigating it.'

'Mmm. I'm not sure they saw it that way,' Tess said. 'I think the biggest issue wasn't that I cooperated; it was that I didn't know I was cooperating. That I allowed myself to be tricked into giving information.'

'Tricked in what way?'

'The investigator I talked to was working undercover. He . . . wormed his way into my confidence. I was taken in by him and I told him more than I ought – long before I knew my boss was on the take.'

'Surely that could have happened to anyone,' Miss Ackroyd said.

'Yeah. Only it didn't – it happened to me.' Tess paused while she selected an eyeshadow from the box, wondering how she could bring the subject back around to Clemmie and the Ling Cottage spook. 'So if I ask how things are, will you bite my head off again?'

Miss Ackroyd smiled. 'I'll try not to.'

'Are you OK up at the cottage on your own?'

'I'm not at home at the moment. I'm staying with Peggy. Beverley offered to feed Nelson for me while I was away.' She shuddered. 'I had to get out. I simply couldn't bear the place another minute.'

'With Peggy?' Tess asked, surprised. Peggy Bristow had definitely been first among equals in the Prue-Ackroyd-killed-her-sister gossip gang.

'Yes, she was kind enough to invite me to stay. Anyway, it will only be until—' Miss Ackroyd stopped herself. 'I'm waiting for some work to be done at the cottage.'

'It must be so stressful for you. Losing someone you love is horrible enough, but then to have had the police sniffing around . . .'

Miss Ackroyd looked at her sharply. 'The police were just doing their job. As they ought, since I pay my taxes.'

'I know,' Tess said gently. 'I wasn't implying anything. I just meant it was added worry you didn't need.'

Miss Ackroyd relaxed. 'Yes. I suppose it was.'

'At least they've got their man now. That must be a big relief.'

'Mmm.'

Tess studied the make-up brushes. 'You'll have all Aunty Clemmie's affairs to sort out as well, I suppose,' she said in a tone she hoped was both casual and sympathetic. 'Are you an executor?'

'Executor?'

'Of the will.'

Miss Ackroyd laughed. 'Clemmie make a will? She wouldn't have known where to begin, dear.'

'So she died intestate?'

'Of course.'

'That makes it easier, I suppose. Since you're her next of kin, I guess everything will go to you automatically.'

'Yes, I suppose it will,' Miss Ackroyd said absently. 'Not that Clem had anything to leave, apart from that pile of tat she treasured so much in the sideboard.'

'Tat?'

'Her coin collection and some other bits and pieces. Completely worthless. Her half of the cottage was the only thing of value that she owned.' Miss Ackroyd gazed into the distance. 'And I ought, I suppose, to be grateful to have a home for what remains of my life. If only I didn't have to share it.'

The last sentence was mumbled almost under her breath. Tess studied her make-up box, pretending she hadn't heard.

The effect of the makeover was startling. It made Tess's flesh creep to see the finished product. With her skin silver-white in the hard illumination of the spotlights, powder seeping into the deep lines of her face and her eyes ringed with purple, Miss Ackroyd looked ghoulish and unearthly – like a corpse.

'How do I look, darling?' Raven called to Tess, pouting. Marianne had gone a bit mad with the foundation. Raven was shiny and deathly pale, with deep scarlet lips.

'A bit like one of those sex dolls,' Tess called back.

'Get lost. I'm a puritanical babe.'

When they were done, Gerard called for them to swap partners. Miss Ackroyd shifted over a couple of chairs to do Peggy's make-up, while Raven – rather reluctantly, judging by the expression on her plasticky new face – allowed herself to be paired with her grandmother. Tess, meanwhile, found herself face to face with Marianne Priestley.

Chapter 9

'OK, ladies, brief number two,' Gerard said, holding up another photo. 'I know you'll have fun with this one, from our recent production of *Oliver!* Let's see what you can do with the working girls of Victorian London.'

'Oh, wonderful,' Marianne muttered to Tess. 'I've always wanted to learn how I can achieve that authentic "syphilitic prostitute" look.'

'I'm the one who'll have to head home looking like I'm going out on the game in 1835.' Tess paused. 'Maybe I should make the most of it and go clubbing.'

Marianne laughed and started selecting the make-up she thought would really capture the essence of nineteenth-century sex worker.

Tess glanced at Raven and Candice. Raven was smirking as she added a generous sprinkling of facial sores to her grandmother's face, and Tess actually heard Candice giggle when she caught a look at herself in the mirror.

'Looks like they're getting along for once,' she said to Marianne.

Marianne smiled. 'Nice to see, isn't it? Nearly thirty years I've been trying to build bridges between those two.'

'They love each other really. They're just not good at showing it.' Tess sneaked another look at them laughing together. 'Something like this is exactly what they need.'

'I'm glad the pair of you decided to stay on. Looks like that young gardener has done us one favour, eh?'

'I suppose we do have that to thank him for.' Tess closed her eyes to let Marianne add some eyeshadow. 'I can't believe you've been at Cherrywood Hall thirty years. Didn't you think about getting another nannying position after Raven was grown up? You were young enough.'

'Oh, no. I couldn't leave the two of them together. They'd have ended up killing each other without me to stand between them.'

'Are you close to the other kids you've looked after?'

'Not like I am to Raven,' Marianne said as she attacked Tess's cheeks with blusher. 'Well, she was such a lost little girl – no siblings, no parents. And as much as I adore Candice, she's always struggled with showing affection. Children need love just like they need food and drink.' She pulled Tess's hair back so she could sweep the blusher over her cheekbones. 'I get letters from the two I had before, Laurel and Francis King, but it isn't the same as it is with Raven.'

'Who were you with before them?'

'I wasn't. I worked for the Kings as their housekeeper before that. The children became fond of me, and when their old nanny left I lobbied Mrs King for her job. I was practically doing it anyway. The kids had never taken to their previous nanny, so she'd often left them with me.'

'Oh, right. So you weren't always a nanny,' Tess said, feeling like the worst person alive for trying to trick her old friend into sharing information.

Bloody Liam. What had he turned her into? Someone quite devious, clearly. Someone like him.

Marianne smiled, obviously pleased to have an engaged audience to share her life story with. 'No. I kept house for the Kings, and I was a general maid and dogsbody before I got promoted. I was with them twenty-nine years, all in all. Before that I was in service with a military family, Colonel and Mrs Harris.'

Parents of the unknown Nadia, of course. Tess feigned surprise.

'Locally? I didn't know we had any military types in the village.'

'Oh, they weren't in Cherrywood long – just over a year,' Marianne said. 'The wife, Betty, was rather a silly thing: a lot younger than her husband, and often sickly. The colonel had brought her here to see out her first pregnancy. She'd had scarlet fever and a doctor thought the moorland air might do her good. I think there was a worry she could lose the baby.'

'Did she?'

'No, the little girl was delivered healthy and bouncing,' Marianne said. 'Beautiful thing, born with a thick head of hair. My mum used to say that was a sign of genius. Anyway, once mother and child were out of danger, they moved on. The colonel was posted abroad not long after.'

100

'Do you still hear from them?'

'No. Betty promised to write, but her letters soon dried up. She was that kind of person – full of gushing promises, quickly forgotten.'

'I wonder where they are now.'

'The colonel must be long dead, unless he lived to an exceptionally old age. Betty was always ailing, but she might still be around.'

'Did they have friends in the village?'

Marianne shrugged. 'They kept themselves to themselves mostly – never socialised. The colonel was rather a snob. He called once on Roland Walton-Lord, Candice's future father-in-law, but the villagers swore they could barely get the time of day from him. He was always polite to me though.' She stopped with her make-up brush poised in mid-air. 'I often wonder what became of their little girl.'

'How old would she be now?'

'Mid to late fifties. I always had the strangest feeling she'd go on to great things – that I'd hear of her one day. Nadia Harris. But I never did.' She laughed, shaking her head. 'Now listen to me, I sound like Peggy Bristow with her book of dream meanings. Let's get you finished off. I think you'd look fabulous with a really impressive skin disease, don't you?'

*

'That's the most fun I've had with Grandmother since Boxing Day 2010,' Raven announced as she drove them to Cherrywood Hall. Feeling gregarious after the makeover session, Candice had invited them and the other ladies back for a drink or two.

'Why, what happened in 2010?' Tess asked.

'That was the year Marianne introduced her to Bailey's. We played drunken charades – the old-fashioned way, with dressing up – and she fell asleep dressed as Cleopatra.' Raven smiled. 'She's not a bad old stick when she lightens up a bit.'

'I think Marianne brings out the best in her.'

'Mmm. I dread to think what my life might've been like without Marianne in it.' Raven shuddered. 'Imagine if Grandmother had packed me off to some horrific boarding school. You know I was the first Walton-Lord to be state-educated? That was thanks to Mari's influence. She didn't want me to grow up detached from local kids my age.'

'You mean from plebs like me.'

Raven grinned. 'Yep. You lucky girl.'

'I always thought boarding school sounded fun,' Tess said as Raven swung the car up the drive to Cherrywood Hall. 'All the midnight feasts and lacrosse.'

'Enid Blyton propaganda. I bet it's awful. And if I'd gone then I'd never have met you and Ol, would I?'

'Or Miss Ackroyd.'

'Well, life can't be all fun and games.'

Tess smiled. 'She wasn't so bad.'

'You would say that. Teacher's pet.'

Tess glanced at herself in the rear-view mirror. Marianne had really gone to town with the facial sores, which clustered round her mouth and nose. Raven, meanwhile, looked like a Barbie with leprosy.

'Look at the state of us,' Tess said. 'I hope your nan's got wet wipes.'

Raven shook her head. 'You're not allowed to take it off. That's half the fun.'

'Oh God,' Tess muttered as they parked up outside the manor house. 'Not him again.'

Liam was out front with a pair of clippers, giving a haircut to one of the topiary greyhounds that flanked the doors.

'He's not supposed to be working at this time.' Raven's hands flew to her cheeks. 'Jesus, look at me! Darling, do you have any tissues?'

Tess grinned. 'Oh no. You're not allowed to take it off, that's half the fun.'

They got out of the car and headed towards the house, trying not to catch Liam's eye. He put down his clippers and looked them up and down.

'Did you girls change your hair?'

'Funny,' Tess said.

'I'm a puritan.' Raven nodded to Tess. 'She's a prostitute.'

'Wow. The Women's Guild really has changed.' He flicked at the side of his mouth. 'Something on your face there, Tess.'

'That's just my syphilis.'

'Ah. Of course.'

'Come on,' Raven said, grabbing Tess's arm. For once she seemed to be in a hurry to get out of Liam's presence. 'See you around, Sam.'

'Hang on,' he said. 'Raven, are you free tomorrow night? I forgot I promised to have a chat about some greenery for your flat. I've got a few ideas, if you want to discuss it over a drink.'

Tess glared at him. So much for having changed. Raven, on the other hand, looked ecstatic.

'My diary's pretty empty,' she said.

'Great. Send me a text and we'll arrange it.' He handed her a business card, the same one he'd previously given Tess, and went back to work.

'Oh my God!' Raven whispered as she dragged Tess inside. 'Did you hear that?'

'Now, Rave, don't get carried away.'

'He asked me out! On an actual date!'

'Maybe not. He said he wanted to talk plants. He's been freelancing for practically half the village; he might just be after another job.'

'Oh, tosh. He's not buying Peggy Bristow drinks at the pub, is he? I told you all those "accidental" meetings were set up.'

Tess sighed. 'I know you're excited but . . . just be cautious, all right? I don't want to see you get hurt.'

'I'll be fine, Tess. I'm a big girl.'

Still, Tess resolved to make sure she was working whatever shift at the pub coincided with Raven and Liam's date.

It was a jolly evening. Candice popped open a couple of bottles of fizz. With barely an arm-nudge, let alone an arm-twist, the drivers among them were talked into abandoning their cars until the next day, and it became a regular knees-up. Even Prue Ackroyd lightened up, with whispered rumours abounding that she'd actually been heard giggling. Not even Gracie's surprise announcement that, thanks to their new expertise, she'd volunteered them to do the make-up for Cherrywood Players' summer *Mamma Mia* production could kill the mood.

When the bubbly was all gone, Marianne raided the Walton-Lord liquor cabinet and Candice started mixing some weird and wonderful concoctions from the assorted spirits that lived there.

'Where did you learn to make cocktails?' Raven asked as her grandmother presented her with something called a Grasshopper.

Candice winked. 'Wouldn't you like to know? Your grand-mother has her secrets too, young lady.'

Tess stared as Candice went back to her table of spirits to mix Gracie a Rob Roy, whatever that was. 'Did she just . . . wink?'

'I feel like my whole world's been turned upside down since I found out what the Women's Guild get up to after dark.' Raven nudged her. 'Hey. Want to hear some juicy gossip?'

Tess stifled a groan. She was a bit sick of gossip, and of secrets generally. Plus she was far too tipsy to be in sleuth mode.

But she nodded as enthusiastically as she could manage. She'd already made up her mind to pay Liam a visit tomor-row, mainly to warn him off Raven, but also to pass on what she'd found out in the hope of getting rid of him a bit faster.

Raven linked her arm and guided her out of the room, where they wouldn't be overheard.

'You'll like this. Look what I found when I went to the loo,' she said, producing something from her pocket.

Tess blinked as she tried to focus. Raven was holding a small blue book with an ornate Arabic pattern embossed on it.

'What is it?'

'It's Gracie's notebook, the one she claimed was full of shopping lists,' Raven said with glee. 'Sweetie, you'll never guess what's really in it.'

'You read it?' Tess said, frowning. 'Naughty. That's private, Rave.'

'I couldn't be sure it was hers, could I? I just flicked through to see if the owner's name was in there so I could return it.'

'Like hell you did.'

'You know you'd do the same. Do you want to know what's in it or not?'

Tess hesitated. But eventually her curiosity got the better of her.

'Go on, since you've looked already,' she said. 'She isn't really writing her memoirs, is she?'

'More embarrassing than that. She's writing a novel.'

'No!'

'Yep,' Raven said, looking pleased with herself. 'And a rather saucy one too. All that Jackie Collins must've gone to her head.'

'Gracie Lister's writing a steamy book? You're winding me up.'

'I'm not. Listen.' Raven flicked to a random page. '"His breath a feverish pant, Hunter pushed his body against Clara's throbbing maiden flesh. She stopped resisting and wantonly gave herself to her warrior lover, a virgin no more." I can't read you the rest, it's a bit much for pre-watershed.'

Tess blinked. 'Gracie wrote that? I mean, with the throbbing maiden flesh and everything?'

'You think you know someone, eh?'

'That's racy enough to be something you'd read.'

'I would, actually,' Raven said, leafing through the notebook. 'It sounds rather good.'

'We'd better put it back where she left it,' Tess muttered, glancing over her shoulder to make sure none of the others were around. 'She'll be mortified if she knows we've read it. Hopefully she'll realise it's missing and grab it before she goes.'

'You do it then.' Raven handed her the book. 'It was on the window ledge in the upstairs loo.'

Tess headed up the stairs, trying to remember the way to Candice's upstairs loo among the maze of bedrooms and studies. The place was hard enough to navigate sober, let alone after three glasses of champagne and a couple of Harvey Wallbangers. Tess didn't know what went into a Harvey Wallbanger, but the Walton-Lord recipe seemed to be about ninety per cent vodka.

'OK, third time lucky,' Tess muttered as she pushed open yet another door. 'Oh. Sorry, Miss.'

Prue Ackroyd jumped back, her face a picture of guilt under the puritan make-up she was still wearing. Tess concentrated hard to bring the scene into focus.

A jewellery box was open on the dressing table, necklaces

and bracelets spilling from it. A string of pearls lay forlornly at Miss Ackroyd's feet.

Tess felt herself sobering up as she worked out what she'd just walked in on.

'This is Candice's room,' she said slowly. 'You're not Candice.'

'What are you doing in here, Teresa?' Miss Ackroyd said, her voice faltering despite attempting her usual stern tone.

'Looking for the bathroom. Why are you going through Candice's things?' Tess shook her head. 'You know, Bev said . . . only I thought she was just gossiping. But it's true, isn't it?'

'It isn't what you think. There was . . . something I had to know.'

'What can you possibly have to know that lives in Candice's jewellery box?' Tess demanded.

'I just . . . had to be sure.' There was a note of pleading in Miss Ackroyd's voice. She wasn't looking at Tess but staring past her. 'I had to be sure. Do you understand?'

'Sure of what?'

'I think she's talking to me,' said a soft voice behind Tess.

Marianne guided Tess to one side so she could enter the room. She put an arm around Miss Ackroyd, who visibly sagged into it.

'I'm sorry,' she whispered. 'Marianne, I'm sorry. I had to be sure.'

'We understand,' Marianne said in a soothing tone, rubbing her back. 'Let's get you back to Peggy's. I think the party's over.'

Tess watched as Marianne guided Miss Ackroyd out of the room.

'What's going on, Marianne?' she asked.

'Prue's had a difficult time lately,' Marianne said, without turning to look at her. 'The strain's started to get to her. It's going to be OK.'

Tess followed them downstairs in a daze, thinking about the scene she'd just witnessed. She was so intent on trying to work out what it meant that she completely forgot about Gracie's notebook, tucked into her back pocket.

Chapter 10

Liam Hanley put down his weeding fork and stopped a moment to rest, wiping the sweat from his brow.

Spring was a time for the emergence of new life, of course, which was why ninety per cent of his work on the Cherrywood Manor estate involved dealing with the weeds that had started popping up everywhere now the warmer weather was upon them. Did people have to get murdered in the spring? Could they not manage to do it in the autumn, when the job of a detective posing as a gardener might at least be a little cooler?

He struggled out of his T-shirt and chucked it down next to Cherrywood Hall's ornamental fountain. God, but weeding was warm work. If common decency would let him take his trousers off and garden in his boxers, he would.

While he got his breath, still on his knees, his gaze wandered over the estate.

It had a beauty different from the average country house; a beauty born of contrast. There was something sort of . . . powerful, he supposed, about the civilised little house with its civilised little gardens, clipped and pruned and

110

landscaped to within an inch of their lives and then set in the midst of the wild moors.

It reminded him of that quote about society being four meals away from anarchy. Impose any amount of English country garden civility on your little patch of world, but there was always Nature, untamed and brutal, waiting for a chance to snatch it back. Just like human beings: outward gentility battling the animal inside. The animal that he knew all too well could kill, given the right circumstances.

But that was getting into the realms of philosophy. Liam's business was pulling up these uncivilised little weeds, ready for a big bonfire later. The animal inside Liam Hanley had pyromaniac tendencies, apparently.

Before he carried on, he pulled out his phone to check his messages.

Nothing. He'd been hoping he might hear from Tess. When he'd seen her outside the house the evening before, she'd definitely looked like she had something other than syphilis to give him.

And Christ, did he need it – information, that is, not syphilis. It felt like his investigation was getting nowhere. Six weeks in and he was no closer to finding out who'd been sending the poison-pen letters. He'd arranged to meet the Walton-Lord girl this weekend in the hope she might know something, but he wasn't optimistic. Just desperate.

There'd been a new letter that morning; he'd seen the postie drop it in. The same style of address, done on an old manual typewriter. The same envelope, with the red and blue airmail border round the edges. He'd have made a grab for it if there'd been no one around, but the mumsy little woman with the snow-white hair, Marianne, had been waiting at the door and snatched it up as soon as it hit the mat. Liam knew that by the time he got to see it, it would have been tampered with. Pretty hard to solve a case when your client was refusing to give you all the facts.

He'd spent the past week and a half trying to find out anything he could about Nadia Harris, Clemency's mysterious heir. There was a long paper trail for her up until 1980, the year her father died. Birth certificate, records of barracks she'd lived at in every corner of the globe, even O-level certificates. Bright kid.

But after that, the woman was a ghost. Not only that: he couldn't find anything to suggest a link to the Ackroyds. As far as he could tell, Clemency Ackroyd had never even met the Harris family.

Could he call on Tess, see if she had anything to tell him? Bit awkward when she was rooming with Raven Walton-Lord. Raven was the last person he wanted finding out who he really was.

Perhaps he could corner Tess at the pub that evening. He knew it could give rise to gossip, singling her out again, but he needed to find out what she knew. And if she wasn't going to come to him . . .

Oh . . . hell. OK, so if he was being completely honest with himself, he wanted to see her. Not for information but for her own sake. Liam hadn't realised, until he'd got to Cherrywood, just how not over Tess Feather he really was.

It was the great regret of his life, the way things had worked out. Meeting someone, falling for them, and not being able to tell them who you really were – wasn't that just a kick in the nuts? And then the way it had all come out, after Porter collapsed. The way she'd looked at him . . .

Had it been worth it, to bring the company down? Jackie Murdoch had been a nasty piece of work. Her embezzlement scam had ruined lives, and thanks to him she was now inside, where she belonged.

But Tess had lost her job – as had many other innocent employees – and Liam had lost Tess.

No. In the end, he wasn't sure it had been worth it.

It was less than ten minutes later that he spotted Tess striding through the Italian garden, looking kind of adorable in white skinny jeans and her Little Miss Grumpy hoodie with her dark hair piled untidily on top of her head. And for once, he was delighted to see, not accompanied by Raven Walton-Lord making pouty faces at him.

He got to his feet and smiled at her.

'You know, I was just thinking about you.'

'Well, don't,' Tess said shortly.

'Hungover?'

She frowned. 'No. Shut up. How do you know?'

'That's your hangover hoodie, isn't it?'

Tess looked down at it. 'Might be.'

She seemed to be doing something weird with her eyes. They were darting all over the place, looking anywhere but at him.

'What?' he said.

'Liam, why are you half naked?'

He glanced down at his shining midriff. 'Oh. Right. Sorry, I got a bit sweaty.'

'Put your shirt on, can you? I can't talk to you when you're like that.'

'Why not? You've seen it all before.'

'Liam, please.'

'Fine.' He grabbed his T-shirt and pulled it over his head. 'So to what do I owe the pleasure of this visit?'

'I came to tell you to stay the hell away from Raven,' she said. 'She doesn't know anything about either the letters or the murder, so you're wasting your time trying your tricks on her.'

'How do you know she doesn't know anything?'

'Because she'd tell me. She's my best friend; she tells me stuff.'

'Not if it could hurt someone she cares about.'

Tess frowned. 'What does that mean?'

'Come back to the cottage where we can have some privacy. Then I'll tell you everything.'

She hesitated.

'Look, I know you don't trust me, but I'm not going to try to seduce you, I promise,' Liam said. 'I'm knackered, for a start.'

'Well . . . ten minutes.'

'Where is your friend today?' he asked as Tess followed him through the gardens to the groundskeeper's cottage. 'I was starting to think you two were joined at the hip.'

'Never you mind. Stay away from her, that's all.'

'Trust me, Tess, Raven Walton-Lord's in no danger from me – not in that respect,' Liam said. 'Despite what you think, I don't bed women for work purposes. Plants, yes.'

'Hmm.'

He unlocked the door to the old red-brick lodge and ushered her in.

'This way.' He guided her upstairs to the room he was using as an office, which he unlocked with another key. 'I set up the Batcave in here.'

Inside was his desk, covered in newspaper cuttings and printouts with his laptop plonked in the middle. A large whiteboard had details of the case stuck to it with coloured magnets.

'Very CSI,' Tess said, nodding to the whiteboard. 'I'm assuming you set this up to impress me?'

'Naturally.'

She went to examine it. 'These are your suspects?'

'Let's call them people of interest.'

There were photographs of faces that were familiar to her, their names written underneath. Colour-coded lines linked them to one another.

Nadia Harris – no photo for her, just a big question mark. Clemency Ackroyd, of course. Gracie Lister, Marianne Priestley, Beverley Stringer, Prudence Ackroyd, Peggy Bristow, Candice Walton-Lord and, finally, Raven Walton-Lord.

'Come on, Liam,' Tess said. 'Raven can't possibly be a suspect. Why on earth would she be writing poison-pen letters? As for killing Aunty Clemmie . . .'

'I told you. They're not suspects, they're people of interest.'

He finished arranging papers and walked over to join her. 'And if there's one thing I've learnt in this job, it's that everyone can be a suspect.'

'Then how come I'm not on there?'

'Because your name's not Walton-Lord.'

Tess frowned. 'You think this is about them?'

'I know it's about them. What I don't know is how, or why. That's the reason I wanted a quiet chat with your friend – to see if I can find out more about the family. Nothing more nefarious than that, I promise.' He indicated she should take a seat at his desk, planting himself on the other side. 'There's a reason I'm undercover here, Tess, at Cherrywood Hall.'

'Candice,' Tess muttered. 'She's your client. She's the one who's been receiving threatening letters.'

'You're good.' He reached into his desk drawer for a photocopy of the most recent letter. 'She's not the one getting the letters. But you're right: she is my client.'

'Marianne, then.'

'Yes, her partner.' He paused. 'That's right, isn't it?'

'No one knows. Officially, Marianne's her companion. That's a thing lonely posh people had in the olden days.'

'I see.' He passed her the letter, tapped out on an old typewriter. 'Take a look at this.'

' "Dearest Marianne, sin will out," ' Tess read aloud. ' "Forgotten but not gone. Wait for me. Kindest regards . . ." ' She looked up at Liam. 'Rather sweet manners for a blackmailer. Just because you're sending hate mail doesn't mean you can't observe the common courtesies, right?'

116

'There's no attempt at blackmail. It's either a threat or a warning; I haven't quite worked out which.' He nodded to the paper. 'Anything else you notice?'

Tess narrowed one eye. 'Is this a test?'

'Might be.'

She held the letter up in front of her, squinting as she tried to see what she might be missing.

'The quality's very poor,' she said. 'I'd say it was a copy of a copy.'

'Well done. Yep, someone's copied the original, doctored it, copied it again.'

'Doctored it how?'

'See the "Kindest regards" at the end there? What do you notice?'

Tess scanned it again. 'Nothing.'

'Look harder,' Liam said. 'Look with the eyes of a grammar pedant.'

'There's . . . a comma,' she said at last. She looked up. 'Someone fussy enough about formal language to end a threatening letter with "Kindest regards" knows how to use punctuation. Whoever tampered with it removed a signature.'

'Signature or name, yes.'

'Who's done it? Marianne?'

'Mrs Walton-Lord, I expect. Marianne Priestley doesn't know who I am.'

'Candice didn't tell her she'd hired you?'

'No. As far as she's concerned, I'm just the new gardener.'

Tess was silent.

'I don't get it, though,' she said finally. 'If Candice knows who sent the letters, why hire you to investigate? Why not confront them herself, or go to the police?'

'My guess is, because it's a signature she doesn't trust. Perhaps one that can't exist – a fictional person, or someone she believes is deceased.'

'And one she's not willing to share with you, for some reason. Does she know you've worked out they've been tampered with?'

'I'm not sure. But she's refusing to let me see the originals, which confirms she's hiding something,' Liam said. 'The other possibility, of course, is that she's covering for her own guilt or that of someone she cares about.'

'She's a suspect too? Your own client?'

'Everyone's a suspect, Tessie.'

'How many letters are there?'

'Three that I know of – four with the one that came this morning. All with the same first sentence – "sin will out".'

'Dating back to . . .?'

'Six weeks ago. Just after Clemency's death.'

'And that's what makes Candice think the death and the letters are linked?' Tess asked.

'So she claims. Personally, I wonder if the mysterious signature might be part of the connection.'

'"Sin will out",' Tess muttered. 'A hate crime, maybe? Some religious nut who doesn't like the idea her and Marianne might be a couple?'

'I don't think so. "Forgotten but not gone" – that doesn't sound like a general threat; it sounds personal.'

'Who delivers them?'

'They arrive with the regular post. Always typewritten and in an airmail envelope.'

'What, they come from overseas?'

'According to the postmark, they come from central Leeds.' He stashed the letter back in his desk. 'If you want to spare your friend my oh-so-odious company this weekend, you could do me a favour while you're here and tell me about the Walton-Lords.'

Chapter 11

'Well, there's not many of the Walton-Lords left now,' Tess told Liam. 'Just Raven, her grandmother – she married in, of course – and Raven's Great Uncle Andrew. Local squires. I think there was a title way back, but it died out or something.'

'What happened to Raven's dad?' Liam asked.

'Died when she was a baby. Car crash. He was a speed junkie – used to ride in rallies.'

'And that's when her grandma adopted her?'

'Yes. Candice's husband had passed away and Andrew, her brother-in-law, was in an institution so she was all alone here. Andrew was the elder brother. Technically this is his estate, although he hasn't lived at Cherrywood Hall for at least fifty years.'

'No children for him, I'm assuming?'

'No, he never married. It's all coming to Rave. Candice is desperate to get her married off and producing more heirs.'

Liam hunted around his desk. Finally he located the piece of paper he was searching for.

'Says here that Andrew Walton-Lord is a resident at Rowan House,' he said. 'What sort of place is that?'

'The sort for people who . . . can't look after themselves,' Tess said.

'Sorry?'

'He's a drunk.'

'Ah. And what do you know about Marianne Priestley? Any family – love affairs?'

'Not that I know of. She's never been married – no kids. Been with the Walton-Lords for nearly thirty years, and worked for a family called the Kings before that. Before she became a nanny for the Kings she was their housekeeper, and a maid before they promoted her.'

'And before that she was maid to the Colonel Harrises,' Liam muttered. 'They're the key to all this somehow.'

'Any trace of the child yet – Nadia?'

'A whole lot of nothing,' he said glumly. 'I can tell you how she did in O-level English, but not where she's been since 1980. Did Marianne know Clemency Ackroyd well?'

'Very – they were lifelong friends,' Tess said. 'Marianne and Prue, not so much.'

'Which of the Ackroyds was older?'

'Clemmie, by a year, although you'd have thought it must be the other way round, the way her sister dominated her.'

'You were right about the passport, by the way,' Liam told her. 'Clemency didn't have one. Never been out of the country.'

'Then why wear a St Christopher?'

'That's just one of many, many things about this case I haven't managed to work out,' he said, sighing. 'Anything you can pass on that might help?'

'A few odd bits I've found out. I don't know if any of it's important, but you did say to be alert for anything unusual, and if it'll get you out of here faster . . .'

'Hang on.' He dug out his pencil and notebook. 'OK, shoot.'

'Well, for one thing I'm almost certain Prue Ackroyd had no idea her sister had two hundred grand squirrelled away,' Tess said.

'How can you be sure?'

'I can't, but she definitely seemed genuine when I sounded her out about the will. She had no idea Clemmie had made one – seemed to think she wouldn't have the know-how. She always treated her sister like a child.'

'Was there anyone else who had a reason to dislike Clemency Ackroyd?' Liam asked. 'Anyone who stood to gain from her death, other than her sister and Nadia Harris?'

Tess shook her head. 'Not a soul. She didn't have an enemy in the world.'

'I'd say she had at least one. Anything else?'

'Just this thing with Ling Cottage. Miss Ackroyd thinks it's haunted. She's gone to stay with Peggy Bristow until Oliver does an exorcism for her.'

Liam chewed his pencil thoughtfully. 'Yeah, you mentioned that before. Haunted by her sister? Not unusual for someone recently bereaved to entertain that sort of magical thinking.'

'No, it's the spook who finished Clemmie off, according to Miss Ackroyd. Then it turned her St Christopher into a Madonna and child. You know, in that way ghosts have of messing about with your jewellery.' Tess leaned towards him. 'And this is the weirdest thing of all, Lee. Last night, after we saw you, we had an impromptu cocktail party up at the house. And Miss Ackroyd . . . it was so strange.'

He suppressed a smile at hearing Tess lapse into the familiar form of his name – the one she'd used when they'd been together. She was so absorbed, eyes glittering as she tried to puzzle it all out, that she didn't seem to notice the slip that reminded him of happier days.

'What did she do?' he asked.

'I found her rifling through Candice's jewellery box.'

He frowned. 'Stealing?'

'That's what I thought. Bev was gossiping recently about Miss Ackroyd having light fingers. She's stony broke, apparently – that was why she moved in with her sister.'

'Broke?'

'So Bev claims.'

Liam scribbled that down. 'So what did she do when you caught her?'

'She looked pretty guilty. But then Marianne came and she . . .' Tess shook her head. 'It was weird. Miss Ackroyd said she had to be sure of something, and instead of bawling her out, Marianne just told her she understood – "we understand", those were her actual words – and gave her a hug.'

'You said they weren't exactly friends?'

'Well, they get on OK – I mean, they've known each other all their lives – but it was Marianne and Aunty Clemmie who were close. I'm not sure Miss Ackroyd has got anyone who'd call her a friend. Too prickly.' Tess paused. 'And another thing. Before, at that meeting you came to. I over-heard the end of something Marianne was whispering to Miss Ackroyd, about the two of them not being so innocent in this. What do you think that means?'

'Wish I knew. The more I learn about these people, the less sense they seem to make.' Liam fell silent, looking over Tess to his whiteboard. 'Tessie, I'm going to tell you some-thing and you're going to laugh. And when you've finished laughing, you're going to listen, and then you're going to believe me.'

She raised an eyebrow. 'Don't tell me you think the Ling Cottage ghost did it.'

'No. It's my belief that Clemency's murder is connected to the Cherrywood Women's Guild.'

He was right. Tess did laugh, through shock as much as anything.

'Don't be ridiculous,' she said. 'You can't think the mur-derer's one of those little old ladies.'

'It's my job to think of everything,' he said with a shrug. 'The six who were at Ling Cottage that night were the last people to see Clemency Ackroyd alive – the last apart from her murderer. For now I'd like to keep the whole group under close surveillance. The threatening letters, this sin or secret, the Harris family – it all seems to revolve around that group of women.'

'Come on, though, the Women's Guild? They've got an average age of about sixty-five. I doubt Gracie Lister could even lift a carriage clock, let alone batter someone to death with one.'

124

'I'm not necessarily suggesting one of them did it, just that they're involved,' Liam said. 'And killers come from all age groups, classes and genders, believe me. It's a great leveller, murder.'

Tess shook her head. 'It sounds so absurd. I've known them all years.'

'Nevertheless, that's the route I'm heading down.' He looked at her. 'What I could really use is a woman on the inside.'

'Oh no. Not me.' She stood up. 'I told you before, Liam, I'm not doing your job for you.'

'I don't want you to,' he said, standing too. 'I just want you to keep your eyes and ears open. You know these people. They'll drop their guard with you in a way they won't with me.'

'Right. But I won't be paid for getting my hands dirty, unlike you. What is your fee for this case?'

He shrugged. 'Ten grand, plus my gardening fee. Weeding's extra.'

'Ten grand!'

'Yeah, and a bonus if I solve it.'

'OK, then I want ten per cent,' Tess said, folding her arms. 'A grand or no dice, cupcake. Plus, your solemn promise that you'll leave Raven Walton-Lord alone.'

'A grand? You're joking.'

'I am not. I have to do a lot of shoop-shooping to make that kind of cash. Plus I'd have to work with you, which ought to earn me some kind of danger money.'

Liam couldn't help smiling. 'All right. I suppose you're worth it.'

She jabbed a warning finger in his direction. 'And I do mean it about Raven – she's part of the deal too. She's not to be treated as a suspect or used for your investigation in any way. She's to be protected and kept safe, if this involves her family.'

'I can't promise that, Tess. I have to investigate thoroughly; it's my job. Everyone can be a suspect.'

'Not Raven.' She looked up to meet his eyes. 'I'm asking you to protect her, Liam,' she said, her voice ever so slightly softer. 'I care about Raven and I don't want her dragged into this. If she gets hurt because I hid who you were from her then I'll never forgive myself. Please.'

Liam hesitated. 'This is someone you've known a long time? Someone you trust implicitly?'

'I've known Raven Walton-Lord since nursery and I'd trust her with my life,' Tess said firmly. 'She's kept out of the investigation or it's no deal, fee or not. Those are my terms, Liam, take it or leave it.'

'I can't guarantee there won't be information I need from her, but if it's important to you then . . . all right, for your sake I'll back off.'

'You mean it?'

'You can have my promise on it. Any questions I might have for her can go through you. How does that sound?'

'That's all I wanted,' Tess said, with the hint of a smile. 'So, is it a deal?'

'OK, it's a deal. A grand on solution of the case, and I'll find an excuse to cancel my date with Raven. But I'll expect you to earn your fee.' He held out his hand. 'Put it there, partner.'

She looked at the hand. 'I'd rather not.'

'Come on. If you're going to be my Watson, you're going to have to start trusting me.'

Tess scoffed. 'No way am I the Watson. You're the Watson. In fact, you're the Hastings. You can only dream of being the Watson.'

'I'm the professional, sweetheart. You're the doe-eyed civilian blown away by my masterful powers of deduction.'

'I think you'll find I'm the unbelievably talented amateur sleuth the bumbling professional has to turn to when he's too thick to solve his own cases.'

Liam laughed. 'God, I missed you. Go on, Tessie. Shake and we've got a gentlemen's agreement.'

'Well, an agreement anyway.' She took his hand and gave it a firm shake.

'When's your next Women's Guild meeting?' Liam asked.

'Not for a few weeks, but there's the spring show next weekend. The ladies are running some of the stalls. I'll let you know if I find anything out.'

'All right. By the way, are you free this afternoon?'

She narrowed one eye. 'Why?'

'Nothing dodgy, don't worry. I've got an appointment to visit Terry Braithwaite, see if I can get his side of the story. I thought you might be interested in joining me.'

'Oh.' She hesitated. 'Well, I suppose I could. It would be useful to have all the facts.'

'Great. I'll pick you up outside the bakery at one.'

After he'd locked up Detective HQ, Liam followed Tess downstairs. On the step, she turned to face him.

'I want half of my fee in advance,' she said.

Liam smiled. 'I don't remember you being this mercenary.'

'You don't remember me being this skint either. Lost my fancy PA job, didn't I?'

'I know, I know, all thanks to me. OK, I'll sort you out a cheque.' He gave her elbow a squeeze. 'It's actually been sort of fun, having someone to bounce ideas off.'

She almost smiled, but not quite. 'Are you kidding? It's been murder.'

'Tess,' a clipped, well-spoken voice behind them said. 'I hadn't expected to see you again so soon.'

Tess winced.

'Candice. Hi,' she said, turning round. 'I was just . . . in the neighbourhood.'

'Is Raven with you?'

'Er, no.' Tess summoned a smile. 'I'm not sure what was in that Grasshopper, but she was a bit the worse for wear this morning. She hadn't made it out of bed when I left.'

'Right.' Candice's lips tightened. 'Well, I'm sure she'll be grateful to know you let her sleep in while you . . . went visiting.' She glared at Liam. 'You should be at work, young man.'

'I was at work,' Liam said. 'Tess just came to ask my advice on the best cuttings for her garden.'

'Tess doesn't have a garden. She lives in a flat.'

'Exactly,' Tess said. 'And it's about time we did something

with our balcony – Raven's always saying so. I thought it would be nice to . . . surprise her.'

'I'm sure.' Candice gave her a curt nod before stalking back towards the house.

'Bollocks,' Tess muttered.

Chapter 12

Raven was still in bed when Tess sneaked out later that day to meet Liam. She'd declared her intention earlier to make this Saturday a duvet day when Tess had brought her in a cup of tea, and she was currently propped up on pillows, sobbing over a *Grey's Anatomy* binge. Evidently Candice hadn't been in touch yet to tell her granddaughter what she'd witnessed that morning, but Tess was sure it was only a matter of time. She was grateful her flatmate was keeping to her room while she nursed her hangover, buying Tess a little more time to work out how she was going to handle the inevitable shitstorm.

With that on the horizon, it was almost certainly a bad idea to be going out with Liam this afternoon. If space was where no one could hear you scream, Cherrywood was where everyone could hear you whisper. There was always a curtain twitching or an unseen pair of ears listening – especially if you were getting up to something you oughtn't to be. Tess wasn't doing anything wrong, but the village didn't know that. All they'd see would be Tess Feather on a date with the object of her best friend's affections while said best friend was in bed nursing a hangover. News like that travelled fast.

She had to go, though. Ever since she'd heard that Terry Braithwaite had been arrested and charged with Clemmie's murder, it hadn't sat right with Tess. She'd known Terry all her life – he'd been in her eldest brother Mikey's year at school, and the two had been thick as thieves for a time – and while he was certainly a weasel and a crook who'd sell his own grandmother for weed money, by her reckoning he was no killer. The idea that for the sake of a few trinkets Terry would kill Aunty Clemmie, who'd been so widely beloved by all who knew her, made no sense at all.

Tess left the flat early, deciding she'd take a walk around the village to clear her head before meeting Liam. It was the sort of fragrant spring day that made every problem seem small, and she soon found her worries about how she was going to deal with Raven lessening as she sauntered along the main street. They'd work things out. They'd been friends since they were infants, and they'd weathered bigger storms than this. She even found her constantly simmering anger towards Liam softening slightly as she inhaled the warm, blossom-scented air.

She did miss London. City life had felt like an exciting new adventure after growing up in sleepy old Cherrywood, and in London there'd always been something to do, some excitement going on. Until the recent drama surrounding Aunty Clemmie's murder, the most excitement Cherrywood ever saw was the annual spring show, which boasted a bouncy castle, brass band and two different types of scone.

After that there was little to look forward to until the high-octane thrill-ride of the village scarecrow festival in the autumn. Still, Tess was forced to admit there was nothing like Cherrywood in the springtime, when the cherry blossom trees that gave the village its name dropped their petals like confetti along the main street and the air filled with fragrance and birdsong.

There was the bakery, the door open so that the scent of fresh bread and cinnamon buns wafted invitingly out into the street, and the post office with its window full of advertisements for second-hand buggies and Keep Fit classes at the village hall. There was Oliver's church, St Stephen's, with the iconic medieval tower that occasionally drew churchspotters and their cameras to the village. There was the Star and Garter, and the village tearooms, and Cherrywood Hall in the distance amid its fine gardens. All the little cottages, clustering above the beck and climbing higgle-piggledy up the hill like wayward sheep. The allotments, where the veg-growers of the village nurtured their darlings like precious children until they could flaunt them at the spring show. And rising above all were the moors, bleak and intimidating even on a fine spring day like this, as if to remind the villagers there was a darker side to life in spite of cherry blossom and cinnamon buns.

'Morning,' Tess said cheerily to Peggy Bristow, who was locking up the village hall. Peggy fumbled the key so that it clattered to the pavement, and Tess bent to pick it up.

'Thanks, love,' Peggy said when Tess handed it back. 'Off anywhere nice?'

'Just out for a walk. Have a good day, Peg.'

Tess hummed a tune as she turned up cobbled Royal Row to walk past Gracie Lister's cottage, the Old School House, easily identified by the low hum of bees as they tended their combs in the immaculate white wooden hives on the front lawn.

By the time Tess had circled back to the main street, Liam was waiting outside the bakery in his car. Tess took a hasty look around before sliding into the passenger seat.

'Don't worry, there's no one around,' he said. 'I checked.'

'You don't know Cherrywood. There's always someone around.'

'Well, never mind. You can tell them I was driving you to the garden centre to advise you on shrubs or something.' He started the engine and drove off. 'You'll be pleased to know I texted your friend back to cancel our date after she messaged me about it this morning. Told her I was washing my hair.'

Tess frowned. 'You cancelled?'

'That was what you wanted, wasn't it?'

Tess thought of Raven in her room, sobbing over *Grey's Anatomy*. Perhaps it hadn't been her favourite comfort watch that had caused the tears. Of course Tess wanted Liam to leave Raven alone, but she hated the thought of her friend getting hurt.

Still, better a little hurt now than a big one later on. Raven would be all right in a day or two, no doubt. Whereas Tess was still reeling from her involvement with Liam Hanley over a year later.

133

'Yeah,' she said vaguely. 'So, um, does Terry know I'm coming?'

'I told him I was bringing someone.'

'He knows you're not a gardener, then?'

'Yes. I talked to his dad in that guise, but I've got a feeling Terry's likely to give a different version of events to a detective trying to get him off the hook than the one Fred gave to the local gardener. I'll fill you in on what to expect when we get to the prison, shall I?'

'No need,' she said absently as she watched the country-side flash past her window. 'It's not my first time.'

He raised an eyebrow. 'No?'

'None of your business.'

'I didn't ask, did I?'

'Well, don't.'

It was over an hour's drive to the prison where Terry Braithwaite was being held on remand while he awaited trial. Tess was grateful that Liam didn't try to make further conversation.

When they arrived at their destination, they were subjected to security checks before being shown to a visitors' room. Numerous others were already there, sitting at tables while they spoke to their loved ones. Liam and Tess were shown to a table, and, after a short wait, one of the wardens led Terry to the empty chair on the other side.

Terry Braithwaite was a lean, stringy man of thirty-five, with a ferret-like face and a hunted expression that suggested he'd spent his life fighting to survive. He frowned when he saw Tess.

'What're you doing here?' he asked.

'I did say I'd be bringing someone,' Liam said. 'Don't worry, you can trust her. She's helping me out.'

Terry was still staring at Tess.

'Doesn't he know, then?' he asked her.

She flushed slightly. 'No.'

Liam frowned. 'Know what?'

'Terry and me have got history,' Tess said. 'Well, not me. He's an old mate of my brother's. It's really not important, Liam.'

'Is it going to be a problem?' Liam asked Terry.

'No problem. Surprised to see her, that's all.' Terry sank back wearily in his chair. 'You worked it out yet, Hanley? This place was bad enough when I'd earned my cell.'

'I'm . . . getting there,' Liam said.

Tess had never liked Terry much. He'd often been around the house when her brother Mikey had been a lad and she'd distrusted him then, young as she'd been. The keen, calculating, hungry expression in his eyes whenever he'd looked at her had unnerved her, and she'd taken to hiding in her room when he visited. Still, she couldn't help feeling sorry for him. He looked exhausted – hollow-eyed and very thin. This was his first trouble with the law in years. His family had been convinced that this time he'd really managed to go straight.

'What do you want, then?' Terry asked Liam. 'I was hoping you were coming to tell me you'd cracked it.'

'I want you to go through with me exactly what happened that night,' Liam said, taking out his notebook.

'I thought you were going to ask our dad.'

'I did, but I'd like to hear your version. Step by step, please.'

Terry glanced warily around the room.

'I'll be in for it if this lot see me talking to a copper,' he said in a low voice. 'They already think I'm a granny killer. Christ knows what'll happen to me if they think I'm a nark as well.'

'I'm not a copper, I'm freelance. You want to get out of here, don't you?'

But Terry still seemed reluctant, his eyes darting nervously and at random around their sockets. Tess watched him warily.

'Did you do it, Terry?' she asked quietly.

He scowled at her. 'You think I could, do you? I'd no more brain that old lady than your Mikey would.'

'They must have some solid evidence to charge you.'

He ran a hand over his forehead. 'Evidence is easy to find when you've got someone with a record you can prove was on the scene, right?'

'Then tell us what happened and help us get you out of here. Your dad's worried sick.'

Terry glared at the table for a moment, then looked up. He spoke quickly, in a low voice.

'I'm not proud of it,' he muttered. 'Dad sent us up with some eggs for the two old girls. He sells them a dozen a week. I'm only human, Tess.'

'What do you mean by that?'

'I've tried to stay straight, for our dad's sake. God knows I never meant to let him down again. But when I saw the back door was off the latch, car gone and no one answering my knock . . . it was more than I could resist.'

'I understand,' Liam said levelly, writing in his notebook. 'What happened next, Terry?'

'I wasn't thinking straight,' Terry murmured, his fingers twisting each other feverishly. 'It was like . . . like I was a puppet, you know, one of them with the strings. Like I was hardly in control of my body while I was doing it; just this instinct driving me. I went into the kitchen and out into the hall. There were a couple of silver candlesticks sitting on the bureau at the foot of the stairs so I grabbed them, then I opened the bureau and pocketed an old watch that looked like it might be an antique. And then . . .'

'Then?'

'That's when . . . when I saw her. I was hunting about for anything else worth taking when I looked through a door and there she was, head bashed in like an egg.' His colour turned as he revisited the scene in his memories. 'All my life, I'd known that woman. Bounced me on her knee at nursery. Nearly made me vomit to look at her lying there in her own blood, and I've got a stronger stomach than most.'

'Did you see anything else?' Liam asked.

'I didn't see nowt after that. I legged it and never looked back.'

Tess shook her head in disgust. 'Christ, Terry. You mean you just left her there?'

'Panicked, didn't I? Don't see what difference it made by then. She was dead.'

'You don't know that!'

Tess had half risen from her chair, and Liam put a hand on her arm.

'Tess. It's OK,' he said gently. 'We just want the facts, remember. No need to get upset.'

She hesitated, then sat back down.

'But if you'd called for an ambulance, maybe they could've saved her,' she said to Terry.

Terry scoffed. 'Are you not hearing me or what? Half her head was smashed in, Tess. She's not getting up and walking away from that.'

'Well you could have contacted the police. Perhaps they might have caught who did it right away, if they'd got to her sooner.'

'Oh, and they'd believe me, would they? With my record I'd have been banged up before I'd finished talking.'

'You're banged up anyway.' Tess shook her head again. 'And you took the candlesticks and watch. Jesus.'

'I told you, I panicked. Soon as my brain caught up with what I'd seen, I took them home and hid them until I could get rid.'

'As soon as you realised they were too hot for you to sell, you mean. What about the money?'

'Didn't take no money.'

'Come on, Terry. Prue Ackroyd said she was missing a hundred quid.'

'She might well be, but it didn't go in my pocket.' Terry leaned across the table. 'Look, Tess, you've known me a long time. I might be a lot of things but I'm no killer – you know

138

that. I don't deserve this, any more than that old girl deserved what happened to her.'

A warden approached them. 'Time's up, Braithwaite.'

Reluctantly Terry stood up.

'I don't deserve this,' he repeated before he was led away.

Liam was silent and thoughtful as they drove back to Cherrywood. Tess was silent too, still seething about Terry's callousness in leaving Aunty Clemmie's body there while he made a run for it with her silverware.

'So you've got a previous acquaintance with Terry Braithwaite,' Liam said after some time had passed.

'It's Cherrywood,' Tess said vaguely. 'Everyone's got previous acquaintances.'

'Perhaps, but it sounds like you know him a bit better than that. How come you never mentioned it?'

'He was my brother's best friend. It's not something I'd brag about. Now you've met him, I'm sure you can see why.'

'And would you say he's the sort to be capable of murder, in your opinion?'

Tess sighed. 'Terry's a scumbag, but . . . no. Theft, brawling, GBH, perhaps even sexual assault, but he's not a killer. He wouldn't have the guts.'

'So you believe his story?'

'Yes, I believe him. He's not a murderer, but he's exactly the type to burgle a dead neighbour. Weaselly little bastard.'

'Then that raises an interesting question, doesn't it?' Liam said.

'Right. If Terry didn't take it, then what happened to the missing hundred quid?'

Chapter 13

By the time Raven tired of *Grey's Anatomy* and emerged from her pit, Tess was ensconced on the sofa, wrestling with a pair of knitting needles.

'So, what do you think?' she asked, holding up her creation. 'For the Guild's shoebox thing.'

Raven gave it an underwhelmed look. 'It's got one leg shorter than the other.'

'I'm definitely getting the hang of it, though.' Tess squinted at the sad-looking bear. 'Ugh, I dropped a stitch. Now little Spinky's got a hole in his knee.'

'Spinky?'

'Yep, that's his name.'

'Those poor kids are already fleeing war zones. What the hell they've done to deserve your knitting skills on top of that I don't know.'

Tess looked up at her, sensing something off in her tone. 'You OK?'

'No. I need some hair of the dog.' Raven went into the kitchen, pointedly not offering to fetch Tess a drink too.

Was her friend still sore about 'Sam' having cancelled their date? Or had she spoken to her grandmother? She wasn't giving much away, other than that for some reason she was in a foul mood.

'So. Ol's got his date a week on Monday,' Tess said when Raven came back in nursing a generous tumbler of gin. 'What do you reckon to his chances?'

Raven shrugged.

Tess waited a second, but apparently that was all she was getting.

'I was thinking film night tonight – what do you think?' she said. 'I got popcorn.'

'Not really in the mood.' Raven nodded to her flatmate's skintight white jeans. 'You've been out in those, have you? You look like a Bodyform advert.'

'These're yours.'

'Where have you been all day?'

'This morning I went for a walk to clear my head, then this afternoon . . . there was an old friend I wanted to visit.'

'Where did you go for a walk?'

Tess put her knitting down and looked up at Raven, who was watching her through narrowed eyes. 'I had a stroll around the gardens up at your nan's.'

'How is the groundskeeper's cottage looking these days? Because from what I hear, you were in there a good while. I do hope you got to inspect the bedroom.'

Tess groaned inwardly. So that was it then. Raven had been talking to Candice.

'And I do hope you enjoyed visiting your friend,' Raven said sourly. 'I heard you were seen getting into a car with him this afternoon, shortly after he texted to postpone our date indefinitely. Quite an eventful Saturday you've been having.'

Ah, the old Cherrywood grapevine: you could always count on it. This was one aspect of village life Tess hadn't missed at all.

'Rave, come on,' she said in a conciliatory tone. 'I wanted some advice, that's all. You know, about this balcony garden we've been planning for ever. He offered to come with me to the garden centre to pick out some plants.'

'OK. Where are they then?'

'I . . . left them with Sam. He's going to bring them round another day.'

'He doesn't keep them in the cleaning cupboard at the Star, by any chance?'

Tess winced. 'Bev told you about that?'

'Course she did, she's Bev. Anyway, she didn't need to. Everyone's talking about it. I'd given you the benefit of the doubt too – that's how chronically naive I am. Until I heard all about your cosy Saturday together while I was out of action.' Raven knocked her gin back in one and slammed the glass down on the table. 'I can't believe you, Tess! You knew I liked him – you *knew* it. Of all the . . .' She laughed bitterly. 'Do you know, you were the one person I thought I could trust to have my back? I never thought you'd knife me in it for the sake of some boy.'

'I didn't—'

'I guess there's only one kind of friend after all,' Raven went on, ignoring her. 'The ones who've let you down and the ones who are building up to it.'

'Rave, please! I swear to you, it wasn't like that.'

'Right. So you haven't slept with him.'

'No. No, of course not.'

But Tess couldn't quite suppress a facial spasm. She'd never been good at lying under pressure.

How could she explain to her friend that yes, she'd slept with Liam – long before he and Raven had ever met? But if she blew his cover now, she could be blowing his chance of finding out who killed Aunty Clemmie. When the murderer was safe behind bars and Liam out of their lives again, she could tell her friend everything.

'Oh God. You have.' Raven was white with anger and hurt.

'It wasn't like you think,' Tess said helplessly.

A single tear slipped down Raven's cheek.

'You know, it's not even that you shagged him; not really,' she said in a quiet voice. 'If you'd told me you liked him, if I'd known he preferred you, I'd have stood aside gladly.' Every word was like a knitting needle through the heart for Tess. 'It's that you lied to me. I thought we were solid, you and me. I thought we were . . . family.'

'We are,' Tess whispered. 'Raven, I promise you that one day soon this will all make sense. I'm an idiot, yes, but I'm not a bitch.'

'I don't know what to think any more,' Raven whispered. 'Just . . . leave me alone for a few days. I need time to think.'

That was the last Tess saw of her for over a week.

*

143

'Rave?' Tess knocked on her flatmate's bedroom door a third time. 'Aren't you coming to the show? You're supposed to be on the jewellery stall.'

There was no answer.

'Still the silent treatment?' she said. 'Please, Raven. I miss you. I swear to you, you mean more to me than a dozen Sam Mitchells.'

Still nothing. Tess pushed open the door and peered in.

Typical. There was no one there. She'd bloody gone, hadn't she? And Tess had been talking to herself for the last ten minutes. She sighed and pulled on her jacket to head down to the park, where she'd volunteered to help Peggy Bristow serve up scones and gossip on the cake stall at today's Cherrywood Spring Show.

When she arrived Tess could definitely sense a coldness, and it had nothing to do with the weather. Eyes were fixing on her from tables all around the field.

From the smellies stall, Candice's gaze flickered to her, then quickly away. Beside Candice, Marianne smiled ever so briefly before she, too, looked away. Even Prue Ackroyd on the tombola seemed to be avoiding Tess's eye, although with her it was hard to tell whether the coolness was pointed or just her usual reserve. Tess got a terse nod from Gracie manning a table of squashes too. Only Bev, the village's other scarlet woman, had a beaming smile for her. Apparently man-stealing, like misery, loved company.

And – oh, fantastic. Liam was here, queueing inside the refreshment marquee to get himself a hot drink. Just what she needed.

'Why do I get the feeling I'm not flavour of the month round here?' she muttered to Peggy Bristow when she'd joined her on the cake stall.

'What did you expect?' Peggy asked as she arranged a batch of Bev's famous fairy cakes on a stand in front of her.

'Does everyone know?'

'Thanks to Beverley, of course they do,' she said in the faint foreign lilt that no one had quite managed to place since she'd moved to the village with Ian sixteen years ago – an affectation, Tess suspected, put on to accessorise her tarot cards and palm reading.

The brass band on the bandstand struck up an arrangement of 'Delilah', which Tess felt really didn't help matters. Had they selected their special cheating backstabbers' playlist, just to rub it in?

'There's nothing going on with me and him, you know,' Tess told Peggy. 'The evidence against me was completely circumstantial.'

Peggy looked up from the cakes to smile at her. 'I know.'

'Right. Your second sight.'

'No, I just don't believe you have it in you. I know people. And it takes a special kind of person to do something like that to a friend.' Her eyes narrowed in Bev's direction. The landlady was giggling with Ian as they laid out flower arrangements on the gardening association stall.

'What do I do, Peg? No one believes me.'

'Wait it out. All things come right in the end.' She picked up one of Bev's cupcakes and sneaked it into Tess's hand under the table. 'Here. On the house.'

'Cheers,' Tess said, smiling. 'So what've we got for the judges this year?'

While the biggest competition at the annual spring show centred around home-grown vegetables, there were also prizes for the best cakes, preserves, flower arrangements and so on. Peggy, who wasn't all that green-fingered, always focused her attention on the rosettes for the best baked goods.

'A poorer selection without Clemmie,' Peggy said. 'Her contribution always took the blue rosette. Still, that does mean I might actually be in with a chance for once.' She clamped a hand to her mouth. 'Oh goodness, that sounded awful. I only meant . . . well, it's a fact, that's all.'

'It's OK.' Tess nodded to the table of cakes. 'Which one's yours?'

'This handsome devil.' Peggy indicated the largest cake with some pride.

Tess blinked. 'Is that . . . Poldark?'

Peggy grinned at her. 'It certainly is. In the flesh, so to speak – well, the sponge.'

'He looks delicious.'

'Doesn't he always? He's fully edible. And, I might add, fully lickable.'

Peggy looked like she was in danger of making a start on him right there and then. Tess wondered what the village's reaction would be to a middle-aged woman hungrily licking an iced Poldark in the middle of the park. Knowing Cherrywood, they'd probably seen worse.

'Um, how did you make the chest hair?' she asked, regretting the question the instant it popped out.

'Chocolate shavings,' Peggy told her proudly. 'I spent hours getting it exactly right. He's a perfect to-scale replica of the real Ross in cake form. And he's gluten-free.' She gestured along the cake's naked torso with her finger. 'You know, the hair goes all the way down to his—'

'So I see,' Tess interjected hastily. 'He's, er, certainly a sexy beast. I mean, as cakes go. What do you think his chances are?'

'Oh, he's a sure thing. I dreamed last night of flight; that's a definite sign of success. Also, just look at him. How can he fail?'

But Tess's attention had been drawn away from Captain Ross Polcake by something else – Liam, leaning over Raven's stall chatting to her as he examined the jewellery she had on offer. Raven was glowing at the attention, resting her fingertips on his arm. The whole scene screamed flirting.

Oh yes, that man was Tricksy with a capital T. Tess had almost believed him when he'd promised to leave Raven alone – for her sake, that's what he'd said. Her simmering resentment had softened just the smallest amount. But clearly Tess couldn't trust him any further than she could throw him – a metaphor which right then involved images of tall cliffs and a cackling Tess rubbing her hands as Liam bounced all the way to the bottom.

'Trouble?' Peggy said quietly.

'You tell me. You're the psychic.'

Tess watched Liam walk away from Raven's stall. Raven caught her eye, and Tess was certain she saw her mouth 'love and war' before going back to arranging jewellery.

'I don't need to be psychic for that one, I think,' Peggy said.

'What a mess,' Tess said with a sigh. 'Hey, when the judges are done with Poldark, can I buy him? I'd get a lot of satisfaction out of slicing his stupid man's head off this evening.'

'Better than doing it to the real thing, I suppose.' Peggy turned to face Tess full on. 'So are we sweet on the young man or aren't we? Because I think you might like to figure that out before you talk to your friend.'

'We aren't.'

Peggy tilted her head like a bird. 'Aren't we though?'

'No.'

'But aren't we though?'

'You know, just asking me that over and over isn't going to change the answer. Why don't you consult the spirit world if you won't believe me?' Tess smiled, partly with relief, as their conversation was halted by a customer. 'Yes, Mr Judson, what would you like?'

The green started to fill with villagers. The cake stall proved particularly popular, especially Bev's cupcakes, and with no Clemmie Ackroyd to compete with, Peggy finally achieved her dream of a blue rosette for her Poldark cake.

They were about an hour in when Tess first noticed the mysterious figure. It was dressed all in black, although its face was bright red, and it seemed to move in a crab scuttle with its hands around its throat.

'What on earth's wrong with young Oliver?' Peggy whispered.

Tess watched him as he sidestepped around the green behind Fred Braithwaite. Eventually, the farmer turned to look at him.

'Something wrong, son?'

'Just admiring your, er . . . jacket,' Oliver said. 'Barbour, right? Lovely stuff.'

Fred looked bemused. 'Right. Well, I just need to get a cuppa. I'll see you next Sunday, Reverend.'

'What, is it Christmas already?'

'Er, ha ha.' Fred moved away, keeping his eyes fixed on Oliver until he was lost in the crowd.

Tess beckoned to her friend, who sidled over, his hands still at his neck to cover his dog collar.

'What's up with you?' she asked.

'Tammy's here,' Oliver whispered.

'I haven't seen her.'

'She's somewhere. Rave said she bought something from the jewellery stall.'

'What's going on?' Peggy asked.

'Oliver hasn't told the lass he fancies that he's a vicar,' Tess told her.

'I'm going to,' he said. 'I just want to achieve maximum sex appeal before I spring it on her.'

Tess shook her head. 'Just tell her, Ol. You know it's only a matter of time till she finds out.'

'After our date tomorrow night. I'll know then if she might be soulmate material.'

'What, after one date?'

'Have you ever known me to waste time when there's a

chance to get my heart broken?' Oliver glanced behind him at the crowd. 'Tessie, why is everyone looking at us?'

'They're looking at me. You've probably been too distracted to notice, but I'm public enemy number one around here today.'

'You? Why?'

She sighed. 'Misunderstanding. Me and Rave have had a falling out.'

'About what?'

She nodded to Liam, who was making his way over. 'That pillock. Told you he was trouble, didn't I?'

'Come on, Oliver,' Peggy said. 'Let me buy you a cuppa. I'm sensing Tess needs a quiet word with her chap.'

'He is most definitely not my chap,' Tess said. 'Do you have to leave me?'

'I always follow my gut,' Peggy said, patting her little pot belly. 'Sorry.'

Peggy nodded hello to Liam as she guided a still jumpy Oliver to the refreshment tent.

'Hiya,' Liam said to Tess. 'Can I have one of these famous cupcakes? I hear they're today's big hit.'

'What're you doing here?' Tess muttered, handing one over.

'I felt like I should get involved with village events now I'm a Cherrywooder. Hey, is that Poldark?'

'I said I'd handle the show, didn't I?'

He lowered his voice. 'Well, come on. I'd be a mug not to turn up while they're all in one place.' He took a bite of cupcake he'd just bought, then looked at it. 'God, that's good. What's in it?'

'Crack, judging by the rate they've been flying off the stands,' Tess said. 'Look, do you know how much trouble I'm in thanks to you?'

'Me?'

'Yeah, you. Everyone thinks I'm shagging you.'

'So tell them you're not.'

'They don't seem to believe me. That's what happens when you're caught playing Postman's Knock in the pub's cleaning cupboard after dark.'

He shrugged. 'I'm sure between us we can handle a bit of gossip.'

'You see all those female eyes looking daggers in this direction, Sam the Gardener?' Tess demanded. 'Those are the sort of eyes you get in this village when people think you've used underhanded methods to steal your best mate's potential new boyfriend. Cherrywood women stick together.' She glanced at Bev. 'Mostly.'

'It's not my fault, is it?'

'Yes, it's your fault. Why the hell are you still flirting with her? You promised me, Lee.'

'She was flirting with me. There isn't much I can do about that. I was just browsing the stalls, I swear to you.'

Tess shook her head. 'All that bollocks you fed me about not wanting people to get hurt any more. But you haven't changed a bit, have you?'

'That's not fair, Tess.'

151

'Go on, bugger off. You're only making it worse by lingering here,' she said. 'Oh, and Sam?'

'Oh right, that's me. Yeah?'

'Please don't speak to me in public for anything other than ordering a drink. If I find anything out, I'll text you.'

Liam actually had the gall to look hurt. 'Right. Bye then.'

'Bye.'

Tess tried not to catch Raven's eye as he left.

Chapter 14

As the afternoon wore on and stalls emptied of their produce, the crowd in the park started to thin. Customers to the cake stall became fewer and further between. Tess and Peggy found themselves chairs for the final hour and Tess leaned on her elbows, nibbling one of Bev's cupcakes as she let her mind wander.

It was all so civilised; so very British. If it wasn't for the presence of Liam Hanley in their midst, a constant reminder of the fact that a woman was dead – brutally killed, right there in the village – Tess would never have been able to make her brain comprehend the fact that anyone on the park's clipped lawn was capable of committing a murder.

But still, the Women's Guild? Liam had to be barking up the wrong tree there. Tess had known them all years – even those like Bev, Gracie and Peggy, who weren't native Cherrywooders. Some of them, like Marianne, Miss Ackroyd and Candice, she'd known her whole life. Yes, they had their peculiarities, same as anyone. But when she tried to picture one of them taking a carriage clock and planting it in poor Aunty Clemmie's head, her imagination just refused to stretch that far.

And yet Liam had sounded convinced that the murder, the threatening letters and the Women's Guild meeting on the evening of Clemmie's death were all connected. Of the seven women who'd met at Ling Cottage that night – Candice, Marianne, Peggy, Bev, Gracie, the Ackroyd sisters – one was dead. Could another one be a killer?

Liam wasn't from Cherrywood, and he had a cynicism born of years as a copper and PI. He didn't look at things the way Tess did. What did she know about these women, really? She tried to see them through the eyes of a Liam-type person instead of a Tess-type person.

Candice and Marianne, both in their seventies, Raven's family. Devoted to each other, although whether as close friends or romantic partners no one was quite sure. That they were sitting on a secret, Tess was certain of – 'sin will out', the letter had said. It couldn't be murder, could it?

Bev Stringer: terrible gossip, am-drammer, proud of her reputation as the local vamp. A loud, friendly fifty-something: good company as long as you remembered to lock up your husbands. What could her connection be to her friend Clemmie's death?

Peggy Bristow, Bev's husband's ex-wife. Self-professed psychic and ambitious baker, with a mousy exterior that hid a dry sense of humour. She'd been the leading voice when it came to pointing the finger at Miss Ackroyd as the possible killer of her own sister, yet now she'd offered her a place to stay – why? And why would she want to kill Clemmie? Surely not just to have a big blue rosette to hang next to the ten years' worth of reds over her fireplace?

Gracie Lister, the Guild's great moderniser. A widow who'd been at the heart of the village since moving there ten years ago, addicted to being in charge, excitable and a little dippy. Aspiring romantic novelist, apparently. What motive could she have to kill Aunty Clemmie? Had Clemmie, too, forgotten the all-important friendship horseshoe at the Guild meeting right before her death?

And Prue Ackroyd, their lead suspect. Disliked by the village and the children she'd educated, feared by her sister, estranged from the mother she'd barely spoken to in the decades before her death. She certainly did have something to gain from Clemmie's demise – the other half of Ling Cottage. Was that enough to drive her to murder? Might she also have believed she'd inherit two hundred thousand pounds? And what connected her to the still unidentified Nadia Harris?

It was no good. Tess just couldn't see what there was in these myriad personalities and relationships that could have led to Clemmie's death. And despite Liam's insistence that there was no such thing as a typical murderer, none of them, not even stern Miss Ackroyd, seemed like someone who could take a life.

'Do you really think she did it?' she whispered to Peggy, nodding in Miss Ackroyd's direction. 'Killed Aunty Clemmie?'

'Prue? No, of course not.'

Tess frowned. 'But you've been telling everyone she did.'

'That's just a game,' Peggy said, shrugging. 'In a sleepy place like this we must have our drama, dear – our whispers of scandal. Otherwise, where's the excitement in life? No one takes it seriously.'

'Somebody killed Clemmie, though, didn't they?'

'Somebody did. But that person wasn't Prudence Ackroyd.'

'Do you believe it was Terry?'

'Certainly not,' Peggy said. 'The cards have been quite clear on that. Terry Braithwaite may be guilty of many things, but he didn't kill Clemmie; I'm certain of it.'

'Then who do you think it was?' Tess asked.

'I wish I knew. I've tried using my gift, but something seems to be blocking me. The ghost, perhaps.'

'You believe in it too?'

'Oh yes. I'm certain there's something at Ling Cottage; I've sensed it myself. And something that doesn't want the murder solved is drawing a curtain across the answer.' Peggy glanced at Ian, sitting with his new wife on his lap behind the flower stall. 'Secrets and lies – we all have them. But sin will out.'

Tess stiffened. 'What did you say?'

'Sin will out, I said. Nothing truly wicked stays hidden for long.'

Tess stared at her.

'So you're not worried about having Miss Ackroyd stay with you?' she asked finally.

'No. Still, I hope she's ready to move back home soon. It's rather disruptive having someone else in the house.' Peggy winked. 'You never know, I might want to receive a gentleman caller.'

Tess laughed. 'Not Captain Poldark, surely?'

'That would be telling.'

'What happened that night, Peg?' Tess asked, her gaze wandering dreamily from Candice to Marianne, Marianne to Gracie. 'The night Clemmie died.'

'Like I told the police, there was nothing out of the ordinary. We were wrapping shoeboxes for the Christmas charity campaign. Mundane work, so out of twenty members only the seven of us had turned up. The meetings at Ling Cottage are never that well attended – something about the place seems to put people off. Anyway, there was coolness between Prue and Clemmie – I think there'd been a bit of a row, before we arrived. They were like children sometimes, the way they bickered.'

'So they weren't talking?'

'Oh, worse than that. They were being terribly polite to each other.'

'That bad, eh?'

'Yes. We could all feel it, this oppressive atmosphere. The meeting wound down after an hour – none of us could stand it any more. Beverley made the excuse of a headache and went home, then Candice, Marianne and Gracie. I was going to walk, but I thought Clemmie and Prue could probably do with a break from each other so I asked if one of them would mind running me home.' Peggy looked thoughtful. 'Strange to think what might have happened if Clemmie had taken me. I wonder which one would still be alive?'

Tess experienced an involuntary shiver. 'I never thought about that. Did you invite Prue in when you got home?'

'I did, but she turned me down. She was still in a sulk with

Clemmie. She said she'd drive to Plumholme Morrison's and get a few bits of shopping while she was out – I think she wanted to avoid going home for a while, personally.'

'And that gave the murderer time to strike,' Tess muttered. 'If she'd gone straight home, Clemmie could still be alive.'

Unless, a Liam-sounding voice in her head whispered, she was the one who did it. Had she gone to the supermarket? Or had she gone straight home, murdered her sister, then carefully covered her tracks before calling the police? It wasn't impossible. Terry had said the back door was open and the house empty when he'd gone round with some eggs, but that didn't mean Prue hadn't been on the property somewhere, staying out of sight until he'd gone. By the sound of it he hadn't been in more than one room. The car hadn't been parked outside, but then concealing it somewhere else in order to give herself an alibi could all have been part of Prue's plan, as could leaving the back door open. Perhaps she'd always intended Terry to take the blame – after all, she must have known he brought their eggs over at that time every week.

Tess's wandering gaze settled on the display of squashes being manned by Gracie. Remembering something, she patted her jeans to make sure it was still there.

'I'll be back in a sec, Peg. I need to talk to Gracie.'

Tess sought out Gracie on her table.

'Oh. Hello,' Gracie said in a disengaged tone.

Tess sighed. 'Not you too. Look, I'm not having it off with Candice's gardener, OK?'

Gracie frowned. 'Why, did somebody say you were?'

'Oh,' Tess said, blinking. 'Sorry. I thought you must have heard the gossip that's been doing the rounds.'

'Was there some gossip? I'm sure I never heard any.'

Gracie seemed distracted, her eyes darting around the park. She was twisting a lace-bordered handkerchief in her hands as if determined to choke the life out of the thing.

'Yes, but there was nothing to it. Hearsay and rumours.' Tess glanced at the handkerchief. 'Gracie, are you OK?'

'I'm . . . fine,' Gracie said absently. 'Did you want to buy a squash, Raven?'

'Tess. I'm Tess.'

'Yes, I know who you are.'

'Er, right,' Tess said, blinking. 'No, actually I just wanted to give you something. I found it at Candice's that night we were having cocktails, but I forgot all about it till this morning.' She took out the blue notebook. 'Yours, right? I remember you writing in it at the theatre.'

Gracie's face lit up. She snatched the book from Tess and cuddled it to her like a newborn.

'Oh my goodness, you found it!' she said, beaming. 'Oh, you wonderful girl, I could kiss you. I've turned my house upside down looking for it. Where was it?'

'Like I said, at Candice's. You'd left it on the window ledge in the upstairs loo. I meant to give it straight back but I got distracted, sorry.'

'You didn't read it, did you?'

'Of course not.' That was technically true: Raven had read it to her, but Tess hadn't so much as opened it.

'I can't tell you how pleased I am to have it back. Not just what's in it, but the book itself is so precious. It was a gift from my father.' Gracie tucked it into her handbag as if it was made of fine bone china, then nodded towards the cake stall. 'You'd better get back to your place, dear. I think Peggy may need someone to keep the top of her head from popping off.'

Tess turned to look. Bev and Ian had wandered over to Peggy's stall and were examining her Poldark cake. Bev looked like she was trying – but not too hard – to suppress a sneer.

'Well done, hun,' Bev was saying when Tess slipped back into her place beside Peggy. 'After all these years of wanting it. I couldn't be more pleased for you.'

'Thank you,' Peggy said from behind a strained smile. 'Yes, I do feel it's my best work.'

'Clemmie would be proud as anything of you, I'm sure. I certainly don't think it was in any way disrespectful to her memory, you entering this year.'

Peggy frowned. 'Why, is that what people have been saying?'

Bev held up her hands. 'Oh, no! No, of course not. Honestly, no one thinks that.'

'Then why did you say it?'

'Well, I'd hate for any idea like that to be on your mind, take the shine off your lovely win.' Bev patted her arm. 'So well deserved.'

'Right.'

Bev smiled wistfully. 'Do you remember the jubilee fete? Clemmie did the most amazing corgi in a little sugar crown.

You'd almost swear it was a real dog.' She turned to Ian. 'Now there was a baker. She could've been on *Bake Off*, I always said.'

Ian ran one finger under his shirt collar.

'Let's buy something for tea and get back to the pub,' he muttered. 'Tessie, are there any of Bev's fairy cakes left?'

'We sold out of those the first hour,' Tess said.

Bev drew herself up. 'Of course you did. I might not be flashy, I might not take home any rosettes, but I've never had a dissatisfied customer in the bun department.'

'And what's that supposed to mean?' Peggy demanded.

'Well. It's just that the name rock cakes is supposed to be whatsit, isn't it? Figurative. I was constipated for a week last time you hosted a meeting.'

Usually scrupulously polite, the pretence of civility between the two women finally seemed to have combusted in the glow of Peggy's blue rosette.

'My rock cakes are very popular,' Peggy snapped. 'Candice requests them every time I host.'

'I'm not surprised. They probably come in handy on her clay pigeon range.'

'Ladies, please,' Ian said, but they both ignored him.

He cast a helpless glance at Tess, who shrugged. It'd been a long, mostly dull afternoon, and if she was being perfectly honest, she was enjoying the fireworks.

'At least I don't have to resort to cheating,' Peggy said to Bev.

'What are you implying?'

'You know exactly what I'm implying.'

'You'd do well to keep your mouth shut, Peggy Bristow,' Bev muttered.

'And you'd do well to keep your hands off other people's husbands,' Peggy shot back. Everyone around them had turned to watch now, and there was an audible gasp.

Bev shrugged. 'Is it my fault you can't keep a man? He was obviously getting something off me he couldn't get at home. You should bin the crystal ball and try spending a bit more time in the land of the living, love.'

'Right. I hate to do this, but . . . Oh, who am I kidding?' Peggy said. 'I've been dying to do this for ages.'

Carefully she picked her blue rosette off Cake Poldark's hairy, chocolatey chest and put it down on the table.

'Um, Peg. What're you doing?' Tess whispered.

'Something I should've done a long time ago.'

With a bright smile, Peggy picked up her cake with both hands and shoved it firmly into Bev's face.

Chapter 15

Tess rapped at Raven's bedroom door. 'Rave, please. We need to talk about this.'

'Sod off, Tess.'

'Come on. We just saw Beverley Stringer get a faceful of gluten-free Poldark. That's got to be worth breaking your vow of silence for.'

'Can you just go?'

'I got pizza for tea, your favourite,' Tess said in her most wheedling tone. 'And I started work on our balcony garden. I'd love to know what you think.'

'Your boyfriend help you, did he?'

'How many times? He's not my boyfriend.'

'Whatever.'

'Rave, please come out. I can't live like this.'

'You won't have to. Not for much longer.' The door finally opened and Raven stood there, pale and grave. 'I talked to Marianne and Grandmother today. I'm going back to Cherrywood Hall.'

Tess blinked. 'Not for ever?'

'Maybe.'

'But you always said you hated living there.'

Raven shrugged. 'I'll have to live there someday. Might as well get a feel for the place.'

'Raven, come on. Can't we just talk about this? We've been friends twenty-eight years. We're not going to chuck that away over some lad, are we?'

But the door had already closed in her face. Tess sighed and retired to her room, wondering what the hell she could do to make things right again.

She couldn't sleep that night. All she could think about was Raven, lying on the other side of the wall. Raven, her best friend, who thanks to Liam sodding Hanley was about to move out and quite possibly never speak to her again.

The last time they'd fallen out over a boy had been Danny Trueman when they were eight years old. He'd tried to worm his way into their affections with carefully selected Love Hearts. *You're the tops*, her one had said. Raven's was bright pink and said *My love*, which she claimed beat Tess's one hands down.

The feud between them had lasted two whole breaktimes before they'd discovered Danny's mum owned a sweet shop and he'd been giving out hearts to most of the girls in their class. Never again would they let a stinky boy come between them, they'd promised, and sealed the pact with a wet-willy swear.

Why was her friend a person of interest in Liam's investigation anyway? Raven hadn't been there the night Clemmie was killed. Tess was certain Rave knew nothing about Aunty Clemmie's murder, no matter what connection Liam believed there was to the Walton-Lords.

Oh, bugger him. She didn't owe Liam anything. But she did owe Raven something – a warning, in case their flirtation went any further.

Tess went to the kitchen and made a couple of mugs of hot chocolate. Then she knocked on the door of Raven's room and, without waiting for an answer, barged in.

'What part of "not talking to you" did you not understand?' her friend mumbled as Tess plonked herself down on the edge of the bed.

'I don't care. I'm an innocent party and I demand to have full best-friend privileges restored.'

Raven groaned and sat up. Tess shoved a mug of hot chocolate into her unresisting hands.

'Is it poisoned?' Raven asked, eyeing it warily.

'It's non-alcoholic. I guess to you, that amounts to about the same thing.' Tess met her eye. 'Rave, there is nothing going on between me and Sam Mitchell. You need to listen to me.'

'So you're going to tell me you didn't sleep with him, are you?'

'No, I'm going to tell you with clear and brutal honesty that I did sleep with him. Lots, actually, and quite enthusiastically too. But I haven't slept with him for well over a year, and the chances of me ever doing so again are exactly nil.'

Raven blinked the sleep out of her eyes. 'Pardon?'

Tess sighed. 'I've got a confession to make.'

'OK,' Raven said slowly.

'You remember when I was down in London, that lad I told you about?'

'Course. Lush Liam, the sexy architect. It was getting serious, then after you lost your job it all went belly up.'

'And I never told you exactly why, did I?'

'No.' Raven was fully awake now. 'Tess, what's this all about?'

'Liam . . . well, I guess you could say he wasn't the man I thought he was.'

'Was he married or something?'

'He was a private investigator, Rave. He was leading the Porter investigation – he was the one who brought them down.'

'Eh? I thought he was an architect.'

'That was what he told me. Undercover, see.' Tess felt her throat convulse as memories of her time with Liam came flooding back. 'He was playing me, the whole time – our entire four-month relationship, just a trick to screw information out of me and get him access to Jackie, my boss. As far as he was concerned, I was never anything more than a means to an end.'

'Bloody hell! And you never told me?'

'I never told anyone. I was humiliated. Ashamed that I let myself get duped – let myself fall for him.'

'Oh, darling. What a scumbag.' Raven put an arm around her, all differences forgotten. 'He really slept with you just to get information about Porter? That is sick.'

'Slept with me. Told me he loved me. On that holiday we took to Las Vegas, he was even joking about marriage.' Tess scowled, angry at her past self for her credulity. 'Nearly as soon as we got back from America, out it all came – how

166

he'd lied to me, used me. Within two months, Porter had collapsed and I was back here, desperate to put it all behind me. Until the day he showed up at your nan's.'

'So Sam Mitchell is . . .'

'Liam Hanley. Yes.'

Raven was silent for a while.

'Well, darling, no wonder you're off men,' she said at last. 'Why is he undercover here?'

'Why do you think? He's been hired to look into Clemmie's murder.'

'Hired by whom?'

'I'm . . . not sure,' Tess said, deciding she'd spilled enough of Liam's secrets for one night. As much as she still resented him, she didn't want to jeopardise his case now he seemed to be getting closer to finding out who might have murdered Clemmie. She looked up at Raven, whose eyes were damp with sympathy. 'I'm sorry, Rave. I promised not to blow his cover and it nearly cost me my best mate – until I realised some things were more important.'

'Aww, Tessie. Here.' Raven licked her finger and wiggled it in Tess's ear.

'Ah! Bitch!' Tess said, giggling. 'Don't wet-willy me when I'm not expecting it.'

'I'm renewing our vow. No boy, whether it's Danny Trueman and his Love Hearts or Liam Hanley and his . . . arms, will ever come between us again. Right?'

'Right. And you won't move back to the hall?'

'Nope. I'm staying right here.'

'Or cake me in the face with a Poldark?'

167

Raven laughed. 'God, wasn't that hilarious? You can't say Bev didn't have it coming.'

'Ian deserved the biggest share of it, if you ask me. He was the one who promised to love, honour and cherish. Plus, that moustache.'

'Fair point.' Raven frowned. 'What will I tell Grandmother about Liam? You're not her favourite person at the moment. Or Marianne's either.'

'Yeah, I had noticed,' Tess said, grimacing. 'We can't expose him now. Can't you just tell them it was a misunderstanding? That I was consulting with him about the balcony garden to surprise you or something?'

'I can try. Why were you really spending time with him?'

'I'd noticed a couple of relevant things I wanted to pass on, then he asked me to go speak to Terry Braithwaite with him. I'm sort of helping with the investigation.'

Raven raised an eyebrow. 'But you hate him, don't you?'

'Yeah, but I still want him to catch whoever killed Aunty Clemmie. Not to mention that the faster he solves it, the sooner he goes.' Tess smiled. 'Plus I negotiated a share of his fee.'

'Ha! You never! So who do you think did it then?'

'We don't know yet. Lots of odd little facts that might be connected but nothing pointing to a single person.' Tess looked at her. 'Rave, can I trust you to keep your mouth shut on this?'

'Of course, darling. I'm not Bev Stringer.'

'Liam thinks it might involve our Women's Guild – I mean, the six who were there that night.'

'No! He thinks one of them did it?'

'Possibly, yeah.'

When Tess had filled her in on what they knew about Clemmie's murder so far, Raven shook her head.

'Seriously though, one of that bunch?'

'That's what Liam thinks. I know what you mean though; I can't get my head around it either.'

Raven counted silently on her fingers as she mentally listed the women who'd been there that night.

'Well it can't be Grandmother or Marianne, that's a given.'

Tess didn't know that anything was a given any more. The world seemed liked a strange parallel universe to the one she thought she'd known. And she'd kept quiet to Raven on the subject of the threatening letters and anything else that involved the Walton-Lords too closely.

'And the others . . . Gracie, Bev, Peggy,' Raven said. 'It couldn't be any of them.'

'Why couldn't it?'

'It just . . . couldn't, that's all. I mean, come on. So that means it must be either Miss Ackroyd or the ghost. And I don't believe in ghosts.'

'I know Miss Ackroyd's difficult, but you really think she could've killed her own sister?'

'If Liam says it's one of them, she's the only one I could picture doing it. She was like that in class – calm and stern, then suddenly she'd just snap and you'd be getting screamed at.' Raven swallowed down the last of her hot chocolate. 'Plus she's the one with the motive, right?'

'What about this Nadia Harris?' Tess said. 'What's she got to do with it?'

'There is that,' Raven admitted.

The two women mused silently, Tess's head on Raven's shoulder as she sipped her hot chocolate.

'Nope, I'm getting nothing,' Raven said at last.

'You and everyone else. Liam, the police, Peggy's spirit guide . . .'

'Well, let me know if you find anything else out. Maybe me and you can crack it. We're just as smart as Liam Hanley.'

'Damn right we are.'

'Hey. You working tomorrow afternoon?' Raven asked.

'No, why?'

'I'm going to visit Great Uncle Andrew. You want to come? I wouldn't mind some company.'

Tess smiled. 'I'd love to. Thanks, Rave, it's good to be friends again.'

Chapter 16

Rowan House was an old mansion, repurposed as a private residence for . . . well, for people like Andrew Walton-Lord. The place had extensive gardens, tennis courts, indoor and outdoor pools, a hot tub, games room – even a sauna. It really was the Rolls Royce of homes for recovering alcoholics.

'How much do you have to drink to get into this place?' Tess whispered to Raven as they made their way across the immaculate lawn. 'I'm thinking I might take a whack at it.'

'Even by my standards, a fair bit. Plus the seventy grand a year residence fees.'

'How much?'

Raven shrugged. 'Andrew can afford it. Poor old soak, I'm glad he has his comforts. I've got a lot to thank him for.'

'Your inheritance?'

'My alcohol tolerance. Good old genetics.'

They entered the reception area, where crisp, smiling staff were bustling about. At a table, a couple of residents played poker for ten-pence pieces. Raven and Tess approached the front desk.

'We're here to see Andrew Walton-Lord,' Raven told the receptionist. 'I'm his great-niece.'

'Well, three visitors in one day,' the woman said. 'Andy will be happy.'

'He had another visitor?'

'His sister-in-law was here earlier: they had a nice long chat. She brought him cake from your village show yesterday.'

'Was it in bits and covered in chocolate chest hair?' Tess asked.

The woman blinked. 'Er, no.'

'Not Poldark then,' Tess whispered as they followed the receptionist to Andrew's room.

'I wish Grandmother had told me yesterday she was planning a visit,' Raven said. 'I'd have left mine till next week.'

When they got to Andrew's suite, the receptionist knocked on the door. There was a barked 'Come!'. She gestured for the two women to go in and left them alone.

They entered a sumptuous study that resembled an old-school gentlemen's club. Books lined the walls, the carpets were deep and soft, and a set of winged leather armchairs sat by a blazing fire. There was a mahogany writing bureau in one corner bearing notepaper, pens and an old typewriter, plus a half-eaten apple and a bowl of roasted peanuts.

An old man with wild white hair was sitting in one of the armchairs, tinkering with something electronic. He had a look of keenness and intellect in his dark eyes, although his expression seemed far away from the world around him.

'Hi, Uncle Andrew.' Raven gave him a kiss on the cheek. 'I brought my friend Tess. You remember her?'

'Confounded thing,' Andrew muttered, his hands shaking while he dug a screwdriver into whatever he was taking apart. He was a notorious tinkerer, dismantling and re-assembling anything electronic he could lay his hands on.

'What is it, sir?' Tess asked, sitting down in one of the armchairs. He'd invited her to call him Andrew on more than one occasion, but she knew he secretly enjoyed the formality.

'Damn wireless. You know, when I was a boy I could build one of these blasted contraptions standing on my head. Could've picked up the Home Service from Table Mountain on it, long as I could get the parts.'

'Here. Let me.' Raven took it from his trembling hands and examined the muddle of circuits. 'You've got a loose connection, Uncle. You see? The blue wire's come out of the connector, here.'

She fixed it for him and handed it back. He looked up at her, acknowledging her presence for the first time.

'Clever girl. Who taught you how to do that?'

'You did,' she said, smiling.

He looked puzzled for a moment, then broke into a smile.

'Sarah, my dear! Well, I am glad you've come to see me. I've been desperate for some company.'

Andrew was the eldest of three Walton-Lord siblings, the only one now surviving. The middle child, Cyril, had been Raven's grandfather – Candice's husband. But the youngest, Sarah: she was the family's great tragedy. She'd died of tuberculosis at fifteen, and her brother never had fully recovered from the loss.

Such a waste. Tess rubbed at the dimple in her arm where

173

she'd received her TB jab. Such a senseless waste. The past was full of waste: pointless wars, their causes since forgotten; pointless diseases, now long eradicated; cruel, pointless, painful loss.

Since she was a child Raven had been Sarah to her great uncle, and she'd learnt to accept the name. It was a sign of Andrew's ever-tenuous grip on reality, yes, but it spoke of his deep affection for her too. It wasn't that he thought she was Sarah, exactly. But Sarah was the name of a little girl he'd loved very much who'd been taken before her time, and in his confused mind, Raven was a Sarah to fill that gap.

'You can't have been lonely today, Uncle,' she said. 'My grandmother came to see you, didn't she? You had cake, the nurse told us.'

'Oh. Yes,' he muttered vaguely, focusing on his radio as with fumbling fingers he screwed the case back together. 'Yes, a good girl to visit me. You know, I almost married her.'

Tess blinked. 'Married Candice?'

'No, no,' he said, waving a hand impatiently. 'The girl. Not Cyril's girl. My girl, my own best girl. Father wouldn't stomach it, of course. Stuck-up old fool. But she was too wily for him, wasn't she, always too . . . Oh, what a farce!' He thrust the radio under the chair and folded his arms, bottom lip jutting like a petulant child.

'Don't give up. I know you can do it,' Raven said. 'You taught me how to do it. That's why you're my favourite uncle, you know.'

He managed a smile. 'I'm your only uncle, I think.'

'It's still an achievement,' Raven said, grinning back.

'Oh, bugger it for a game of soldiers. Let's have a drink.'

After peeking outside to make sure no staff were eavesdropping, he shuffled to the writing bureau, mouth curving with schoolboy mischief. He took out a large hardback book and laid it on the desk, then opened the cover to reveal hollowed-out pages. A hip flask and four shot glasses were hidden inside.

Raven shook her head. 'How does he get away with it?' she muttered to Tess. 'He must've made that.'

'Should we get the booze off him? He's supposed to be teetotal, isn't he?'

'He's eighty-six. Let him have his little pleasures,' Raven said, shrugging. 'Anyway, that stuff's more than two-thirds water. It's not much more than a placebo.'

'How do you know?'

'Who do you think smuggled it in for him?'

'Here we are,' Andrew said, handing each of them a generous glass of whisky-and-water with a bon-viveur flourish. 'The best stuff. My sister brought it for me.'

Tess took a sip. Raven was right: it was about ninety per cent water. Still, it clearly fulfilled an emotional need for Andrew, who seemed to enjoy playing host. He watched her carefully as she drank, and for his benefit she smacked her lips.

'Mmm. That is good. Thank you, sir.'

'Of course it's good,' Andrew said, drawing himself up proudly. 'My sister, you know. She keeps an excellent cellar.'

When he'd knocked back his own tumbler, Raven reached under his chair and drew out the radio. She handed it to him.

'Just a few more screws to tighten and it'll be as good as new,' she said, nodding encouragingly.

'Yes. Yes, I rather think so too.' Andrew was quite jolly now he'd had his afternoon tipple.

His hands steadier after the drink, he managed to fix the casing back in place, then turned the dial. He beamed at them when sound started coming through the speaker, even though it was only white noise.

'There!' he said triumphantly. 'Didn't think I could do it, hey?'

'We knew you could.' Raven looked genuinely proud. 'My Uncle Andrew can do anything with electronics.'

'Aww. Little Sarah.' He patted her hand. 'You were always a good girl. Our little girl.'

Tess noticed Raven blinking back a tear and reached out to squeeze her arm.

'Yes, always a good girl,' Andrew mumbled, his eyes becoming unfocused as he listened to the white noise coming from the radio. 'Best girl.'

Tess wished he'd turn the thing off. The formless, high-pitched noise, the heat from the unnecessary fire, the old-fashioned brass-and-oak surroundings of Andrew's study, were unsettling her. It felt eerie; otherworldly. Even Raven, flushed and tearful as she thought about the child-aunt whose name she'd been forced to inherit, was like something from another time.

'Should've saved her,' Andrew muttered, talking to himself. 'Could've, if I'd married the girl. Coward, wasn't I? Couldn't bear the old man's disappointment. Pah!'

'Saved who?' Tess asked quietly. 'Sarah?'

'No. No, not Sarah.' He turned up the volume on the radio, the white noise ricocheting around Tess's brain. 'The other one. Charity.'

'Who's Charity?' Tess whispered to Raven.

'No idea,' she muttered back. 'Sounds like an old girl-friend he's got on his mind. He had a reputation as a ladies' man in his twenties, before Great Aunt Sarah's death drove him to the bottom of a bottle.'

'Who was Charity, sir?' Tess asked him. 'A sweetheart?'

'Hmm?' He finally switched the radio's dial to the off position, and Tess exhaled as the tinny sound in her brain subsided.

'Who was Charity?' she asked again.

'Charity?' he said, blinking. 'Never heard the name in my life, girl. Now come on, let's have another drink.'

Chapter 17

While the two women were paying their visit to Andrew Walton-Lord, Oliver was spending his Monday afternoon crammed uncomfortably into a tiny armchair in the front room of a couple of parishioners, Mr and Mrs Swallow.

'Would he like some tea?' Mrs Swallow whispered to her husband.

'Would you like some tea, Your Reverence?' Mr Swallow asked Oliver with a deferential bob of his head.

'Er, just Oliver's fine.' He turned to Mrs Swallow. 'A black coffee would be lovely.'

'Ask him if he wants a biscuit,' Mrs Swallow whispered to Mr Swallow.

'Would you like a biscuit, Reverence?' the man asked with another little head-bob. 'They're Boasters.'

Oliver was used to a bit of weirdness on those occasions he was called upon to perform a home visit. Most folk encountered vicars only a handful of times in their lives, usually for the purposes of hatching, matching and des-patching, and they were never quite sure what to do with one when they got them on the sofa. But Mrs Swallow's reluctance to address him directly was a new one.

'No, just the coffee is fine, thank you,' he said to her.

Mrs Swallow stifled a nervous giggle and disappeared into the kitchen.

'Now, I know this is a difficult time for you,' Oliver said to Mr Swallow when she'd gone. 'The stress of arranging a loved one's funeral is never a picnic in the park. But rest assured that I'm here to make the experience as easy on you and your wife as possible.' He took out a notebook. 'So. Can you tell me if there's anything you'd particularly like to request?'

'Well, we'd want sausage rolls. And a bar, o' course. He'd want a good booze-up, would Gazzer.' Mr Swallow glanced fondly at a photo on the mantelpiece of a burly, bearded chap in a Black Sabbath T-shirt.

'I actually meant anything you'd like in the church service,' Oliver said. 'Any poems or readings, or music perhaps, that your brother was particularly fond of? Hymns for the main service, of course, but any piece of music can be played when the pallbearers carry in the coffin. Families often choose a favourite song of the deceased.'

'Well . . .' Mr Swallow thought for a moment. 'Could we get some AC/DC? "Highway to Hell"? That was Gazzer's favourite.'

Oliver ran a hand through his hair. 'Um, well, I know I said any piece of music, but I'm not sure it would really be appropriate to—'

'How about "Sympathy for the Devil"? First single our Gazzer ever bought, bless him.'

'I don't suppose he liked Led Zep? "Stairway to Heaven"?' Oliver asked hopefully.

'Not one of his favourites, no.'

'Any hymns at all?'

'Oh, no,' Mr Swallow said, wrinkling his nose. 'No, Gazzer'd have no interest in that kind of thing.'

'It's just, I don't think that in church we could really – oh. Thank you.'

Oliver reached up to take his coffee from Mrs Swallow, but she sidestepped him deftly and handed it to her husband, who bobbed his head so low it nearly touched the mug as he handed it over.

'Um. Yes. Thank you,' Oliver said. 'Now, Mr Swallow. There must be something your brother liked that would be more appropriate to a Christian ceremony. Something without hell or the devil or . . . anything like that.'

Mr Swallow pondered. 'There's the song he lost his virginity to. Back seat of our dad's Cortina, December 1976. I guess he'd like to have that.' He gave Oliver a nudge. 'Bring back a few memories for the old boy, wherever he is, eh, Father?'

'I'm not sure that's really . . .' Oliver glanced at the clock and sighed. 'Oh, why not? What was it?'

'Blue Öyster Cult. "Don't Fear the Reaper".'

Oliver just managed to stifle his groan.

*

And people wondered why he was nervous about telling girls what he did for a living, Oliver reflected as he drove to the restaurant where he'd arranged to meet Tammy for their first date. Who knew how they might react to the socially discombobulating fact of his vicarhood? Maybe Tammy would spend the whole evening whispering small talk to the waiter for him to pass on.

He frowned when he drove by Cherrywood Village Hall. Peggy Bristow was there, unlocking the door. Of course she had her own key – Peggy had cleaning jobs at most of the public buildings in the village, including the post office, St Stephen's and the hall – but seven p.m. was a bit late for dusting.

He was behind schedule, thanks to the late Gazzer Swallow's somewhat demonic taste in music, but he pulled up and hailed her.

'Everything OK, Peg?'

Peggy jumped. 'Oh. Oliver. It's only you.'

'Not working at this hour, are you?'

'Just looking for my reading glasses. I must've left them here this morning.'

Oliver smiled. 'Miss Ackroyd driving you round the twist, is she?'

Peggy's face relaxed into a grin. 'How did you guess?'

'I must be a fellow psychic.'

'Well, you're not wrong. I did feel the need to escape somewhere for half an hour.'

'It's OK, I won't tell the other trustees on you.'

'Are you going to get rid of this bloody ghost or what?'

181

Peggy demanded. 'I'm not sure how much more of Prue as a houseguest I can take before there's another murder in Cherrywood.'

Oliver sighed. 'I know, I have been putting it off. I'll speak to the bishop tomorrow. I just hope he doesn't think I've gone crackers.' He nodded down the street. Ian Stringer was sauntering in their direction. 'You'd better go in and hide. Here comes someone else whose company I'm guessing you're keen to avoid.'

'Have fun with your lady friend!' Peggy called as he drove away.

Ugh. He supposed he had Tess to thank for that. Nothing stayed secret in Cherrywood.

Outside the restaurant, Oliver took off his clerical shirt and dog collar and stuffed them in the glove compartment, leaving him in the plain black T-shirt he'd been wearing underneath. There was still one secret he was hoping he could sit on a while longer.

He'd booked them a table at a tapas place, far enough out of Cherrywood that he was unlikely to be greeted with an 'Evening, Rev' as soon as he walked through the door. Tammy was already seated, sipping a glass of red wine.

'Sorry I'm late,' he said when he joined her. 'Got held up at work.'

'No worries.' She nodded to what he was wearing. 'All in black again. You're not a goth, are you?'

'Er, no.' Oliver ran a finger under his collar. 'I just . . . think it's slimming.'

She laughed. 'Someone as skinny as you worries about looking slim?'

'Well, I was a chubby kid. It had a lasting effect on my self-image.' He scanned her sky-blue pencil dress, colour-coordinated with her nails, shoes and bag. She looked like she'd gone to some effort and he felt suddenly self-conscious about his own, slightly worse-for-wear work clothes. 'You look amazing.'

She flushed. 'Thanks.'

His gaze flickered to the gold necklace she was wearing. 'That's pretty. What's the design?'

'Oh, this? It's a St Christopher,' she said, fingering the little medallion.

St Christopher . . . Oliver wondered why the words should cause a sudden twist in his stomach.

Of course. Aunty Clemmie. Aunty Clemmie and the jewellery-fiddling ghost, and this exorcism Miss Ackroyd wanted him to do. Well, he wasn't going to think about that tonight.

'Do you travel a lot then?' he asked.

'No. I'd like to, though,' Tammy said. 'I thought maybe St Chris could make it happen for me, if I wore him close to my heart.'

There was a pause in the conversation while the waiter took their order.

'So tell me, Tammy McDermot,' Oliver said, relaxing into his seat. 'Where would you travel to right now, if you could go anywhere in the world?'

'That's easy.' Her eyes sparkled in the candlelight. 'The

Rocky Mountains. I'd rent a log cabin with snow on the roof, light a fire and do nothing but read all night and explore all day, just me, myself and I. And maybe the odd grizzly bear.'

'That sounds wonderful.'

'Doesn't it?' She smiled. 'Of course, I wouldn't mind a bit of company. If it was the right sort.'

'What's the right sort?'

'Oh, a big, strapping lumberjack type, I suppose. Someone to fit into the picture.'

'You know, I've got a checked shirt at home,' Oliver said. 'And I know all the words to that Monty Python song.'

She laughed. 'Close enough.'

He glanced at the St Christopher medallion. 'Are you religious then?'

'Not especially,' she said, shrugging. 'It's not something I've thought much about.'

'Right.'

'How about you?'

'Well, er . . . I suppose I've always thought of myself as a spiritual sort of person,' he said, trying not to grimace.

It's not like it was a lie. As far as it went, that statement was one hundred per cent accurate. And it definitely sounded like the kind of thing people said on first dates, rather than plunging headlong into a deep discussion of personal faith. If you want to make friends at parties then stay off politics and religion, his mother had once told him.

Which might've been a lot easier if he hadn't decided to

become a vicar. Oliver wondered fleetingly how the prime minister coped.

The waiter came back with their drinks and tapas. Oliver, who hated black olives, immediately ate four in a row as a penance.

'So do you have family in the area?' he asked Tammy as they ate.

'Yes, I live in Plumholme with my mum. Most of the family are up in Scotland though,' she said. 'How about you? You seem pretty close to Tess.'

'Her and Raven are my oldest friends. My parents live not far away too, in one of those park homes.'

'Brothers and sisters?'

'A brother. Archie.'

'Older or younger?'

'Older. I mean, he would be older.'

'Would be?'

Oliver looked down at his plate. 'Yeah.'

'Oh God, I'm sorry.' Tammy reached out to place her hand on his. 'Sorry, Oliver. If I'd known, I'd never have blundered in.'

'It's OK. It was a while ago now. Not that it doesn't still hurt, but . . . you learn to live with it.'

'How old were you?'

'Sixteen. Archie was two years older.' He swallowed. 'He . . . we always knew we could lose him young. He was born with it, the thing that killed him.'

'What was it?' Tammy whispered.

'His heart. He had Down syndrome. One of the complications was a hole in the heart.' He crumpled his napkin in his fist, then smoothed it out again. 'I still think about him every day.'

'Of course you do,' Tammy said gently. 'Tell me about him.'

'Oh, you'd have loved him. He was an amazing kid. Wicked sense of humour.' He smiled. 'And he was mad on football. Archie could tell you every Leeds United player from the past fifteen years – every single one from memory, with their scoring record, transfer fees, the lot. We were due to go to the match together the day he – when it happened.'

'Oliver, I'm so sorry.' Tammy took his hand, and this time she didn't let it go. 'What a horrific thing for your family to go through. How did you cope?'

'I didn't, for a while. I went right off the rails.'

'Who, you?'

'Hard to believe, right?' He shook his head. 'Selfish little bastard that I was. Never even cared what it was doing to Mum and Dad. But then . . . I found comfort somewhere it never would've occurred to me to go looking for it. It was during that period of my life that I realised what I wanted to be when I left school.'

She blinked. 'You knew you wanted to be a motivational speaker at sixteen?'

Motivational speaker. Yes, that was what Tess had told her, wasn't it? Oliver mentally kicked himself for the slip.

'Er, sort of,' he said, popping another horrible olive into his mouth. 'I wanted to help people going through a tough time, maybe veering towards self-destruction, the way I had been.'

She looked at him for a long moment before she spoke again.

'You know, Oliver Maynard, you're really something quite impressive.'

He felt his cheeks heat. 'I'm really not.'

'Take a compliment, man.'

He smiled. 'OK, then I'm awesome. Back at you, by the way.'

Tammy flushed slightly, poking at her food with her fork. 'So . . . shall we do this again?'

'I'd like that very much.' He squeezed the hand he was holding. 'Very much.'

At the end of the evening, they paid their bill and stood to leave.

'I'd better call a taxi,' Tammy said.

'No need. I wasn't drinking, I can give you a lift home,' Oliver said. 'Where do you live?'

'Thanks. Just drop me off by the church in Plumholme. I can walk to my mum's from there.'

Plumholme was a village some eight miles distant, and Oliver had to pass through Cherrywood to get them there.

He frowned as they drove past the village hall. Peggy Bristow was just leaving, by the back door this time, looking about her as if anxious not to be spotted.

'She's been in there all this time?' he muttered. 'Miss Ackroyd really must be driving her mad.'

'Sorry?' Tammy said.

He smiled. 'Nothing. Come on, let's get you home.'

Chapter 18

'So did it go well?' Tess asked Oliver the next evening in the pub, although she could already tell what the answer was going to be from the gooey expression on his face.

'Yeah. It went really well.'

'But you still didn't tell her, right?'

Oliver sighed. 'Nearly, when I dropped her off, but I chickened out.'

'When are you going to?'

'It's harder now, isn't it? I really like her, Tessie – I mean, *really* like her. What if it puts her off?'

'Does she like you?'

'I think so. She said she wanted to go out again, and she held my hand of her own free will, and she didn't completely recoil when I kissed her goodnight. I'm taking those as positives.'

'Well, there you are,' Tess said. 'She's got to know the real Oliver Maynard and she likes him. She's not going to be put off just because you're a vicar.'

'You don't know that.'

'Right. So you're going to leave the priesthood purely out

of social embarrassment, are you? How unbelievably English of you.' Tess reached up to adjust her Cher wig, which was pinching her scalp. She was in full costume, waiting for Ian to get back from the shops so they could perform their set.

'Don't be daft,' Oliver said. 'I just need a bit more time. Next date, I'll break it to her gently over wine. Lots of wine.' He paused. 'Or maybe the one after that. Three's the charm.'

The conversation halted while Tess served a thirsty customer.

'She's bound to hear on the grapevine before then,' she said when the customer had gone. 'I'm surprised you've managed to keep it secret this long, especially with Bev around. Did you find out if she's a Christian?'

'Yeah.' Oliver took a gloomy sip of his pint. 'I thought she might be when I spotted she was wearing a St Christopher, but it sounds like she hasn't got any strong faith.'

Tess was alert at once. 'A St Christopher? Like Aunty Clemmie's?'

'Lots of people wear them, Tess.'

'Yes. I suppose they do.' She shook herself. 'Ugh. I'm so on edge these days with this murder business. I wish they'd just catch whatever bastard did it.'

'You're still convinced it's not Terry then?'

Bev appeared from the storeroom to refill the bowl of peanuts on the bar.

'Have you not heard the news?' she asked. 'Terry Braithwaite's off the hook. A dog walker came forward to say they'd seen him heading up to the cottage with a box of eggs

189

at around nine-thirty p.m. – more than half an hour after Clemmie was killed, according to the coroner's report. Police've dropped the murder charge pending further investigation and he's been released on bail for the theft.'

'Thank God for that,' Tess said. 'Not that he doesn't deserve to get done for failing to report the murder – if he knew about it,' she added hastily, since her visit to Terry with Liam wasn't something that was common knowledge. 'But scumbag though he is, I'd hate to see him do time for a murder he didn't commit.'

'So have police reopened the murder investigation?' Oliver asked.

The landlady shrugged. 'Suppose they must have. Prue Ackroyd must be having a few sleepless nights over at Peggy's.'

Tess wondered if Liam knew about this development. She wished she could call him, but she was due to perform with Ian any minute.

'Where the hell is that husband of mine?' Bev demanded. 'He should've been back ages ago. I'd better ring him.' She disappeared upstairs.

'Any ideas on suspects now Terry's out of the picture?' Oliver asked Tess as he sipped his pint. 'You seem to be taking a keen interest in solving the case.'

'Well, it can't be Miss Ackroyd.' Tess shook her head. 'I honestly can't imagine it could be anyone – I mean, anyone we know. It feels so strange to think of someone in the village being a killer.'

'Maybe Miss Ackroyd's right,' Oliver said. 'Maybe it really was the ghost.'

'Did you speak to your bishop about her exorcism?'

'I nearly phoned him this afternoon but I wimped out,' he admitted. 'I did look into it, though. I'm in this priests' group on Facebook so I asked in there for some advice.'

'What did they say?'

'Apparently requests for the Church to deal with malevolent presences are more common than you'd think,' Oliver said, finishing his drink. 'I was chatting to a lass who's on the deliverance team for her diocese; she was telling me all about it.'

'Deliverance team?'

'Yeah, the Church favours the term "deliverance" over "exorcism" these days. Every diocese has got a team assigned to it. First they investigate for physical explanations, leaking pipes or whatever. If none can be found they say a blessing and presto, poltergeists banished to whence they came.'

'Bloody hell. I had no idea the Church of England employed its own Ghostbusters.'

'Me neither. Anyway, now I'm reassured he won't think I've gone dotty I'm going to ring Michael – the bishop – and ask him to put me in touch with our team. I'll be glad to wash my hands of the business.' Oliver pushed his glass away. 'Right. I'd better go home and make the call, before Peggy Bristow finally cracks.'

Tess was silent a moment.

'Ol, can I have a word in private?'

'Is it urgent?'

'A bit, yeah.'

She gestured for him to join her behind the bar and led him into the storeroom, where she could still keep an eye out for customers.

'Don't call your bishop,' she said in a low voice. 'Call Miss Ackroyd and tell her you'll do the exorcism – you personally.'

'Me? Why?'

'Because I think she knows more about her sister's murder than she's letting on and this could be our chance to find out what it is.'

'*Our* chance?'

'Yeah. I'm going to come too, hold your crucifix and proton pack for you. She likes me.'

'Tess, come on,' he said. 'You know I can't do that. I could get into trouble.'

'Not if you're helping to solve a murder.'

'We're not the police. Let them deal with it.'

'How are they dealing with it?' Tess said. 'They already nearly sent down the wrong man. God knows who'll be in the frame next. They're looking in completely the wrong place, trust me.'

'You seem to know a lot about it.'

She glanced towards the bar and lowered her voice even further. 'OK. You have to keep this under your cassock, but . . . you know Sam Mitchell?'

'That gardener you hate?'

'Yeah. Well, he's not a gardener. He's an undercover detective.'

192

When she'd filled Oliver in on everything, he looked a little dazed.

'The Women's Guild?' he said, sinking into a chair.

'So Liam believes.'

'Our Women's Guild? Cherrywood Women's Guild?'

'That's right.'

'But . . . they're the Women's Guild.'

'Liam says murderers come in all shapes and sizes. Even Women's Guild shapes and sizes.'

'Do you think one of them did it?'

'I don't know,' Tess said. 'But I do know Miss Ackroyd's hiding something, and if we can find out what it is then it might point us in the direction of the killer.'

'And this private detective, he's really your ex?'

'Sadly, yes.' She sighed. 'But that's a story for another time. So will you do it?'

'I dunno, Tess. It doesn't feel right, lying to Miss Ackroyd.'

'You're not lying, are you? You're doing exactly what she asked you to do.'

Oliver still looked wary. 'I'm supposed to refer it to the deliverance team though.'

'She doesn't want the deliverance team, Ol, she wants you. She trusts you.'

'But I'll be tricking her. I mean, we'll be spying on her.'

'We're trying to help her,' Tess said. 'She's hiding something, but I don't think she's the killer. If we find out who the murderer is, she can finally stop dreaming up goblins and ghouls and lay her sister's memory to rest.'

'I suppose,' Oliver murmured. 'I do think the ghost is

more likely to be a manifestation of grief than anything else.'

'Me too. It's the right thing to do, Oliver.'

'I'm . . . not sure. I think I'd like to have a chat with the boss first.'

'The bishop?'

'He's more of a line manager.' Oliver flicked his eyes upwards. 'I meant the big boss.'

'Ah, right. That guy.' Tess patted his arm. 'Well, you have a think and a pray and let me know, eh?'

'Right.' He stood up. 'I'd better go. I'll catch up with you later.'

'Yeah, see you.' She followed him out to the bar, where a flustered Ian had just burst through the door. 'And look what the cat dragged in.'

Tess beckoned him over.

'You're in trouble, you know,' she said. 'Bev's been trying to call you. We were supposed to be on half an hour ago. Did you forget?'

'Sorry. Got held up.'

Bev came stomping over and glared at him. 'And where the hell have you been?'

'Now, pet, don't overreact—'

'I've been worried sick!' she exploded. 'It's a five-minute walk to the corner shop. You've been gone over an hour!'

'Come on, it wasn't that long.'

'You only went out to get me a pack of B&H. What've you been doing?'

'I bumped into a mate,' Ian said, running a finger under

his collar. 'Thought we'd go for a quick pint at the Green Man. Sorry, love.'

'Well, you'd best get into costume,' Bev said. 'Here, give us my fags.'

Ian blinked at her.

'Come on, Ian, where are they?'

'I, er . . . sorry, I must've put them down somewhere.'

'For God's sake! I give you one simple job.' She shook her head at Tess. 'Never get married, Tess.'

'I'll do a solo number while you get ready,' Tess said to Ian. 'Our fanbase is starting to look pissed off.'

It was true. Old Guy Cartwright, their single fan, was checking his watch impatiently.

Tess treated the pub to a bit of 'Fernando' while Ian got his glad rags on, letting her mind wander while she sang. The release of Terry Braithwaite and reopening of the murder investigation had come as a complete surprise, and she was desperate to speak to Liam about it.

She had a confession to make too – another two people now knew who Liam really was. She suspected he wasn't going to take it well, but what choice did she have? It was his fault, letting rumours get started about him and her.

They could trust Raven and Oliver, and anyway, the two of them were well placed to help with the investigation. Between her and Ol – the barmaid and the priest– they were confidants for most of the village, and Raven had an insight into the Walton-Lord family that no one else could provide.

She just had to convince Liam it was for the best.

Finally Ian joined her in his Sonny Bono suit and they

belted their way through the rest of the set, Tess itching to be done so she could phone Liam. When they were finished, Bev joined them on stage.

'You can get off, love,' she said to Tess. 'Tammy should be here any minute.' She glared at Ian. 'And then me and you are having words.'

Ian shifted uncomfortably on his stool. 'I said sorry. It won't happen again.'

'Won't happen again? That's the second time this week.' Bev turned to Tess. 'I don't suppose you could run us an errand, could you? I'd ask the mister but he's as good as useless lately.'

'No problem. You want me to pick up your cigs?'

'No, I was hoping you might pop up to Ling Cottage and give that mangy moggy of Clemmie's his tea. I told Prue I'd feed him while she was staying at Peggy's, but I've got a banging headache.' She cast a look at Ian. 'Nicotine withdrawal, probably.'

Tess's heart jumped. Ling Cottage – full access to Ling Cottage! The perfect opportunity to do some Scoobying while Miss Ackroyd was away. Liam would be whooping if she could tell him she'd wangled the key.

She tried to look nonchalant. 'I don't mind, yeah. How do I get in?'

'Hang on.' Bev reached into her balconette bra for the key and handed it to Tess, who tried not to grimace.

Ick. Warm . . .

'Cheers,' Tess said. 'I'll just change then I'll head up.'

Chapter 19

Liam was bathed in the sickly glow of Black Moor Farm's security light, jogging on the spot. Spring was fast becoming summer, but the moors at night were chilly whatever the season. At his feet, Candice's Pomeranian Susie sniffed at a suspicious-looking puddle before deigning to splash primly about in it.

The day had got off to an inauspicious start when he'd overboiled his breakfast egg and buckled his soldiers. Then it had taken a turn for the worse when Della, his contact at West Yorkshire Police, had called to tell him Terry Braithwaite had been released and the investigation reopened. Of course it was good news for Terry, and Liam was pleased to think he'd been instrumental in making it happen – it had been one of his freelance gardening clients who had casually recalled seeing Terry walking to Ling Cottage the night of the murder, and Liam had pressed them to contact the police in case it might be significant. But it had been convenient to be able to investigate without the police running around, getting under his feet and limiting his access to scenes and suspects.

But now, things were looking up. Tess had called, for one thing. That in itself was enough to brighten Liam's day. And then she'd told him she'd got the key to Ling Cottage. The plan was to meet here, far enough from the village that they were unlikely to be seen together, and walk up.

Liam had barely seen her since she'd banned him from speaking to her publicly at the show, although several times he'd tried to put himself in her way. He'd seen her at the pub, of course, but she'd made sure the conversation stayed restricted to drinks orders. And he'd had a couple of texts with titbits of information she thought might be relevant to the investigation. There'd been no personal element to them, though. The 'How're you doing?' enquiries he tagged on to his own texts had been ignored.

He missed her. Quite a lot, in fact. The time they'd spent discussing the case had reminded him just how much he enjoyed her company, her conversation, her sense of humour. It had reminded him exactly why he'd fallen for Tess Feather in the first place, and the revelation that he'd never really unfallen for her had surprised him more than it probably should have.

'What have you got there, girl?' He bent down to prise something out of Susie's jaws before she swallowed it. It was a short length of chain: just a few links, probably from a necklace. Liam tucked it in his pocket and ruffled the dog's fluffball ears. 'Trouble, aren't you? Just don't tell your mums where I took you on your walk today, that's all.'

He smiled when he spotted Tess walking towards him.

'Hi,' he said.

'Did you know Terry Braithwaite has been released?' Tess demanded.

'Yeah, I'm good, thanks. How are you?'

'Never mind that. Did you?' Susie jumped up at her leg, yipping with delight, and Tess petted her absently.

'Della told me earlier. It seems the witness I sent her way came up trumps.' Liam glanced at Black Moor Farm, the Braithwaites' residence. 'We don't want to talk about it here. Come on, let's walk.'

Together they headed into the darkness, up the dirt track over the moors that led to Ling Cottage. Susie scampered along between them.

'What else did Della tell you?' Tess asked.

'That they've reopened the case. That's going to clip our wings a bit, but I've got a pretty good relationship with her. If I can keep her sweet, she might pass along information.' Liam glanced at her. 'How did you get the key to the house?'

'It came via Bev's bra. She asked me to go feed Miss Ackroyd's cat.'

'And you're absolutely sure the old lady's not there?'

'No, she's staying with Peggy Bristow until Oliver does her exorcism.' Tess winced. 'Which reminds me. Liam . . . I've got a confession to make.'

He frowned. 'Confession?'

'Look, I know it's important and everything, but Raven's important to me too, and when she said she was going to move out, well, I couldn't bear for her to think . . . I mean, it's not like you've got any right to take the moral high ground, is it? And it is really your fault.'

'Whoa. Tess.' He stopped walking and put his hands on

her shoulders. 'Do you mind telling me what on earth you're jabbering about?'

'Told Raven who you are,' she muttered, eyes down.

'*What?*'

She looked up to glare at him. 'Well I had to, didn't I? Everyone in the village was looking daggers at me, and she was threatening to move back to Cherrywood Hall. I'm not losing an old friend over some stupid misunderstanding.'

'For God's sake, Tess! Raven Walton-Lord's the last person I need knowing why I'm really here.'

'She's not involved, I told you.'

'But someone she cares about might be,' he said, scowling. 'Thanks a sodding bunch, partner.'

'She doesn't know everything. I didn't tell her about the letters, or Marianne's connection to Nadia Harris.'

'Right. But you told her everything else.'

'She can help, can't she?' Tess said defensively. 'Who knows more about the Walton-Lords than she does?'

'Oh, this is bloody perfect, this is,' Liam muttered. 'Tell you what, why don't you put an announcement up on the parish council noticeboard?'

'Don't be daft.' Tess scuffed at the ground with her trainer. 'I, er . . . I did tell one other person.'

'Christ, Tess! Does the term "undercover" mean something different to you than it does to other people?'

'It was only Oliver. We can trust him, he's a vicar.'

'Exactly. Second only to butlers in terms of likelihood of having done it.'

'He's one of my closest friends,' Tess said, frowning. 'He

used to feed sugar syrup to dying bees in the school playground. He's a *Blue Peter* badge holder. Trust me, battering old ladies to death is not one of his hobbies.'

Liam shook his head. 'Why did I ever think you'd be able to keep this to yourself?'

'It's two people, Liam. Miss Ackroyd trusts Oliver; she confides in him. I thought if he did this exorcism, he might be able to find out something significant. I had to tell him or he wasn't going to do it.'

Her cheeks were flaming, her grey eyes sparking with defiance. Liam almost smiled at her expression but stopped himself in time.

'I'm not happy about this, Tess,' he said, resuming their walk.

'Well, I am. And I'm your partner so I'm entitled to make executive decisions on behalf of the both of us.'

This time he did let himself smile. Something about hearing Tess call them partners made his spirits lift, in spite of their gloomy mission.

'I suppose I can't argue with that,' he said. 'And you did get us the key. Not that it in any way cancels out your big flapping gob.'

'I won't tell anyone else. Raven and Ol are my best friends, that's all.'

'Right. Have you got any other best friends? Maybe the town crier, local newspaper editor, anyone like that?'

Tess smiled. 'Just those two.'

They soon reached Ling Cottage. Tess unlocked the door and Liam followed her in, Susie straining at her lead.

'So what avenues have you been exploring lately?' Tess asked him.

'Nadia Harris avenues.'

'You didn't find her?'

'No, but I've been thinking about her. Thinking about motive. Opportunity. Connections.' He followed Tess into the front room, and she flicked on the light. 'Nadia Harris was born on the seventeenth of May 1964. She'd be fifty-eight. There's three of the Women's Guild ladies who are around the right age – Peggy Bristow, Beverley Stringer, Gracie Lister.'

'What, you think one of them might be her? Nadia?'

He shrugged. 'Not impossible, is it? All three are incomers. But I did some research and none of them are a match. They all have their own paper trails pre-1980, when Nadia Harris was still active, so that's one theory eliminated. I also thought a lot about motive.'

'And?'

'Nadia had a motive for murder, a pretty compelling one – two hundred thousand pounds. But if it's the money she's after, then where the hell is she? She can't claim it unless she makes herself known.'

'Biding her time, perhaps,' Tess suggested. 'That way it'll be less suspicious when she does come forward.'

'Could be. Or that's another damp squib theory I'm wasting precious time on when I should be looking elsewhere.'

'So your conclusion to all this thinking was . . .'

'Yeah,' Liam said with a sigh. 'That I still know naff all.'

They were interrupted by ferocious barking from Susie, and an angry yowl in the shadows for answer.

'Nelson,' Tess said. 'Obviously not a fan of canine visitors.'

'Come on then, Suze,' Liam said, picking her up. 'You go have a scamper in the garden while me and Aunty Tess do what we need to do. We can't have you and Nelson destroying the place.'

He carried her through the house to the back garden, peeping through open doors as he went.

It was a miserable little place, like something out of Dickens. What was that book they'd read at school, about the really gloomy, depressing house? Meh, it'd come to him later.

There were no carpets: just threadbare rugs over uneven stone. The walls were stone too, whitewashed in what was probably a futile attempt to brighten the place up. No central heating, only coal fires in the study and front room. Hunched shadows lurked in every corner – God knew what items of furniture they might be in daylight, but now, at night, they were distinctly goblin-like.

Liam shuddered. Yes, he could understand why Prudence Ackroyd dreamed up ghouls to haunt her waking nightmares, living alone in this place with her sister's blood still fresh. He felt a flicker of pity for the woman, whatever secrets she might be hiding.

The back door was at one end of the kitchen. He drew back the latch chain and plonked Susie down on the damp grass.

'You can play out here till we're done.' He ruffled the dog's ears and went back to Tess in the study.

'This place creeps me right out,' he told her.

'I know what you mean. It gives me the willies too.'

He nodded to a black-and-white photo on the rough-hewn wooden mantelpiece. 'I take it that's the Ackroyd family. They look like they match the house.'

'Yeah,' Tess said. 'The sisters as kids with their mum and dad, Connie and Arthur.'

Liam took the photo down to examine it. The two girls, unsmiling, sat on top of a piano in identical sailor dresses, their dad towering over them in army uniform. He had one arm around his wife, who looked uncomfortable at the touch.

'American Gothic, eh?' Liam said. 'They look miserable as sin.'

'They probably were. Connie Ackroyd was . . . well, let's just say I'm glad she wasn't my mum. Arthur passed away when the girls were small so she mostly raised them alone.'

'Why are you glad she wasn't your mum?'

Tess shuddered. 'She was terrifying – proper old-school battleaxe like they don't make any more, thank God. Miss Ackroyd takes after her a bit, but she's nowhere near as bad. I don't think Connie had an ounce of warmth or tolerance in her. She wouldn't put up with a foot out of line, especially from Clemmie.'

'What about Prudence?'

'They weren't on speaking terms – not since before I was born,' Tess told him. 'Prue Ackroyd wouldn't set foot in Ling

Cottage while her mother was alive. I was surprised when I heard Connie had left her half the cottage – I'd thought it would all go to Clemmie.'

'What happened to stop them speaking?'

Tess shrugged. 'No one knows. I always assumed there was too big a personality clash.'

'So Clemency lived all alone with her mum?'

'Yeah, until she died ten years ago. Then her sister moved in and filled the gap. Between them they bullied her something awful, poor soul.'

'Why did she stand it?'

'I used to think she had no choice – no money of her own to break free,' Tess said. 'But if she had two hundred grand sitting around doing nothing, who knows? I guess she stayed from a sense of duty. She devoted her life to her mum.'

Liam looked again at Connie Ackroyd. She had a very distinctive face. Sharp cheekbones, the chin prominent, the eyes hard. He felt a surge of pity for Clemency Ackroyd, trapped with this unpleasant-looking individual her entire life.

He put the photo back and turned to Tess.

'So then, partner. Where shall we start?'

Chapter 20

'We'd better look in Miss Ackroyd's room first,' Tess said.

Liam hesitated. 'Her bedroom?'

Tess grinned. 'Not shy, are you? Come on, you're a detective. If there's something she's hiding, that's the place we're most likely to find it.'

'Be careful, that's all. We don't want her to know we've been snooping.'

They tried a couple of doors until they found the one that, judging by the open paperback on the bedside table, must belong to Prudence Ackroyd.

'Well, well, well.' Tess picked up the book and showed it to Liam.

'*The Hero's Return*,' he read. 'Looks racy.'

'Yep. Diana Skye, Raven's favourite. She writes these steamy romances about men in uniform.' Tess shook her head. 'You think you know someone. Naughty Miss Ackroyd.' She put it back on the table, careful to place it in exactly the position it had been before.

Liam glanced around the room, unsure where to start. 'Tessie, what exactly do we think we're looking for in here?'

'Anything that looks like it wants to stay hidden.' Tess, less shy than he was, yanked open the cupboard and peered in. 'What do we know about Miss Ackroyd, Lee?'

'Well, she thinks her house is haunted but is cagey about saying why.'

'Might be a petty thief.'

'Was one of the last people to see her sister alive.'

'And in line to inherit half of a property worth, what, three hundred grand or more in the event of her sister's death.' Tess started rummaging through Prue's clothes. 'Let's see what else she's got to hide.'

'Right.' Liam pulled open a drawer in a dazed sort of way. He was starting to wonder who was leading this investigation.

The drawer he'd opened was full of old photo albums and notebooks. Liam took a few out and started looking through.

'Anything significant?' Tess asked.

'I don't think so. Just family photos of them looking miserable in different places.' He took out an old leather notebook and opened at a random page. 'Oh. This might be something.'

'What is it?'

' "Twelfth of June 1964",' Liam read. ' "I went to Ling Cottage to collect my things today. A huge set-to with Mother, of course. I tried again to convince Clemmie to come away with me, but she's weak, the poor soul. I wish Mother would just die and leave us to live the rest of our lives! But we could never be so lucky." '

Tess blinked. 'Prue kept a diary?'

'Seems so.' He weighed the thick volume in his hand. 'This must be five years' worth of entries. Do you think we could get away with taking it? There might be something about Nadia Harris in it – it's from around the time she was born.'

'Where was it?'

'Just stuffed in the bottom of the drawer, under a load of photo albums. It looked like it hadn't been touched in years.'

'Hmm. She might not miss it, but we need to be careful. Miss Ackroyd's the sort of person who notices things.' Tess removed a large, empty bottle from the blanket box she was rummaging in. 'Aha!'

Liam frowned. 'What, the old girl's a drinker?'

'Nope. Bev was right, she has been half-inching. The missing hundred quid – she told the police it was all in coins in an old whisky bottle. Bev said she thought Miss Ackroyd had taken it – and that it wasn't the first thing to go missing from the house.'

'Why report it, then?' Liam asked. 'Her sister was dead. She could just take it.'

'So she could claim it again on her insurance would be my guess,' Tess said, shrugging. 'Bev said she was broke. The question is, why? Where did her money go?'

'Are you thinking blackmail?'

'I'm not thinking anything. Just filing questions away to ponder later. Come on, let's keep exploring.'

But there were no more secrets hiding among Prue Ackroyd's frillies. When they'd put everything carefully back how it was – other than the diary, which Liam pocketed to peruse at leisure – they moved on to the study.

'The sideboard . . .' Tess gazed thoughtfully at the old mahogany chest.

'What?' Liam said.

'Trying to remember something.' She cycled back through a hundred and one conversations until she found the one she needed. 'That was it. Miss Ackroyd said Clemmie kept her treasures in the sideboard.'

'This is where they found the body,' Liam told her.

'What, right here?'

'Yeah. On the rug in front of the sideboard, face down. I saw the crime scene report.'

Tess glanced at the rug she was standing on and shuddered. Liam put a hand on her shoulder.

'I can look if you want,' he said gently. She nodded and moved aside for him.

He opened the top drawer, but there was nothing except junk in there – old receipts, bus tickets and other signs of a compulsive hoarder. When he'd checked for anything significant, he looked at the second drawer. There was a small keyhole.

'Could be locked,' he said. 'Then what?'

'We'll have to hunt for the key.'

But there was no need. The lock was rusted, like it had long since given in to the ravages of time. Liam gave the drawer a couple of firm pulls and it creaked open.

An ancient Ringtons Tea tin turned out to be full of old coins. None, Liam suspected, very valuable, but nevertheless he took a quick inventory in his notebook. Other than that, all the drawer contained were papers – letters, memorandum books, calendars.

He took out a few yellowed envelopes to examine them.

'Must be ten or twelve of these. Typewritten address.' He passed a few of the envelopes to Tess.

'Typewritten?' she said. 'On the same typewriter as the ones Marianne's been getting?'

'Couldn't say just from looking. Different envelopes, though. Hers always come in airmail ones.'

Tess hesitated, looking down at the letters in her hands. 'Would it be wrong to open one?'

'Not if it could help catch a killer.'

Liam lifted one to sniff it. It smelt of cigar smoke and age. Tess followed suit.

'They smell very, sort of . . . masculine,' she observed. 'Could they be love letters?'

'They could be. They could also be income tax demands – the old girl clearly liked to hang on to things. Let's see if there are any with a broken seal.'

Tess turned them over and over, seeming hesitant to pry into the private life of the dead woman.

'This one looks like it might have been opened recently.' She handed one of her envelopes to Liam. 'The flap's a different colour, and it's coming open at the edges.'

'You're right.' He looked at her. 'Shall I?'

'Go on.'

Carefully Liam opened the flap and eased out the letter. It

was written in a very shaky hand, and it took him a moment to decipher it.

' "Darling girl",' he read. ' "I know you forbade me to call you so, but darling you are and darling you must always be." '

'So it is a love letter,' Tess said.

'Sounds that way. Listen. "I can't believe a year has gone by since the whole sorry affair, and our beautiful Charity still mourned. I never can forgive your mother, just as I know you can never forgive me. To take a life is a terrible sin, but by the grace of God I hope you keep it safe for her. Father continues blissful. I'm sorry, my darling. Always your loving Felix." ' He looked up at Tess. 'You know a Felix?'

Tess shook her head. 'Not in Cherrywood; not in my lifetime.' She looked thoughtful. 'Charity, though. Andrew Walton-Lord was rambling about a Charity.'

'What did he say?'

'He talked about saving her, and some girl he should've married.' Tess paused. 'Lee . . . Andrew had an old manual typewriter. In his rooms at Rowan House.'

'You think he wrote these?'

'Perhaps. He's not so much older than Aunty Clemmie that they couldn't have been lovers. Felix might have been a nickname.'

'What about the threatening letters? Could he have written them?'

'Andrew?' She shook her head. 'No. He's just a confused, sweet old man. Harmless.'

'Maybe it's an act.'

'If it is he's been putting it on a long time. Booze and grief addled his brain long before I was born.'

Liam looked at the letter again. 'It's like a riddle, isn't it? As if he was afraid of the letter being intercepted and chose to write in sentences only the recipient would be able to make full sense of.'

'Yeah, you're right, it doesn't quite fit together,' Tess said. ' "Our beautiful Charity still mourned . . . I hope you keep it safe for her." How can Clemmie keep whatever it is safe for someone who's presumably dead?'

'Let me get a photo of it, then we can puzzle it out later.' Liam got out his phone and snapped a picture.

'Can we get away with reading the others?' Tess asked.

'There's no way of opening them without it being obvious the seals have been tampered with. None of these have been reopened since Clemency first received them, by the look of things.'

'But they might give us the clue we need to crack the case.'

Liam hesitated.

'Not today,' he said at last. 'This drawer looks like it's opened regularly. If we take them, Prudence'll know someone's been here and trace that back to you, then bang goes her confidence. And we don't know they'll give us any more than we've got already, if they're all as sphinx-like as this one. We've got the diary.'

'If you're sure.'

'We'll leave them for now, anyway. Perhaps you can wangle the key again if we hit a dead end.'

'We'd better get a move on,' Tess said. 'Candice'll be wondering if you've taken Susie to Timbuktu for her walk.'

'God, Susie, I forgot. I'd better check she's OK.'

'And I'd better do what I'm officially here for and feed the cat,' Tess said, glancing down at Nelson purring hopefully by her feet.

They headed to the kitchen. Tess explored the cupboards for Nelson's biscuits while Liam opened the back door to check on the dog.

'She's making a right mess out here,' he said with a groan. 'Susie! Naughty girl. Come here.'

The little dog came bounding up, evidently impressed with her evening's work and expecting Liam to be impressed likewise.

'What's she done?' Tess asked.

'Dug up half the garden, the little bugger.' Liam took out Susie's lead and clipped it on her, then tied it round the drainpipe. 'There. That should hold you till we're done.' He raised his voice. 'We'd better be quick, Tess, before she starts grumbling.'

'OK, come on. Let's have one last scout, then go.'

'I'll just fix the garden first. There's dirt everywhere.'

There was a monkey puzzle tree by the gate, rather an exotic touch in an otherwise conservative garden, and Susie had really gone to town underneath it. Soil was thrown all over the place, a little hole at the base where she'd dug in with her front paws.

She was already straining at her lead to get back to her work. Liam tickled her behind the ear to make up for spoiling her fun, then filled in the hole as best he could with his boot. Hopefully, if Prue Ackroyd noticed the mess, she'd blame moles or something.

When he was done he went back into the kitchen, where Nelson was wolfing down his tea. 'Right. Let's have a look in the bottom drawer of that sideboard and get out of this godawful place.'

'We already looked in Clemmie's drawer,' Tess said. 'The last one's probably just more receipts.'

'Still, I'd like to check it out.'

They headed back to the study and he tried the third drawer.

'Won't budge,' he told Tess. 'I think this one might actually have a working lock.'

'Oh! I might know where the key is. I saw a tiny one in the kitchen drawer with the cutlery.'

'OK, go fetch it then. Maybe the Ackroyd girls had a treasure drawer each. Who knows what Prue keeps in hers?'

Tess went to get the key. Liam turned it in the lock and the drawer slid open.

'Uh-oh.' He drew out an envelope. It was addressed in a monospace font, red and blue chevrons around the edge. 'This looks familiar. Typewritten, airmail envelope . . .'

'Marianne's letters!' Tess said. 'How did Miss Ackroyd get one?'

'She didn't. This is addressed to her. Looks like our poison pen pal has more than one victim on the go.'

'How many are there?'

Liam searched the drawer. 'Just this one. Either the writer's got more to say to Marianne than Miss Ackroyd or she's destroyed the evidence.'

'Well, go on, open it.'

There was no worry here that Prue Ackroyd might detect tampering. The letter had been opened recently, the flap tucked back in with no attempt made to reseal it. Liam drew out the contents: a single sheet of lavender-coloured notepaper.

' "Dearest Prudence. Sin will out." ' He looked up at Tess. 'Déjà vu.'

'What else?'

' "I've been gone a little while but I won't ever leave you again, I promise. Heartfelt apologies for the long absence." '

'Seriously?'

'Yep. Politest threatening letter writer ever.'

Tess was visibly holding her breath.

'Signature?' she whispered.

'What do you think?'

'Liam! Come on, don't tease.'

' "Kindest regards, Charity." '

'Charity!'

'That's what it says.' He held up the letter to show her. It wasn't a signature: just the name, typewritten in full caps.

'But she's dead, isn't she? The Felix letter made it sound like she was dead, whoever she was.'

'I think we might have found Prue Ackroyd's ghost.' Liam examined her face, white and drained of blood. 'You OK, Tessie?'

'I'm OK.'

'You need a drink? A seat or anything?'

'No. No, I don't need anything.' Despite her pallor, her eyes were glittering. 'This is it, Lee! This is the biggest clue yet.'

'I think you're right.' He pulled out his phone and took a photo of the letter. 'What do you think it means?'

'I don't know. But assuming these letters are from the same source as the others – why would Candice hide the name? Who was Charity? If we can find out more about her, we could have this cracked.'

Liam stared at the letter in silence for a moment.

'OK, so here's a question,' he said at last. 'Was Clemmie's murder premeditated or a crime of passion?'

'How do you mean?'

'Well, we keep talking about motive – the money, the house.' He glanced at the mantelpiece, a dark square indicating the place where Connie Ackroyd's carriage clock used to sit. 'Maybe we're looking at it the wrong way.'

'Go on.'

'If you turn up with the specific intention of murdering someone to get your inheritance, you bring your own weapon, right? Something a bit more efficient than a brass clock.' His eyes flickered to the companion set sitting next to the coal scuttle. 'Not to mention that there's a heavy poker right there. This is someone who used the first thing they laid hands on – didn't even bother trying to make it look like an accident.'

'Where is the clock now?' Tess asked.

'With the police. The killer dropped it by the body, smashed to bits.'

'No prints on the casing?'

'Some, but they belong to the Ackroyd sisters. Our murderer did have the presence of mind to wear gloves, it seems.'

'Which suggests the murder was premeditated to the extent the killer thought to put their gloves on, but not planned far enough in advance for them to have brought along their own weapon. They—'

'They decided to do it while they were here in this house,' Liam finished for her. 'Which adds weight to my theory about your Women's Guild ladies not being as innocent as they appear.'

'Why did they decide to do it, though?'

'Maybe something they found here made them angry.'

Tess nodded to the letter in his hand. 'That?'

Liam shook his head. 'The postmark says this was sent after the murder, same as the others. But the Felix letter – someone had opened it recently, hadn't they?'

'And whoever it was didn't like what they read.'

'Marianne Priestley,' Liam said, tucking the Charity letter back into its envelope. 'She's the key to all this, somehow. And the others who were here that night – every one of them potentially knows something, murderers or not.' He looked at her. 'When's your next Women's Guild meeting?'

'This Sunday. It's not a regular evening meeting. It's a special all-day thing.'

'I wish I could work out a way in that didn't involve doing a drag act,' he muttered. 'I can't give another talk. Aren't men ever allowed at meetings?'

'At the ladies' and gentlemen's open evening, but that's not until the autumn.' Tess grinned. 'Although . . . actually, I've just thought of one way you can get in.'

Chapter 21

'How the hell did I let you talk me into this?' Liam muttered to Tess that Sunday when she and Raven met him in the gardens of Cherrywood Hall.

'You wanted to get access to a meeting, didn't you?' Tess said. 'It was either today's spa afternoon or modelling for the life-drawing class next month, so you're really getting off lightly. At least you get to keep your pants on.'

Raven snorted, and Liam gave her a dirty look.

'But I've never done any massage before,' he protested to Tess.

'Course you have. I mean, it's obviously something I try never to think about now, but I do remember we sometimes had massage before we had . . . other things.'

'Yeah, erotic massage. That's just fumbling about hoping you find the right spot, like everything you do in bed. Candice Walton-Lord seems to think I'm an expert in the proper stuff.'

'Yes.' Tess shot Raven a look. 'My friend here did build you up a bit more than was strictly necessary. I'm not sure why she needed to tell her grandmother you had a Level 3 certificate in Swedish massage. Still, it's done now.'

'Did you read that copy of *Massage for Dummies* we got you?' Raven asked Liam.

He glared at her. 'You're enjoying this, aren't you?'

'Oh, enormously.'

Tess patted his back. 'Relax, Lee. Seriously, how hard can it be? There's the two professionals Candice hired here too. I'm sure you can just lurk about picking up gossip while they do the real work.'

Raven laughed. 'Are you kidding? Bev's already booked three massages off him. Gracie asked me to do the scheduling and I've been charging a fiver a time to reserve him on the sly.'

'You know, I'm really starting not to like you,' Liam said. Raven grinned and blew him a kiss.

'So are we going in then?' Raven asked. 'There are twenty Women's Guild members in there just desperate for you to touch them up, Liam.'

'Hang on,' Tess said. 'Before we go in. How are you getting on with that diary? Any use?'

Liam shook his head. 'No mention of anyone called Charity, or of the Harris family. All I've learnt from it is that Connie Ackroyd was a nasty piece of work who tortured her daughters mentally as often as she abused them physically. Prudence couldn't wait to leave home, unsurprisingly, and begged her sister to go with her, to no avail. Harrowing to read, but I can't see how it relates to the case.'

'Well, hopefully today's massage session will yield a few more clues,' Raven said. 'Come on, they're waiting.'

Liam sighed. 'All right, let's get it over with.'

When they reached the library, a few members of the Women's Guild were milling about in bathrobes, drinking tea. Others, presumably, were outside enjoying the hot tubs Mrs Walton-Lord had installed in her summerhouse, or swimming in the heated pool.

In an adjoining room, where a few pop-up beds had been erected, a couple of members were already receiving massages from the professional masseuses who'd been hired for the day. The women were lying face down, naked from the waist up with a towel to protect their modesty down below. Liam grimaced when he spotted them. While a roomful of oiled-up, topless women all salivating for his hands on their flesh had certainly been a fantasy of his younger days, he'd rarely envisioned them as old enough to be his mum – or, in a few cases, his gran.

All eyes swivelled to the door as Liam entered. Bev grinned and gave him a little wave.

He was immediately commandeered by Gracie.

'Well, are we glad to see you,' she said, beaming. 'Candice tells me you've got quite the magic fingers, whether they're working on geraniums or shoulders. Now, come along with me and I'll show you to your station. There's a long waiting list for you, Mr Mitchell.'

Liam winced. 'I was afraid there might be.'

'I'm really looking forward to this,' Tess whispered to Raven as they watched Gracie lead Liam off.

'I think everyone's with you there, darling,' Raven said, glancing round the sea of unblinking eyes following Liam and Gracie to the next room. 'Don't worry, I did put our names down too.'

'Not the massage.' Tess grinned. 'I just love watching him squirm.'

'Let's go into the dining room – that's the changing room. Grandmother's put robes out for everyone.'

They got changed and went back in, now in just their knickers underneath a towelled bathrobe. Liam was reluctantly rubbing oil into a disrobed Peggy Bristow's shoulders with his fingertips. Tess smirked at Raven and they sidled closer.

'That's it, lad,' Peggy was saying to Liam. 'Get right in between the blades there. I've been feeling my rheumatism flaring up lately. After that you can have a go at my feet.'

Liam's eyes widened in horror. 'Your feet? Um, I don't think I do feet.'

'Oh, you definitely do feet,' Raven called to him. 'I've booked in plenty of feet for you.'

'How are the bunions these days, Peg?' Tess asked.

'Still giving me gyp. A good, firm rub from this young man ought to do them the world of good.' Peggy grinned evilly. 'I might get him working on my varicose veins while he's down there as well.'

'I hate you,' Liam mouthed to Tess and Raven. They each shot him a thumbs up before wandering away to get a hot drink.

'Looking forward to your turn, darling?' Raven asked Tess.

'Are you kidding? I've had all that before and I don't remember it being so hot that I'm mad keen on reliving the experience. What did you have to book me a massage from him for?'

Raven shrugged. 'It'll give you two the chance to compare notes without it looking suspicious. Besides, we don't want to miss out on the fun, do we?' She scanned Liam's bare arms, muscles shifting under the flesh as his fingers pressed into Peggy's shoulders. 'I can't believe you once had those on tap. You lucky mare.'

'I thought you hated him.'

'Well, yeah, after what you told me I think he's a complete arse. I can still enjoy looking at him, though, can't I?' Raven sighed. 'That body. He could get work modelling for Diana Skye covers.'

'For God's sake, don't say things like that around him,' Tess muttered. 'The man's insufferable enough as it is.'

In the massage room, Liam was silently cursing Raven Walton-Lord, Tess Feather, Peggy Bristow's chiropodist, and anyone else responsible for the fact that he was currently faced with a very unappealing pair of feet to rub.

'Don't worry about the flaking,' Peggy told him as she wriggled to get herself more comfortable. 'It's nothing fungal. Not had a chance to take my shoes off all day, that's all.'

Liam grimaced as he got to work. He'd better get some decent results out of today to make up for this whole traumatic experience.

His plan hinged on the break for afternoon tea, when he'd be able to mingle freely with the women. He was going to drop some information into this little gossip circle where everyone claimed to know everyone else's secrets. He was going to set light to a fuse, then he was going to stand back and see what – or who – exploded.

Tess had been briefed and she knew what part she needed to play. Today they were tag-teaming, and after the disappointment of the diary, he was crossing everything that their plan would pay off with at least one lead.

After Peggy, Liam had another six appointments to get through before teatime. Bev Stringer had booked a double session, insisting she liked it 'rough' and begging him to give her lower back a merciless pummelling while she made some very disturbing groaning noises. Raven Walton-Lord just seemed to delight in winding him up. Then after a foot massage for Gracie Lister – who apologised in advance for her athlete's foot – it was Tess's turn.

When they could see Liam was finished with Gracie, Raven gave Tess a little push towards him. 'Go on,' she whispered. Tess reluctantly approached the massage bed, feeling awkward.

Liam smiled at her. 'You booked a session?'

They had the space to themselves – the poor professionals Candice had booked, both female, had barely got a look in since Liam had turned up and wandered off to take a tea break. If they spoke in low voices, they could converse in virtual privacy.

'Raven did, to give us the chance to compare notes.' Tess sat down on the bed. 'I'm not taking my robe off. Just do my neck or something, for the look of the thing.'

'Are you sure? Might seem a bit suspicious. Everyone else has gone for the full upper body job.'

'Neck and that's your lot,' Tess repeated firmly.

He shrugged. 'Your loss. I'm getting quite good. Bev Stringer told me I've got orgasmic fingers.'

'I bet she did.' Tess loosened her robe the smallest amount so she could drop it a little lower. Liam rubbed some sweet-smelling oil on to his hands and started massaging her neck.

Tess felt her eyes starting to close as Liam caressed the skin with firm fingers and hastily forced them open again. She felt very exposed, practically naked under her robe with Liam touching her in that intimate way. It brought back old times – old times she'd tried very hard to forget. Despite what she'd told Raven, he actually was rather good.

'There's a trick to it,' Liam told her, as if reading her mind. 'I just pretend you're a lump of dough. You'll rise lovely once you're in the oven, Tessie.'

'All right, never mind the small talk,' Tess muttered, trying to focus on something other than his hands on her skin. 'Find anything out?'

'Nothing important, I don't think. No one seems that interested in making chitchat while they're being massaged. I suppose they just want to relax and enjoy the experience.' He grimaced. 'All I've learnt is that Gracie can't find anything that works on her athlete's foot – oh, and Bev had a row with her husband this morning. I'd be very surprised if either has anything to do with Clemmie's murder.'

'So it's all down to the tea break then.'

'Yep. Ready to play your part?'

Tess nodded. 'You can count on me.'

Finally, Gracie Lister called for them to break for afternoon tea. Liam breathed a sigh of relief and went to join the women in the next room where a buffet had been laid out, leaving his last customer, Candice Walton-Lord, to re-robe.

He helped himself to a buttered scone and a couple of tiny sandwiches – triangular, of course, because despite the topless massages and occasional murder, these weren't barbarians. They were the Women's Guild.

'So, Sam, how are you finding your new career as a masseur?' Peggy Bristow asked.

'It, er . . . has its moments.'

She glanced at Tess with a knowing smile. 'Yes, I imagine it does.'

'It's an interesting accent you've got, Ms Bristow,' Liam said. 'Where are you from originally?'

'Here, there and everywhere,' she said with a shrug, and he noticed the foreign tones consciously deepened now he'd drawn attention to them. 'I was moved around a lot as a child.'

'Oh?'

'Yes, my family had the travelling bug. I don't think we stayed anywhere more than a year or two at a time.'

Liam glanced at Tess, who was helping herself to a plate of food beside Peggy. She didn't catch his eye, but she gave an almost imperceptible nod.

'I was so sorry to hear about your friend Clemency,' he said. 'Have you heard any more about the heir?'

Peggy frowned. 'Heir?'

Nearby, Marianne Priestley froze with a sandwich halfway to her plate.

'Yes, this mystery woman Clemency named in her will. I've heard whispers she's got two hundred grand heading her way, once they track her down.'

Peggy looked puzzled. 'Who told you that?'

'I'm not sure. Overheard it in the Star, I think,' Liam said vaguely.

'You must've got the wrong end of the stick, lad. Clemency Ackroyd didn't have any money.'

Liam frowned. 'Really? I'm sure it was her I heard mentioned.'

Tess turned to them and nodded. 'He's right, Peg. I heard the same bit of gossip. Someone was saying Aunty Clemmie had a secret savings account full of cash and she'd settled the lot on this woman no one's ever heard of.'

'But where would she get money like that?'

'Search me. Not out of her pension, that's for sure.'

'Did this person have a name?' Marianne asked quietly.

'I didn't hear one, no,' Tess said. 'I wonder who she is. I didn't think Aunty Clemmie had any family apart from her sister.'

Bev was next to Marianne, listening intently to every word they were saying. She put her plate of food down and hurried away.

'Well, that'll be all over the room in a minute,' Peggy said to Liam. 'That woman can never keep anything to herself. Except other people's men, that is.'

'God, I'm sorry,' Liam said, his face a picture of innocence. 'I had no idea it was a secret. I just assumed if it was being talked about in the pub then everyone knew.'

'Well, you weren't to realise.' She glanced at Prue Ackroyd. 'She must have known, anyway. Dark horse, keeping it to herself this last fortnight I've had her at mine. I think I'll go have words.'

'Good work,' Liam mouthed to Tess as Peggy went to talk to Prue.

Tess glanced at Marianne, whose face was deathly white.

'Are you OK, Mari?' she asked.

'Hmm?' Marianne stared at her for a second, then forced a smile. 'Oh. Yes, I'm fine, thanks, Tess. I think I'll go see if either of the hot tubs is free.'

Tess noticed Raven browsing the book swap table, trying surreptitiously to catch her eye, and went to join her.

'How'd it go?' Raven muttered.

'And the Oscar for Best Actress goes to Teresa J. Feather,' Tess whispered back. 'Now we just stand back and wait for the fireworks.' She scanned the table, which seemed to bear a lot of Diana Skye titles. 'Trying to get some converts for your dirty books?'

'Yep. Actually, Miss Ackroyd already helped herself to a couple. For her friend's niece, she said.'

Tess smirked. 'Heh. I bet she did.'

Gracie wandered over and picked one up, her lip curling.

'Utter rubbish,' she said. 'I don't know how you girls read this drivel.'

'Oi. That's *Her Soldier Saviour*. That's my favourite one, that is.' Raven snatched it up as soon as Gracie put it down, cuddling it to her as if worried its feelings might be hurt. 'Anyway, that's a bit rich coming from you.'

Gracie frowned. 'What do you mean by that?'

'Well . . .' Raven faltered. 'You read romances, don't you?'

'Yeah, what about all those?' Tess said, indicating the little stack of Jackie Collins books Gracie had contributed.

'Jackie doesn't peddle the nonsense this Skye woman does.' Gracie cast another withering look at *Her Soldier Saviour*. 'They're always the same, aren't they? Some weak-willed girl waiting for a strong, handsome man in uniform to turn up so she can be swept away by *love*.' Tess could hear the sneer in her voice as she pronounced the last word. 'Rather pathetic.'

'It's not like that. They're beautifully written, and the heroines are always relatable.' Raven glanced at the book's back cover. 'See, in this one there's this orphan, Kathleen. Her parents die and she's left all alone in a foreign country. Then this gorgeous lieutenant saves her from being raped one night and teaches her the real meaning of love.' Her eyes had taken on a misty quality.

'Lies for the chronically naive,' Gracie muttered. 'Real life doesn't work that way, I'm sorry to say. You'd do well to put such sentimental nonsense out of your head, Raven.'

The girls watched her as she marched off.

'What's up with her?' Tess said. 'I've never heard her talk like that before.'

'Me neither. Something's obviously made her bitter.'

Raven put her book back down on the table. 'Do you know anything about her husband?'

No one in Cherrywood had ever met Stephen Lister, who'd died before Gracie moved to the village.

'Not really. Only that he was a bit older than her.'

'I wonder what sort of marriage they had,' Raven said. 'Maybe he did the dirty on her with his secretary or something.'

'And yet she writes romance herself,' Tess said in an undertone. 'More secrets. Cherrywood seems to be chocka with them.'

There was a loud crash. Tess spun around to see what had happened.

Miss Ackroyd was with Peggy Bristow, leaning against the wall for support. The shattered remains of her teacup lay disregarded at her feet.

'I think another one just got out,' Raven whispered.

Chapter 22

'Bev, I'm going to get off,' Tess called through to the bar storeroom when she finished her shift one Tuesday over a week later. It hadn't been her afternoon to work, but Tammy had phoned in sick, so she'd been drafted in to cover.

There was no reply. Tess poked her head through the doorway and saw that the back door leading into Bev's little kitchen garden, where she grew her magnificent marrows, was open. The pub landlady was outside, locking up the shed. She jerked round when Tess approached her, seemingly startled.

'Oh. Sorry,' she said. 'Thought you were the hubby.'

'I've finished my shift,' Tess said. 'You'd better come and mind the bar.'

'Isn't Ian there?'

'No, he went out.'

Bev scowled. 'Again? Why is that man never around when there's work to be done?'

'Don't you know where he's gone?'

'God knows. Drinking with a mate somewhere, probably, while I'm here picking up the slack as usual.' She sighed. 'All right, Tessie, you get home. I'll take over.'

'Thanks, Bev.'

Tess walked out of the Star and Garter, leaned back against the wall and exhaled through her teeth.

Work was tough lately. She didn't know what was going on with Bev and Ian but they were clearly having issues, and it wasn't the pleasantest environment when the landlord and landlady weren't getting along. Gone were the over-the-top public displays of affection. Bev had a perpetually thunderous expression on her face these days, and Ian seemed to spend most of his time trying to avoid her.

Still, it wasn't a bad job, Tess reflected as she walked home. The pay was pretty poor but working behind the bar had definitely helped her get back into the swing of village life again. When Tess had first come home to Cherrywood – hurt at the way things had ended with Liam and ashamed that she'd failed in the career she and all her friends at home had had such high hopes for – she'd felt she would never be able to settle back into the slower pace of rural life. She hadn't wanted to. All she'd wanted had been her old life back, down in London.

But after a year of pulling pints, sympathising with all the little worries and triumphs of people she'd known most of her life, Tess had found with surprise that she was actually rather glad to be back. Her life in London had been exciting, yes, but she'd never felt part of a community there. After growing up surrounded by the wide-open spaces of the moors, she'd often felt hemmed in by the buildings and crowds of the city. The best thing about her life down south, other than a job with excellent pay and prospects, had been Liam – but of course, he'd turned out to be a lie.

And now he was here, just when she'd finally managed to put him out of her mind and move on. Tess had had to be quite stern with herself lately. Too often she'd caught herself checking her phone to see if he'd texted, or peering into gardens wondering if he might be there doing some work for one of the villagers. When he occasionally came into the pub, her stomach flipped – reflex, she told herself; an old habit that would disappear as she grew accustomed to him being around.

Anyway, the investigation would be done soon and he could go back home. Life in Cherrywood could go back to how it had been before Aunty Clemmie's murder – cosy, genteel and predictable. The sooner Liam Hanley sodded off back where he came from the better, as far as Tess was concerned.

Automatically she reached into her pocket for her phone. Her fingers clasped around it, until she realised what she was doing and dropped it again.

It was the investigation. That was what kept her glued to her mobile. What Miss Ackroyd had said that night at the theatre was right – Tess needed exercise for her brain and she hadn't been getting it pulling pints. But now – making connections, exploring theories, plotting and scheming with Liam – her brain was getting all the stimulation it needed and then some.

And OK, so Liam was pleasant company. So he was nice to look at, and he made her smile in spite of herself. She knew all that; she always had. She also knew he'd lied to her, hurt her more than she'd known it was possible to hurt – beyond repair, it had felt like at the time. *Fool me once, Liam Hanley, shame on you. Fool me twice* . . . well, Tess was nobody's fool; not any more.

It had been just over a week since the spa afternoon and Clemmie's secret fortune had become common knowledge around the village, although the name of her mysterious heir was still unknown to any but Liam, Tess and their co-conspirators. Miss Ackroyd's reaction had been enough to confirm what Tess had already suspected: that the existence of the money and its heir were news to her. That meant she was now an unlikely suspect in her sister's murder.

Marianne's reaction had been significant too – the way she'd paled, then sagged with relief when Tess had said the heir hadn't been named. Marianne knew Nadia Harris was Clemmie's heir, Tess was sure. What was she hiding, and why?

Tess was hoping to find out more the following evening, when Oliver – finally convinced after his chat with the Almighty that it was the right thing to do – was allowing her to assist him with the Ling Cottage exorcism.

She'd been to talk to Andrew Walton-Lord too, hopeful he could tell her about Charity. But the old man's lucid moments were fewer and further between these days, and the name was greeted only by a blank stare.

When she got home, Tess jumped in the car and headed for the nearest supermarket. It was on the other side of Plumholme in a built-by-numbers retail complex: shops, cinema, bowling alley, that sort of thing.

Tess hated grocery shopping, although it was generally left to her. Raven probably wouldn't have recognised their local supermarket if it had accosted her in a dark alley and bitten her on the bum – admittedly a pretty unlikely occurrence, although you never knew these days.

Tess whizzed round the aisles as quickly as she could, chucking essentials into her trolley – bread, baked beans and gin being the key items when you shared a flat with Raven. When she came out, she was surprised to spot Miss Ackroyd exiting the gaudy amusement arcade opposite. It was a warm day, yet the old lady was wearing a long coat with the collar turned up and a brimmed hat that cast a shadow over her face. Tess recognised the hunched figure and shuffling walk straight away, however.

'Miss!' she called, waving, but Miss Ackroyd didn't seem to hear. She hastily unlocked her Mini and drove off.

Tess headed back to her own car, chucked the shopping in the boot and started the engine.

She sat for a moment, staring at the dashboard lights, then turned the engine off again.

'Damn it,' she muttered. 'And I got frozen stuff too.'

But she had to know. What had Prue Ackroyd been doing in an amusement arcade? Was that it, the secret to her money problems – had she flushed her pension away on the fruities? Tess couldn't picture it somehow.

She got out of the car again, took out the red and white polka-dot umbrella she kept in the boot and headed for the arcade.

Inside, she was greeted by an ocean of flashing LEDs, the

machines beeping out their invitations to throw your money away. Fruit machines, coin cascades and one-armed bandits lined every wall, where gangs of dead-eyed teenagers mechanically fed coins into the slots. Tess approached the manned kiosk where money could be changed.

'Hi,' a young woman said from behind a false-looking smile. 'How much would you like today?'

'Nothing, thank you. I just came in with some lost property.' Tess held up the umbrella. 'I saw one of your customers leave this on the wall outside, but she'd driven off before I could give it back. If she was a regular, I thought you might be able to return it.'

'Yes, of course. Did you see who left it?'

'It was an older lady, in her sixties or seventies, I'd guess. About five foot five, short grey hair, glasses. Long blue coat with a matching brimmed hat, driving a green Mini. Does she sound like someone you know?'

'Oh, that'll be Prudence Ackroyd; she always comes on Tuesdays,' the woman said. 'That's when we have casino night in the upstairs function room.'

'Casino night?'

'Yes, Miss Ackroyd never misses it.' The girl leaned forward, clearly keen to break up her boring work day with a bit of a gossip. 'You'd never think it to look at her, but she's something of a high roller. Came into some money when her sister died recently – did you hear about it, out in Cherrywood? Shocking really: she was brutally murdered during a burglary.' The girl's tone suggested sympathy, but her eyes sparkled with voyeuristic glee.

235

'Yes, I remember reading about it,' Tess said, not quite managing to suppress a degree of coldness in her tone. The girl didn't seem to notice, however.

'Well, we didn't see Miss Ackroyd for a week or some after. But then she was back in her old chair, same as always. She almost never misses.' The girl laughed. 'I even wondered if we might see her the day after she found the body.'

'Is she lucky?'

'Not as lucky as she'd like to be. Still, we all need our guilty pleasures, right?'

'I suppose we do,' Tess said, turning to go. 'Er, thank you.'

'What about the umbrella?' the girl called after her.

'Oh. Yes.' Tess came back and placed it on the counter. 'Thank you.'

As soon as she was driving back to Cherrywood, she called Liam on the hands-free.

'Can you talk?' she said.

'Yeah, what is it?' Liam asked.

'Prue Ackroyd. She's a casino junkie.'

'Seriously?' She could practically hear his raised eyebrow.

'I just did a bit of Scoobying at that amusement arcade next to Plumholme Morrison's. Sounds like she's their best customer – last of the big spenders.'

'You positive it was her?'

'I saw her coming out. The girl in the kiosk said Miss Ackroyd hardly ever misses a game.'

'So not blackmail,' Liam said. 'Just theft to feed a habit.'

'Looks like.'

Liam sighed. 'And we've learnt exactly nothing that helps with the murder investigation. Again.'

'We've learnt she needed cash,' Tess said. 'Addicts aren't rational, are they? They can do drastic things to get their fix. Maybe we were too quick to scrub her off the suspect list.'

'Terry Braithwaite said she wasn't at home when he discovered the body. That suggests she's unlikely to have done it, unless she came home, killed Clemency and then went out again.'

'Not necessarily. If she knew he was coming with the eggs, she might have hidden deliberately to give herself an alibi.'

'You and Oliver are seeing Prudence tomorrow, aren't you?' Liam asked.

'Yeah. I'll let you know what we find out.'

'Right.' He paused. 'You free tonight, Tessie?'

'Hmm?'

Tess's gaze had fixed on a car that she knew she'd seen before: a red Toyota. She watched as it turned down Plumholme high street.

'Are you free? I thought you might like to come over for a drink. Strictly business. We can go over what we know so far, see if there's something we're missing.'

'I've got freezer stuff,' she mumbled absently. Following a feeling in her gut, she made a snap decision and swung her car round to follow the Toyota.

'Well, go home first and put it away. But for God's sake, don't bring Raven with you.'

'Not tonight, Lee. Sorry, I have to go. I've got a hump.'

237

'A hump? What, like Quasimodo?'

'Not that kind of hump, the other kind.' She frowned. 'No, not hump. One of those sixth-sense things you coppers set so much store by. A hunch, that's it.'

'OK,' Liam said slowly. 'Fancy sharing this hunch with me?'

'Well, it might be nothing. Talk later, OK?'

She hung up and pulled into Plumholme Village Hall's car park. The other car was there too, although its resident had disappeared.

This was what happened when you hung out with detectives. You started getting humps or hunches or whatever they were called. And when you started getting hunches, you ended up losing your best umbrella and with a boot full of soggy fish fingers.

Why had the sight of the car set her stomach hopping? It didn't belong to any of the Women's Guild ladies.

After pondering a second, Tess finally put her finger on why her Spidey sense was tingling.

It was Tammy's car. Tammy, whose shift she'd just covered at the pub because the other girl had phoned in sick. Yet here Tammy was, palpably not cocooned in her duvet nursing a Lemsip.

Tammy wasn't on Liam's persons of interest list. She wasn't in the Women's Guild and she had no connection with either the Walton-Lords or the Ackroyds. But ever since Oliver had told her Tammy wore a St Christopher, Tess had been ever so slightly on her guard.

OK, lots of people had them, but it seemed a bit of a coincidence that Tammy should suddenly start wearing one right after Aunty Clemmie's was reported missing. Tess sincerely hoped, for Oliver's sake, that Tammy wasn't involved in this whole messy business. But her recent foray into sleuthing had made her very aware that no one, no matter how pure they seemed, was without their dirty secret.

The village hall was closed when she tried the door. Tess glanced around, wondering where Tammy might have gone.

There was the pub, the Green Man, its beer garden humming with people – could Tammy have gone for a drink? Maybe she was playing hooky to go out with Oliver.

The only other building active at this time of night was St Michael and All Angels Church, the bells ringing out to welcome people to evensong. After another glance at the pub, Tess headed in the direction of the churchyard.

She wandered among the gravestones, watching people enter the church. Should she check and see if Tammy was inside? The pub seemed the likelier option, but something had drawn her here.

'Can I help you there?'

Tess swivelled to face the friendly vicar who'd appeared at her shoulder.

'Oh. Sorry, I didn't realise there'd be a service on.'

'Will you be joining us?' the woman asked.

'Um, no. I actually just came to . . .' Tess cast about for an excuse as to why she was wandering among the graves. '. . . to, er, research my family tree. I think I might have ancestors buried in here. It'd be nice to pay my respects and find out a bit more about them.'

'Ah yes, of course. We get a lot of family history research-ers,' the vicar said in her pleasant Scottish lilt. 'Some of our graves date back to the sixteen hundreds, you know.' She put a hand in Tess's and gave it a vigorous shake. 'Alison.'

'Tess. Tess Feather.'

'I think we do have some Feathers. Try the top corner, by the yew.' Alison smiled. 'You never know, perhaps you'll dis-cover you're related to royalty. My father claims he can take us all the way back to James the First.'

'Knowing my luck, I'll turn out to be a direct descendant of some famous murderer,' Tess said with a smile. She did a double-take when she spotted Tammy, heading for the church door. 'Alison, do you know that girl? She looks a lot like someone I work with at the Star and Garter in Cherrywood.'

'That's right.' Alison laughed. 'I shouldn't have favourite members of my congregation, should I? But I think in that case I'm allowed to be a little biased.'

'She's a regular then?'

'Certainly,' Alison said with a proud smile. 'Although Tammy's something of a captive audience. She's my daughter.'

Tess's gaze flickered over the surplice and dog collar. 'You're not serious. You're Tammy's mum?'

'Why so surprised? Most people have one, you know.'

'No. Sorry. She just never said you were a vicar.' Realising how this must sound, Tess back-pedalled hastily. 'I mean, not that I have a problem with that. Some of my best friends are vicars.'

Alison laughed. 'That's what they all say.'

'But in this case it's true. Oliver Maynard. I've known him since nursery.'

'Have you now? Well, he's a good lad. I know him well, of course.' Alison glanced at the church door as the last few made their way in. 'I have to go take the service. If I didn't, I'd press you for some details on this mysterious new boyfriend Tammy's refusing to tell me anything about, but time's getting away from me, I'm afraid.'

'It was lovely to meet you.'

'And you. I'm glad Tammy's making friends in her new job.' Alison nodded to something behind Tess and lowered her voice. 'Here's another regular visitor to our little churchyard. Every year in May, like clockwork. Cemeteries are fascinating places if you're a student of the human condition.'

Tess turned to look. A hunched figure was laying flowers on one of the graves.

'Someone she lost?' Tess asked.

'I don't believe so. She leaves flowers on a different grave every year – always infants,' Alison said. 'I often wonder why – if there was a child she lost in pregnancy, perhaps, who has no marker where she can mourn.'

The figure remained, head bowed, for a moment after depositing the flowers. Then as it stood upright, the light from the open church doorway illuminated its face. Tess's hand flew to her mouth as she stifled a gasp.

It was Candice.

Chapter 23

'You can go if you want, Tess,' Tammy said the next night in the pub. 'Your shift ended five minutes ago.'

'That's OK,' Tess said. 'I'm just waiting for Oliver.'

Tammy's cheeks pinkened. 'Oliver's coming?'

Tess smiled. 'Yeah. How's it going with you two?'

'Pretty well. At least, I think so. What did he say about it?'

'Now what kind of mate would I be if I told you that?' Tess said, laughing. 'All good things, though, I promise. How many dates have you been on now?'

'It'll be our fourth tomorrow.'

'Fourth?'

Tammy nodded. 'You know, it's been a while since I made it past a first one. I don't want to jinx it, but I really think this could be going somewhere.'

'How was the last date? Anything exciting happen?' It was the third date that Oliver had earmarked for coming clean to Tammy about his job.

Tammy laughed. 'Yeah, I know, third date, right? You're trying to find out if we jumped into bed with each other, aren't you?'

'Actually, no.' Tess paused. 'Did you?'

'We didn't, actually.' Tammy flushed, fiddling with the St Christopher round her neck. 'He's very sweet about that stuff. I can't remember the last lad I went out with who didn't start pressuring pretty much straight away, but Oliver seems happy to take things slow. We only kissed properly for the first time last week.'

'Told you he was worth a shot, didn't I?' Tess glanced at the necklace she was playing with. 'That's nice. Is it new?'

'This?' Tammy said, glancing down at it. 'New to me. I bought it at the spring show.'

Tess blinked. 'The show?'

'Yes, from the jewellery stall. I had to replace the damaged chain, but it was only a few quid so I can't complain. Anyway, I thought the medallion was sort of appropriate. Something to protect me on my travels, if I ever get to go on them.'

'Is that the plan?'

'When I get enough in the piggy bank.'

'Are you a Christian then, Tam?'

'Suppose,' Tammy said vaguely. 'I've not thought much about it.'

Tess decided it was time someone bit the bullet. 'And how does your mum feel about that?'

Tammy frowned. 'My mum?'

'Alison, right? The vicar at St Mike's?'

Tammy glanced around to check no one had heard and lowered her voice. 'All right, Tess, who grassed me up?'

'She did. Your mum. I spotted you going to evensong last night when I was . . . doing family history research in the graveyard.'

'You didn't tell Oliver, did you?'

Tess frowned. 'Well, no. Why the big secret though? You're not ashamed of your mum, are you?'

'Of course not! My mum's amazing. It's just . . . early days,' Tammy said. 'I don't want to scare him off with religion. People think vicars' daughters are weird.'

Tess shook her head. 'Oh my God.'

'What?'

'Right. This is for his own good.' She took a deep breath. 'Tam, I need to tell you something about Oliver.'

'What is it?'

They were interrupted by the arrival of the man himself, zipped up to the chin in a highly unseasonal fleece and with a rucksack over one shoulder. He beamed at Tammy.

'Hello, beautiful.'

'Evening, sexy,' Tess said.

'Not you. You're just lucky I stopped calling you Snotface.' Oliver leaned over the bar to give Tammy a kiss. 'Looking forward to tomorrow?'

'Too right,' she said. 'I can't believe you got us Monster Trucks tickets. Those things are like gold dust.'

Oliver shrugged. 'Some of us just have friends in high places.'

'He's not kidding,' Tess said. 'Tam, Oliver here's got something he needs to tell you.'

Oliver glared at her. 'No I don't. Shut up, Tess.'

'Ol, just tell her. Come on.'

'Tell me what?' Tammy asked.

'I don't know what she's talking about,' Oliver said,

although the panicked bunny look was a dead giveaway that he had something to hide.

Tess nodded to his fleece. 'Unzip that.'

'Eh? No.'

'Go on, Ol, get it off.'

Tammy shook her head. 'This is getting weird.'

'Right. If you won't do it, I'm going to.' Tess gestured to Tammy. 'Oliver, meet Tammy McDermot, daughter of the Reverend Alison McDermot of St Michael and All Angels, Plumholme. Tammy, meet the Reverend Oliver Maynard of St Stephen's, Cherrywood.'

Silence reigned while the young lovers stared at each other.

'Your mum's a vicar?' Oliver said at last. 'Alison's your mum?'

'Yeah. You're a vicar?'

'Yeah.' Oliver unzipped his fleece to reveal his dog collar.

'Why didn't you tell me?'

'Why didn't you?'

Tammy flushed. 'I thought it might scare you off.'

'Likewise.'

'I was going to tell you. When I was sure you liked me enough not to mind.'

'Also likewise.'

Tammy blinked at him. 'Then all these weeks we've been . . .'

'Apparently so.'

They stared at each other. Then they burst out laughing.

'So I suppose we should talk about this,' he said when the

laughter had died down, leaning over the bar to kiss her again.

'I suppose we should. Are you free later?'

'Not for an hour or so.' He grimaced. 'I have to go perform an exorcism.'

*

'Tessie, I don't know whether to strangle you or kiss you,' Oliver said as they walked up to Ling Cottage. An overwhelming feeling of relief had filled him, like a great weight had been lifted. 'How did you know Alison was her mum?'

'Spotted her going to evensong last night. Alison told me when we fell into conversation.'

'I've nearly worried myself into an early grave wondering how to break it to her.' Ling Cottage loomed in the distance, an intimidating black speck against the setting sun. 'What exactly are we hoping to find out tonight?'

'Whatever there is to find out.' Tess glanced at him. 'And you'd be doing me a big favour if you could work the name Charity into the ritual somehow.'

'Charity? Why?'

'Because Miss Ackroyd knows who she is, I'd bet my life. Charity's the missing link – the connection that could shed light on everything.'

'I'm not masquerading as a medium, Tess,' Oliver said sternly. 'If I'm skipping the deliverance team, I want to do this properly.'

'OK,' she said, sounding disappointed. 'You know, your

246

professional ethics are a real drag when it comes to solving murders.'

'Well excuse me.'

'We love you for it though, darling,' a voice said.

They turned to look at a dark-haired figure leaning against the drystone wall that flanked Black Moor Farm.

'Raven! What're you doing here?'

'Just getting my daily exorcise,' Raven said. 'You see what I did there?'

'You're not coming too?' Oliver asked.

'Don't want to miss all the fun, do I? I quite fancy a bit of ghostbusting.'

He shook his head. 'I don't know if this is shaping up to be an exorcism or a party.'

'It can be both.' Raven joined them and linked his arm. 'Try to see us as moral support.'

'How I'm going to explain turning up to perform a deliverance with a couple of unbelievers like you two, I don't know.' He sighed. 'Well, let's get it over with.'

'Rave, I don't suppose you remember selling Tammy a St Christopher at the spring show?' Tess asked as they continued their walk.

Raven frowned. 'I remember her buying something. Couldn't tell you what it was.'

'She said she bought it off you – a gold medallion with a broken chain. I just wondered if you remembered where it had come from.'

'From Grandmother, I should think. She donated most of what was on the stall, apart from the handmade stuff from the Guides. Gave me an old jewellery box and told me to help myself.'

'And that's where you found the St Christopher?'

'God, Tess, I can't remember. I just tipped the lot out on the table for people to rummage. Why?'

'Aunty Clemmie had one that's disappeared,' Oliver said. 'Miss Ackroyd thinks the ghost transformed it into a Madonna and child.'

'Right,' Raven said, sounding puzzled. 'For its own amusement?'

'Who knows? It's a funny bugger, this spirit.'

'Well, I can't imagine it's the same one. There're plenty of them about, aren't there?'

'I guess so,' Tess said. 'Did anyone else donate apart from your nan?'

'Peggy brought a few bits along. That was it, I think.'

When they reached Ling Cottage, Oliver swung off his rucksack.

'I'd better suit up.'

He took out the little bundle of clothing he'd brought, removed his fleece, then threw on his cassock, surplice and tippet.

'Does it need to be the full gear for an exorcism?' Tess asked.

'No, but this is Miss Ackroyd,' Oliver said. 'She'll expect to get her money's worth.'

'Really, darling, you could've given the old vicar dress an iron,' Raven said, brushing a few specks off his attire. 'What will the ghost think of you?'

'Please can you call it a surplice? I'm not sure my dignity can stand "vicar dress".'

When he'd finished, Oliver smoothed back his hair and knocked on the door. A haggard-looking Miss Ackroyd answered.

'Oliver. Thank God.' Oliver thought for a second she was going to hug him, she looked so pleased to see him. 'Come in, please, all of you.'

The presence of Raven and Tess didn't seem to faze her – if anything, she looked grateful for a crowd. Perhaps she felt that when it came to banishing phantoms, there was strength in numbers.

She showed them into the front room. A coffee table had been dragged into the centre, the Madonna and child necklace that had been found on Clemmie's body laid in the middle. A couple of candles flickered beside it.

'I hope you don't mind me bringing Tess and Raven for prayer support, Miss Ackroyd,' Oliver said. 'It helps cleanse the, er . . . the auras, you know.'

'Not at all,' Miss Ackroyd said. 'I'll get a pot on before we start.'

'Tea and exorcism, how very C of E,' Raven muttered when Miss Ackroyd had disappeared into the kitchen.

Tess raised an eyebrow at Oliver. 'Cleanse the auras?'

'Look, it's my first time, all right?'

'I thought you had to shake holy water everywhere and yell, "The power of Christ compels you!" '

'Well? Have you got any holy water?' Raven asked Oliver.

'No, I haven't got any holy water,' Oliver said. 'Where on earth would I get holy water?'

'You make it, I guess,' Tess said. 'Just wave your arms over it and say a blessing, same as the communion wine.'

'In that case, yeah, I've got an unlimited supply. It's right there in the tap.'

'Great,' Raven said, rolling her eyes. 'Holy water with extra fluoride, for healthier teeth and bones.'

'What do you want, sacred Evian?'

The three of them fixed on forced smiles as Miss Ackroyd came back in with their tea.

'Right,' Oliver said when they were all furnished with drinks. 'So first I'm supposed to investigate for non-supernatural explanations.'

Miss Ackroyd frowned. 'I told you, Oliver, the only explanation is supernatural. You assured me you believed me.'

'I do, of course, but the Church requires that I investigate. I have to follow correct procedure, Miss Ackroyd.'

Her expression lifted slightly. 'Well, I suppose if that's the way things are done. Go ahead, young man.'

'OK, can you tell me about this ghostly activity? Other than your sister's murder, I mean. You mentioned things being moved.'

'Yes. My glasses, for one thing. I left them on my bedside table a few weeks ago before I went to sleep. When I woke up, they were on the dressing table.'

'You couldn't just have forgotten that's where you put them?'

She glared at him. 'No, I could not. I'm not senile just yet, Oliver Maynard.'

Oliver cleared his throat. 'OK. So there's that. Um, anything else?'

Miss Ackroyd glanced fearfully out of the window to the garden. She did look genuinely terrified. Oliver found it hard to believe that there was any ghostly presence in Ling Cottage, but he hoped his prayer for deliverance would help settle the old lady's mind.

'Miss Ackroyd?' he said gently, drawing her attention back to the three of them.

'Oh. Yes. The key.'

'Key?'

'The little key for the sideboard,' she said. 'When I left to stay at Peggy's, it was in the cutlery drawer in the kitchen. When I came home this evening, lo and behold, there it was in the lock. And there are . . . things missing. Private things. Things that couldn't possibly be of interest to . . . to anyone living.'

Oliver glanced at Tess, who had a faintly guilty look on her face. Did she know something about this?

'Anything further?' Oliver asked Miss Ackroyd.

Miss Ackroyd lowered her voice. 'Yes. The garden. Follow me and I'll show you.'

'All right, Tess, why've you got that look on your face?' Oliver asked in a whisper as they followed Miss Ackroyd out to the back garden.

Tess grimaced. 'Look, I might've . . . accidentally, I mean, I might've been behind some of that.'

'Eh?'

'The key for the sideboard. I left it in the lock by mistake, and Liam borrowed an old diary of Miss Ackroyd's we thought she wouldn't miss to help with the investigation. I was here with him last week, Nancy-Drewing.'

'Out here by the tree,' Miss Ackroyd said when they reached the back door.

She flicked on the porch light and they followed her to the monkey puzzle tree.

'There,' she said, pointing to the ground. Oliver couldn't help noticing that she stood a little back, as if afraid to get too close to the spot.

He looked where she was pointing. 'What am I looking for, Miss Ackroyd?'

'The ground, don't you see? The soil's been disturbed.' Miss Ackroyd visibly shuddered. 'Like . . . like something's clawed it away.'

'A mole or a fox, I expect.'

'No,' she said sharply. 'No. I know exactly what did this.'

'What did it?' Raven asked.

Miss Ackroyd shivered again. 'Something that wants me dead. Just like it wanted Clemmie dead.'

'Why should it want you dead?'

'Sin will out,' Miss Ackroyd muttered. She looked up, resuming the stern mask of their old schoolteacher as quickly as it had slipped away to reveal the frightened, vulnerable person beneath. 'We'd best go in. Your teas will be getting cold.'

'Um, Ol?' Tess muttered as they followed her back inside.

'Yeah?'

'That one was me too.'

'What? You dug up the garden?'

'Not me personally. Susie, Candice's dog. Liam had brought her out for her walk.'

'Tessie, are you trying to tell me you're the Ling Cottage ghost?'

'I think I am, yeah.'

'Great,' Oliver muttered. 'There's nothing like exorcising old friends of an evening.'

Tess shrugged. 'Well, maybe I'll enjoy the demon dimensions. I bet there's a free bar.'

Back in the front room, Miss Ackroyd turned to them.

'I assume we all need to sit down and hold hands. I'll turn off the big light.'

'No need for anything like that,' Oliver said. 'It's not a seance.'

'What's the difference?'

'Well, do you want to get rid of the ghost or have a chat with it?'

'Oh,' she said. 'Yes. Still, we ought to sit down, at least. We don't all have young legs.'

When they were seated, Oliver nodded to the Madonna and child medallion on the table. 'Why is that there, Miss Ackroyd?'

'It's a focal object. Something connected to the ghost,' Miss Ackroyd said. 'That's right, isn't it?'

'Did Peggy tell you that you needed a focal object?'

'Well, yes.'

'I thought as much,' he muttered.

'So is it wrong?' Miss Ackroyd asked, looking worried.

Oliver summoned a smile. 'No. But it's not strictly necessary for the deliverance.'

'What is the significance of the necklace, Miss Ackroyd?' Tess asked. 'I know it was your sister's, but I don't see how it's connected to the ghost.'

'That's just it,' Miss Ackroyd said in a low voice. 'It wasn't Clemmie's – she had no such necklace. The ghost put it on her.'

'How can you be sure it wasn't hers?'

'I have reasons,' Miss Ackroyd muttered darkly. 'My sister would never wear a necklace like that.'

'Why that icon?' Oliver asked. 'I'd expect a Madonna to be worn by a Catholic.'

'Charity,' she whispered. 'It's . . . it's hers.'

'Is Charity the ghost?' Raven asked.

Miss Ackroyd looked at her sharply. 'Who told you that, child?'

'I just thought . . . the way you talked about her.'

'Can we get on with this? I would like my house back some time tonight.'

Oliver glanced at Tess. 'Miss Ackroyd, I want to help you, but this is all very odd. Isn't there anything else you can tell us that might help focus our prayers while we ask for deliverance?'

'Can't the three of you feel it?' Miss Ackroyd was becoming distressed now, shaking all over. 'The threat – the danger? Don't you sense there's something here that wants to hurt you?'

Oliver looked worried. 'Not to the extent you do, I think. There isn't any more to this, is there?'

'How do you mean?'

'There have been rumours . . . your sister, money she left to a woman no one seems to know anything about. Is there a connection?'

Miss Ackroyd's absent gaze had fixed on the window, looking out into the garden as if she could see something there. Her lips moved silently.

'Miss Ackroyd?'

'Hm?' she said.

'This isn't about your sister's legacy? There was a beneficiary . . .'

'Nadia,' Tess said. 'Nadia Harris.'

'Nadia Harris,' Miss Ackroyd repeated, her eyes still fixed on the garden. 'That's right. Clemmie left her everything.'

'Who is she?'

'I don't know. Some child my sister had made a favourite of, no doubt.'

'Do you know where Clemmie got the money?'

'From him, I suppose. It seems she was more sly than I gave her credit for.'

'Him?'

'Mmm.' Miss Ackroyd shook herself out of her reverie. 'What do we need to do, Oliver?'

'Well, I say a blessing for the house, asking for it to be delivered from anything harmful,' Oliver told her. 'If you could all bow your heads and support me in prayer, that would be helpful. And then that's it, you're all sorted.'

'That's all there is to it? I thought you needed crucifixes and incense and . . .'

'Holy water?' Tess supplied.

'Yes, that sort of thing.'

Oliver shrugged. 'It doesn't need to be flashy. Just a simple request to God to cleanse the house of anything that might want to hurt you.'

'And then she'll – *it* will be gone?' Miss Ackroyd asked.

'That's right.'

'Where will it go?'

'To wherever it belongs.'

Miss Ackroyd breathed deeply for a moment.

'All right. Go ahead, young man.'

'Right.' Oliver reached into his rucksack for his prayer book. 'If you can all bow your heads, please.'

'Do we hold hands?' Raven asked.

He shrugged. 'If it gives you joy.'

Raven took his hand, and Oliver reached for Miss Ackroyd on the other side. It might not be strictly necessary for the exorcism, but in the gloomy setting of Ling Cottage, it did feel reassuring.

'Father, we ask that you visit this house and free it from the snares of the enemy,' Oliver said in a low, gentle voice. 'May your holy presence dwell here and guard its occupants in peace and serenity, and may your blessing rest upon us all. Amen.'

'Amen,' the others echoed. Oliver kept his head bowed for a moment, then crossed himself and looked up.

'Is that it?' Miss Ackroyd demanded.

'Um, yeah.'

'You're sure that's enough? We don't need to take communion or anything?'

'No, the blessing is all that's required.'

'Can't you feel the difference?' Raven asked.

Tess nodded. 'I think I can. More peaceful, as if the place
is at rest. Don't you think so, Miss Ackroyd?'

'Yes,' Miss Ackroyd whispered. 'Yes, you know, it does
feel as though there's been a change. The atmosphere . . . yes,
it's less oppressive altogether, isn't it? Thank you.' In a rare
display of affection, she patted Oliver's hand. 'Thank you,
Reverend.'

*

Outside, Tess rubbed her arms to warm up, glad to be free of
the house's gloomy atmosphere. The inside of Ling Cottage
somehow always managed to feel colder than the moors
around it.

'Did you hear that?' Oliver said, looking rather dazed.
'Did you hear what she called me?'

Tess smiled. 'Looks like you've finally supplanted the
sainted Reverend Springer in her affections.'

'Son. Lad. Young man. But never Reverend,' he muttered.
'Tell you what, I haven't felt this priestly since my ordination.'

'Poor Miss Ackroyd,' Tess said with a sigh. 'Her mind's all
over the place, isn't it?'

'You think that's true?' Raven asked. 'Her not knowing
who Nadia Harris is? I thought if anyone knew, it'd be her.'

Tess shrugged. 'She didn't seem in much of a state to lie.
Seemed like she was half in a dream. Or a nightmare.'

'This Charity. Whoever she was when she was alive, it's clear Miss A thought she had it in for her in death. Who do you think she might've been?'

'Someone connected to her or her sister, that's clear.'

'When Uncle Andrew mentioned Charity, I thought it must be some girl he was knocking about with, but . . . you think it's the same one?' Raven asked.

'Definitely.' Tess paused. 'Rave, did your great uncle ever have a nickname?

'Andrew? Not really. Marianne calls him Andy, but I'm not sure he approves.'

'He wasn't known as Felix?'

'Not since he was a kid, no. Why?'

Tess blinked. 'How do you mean, not since he was a kid?'

'What, didn't you know?' Raven said. 'That's his first name. Andrew's his middle name. He hated Felix – he's been Andrew since he was ten.'

'Why did he hate it?'

'He never got on with his father – Roland Walton-Lord was an old-school toff. Uncle Andrew associated the classical name with him and his affectations.' Raven smiled, a little sadly. 'And it didn't really suit him. It means lucky, you know.'

'Then why use it with her?' Tess muttered to herself. 'Perhaps she made him feel lucky.'

'Who?' Raven asked.

Tess hesitated. But Raven was in too deep now to be kept in the dark.

'Clemmie,' she said. 'They were lovers, I think. Liam and

me found a letter he'd written to her. He talked about Charity being mourned and keeping something safe for her. And he signed it Felix.'

'Lovers? Clemmie and Andrew?' Raven blinked. 'Wow. So what was it he wanted her to keep safe?'

'I'm not sure. The language in the letter was cryptic – deliberately so. If this Charity was being mourned then presumably she was dead, so I don't know how Clemmie could be expected to keep anything safe for her.'

'Could Charity be this girl – this Nadia Harris?'

'Not impossible,' Tess said. 'How old would Clemmie have been in May 1964? Late teens?'

'Seventeen,' Oliver said.

Tess shook her head. 'God. Just a kid.'

'A kid who was old enough to be a mother.'

'Yes. My thoughts are tending that way too.'

'And Andrew would've been twenty-seven. At the peak of what the family called his "little problem",' Raven said. 'But Miss Ackroyd seemed certain Charity was the ghost. So she couldn't be Nadia, could she?'

'Hmm,' Tess said. 'Something's rotten in the state of Cherrywood, guys.'

'What will you do next, Tessie?' Oliver asked.

'Talk to Liam. I've got a freelance gardening job for him.'

Chapter 24

'Come on, pick up,' Liam muttered as he waited for Tess to answer her phone. At his feet sat the evidence of his night's work.

'What?' she demanded when she answered. 'I'm busy.'

'I know you are. This is urgent.' He paused, registering the slight slur in her voice. 'Tessie, are you drunk?'

'No. A bit.'

In the background, he heard Raven Walton-Lord. 'Come try the elderflower, darling, it's lush.'

'There in a minute!' Tess called back.

'What, the pair of you are out on the razz?' Liam said. 'I thought you were at a Guild thing.'

'I am. Gin-tasting at the village hall,' Tess said. 'Raven's having the best night of her life.'

'Gin-tasting with the Women's Guild?'

'You'd be amazed what they get up to. It's a brave new world, Lee. Gin and Jerusalem.'

'Prue Ackroyd's still there, isn't she?'

'Yeah, why?'

'Will she be there a while longer?'

'There's an hour left.' Tess lowered her voice. 'What's going on? Are you up at the cottage?'

'Yes. I need you to sneak out and meet me.' He glanced at the Quality Street tin on the ground in the light of the head-torch he was wearing. 'Your hunch was right, Tess. I've found something.'

★

It was about twenty-five minutes later when Tess joined Liam in the garden at Ling Cottage.

'What is it?' she asked, nodding to the tin at his feet.

The big advantage of the last couple of months Liam had been undercover, taking on gardening jobs for anyone in Cherrywood who'd hire him, was that he could be spotted digging in a garden at eight at night without it raising any eyebrows. He'd timed it for this evening, when he knew Prue Ackroyd wouldn't be at home, to carry his shovel up to Ling Cottage and do a little investigating.

'I don't know yet,' he told her. 'I wanted to wait for you before I opened it. This was your hunch; I'm just here to provide the muscle.'

'Was it where I said?'

'Yep, under the monkey puzzle tree.'

'Well, whatever's in there, Miss Ackroyd must have known about it,' Tess said, eyeing the tin. 'Any guesses?'

Liam shrugged. 'Evidence, maybe. The missing St Christopher, or more poison-pen letters.'

'I don't think so.' Tess picked up the octagonal tin. 'Look

261

at the logo, and how faded it is. This is old. I'd guess it's been down there a good while.'

'I didn't examine it that closely.' Liam glanced around the garden, where strange shapes lurked in the shadows. 'I bloody hate this place, Tess.'

She smiled. 'Did you call me because you were scared, Liam Hanley? A big, tough ex-copper like you?'

'If I say yes, will you keep it to yourself?'

She patted his arm. 'Your secret's safe with me.'

'So did Prudence give you any clues about what's in the tin?' he asked.

'No, but her eyes were drawn to that tree the whole time we were here. It clearly freaked her out that the soil had been moved. It was all very "Telltale Heart".' Tess handed him the tin. 'You can do the honours.'

It was sealed with a couple of layers of parcel tape, surprisingly still holding strong despite their obvious age. Liam peeled them off and took out a penknife to prise open the rusted lid.

'What is it?' Tess asked, standing on tiptoes to try and get a look.

'Tissue paper. Or the remains of tissue paper. And . . .' He plucked something out and dangled it in front of her.

'A Madonna!' she said, staring at the medallion. 'Is it the same one?'

'I don't think so. This one's all tarnished.'

'It's an identical design though, isn't it? What's in the tissue?'

'Let's find out.'

He unwrapped it, Tess craning to see.

'Jesus Christ,' he muttered when he'd peeled it away.

'What? Lee, what is it?'

'Tessie, don't look. For God's sake, don't look.' He turned his body to shield the tin's contents from her view.

But it was too late. She'd already caught sight of what had been hidden in there. And it was enough to send her reeling towards the ground.

*

'Nearly there.'

Tess opened her eyes. She was slumped in a car seat with her head against Liam's shoulder while he drove. Her brain felt like a sack of coconuts.

She didn't remember getting in his car, or anything much after she'd seen what was in the tin. She guessed she must have fainted.

'Lee, where're we going?' she mumbled.

'My cottage. You've had a shock; you need to rest.'

'But you're OK.' She blinked him into focus. 'You saw it too. How can you still be OK?'

'I've been doing this job for five years, Tess, and I was a copper for six before that. I'm sorry to tell you, this isn't my first time.' He glowered at the road. 'But if you think I'm OK, you're very, very wrong.'

Tess examined his face. His expression was set and determined, but he was deathly pale.

'I'm sorry,' she whispered.

He glanced at her in the mirror. 'You ever seen a dead body before?'

'Once. Just once. But it wasn't like . . . it was so tiny, Lee.'

'I know,' he said quietly. 'I'm sorry you had to see that.'

'The tin. Where . . .'

'Where we found it. After you fainted my first thought was to get you out of there. Suppose I panicked a bit.'

'We need to tell the police.'

'We do. But not just yet.'

When he'd parked up, he supported a still shaky Tess to the groundskeeper's cottage. The first thing he did when he got in was turn on nearly every light in the place, then take a match to the big candles in the old fireplace.

Tess understood. He wasn't the only one who suddenly felt afraid of the dark.

He went into the kitchen, coming back a minute later with two mugs of something musky and steaming.

'Here,' he said, handing her one.

'What is it?'

'Cure for shock.'

She took a sip and pulled a face. 'Irish coffee?'

'Yeah, heavy on the whisky. It'll go right to your toes.'

'I feel sick,' she mumbled.

'It should help with that too. Drink up while it's hot.'

Liam sat next to her on the sofa, and when he put an arm around her, pulling their bodies close, she didn't object. Whatever her feelings towards him currently were, human contact was what she needed right now. As the hot coffee and alcohol seeped through her veins and the warmth of Liam's body flowed into hers, the sharp, sick feeling in Tess's gut started to numb.

'What do we do?' she asked, nursing the warm liquid in both hands.

'Call the police,' Liam said grimly. 'But first I want to speak to Prudence Ackroyd.'

'She knew,' Tess muttered. 'God, all the time she lived there she knew it was right there in the ground.' She looked up at him. 'Lee, you don't think she . . .'

'I hope not. But there's a story behind this and she knows what it is.'

A vivid image of what had been in the tin rose up in Tess's mind, and the shock and nausea hit her afresh.

It had been so tiny, so perfectly formed; curled as if sleeping. Every bone just as it ought to be – little fingers, little toes. She didn't think she'd ever forget that image, the tiny baby skeleton, hugging its knees as it slept.

Whatever she'd thought might be hiding under Miss Ackroyd's monkey puzzle tree, it hadn't been that.

'It is definitely human?' she whispered.

'I'm sorry. It is.'

'Do you think it was hers? Miss Ackroyd's?'

'More likely her sister's, based on what we know. And I'd lay down money its name was Charity.'

'Poor little love.' Tess choked on a sob. 'It must've been so . . . so frightened, all alone in the dark.'

Liam pulled her closer and pressed his lips against her hair.

'Try not to think of it that way,' he said gently. 'It was very likely a stillbirth, at a time when out-of-wedlock pregnancies were often covered up.'

'But what if it wasn't? You remember what the letter said. "To take a life is a terrible sin."'

'Well, we'll know soon enough.'

She looked up at him. His eyes were soft and reassuring in the candlelight.

'You weren't thinking of confronting Miss Ackroyd tonight?' she asked.

'I'll have to. I can't keep this from the police. I need to let them know as soon as possible.'

Tess thought for a moment.

'Let me and Oliver do it,' she said. 'He'll come straight over if I tell him he's needed in a professional capacity.'

'Vicar Oliver? Why?'

'Because Miss Ackroyd trusts him more than anyone, and I'm one of the few people in Cherrywood she doesn't actively dislike. She'll talk to us.'

'I don't know, Tess.' He scanned her face, concern in his eyes. 'You're as white as a ghost, if you'll pardon the expression.'

'I'll be OK. Please, Liam. You're a stranger; she won't open up to you like she will to us.'

'Are you sure you're up to it?'

'I'm fine, I promise. Anyway, you don't really want to blow your cover at this stage, do you?'

'There could be danger, Tess.'

Tess smiled weakly. 'From Miss Ackroyd? Not to us, I'm certain of it.'

'Well . . . if you're sure,' Liam said reluctantly. 'Call me as soon as you're done. I want to know everything.'

★

Tess shivered as she went out into the hall to ring Oliver.

She couldn't believe she was really in any danger, not from Miss Ackroyd, but . . . the dead child. And Aunty Clemmie. For the first time, it was starting to hit home that her old teacher might have taken a life.

Maybe more than one.

'Ol?' she whispered when he picked up.

'Tess.' Oliver sounded surprised. She guessed she sounded pretty shaken still. 'What's up?'

'You're needed. Can you meet me?'

'Now? I'm supposed to be going out with Tammy.' He paused. 'Are you OK, love? Your voice is trembling.'

'I need you to meet me at the groundskeeper's place at Cherrywood Hall, right away,' Tess said. 'Can you ring Tam and tell her something's come up? We have to be at Ling Cottage in half an hour.'

'Ling Cottage? Why, what else has happened?'

'Oliver, you're going to need every ounce of faith you've got for this. Something horrible's been hiding up there.'

*

'Oh my God,' Oliver whispered when Liam and Tess had filled him in. 'A child?'

Liam nodded. 'A newborn.'

'Is it – was it Miss Ackroyd's?'

'Most likely Aunty Clemmie's,' Tess said.

'Charity,' Oliver said slowly. 'You think it's her.'

Tess nodded. 'Maybe a stillbirth – or maybe not.'

267

'Why call me? It sounds like a matter for the police.'

'Because she trusts you. I want you to come talk to her with me before we get the police involved.'

Oliver shook his head. 'Cover it up? You know I can't.'

'No one's asking you to do that,' Liam said. 'We just want to find out what happened.'

'How long . . . I mean, when did it – she – die?'

'Hard to say. Fifty years at least, I think.'

'She's been up there all this time.' Tess shuddered. 'Can you imagine, living in the house knowing that was there? No wonder Miss Ackroyd believes in ghosts.'

'Why wouldn't Clemmie report it, if it was a stillbirth?' Oliver asked.

Liam shrugged. 'I'm assuming since neither of the Ackroyd girls have been married that it wasn't a planned pregnancy. Half a century ago in a place like this, a baby and no husband would've made her a social pariah.'

'We found a necklace with the body,' Tess said, fighting back the wave of nausea she felt whenever she thought about what had been in the Quality Street tin. God, what a coffin for the little thing . . . 'A Madonna and child, like the one they found on Aunty Clemmie, but old and rusty.'

Oliver looked dazed. 'This is . . . macabre,' he muttered. 'I'm a village vicar, guys, and a young one at that. I don't know if I've got the experience to deal with this.'

'You don't need experience. Just compassion.' Tess smiled. 'That's something you've always had plenty of.'

'I'm afraid, Tessie.'

'So am I, Ol. But Miss Ackroyd's a tormented soul. We

should talk to her before the police start asking questions. See what we can do to help.'

'Yes.' Oliver squared his shoulders. 'You're right. This is my parish and Miss Ackroyd's my responsibility. I can't hide from that when the going gets tough.'

'Let's say it's our responsibility,' Tess said. 'We'll go together.'

He smiled. 'You ever thought of a curacy, Tess? You seem to be my right-hand woman these days.'

'As long as it wouldn't interfere with my Cher-impersonating,' she said, smiling back. 'Come on, let's get up there. She could be back any time.'

Chapter 25

By the time Miss Ackroyd arrived home, Tess and Oliver had been waiting nearly ten minutes, lurking out of sight.

'This is going to be horrible,' Tess whispered to Oliver. 'I mean, I knew Aunty Clemmie had been killed, but until tonight . . . I was so focused on solving the puzzle, I hardly thought about how scared she must've been. About death.'

'It'll be OK. Trust in God.'

'You know I don't believe.'

'Then I'll trust in Him and you trust in me.' He squeezed her hand in the darkness.

'You think she did it?' Tess whispered. 'Miss Ackroyd?'

'No.'

'You sound very sure.'

'I am. Prue Ackroyd is not a killer; I'd stake my soul on it.'

They waited until the old lady was unlocking the front door before making themselves known.

Tess stepped towards her. 'Miss Ackroyd.'

She started. 'Teresa! Goodness, you gave me the fright of my life. Where on earth did you disappear to tonight?' She peered into the darkness. 'Is that Oliver?'

'Can we come in, please?' Oliver said. 'We need to talk to you about something.'

'Is it about the . . . procedure?'

'We're not sure,' Tess said. 'Let's go in, shall we? It's rather delicate.'

Looking puzzled, Miss Ackroyd unlocked the door. She gestured for them to follow her into the front room.

'Do you want tea?' she asked.

'Not right now,' Oliver said. 'Sit, please.'

'What is it? Why do you both look so solemn?' she asked, taking a seat. She looked concerned, and a little afraid.

They sat down opposite her. Tess glanced at Oliver, unsure where to begin.

'We know, Miss Ackroyd,' Oliver said. 'We know about Charity.'

The colour drained from Miss Ackroyd's face.

'Charity?' she said in a barely audible whisper. 'No. You can't do.'

Tess nodded. 'We know who she was. We . . . found her.' She couldn't help flinching when she thought about the contents of the tin.

'I don't know what you mean,' Miss Ackroyd mumbled.

'It's no good, Miss Ackroyd. We know. You can take a look at the tin under your monkey puzzle tree if you're in any doubt.'

There was a look of horror in the old woman's face. 'You . . . you dug it up?'

'I'm sorry. We did.'

'It's all right,' Oliver said gently. 'We want to help. We know you didn't hurt her. Tell us what happened.'

Miss Ackroyd's face convulsed with a sob.

'It wasn't me,' she whispered thickly. 'I never could, not to a little child. It was her.'

'Who?' Tess asked.

'*Her*. She . . . she did it to her. In the letters she said . . . but it was all her.'

'Letters?' Oliver said.

'She wrote to me. Charity.'

'Miss Ackroyd, she's dead. Whoever's been sending you letters, it's not Charity.'

'Did somebody hurt her, Miss Ackroyd?' Tess asked quietly.

'Yes. Yes, she . . . she . . . I couldn't stop it. Clemmie never did forgive me. Oh, she said she did, but I knew. It was in her eyes, always there in her eyes. I hated her for it sometimes – I couldn't help it. Even though I loved her, I . . .' Her voice broke in a sob. '. . . hated her.'

Tess shot a worried look at Oliver. Miss Ackroyd was sobbing uncontrollably, her rambling nonsense speech lost in gasps. It felt frightening, seeing someone who in childhood they'd viewed as an authority figure, grown up and strong, reduced to that level of helplessness.

Oliver stood and went to rest a hand on her shoulder.

'It's OK,' he said softly. 'The past's where you left it; it can't hurt you now. Let us help you lay it to rest.'

He nodded to Tess, who understood. She rose from her chair.

'You know, I think we could use that tea,' she said. 'Let me make it while you two take a minute.'

It was strange, she reflected as she brewed three cups of strong, milky tea in the kitchen. Oliver had always been afraid of Miss Ackroyd, ever since schooldays. But out of everyone in the village, she trusted him most – even loved him, in her way. He was the only person who could be where he was right now, comforting her as she sobbed.

When Tess returned with the tea, Oliver was in his seat again. Miss Ackroyd was deathly pale, but the tears had dried and she seemed calmer.

'Everything OK?' Tess asked.

Oliver nodded. 'Miss Ackroyd's ready to tell us what happened.'

'I think at this stage, the two of you might call me Prue,' Miss Ackroyd said with a weak smile.

'Go ahead, please,' Tess said, sitting down with her tea. 'Take as many breaks as you need.'

Miss Ackroyd sighed, dabbing at her eyes with a lace-edged handkerchief. 'It was just Clemmie being Clemmie – that's how it started. Foolish child she was, her head full of dreams – romance. Well, I should have guessed how it would all end when she went into service up there. She was desperate to be in love.' She shook her head. 'Oh, I do wish she'd never confided in me. I don't know why she had to make it my problem too.'

'Where did she go to work?' Tess asked.

'At the hall. Roland Walton-Lord needed kitchen staff. Of course we ought to have known what would happen. The rumours we'd heard about him.'

'Roland?'

'Not him, the son.' Miss Ackroyd curled her lip. 'His eldest: the handsome drunk with the dreadful reputation. They had him in the asylum a year or two later. Drank his sanity away, they say. But not before he got our Clemmie into trouble, oh no. Swore he'd marry her.' She scoffed. 'Well, don't they always?'

'But he never did,' Tess said.

'Of course he didn't. I doubt he ever intended to, and when his father found out what had happened, he banned them from seeing each other. Andrew was too weak to fight it, even if he could have sobered up long enough.'

'So what happened?'

'Roland told Clem to . . .' Miss Ackroyd swallowed. '. . . to sort it out. Said he'd pay.'

Oliver glanced at Tess. 'Abortion? Wouldn't it have been illegal?'

'But it happened, all the same. Knitting needles, castor oil, greasy back-alley quacks. It was a death sentence for too many women.' Miss Ackroyd looked down at her hand, clutching the handkerchief in white knuckles. 'Girls I knew amongst them.'

'So Aunty Clemmie decided to keep the baby rather than risk it,' Tess said.

'Oh, she'd never have gone through with it. Not Clemmie. She idolised children – wanted the baby far more than she cared about saving her reputation. Foolish girl.'

'She took the money, though,' Oliver said.

'She never told me she had, although I'm assuming that's where it came from,' Miss Ackroyd said. 'I suppose she told

Roland it had all been taken care of. She managed to hide her condition until the end, with my help.'

'How?'

'She was always a curvy girl. Loose-fitting clothes, staying away from the village – the Walton-Lords had let her go, of course, although I know the young man still wrote to her until they packed him off to the madhouse.'

'Did you see the letters?' Tess asked.

'No, she wouldn't let me. Not that I cared what was in them.' Miss Ackroyd sneered. 'She actually had the nerve to accuse me of going through them, the night she died. She could be quite arrogant sometimes.'

'You didn't like your sister very much, did you?' Oliver observed.

Miss Ackroyd looked shocked. 'What a thing to say! Of course I did, I loved her.'

'And yet I've never heard you say a kind word about her.'

'She was weak,' Miss Ackroyd muttered. 'We both were, and I despised us for it. If we'd stood up to her . . .' She shook her head. 'Sin will out, that's what she said. She knew we couldn't keep her buried for ever.'

'Charity?' Tess said, lost in a sea of pronouns. 'That was what your sister called the baby, wasn't it?'

'Yes.' The name seemed to have an unsettling effect on Miss Ackroyd. Her voice sank to a whisper, and she trembled through her whole body. 'I came home and she . . . It was done, all over. Clem had delivered it alone in her room.' She broke into sobs again. 'You say I never cared for her, but I would have done anything for my sister. At least,

I believed so then. But when she put me to the test . . . I let her down.'

'How do you think you let her down?' Oliver asked.

'I killed her,' she whispered. 'Charity. It was my fault.'

'You mean the baby was alive when you came home?'

'Yes. A mewling, runtish thing; a four-pounder or less. Perhaps . . . perhaps she wouldn't have been long for this world. She didn't look fated to survive. But Clemmie cradled her and crooned over her like she was the most beautiful child ever created.'

'When was this?' Oliver asked.

'Oh, I'll never forget that day,' Miss Ackroyd said. 'I wish I could. Thirteenth of May 1964.'

Thirteenth of May. Nadia Harris had been born just days later. Two babies, four days between them, one who lived and one who died . . . what was the connection?

'What happened to her?' Tess whispered, dreading to hear the answer. 'What did you do?'

'That's just it. I didn't do anything.' Miss Ackroyd's face twitched feverishly. 'Clemmie begged me to take the child and smuggle her away. But I hesitated. I was afraid. And then . . . then I'd hesitated just a moment too long.'

'You mean the baby died?'

'No.' Miss Ackroyd's brow lowered. 'I mean that Mother came home.'

There was silence for a moment.

'She did this?' Oliver whispered. 'Your mother, Connie Ackroyd, did this?'

'She was a hard, brutal monster of a human being,' Miss

Ackroyd said with a bitter simplicity. 'I hated her. I hated her before, and after – well, I swore I'd never set foot in this place while she was living, and within weeks I'd found a position elsewhere and got myself out. I begged Clemmie to come away with me, but she couldn't leave. Like I told you. Weak.'

'What did your mother do?' Tess asked.

'She . . .' Miss Ackroyd paused while she struggled to get her sobs under control. 'At first, she demanded the child from Clemmie. Called them names, both of them. Whore. Bastard. Horrible, ugly words that made Clemmie and the baby cry, and me too. I screamed at her to stop, and—' She drew her fingers along her cheek, over a long, thin indentation Tess had noticed before. 'Back of the hand. It could have been worse – she had a stick for when we'd been very bad – but it was hard enough to make me fall to the floor. Her wedding ring cut my cheek so I was dripping blood, and then . . .'

Tess could guess what was coming. 'And then your mother took Charity from Clemmie.'

'Yes,' Miss Ackroyd whispered. 'Clemmie struggled but she was drained after the birth; it wasn't difficult. Mother snatched the child away; said she'd be better off dead than the worthless thing she was. And she threw the baby on the bed, and she . . . she . . .' Her speech was breaking, but she forced herself on. 'With the pillow.'

Exhausted, Miss Ackroyd sank against her arms and shook with tears.

'It's all right,' Oliver said gently. 'You don't need to tell us any more. We understand.'

'It was my fault. I could have stopped it, if I'd only done what Clemmie had asked me right away.'

Oliver went to rest a hand on her shoulder.

'It wasn't your fault. You were a child yourself. You acted the way any girl your age would in the same situation.'

'Charity doesn't think so. In the letters, she said . . .'

'Whoever wrote those letters, it wasn't her.' Oliver squeezed her shoulder. 'You know, in the new Bible translations you dislike so much, the Greek word translated as "charity" in King James's time is given as "love". No innocent child could be so malicious, Prue, in this life or the next. Charity's at peace now – with God.'

'Then where did they come from? And the medallion just like Charity's, that Clemmie bought her to be buried with?'

Oliver's brow darkened. 'They came from someone who wants to make you pay for a dead woman's crime. And I promise you, we won't rest until we find out who that is.'

*

'So they buried Charity in the garden with the Madonna medallion,' Liam said when Tess called at the groundskeeper's cottage afterwards.

'Yes. Aunty Clemmie got it for her,' Tess said as she sat on his sofa nursing another mug of tea. 'The mother and child, right? The relationship they were never allowed to have.'

She wasn't actually drinking the tea. Over the course of the evening she'd had tea, Irish coffee and seven different flavours of gin, and currently she was about ninety per cent liquid. But there was something about the feel of a hot drink in your hands. Tea felt comforting, real, simple – far away from corpses and murder and all the gruesome events of that night.

'That's why Miss Ackroyd was so certain Clemmie didn't own any such item of jewellery,' she told Liam. 'Her sister knew she'd never buy another like it. Clemmie was superstitious that way.'

'Then where did it come from, the one they found on her?'

'From someone who knows all about it,' Tess said, scowling. 'Someone who knows the part Miss Ackroyd played and wants to make her suffer.'

'Marianne Priestley,' Liam said. 'She was Clemmie's best friend, right?'

'Marianne?' Tess shook her head. 'No.'

'Someone's messing with Prue Ackroyd, Tess. Trying to make her think this kid's back from the dead and out for vengeance.'

'Well, I know, but—'

'You can't keep dismissing suspects just because they're old friends. If the last six weeks have taught you anything, it should be that there's no such thing as an innocent person.' Liam looked grim. 'Everyone's got something to hide.'

'How can it be Marianne, though? She's been getting letters too.'

'Can we trust that she didn't send those to herself? It could be a ploy to throw us off the scent.'

'But Candice hired you.'

'She also hid key information from me. The name on the letter,' Liam said. 'All that proves is that Marianne has secrets from Candice as well as from us. Or that Candice is part of a conspiracy to pin this whole thing on someone else.'

'I can't believe it. Not Marianne.' Tess paused. 'Candice though . . . she did know. About Charity.'

'How do you know that?'

'I saw her, the same night I found out what Miss Ackroyd's light fingers were chucking their money away on. She was in the cemetery at Plumholme, putting flowers on this little kid's grave. The vicar told me she does it every year – always a different kid. She thought maybe it was for a child lost in pregnancy who didn't have a grave of their own.'

'But you think it was for Charity.'

'Who else?'

'Yeah, you're right.' He sighed. 'I'm turning you into a pretty cynical person, aren't I, Tessie?'

'This case is.' She took a sip of the tea, for something to do as much as anything. 'I mean, Jesus, people I've known since for ever . . . I honestly don't know who to trust any more.'

Liam shuffled round on the sofa. 'You trust me, though, right?'

'In a professional capacity.'

'But not in a personal capacity?'

She sighed. 'Lee, please. I've had a bloody awful night and I'm wobbly as hell. Can we not do this?'

'Sorry,' he said gently. 'I'm trying to earn it, though, Tess. I know I didn't play fair with you during the Porter investigation, but I'm not a bad man. Not really.'

Tess sipped her drink in silence, avoiding his eye. Eventually he took the hint.

'So how did Prue respond when you said it'd have to be passed on to the police?' he asked.

'She was fine about it – actually seemed relieved,' Tess said. 'She went along to the station with Oliver, as docile as a lamb.'

'How is Oliver?'

Tess's brow lowered. 'Angry, and he's not the only one. Can you believe Connie Ackroyd did that to a little baby? I knew she was hard as nails, but Christ!'

'Did you know her?'

'Everyone did. Everyone was afraid of her.' She looked up. 'Tell you a story, Lee?'

'OK.'

'When I was a kid, I was desperate for a pet, but my parents always said no. There wasn't space, we couldn't afford to keep one, we had a houseful . . . For years I begged, and the answer always came back no.'

Liam blinked. 'Right. And?'

'Then one summer, when I was seven, my dad came home with these newborn kittens.' She smiled at the memory. 'Two in his big rucksack, another pair under his arms. One for each of us. I was delighted with my Mitzi – she was this gorgeous tortie fluffball, just perfect. Dad said they didn't have a mum and we kids would have to care for them until they were strong. And we did it too, taking feed shifts through the night, even though we were zombies for school. I loved it – being their mum, watching our babies get stronger every day.'

'I'm not making the connection here, Tess,' Liam said. 'I mean, I'm happy you got your cat and everything, but –'

'Years later, Mitzi died. The last of our little litter.' Tess blinked back a tear. 'It wasn't so sad really. She was eighteen, and she died in her sleep in her favourite spot – dreaming, I hope. After we'd buried her, I rang Dad and asked what had finally changed his mind all those years ago. Where the kittens had come from.'

Liam leaned round to look into her face. 'Where?'

'Connie Ackroyd. He'd found her by the canal with this wriggling bin liner. Her mouser Daisy had had kittens and she wanted rid.'

'You mean she was going to drown them?'

'Yeah. Dad gave her all the money in his wallet to let him take them.' Tess bit her lip. 'A person who could do that . . . It made me feel ill. But I never would've believed she was capable of killing a baby.'

'People like her don't see any difference. All they see is vermin.' With a sudden movement, Liam punched the arm of the sofa. 'What makes me sick is that she got away with it. Died peacefully in her sleep, probably, a stainless pillar of the community. Why the hell didn't her daughters tell anyone?'

'You've seen Prue's diary. Connie as good as brainwashed them. Prue managed to break free, but Clemmie . . . it was like she was in thrall to her, all her life.' Tess shook her head. 'There's so much that makes sense now. The way Aunty Clemmie loved kids, how she used to well up when she saw anyone with a newborn and beg to have a cuddle. Oh God, Lee . . .'

She buried her head in his shoulder as she gave in to sobs, and he wrapped his arms around her.

'Why don't you stay over?' he whispered. 'You've had a rough day – you shouldn't be alone.'

It was tempting. She felt the need to be close to someone tonight and Liam's arms were right there: available, warm and reassuring. But Liam's arms were a dangerous place for her to be.

'No . . .' She lifted her head and wiped her eyes. 'That's not a good idea.'

'No funny business, I promise – just some company. I can put the camp bed up so you can take my double. I don't much fancy being alone myself after . . . well, you know.'

'Sorry, Lee, I really can't. I'd never be able to explain it to Raven.' She looked at him. 'But . . . thanks for looking after me tonight, all the same.'

Chapter 26

Oliver was heading back from Ling Cottage a week later, feeling weary and toying with the idea of calling in at the pub for a drink. Between dropping in to chat with Tess and dropping in to gaze at Tammy, he seemed to spend half his life at the Star these days. His parishioners were probably starting to talk, possibly wondering what happened to the leftover communion wine.

But after the grisly events of the week before, he suddenly felt very alone in his big, empty vicarage. The pub, where dozens of familiar faces were ready with a friendly hello for their village vicar, was a much more inviting prospect.

He'd been up to see Miss Ackroyd again. He called on her most nights now. In fact, he'd been hoping to convince her to go to the pub with him, where she'd have the opportunity to see a few friends. Prue had barely left the house since the facts surrounding Charity's death had come out – of course, a thrilling piece of gossip like that had quickly spread.

Oliver knew it wasn't good for her, hiding away in that miserable old place, but she wouldn't be persuaded to leave the house. She said she needed time to herself, but he knew that in reality she was afraid of what people would say when they saw her out and about. How they'd respond, now they knew she'd been involved in a child's murder.

She hadn't really, of course. A sixteen-year-old girl, beaten and bullied by an abusive parent, had been forced to witness a terrible crime. She hadn't committed the crime – the police agreed with that, no charges were to be brought – and her only sin was in having hesitated in her response to her sister's plea for help.

Over the last week, Oliver had been gently guiding her, reminding her that her faith offered unconditional forgiveness for those who repented. Reminding her of the need, having been forgiven by God, to then forgive herself. She was definitely starting to come to terms with what had happened, but what she really needed was people. Friends.

'I don't need anyone,' she'd told him when he'd suggested breaking her self-imposed exile with a trip to the Star. 'But you may come and see me again, Oliver.'

A month or so ago, he might have been offended by the condescending tone in which the invitation was uttered. Taken it as yet another sign that she didn't consider him a 'proper' vicar like old Rev Springer. But not now. They understood each other now.

There was nothing maternal about Prue Ackroyd, but he'd nevertheless been surprised to discover she was rather fond of him. Oliver, for his part, had overcome his fear and become fond of her likewise. He even found, when he was able to break through her reserve, that she was rather good company. An odd pair of friends they made, but in their own way they seemed to suit.

He was driving along the main street towards the vicarage, planning to drop off the car and walk to the pub for a pint – just one, he promised himself, although if Tammy was working he might hang around – when he spotted Peggy Bristow, once again sneaking into the village hall by the back door. He rolled down the window and called to her, but she didn't respond.

What could she be doing in there this time? Miss Ackroyd was back at Ling Cottage and Peggy had her house to herself for whatever she chose to do in it, whether it was smearing fondant icing over TV hunks or trying to coax Saturday's Lotto numbers out of her crystal ball.

Ah, now he remembered. It was the first performance of *Mamma Mia* tomorrow night, wasn't it? Peggy must have offered to help Bev get the stage set up. Well, it was good to know they were on speaking terms again after the now infamous cake-meets-face incident at the show.

Oliver turned into the vicarage, parked his car and walked back towards the main street, taking a shortcut down Albert Street to bring him out by the post office.

The pub was right opposite, its windows glowing invitingly. Oliver took a step towards it, hesitated, then turned around to head down the street.

If Peggy was setting up for tomorrow, surely there'd be others helping out. And why sneak in by the back like that?

As a trustee of the hall, Oliver felt he ought to check it out. Using the place as a hideout from Miss Ackroyd every once in a while was one thing, but if Peggy was regularly employing it as her personal chill-out zone then he should really

286

have a quiet word. She could get herself in a lot of trouble if the other trustees got wind.

When he reached the hall, he took out his key and let himself in.

'Peggy?' he called. 'You here?'

There was no answer. He peeked into the main hall, but there was no one in there. Just the stage laid out for tomorrow's performance, plastic palm trees bathed in the sickly illumination of the green fire exit light.

He checked the library room, then the youth club area. Nothing there. No reply when he knocked on the door of the ladies' loos either. Perhaps Peggy had gone.

Oliver was about to leave himself when he noticed the deactivated security alarm. If Peggy hadn't set it, she must still be in the building somewhere.

He headed to the basement room where the boilers were kept. It was the last place she might be, although what she could be doing in there he couldn't imagine.

When he got there, he gently opened the door and peeped inside. He stared for a moment, then just as gently closed it again before heading back upstairs and leaving the way he'd come in.

Then he went to the pub. All of a sudden, he badly needed a drink.

*

Tess was not having a good shift. Bev was in a double stress over the opening night of *Mamma Mia* tomorrow and another row with Ian, which had seen him storming out to go meet a friend at the Green Man. It was not a happy time to be a barmaid at the Star and Garter.

Tess was pouring Guy Cartwright a Guinness when Bev came stomping up with the remains of a pint of Best. She slammed it down on the bar.

'Taste this,' she demanded.

Tess left the Guinness to settle and took a tentative sip of the Landlord. 'It's beer. And?'

'It's off is what it is,' Bev said, looking thunderous. 'Must've been a bad barrel, bloody useless brewery. How many of these have you served tonight?'

'I dunno, a few? It tastes fine to me, Bev.'

'Well, then that must be why you're staff and I'm running the sodding place.' Bev held the half-drunk pint up to the light. 'How could you not have noticed that sediment? Half our customers will probably have the runs tomorrow. Go change the barrel, Tess, for God's sake.'

'Now? I'm serving.' Tess nodded to a worried-looking Guy. He was examining his Guinness warily, obviously wondering what his chances of ending up with the runs were.

'Tess Feather, do you need me to hold your hand for everything? Finish that, take the money, change the barrel. No wonder that place you were at in London went bust.' Bev cast another dark look at the dodgy bitter and stomped off.

When she was in a good mood, Bev could be the perfect boss. When she wasn't, she was the devil in leopard-skin.

'Sorry about that,' Tess said to Guy, grimacing.

'What's up with her?' Guy asked. 'Call me oversensitive, but I'm detecting she's not her usual jolly self.'

'Oh, she's just stressed about *Mamma Mia* tomorrow.' Tess handed him his pint. 'I'd better go sort out this barrel before she pops.'

When she got back, Guy had disappeared and Oliver had taken his place. He was staring with unseeing eyes at the spirit optics.

'Back again?' Tess said. 'You're getting to be my best customer, Ol. The usual?'

'Something stronger.'

'Such as?'

'Whatever you recommend, so long as it's solid alcohol.'

'OK, you can have the Raven special. Double gin with gin on top.' She turned to the optic and started pouring. 'What's driving you to drink?'

Oliver watched as the gin squirted into his tumbler. 'Tess . . .'

'Yeah?'

'Tess . . .'

'Yeah?'

'Um, Tess . . .'

'For God's sake, Oliver!'

He looked to both sides, leaned over the bar and lowered his voice. 'Where's Ian supposed to be?'

'Out at the Green Man. Him and Bev had another row so he's hiding there in a sulk. Why, did you need him?'

'No. Anyway, I think he's a bit . . .' He swallowed. '. . . tied up.'

'Eh?'

Oliver lowered his voice still further. 'He's not at the Green Man, Tessie. He's at the village hall.'

'What, dropping off stuff for tomorrow?'

'No. He's . . .' Oliver paused to take a sip of his gin, looking pained. 'OK, so you know that when two people love each other very much, they do certain . . . things . . .'

Tess rolled her eyes. 'Thanks, Ol. I've been waiting years for someone to tell me how all that worked.'

'And sometimes the things might be black, maybe a bit shiny, far, far too tight, obviously, with lots of nobbly rubber bits . . .'

'What are you going on about?'

Oliver knocked back the rest of his gin, glanced behind him, and leaned forward again until they were practically nose to nose.

'I just saw him having . . . they were doing . . . I mean, Peggy Bristow, I never thought . . .' He shook himself. 'Let's just say it's not only outside the bedroom that Ian Stringer has a thing for dressing up.'

Tess's eyes widened as she pieced together the fragments. 'Oh my God!' She lowered her voice to match his. 'You caught Ian having sex with his ex-wife?'

'I think it was sex. It was hard to see which bit was going where with all the leather.'

'You are kidding me!' She looked over her shoulder to check Bev wasn't around. 'You mean *mmm* and *mmm* were doing *mmm* at the village hall?'

'If by *mmm* and *mmm* you mean Peggy and Ian, and by

290

mmm you mean some pretty kinky stuff that no minister of God's Church should ever have to witness, then yes. In the boiler room at the hall, up against the wet sponge-throwing board from the summer fun day.' He shuddered and glanced longingly at the spirit optics. 'Can I get another?'

'After what you've been through? This one's on me, love.' Tess poured him another gin. 'What did they say when you caught them at it?'

'They didn't. I sneaked off again before they noticed me. They were, er . . . a bit distracted at the time.' He swallowed down his drink. 'It can't have been a one-off either. I caught Peggy heading in there a few weeks ago, looking shifty. She fed me some line about needing to get away from Miss Ackroyd.'

'Actually, I saw her coming out not so long ago, ages after she ought to have finished work,' Tess said. 'Why use the hall though? Why not Peggy's place?'

He shrugged. 'Maybe they like the thrill of potentially getting caught.'

'Well, now they've experienced the thrill of actually getting caught. I hope it was as much fun as they'd hoped.' Tess pictured the three of them: dowdy, bespectacled Peggy; larger-than-life Beverley with her loud dress sense; Ian with his Sonny Bono moustache. They were the most unlikely-looking love triangle she could imagine.

'You think we should tell Bev?' Oliver asked.

'I think we should keep out of it,' Tess said firmly. 'It's hard to see Bev as the wronged party after what she did to Peggy. Ian deserves a good kick in the you-know-whats, but

I don't think we're the ones to give him it. Anyway, from the sounds of things he'd probably enjoy it.' She shook her head. 'Peggy Bristow a dominatrix – can you believe it? I thought her only vice was lusting after baked Poldarks.'

'Tessie, you don't think . . . Could it be connected? You know, to Aunty Clemmie and Charity and all this stuff that's going on?'

'I don't see how.' Tess pondered for a moment. 'But Peggy is a person of interest. Liam'll want to know about it. I'll fill him in tomorrow at *Mamma Mia*.'

Chapter 27

'Peggy Bristow?' Liam said after Tess had dragged him backstage at the village hall the next day. 'The little round one who looks like my Aunty Susan, with the bunions and varicose veins?'

'Yep.'

'Peggy Bristow likes dressing up in a crotchless leather catsuit and beating merry Christmas out of fellers with a riding crop?'

'So Oliver says.' Tess frowned. 'Hang on, who mentioned crotchless leather catsuits?'

'I may have been embellishing slightly,' Liam said. 'I should point out that in my imagination, the part of Peggy Bristow is being played by Scarlett Johansson.'

'So you think it's connected, her affair with Ian? Peggy's, I mean, not Scarlett's.'

'I can't see how, but I'll add it to my profile notes.' He sighed. 'Will this stuff ever start adding up? I thought once we found out who Charity was, everything would fall into place. We seem to have kinky adulterers and roulette-addicted petty thieves coming out of our ears, but the only murderer we've managed to catch has been dead for ten years.'

'We know more than we did, at least. Did you go through Andrew's letters to Clemmie?'

Miss Ackroyd, finally convinced her threatening letters had come from a living, breathing human being rather than anything supernatural, had been persuaded by Oliver to part with the contents of her sister's drawer in the ongoing hunt for her killer.

'Yeah. Nothing,' Liam said glumly.

'Nothing about Charity?'

'She's mentioned a few times, but nothing that points to anything we didn't know. No mention of anyone named Harris, which I'll admit is what I was hoping for. Mostly it's just Andrew feeling sorry for himself and begging her to forgive him.'

'For not standing up to his father?'

'Yeah. He did love her – would've married her, if he'd had the guts to break with his family. He blamed his weakness for Charity's death.'

'Him too, eh?' Tess sighed. 'Poor Andrew. And poor Clemmie too. Both conditioned to obey these bullies without question, even if it meant sacrificing their own happiness.'

'Yeah, I couldn't help feeling for the guy,' Liam said. 'The Felix letters get more rambling as they go on. The last one was just nonsense.'

'Raven said that was the peak of Andrew's drink problem.'

'Oh. Here.' Liam took out Prue's diary, the one they'd taken the day they searched the house. 'I thought it might be better if you returned this. She trusts you.'

'No help from that quarter either, I'm guessing?'

Liam shook his head. 'I looked up the entry for the date of Charity's birth, and the one for Nadia's. No mention of either name, or of the birth at all. On the day Charity was born, Prue just hints darkly at a big row with her mum and vows she'll get herself and Clemency out of there. No specific mention of what happened. I suppose she was worried it could get her sister into trouble if someone found it.'

'And yet she couldn't get Clemmie to leave, even after what had happened,' Tess murmured, running her fingers over the old leather. 'What happened to Charity's body?'

'It's been released to the family – I guess that means to Prue, since the biological father's in no state to take responsibility for her. She'll arrange for burial in the local churchyard, I suppose. Do you want to visit her with me?'

'Yes, I'd like to pay my respects. Poor kid.' Tess scowled. 'Makes me angry just thinking about it. If she was alive now, she'd be fifty-nine. She could have kids – grandkids. Who knows what she'd have done with all those years Connie took from her?'

'Makes you value your own years that bit more, eh?'

'I guess it does.' Tess was silent a moment. 'Lee, I was thinking, we really ought to talk to Andrew in person. You never know, he might still have Clemmie's replies to his Felix letters somewhere.'

Liam shook his head. 'She never wrote back. He says so in his letters. Wouldn't have anything to do with him after Charity's death.'

'And yet she kept his letters, all those years,' Tess

295

murmured. She roused herself. 'Anyway, it'd be good to hear his side of the story.'

'Can you get us into this Rowan House place?'

'I wouldn't do it yet. Andrew's . . . not good right now,' Tess said. 'He goes through these periods when his mind wanders and he can't recognise even his own family.'

'Would it be better if you went alone with Raven?'

'Perhaps. It might scare him if I bring a stranger, but he always remembers her. Even if he does think she's called Sarah.'

'Sarah?'

'A sister who died young.' Tess sighed. 'First he lost his little sister, then his baby daughter. No wonder he spent the best part of his life cuddling a bottle.'

'So you know what you're supposed to be doing tonight?' Liam asked.

'Yep. Get into conversation with Marianne, find out what she knows. And you'll be . . .?'

'I'll be enjoying some top-quality ABBA, obviously.'

Tess laughed. 'You really are new around here. And?'

'And keeping my ears open for the buzz in the village about Charity. Is Prue Ackroyd coming?'

'She's supposed to be,' Tess said. 'Gracie volunteered some of the Women's Guild to do make-up, plus the catering for cast and crew. But no one except Oliver's seen anything of Miss Ackroyd since Charity was found.'

'Well, if she does turn up, keep an eye on her, OK?'

'OK.'

He disappeared out into the hall while Tess waited for the rest of the Women's Guild volunteers to arrive.

Marianne and Candice turned up first, with Raven in tow. Gracie was hot on their heels.

'Tess. Here already?' Marianne came over to embrace her.

All had been forgiven now Tess and Raven were friends again, the 'Sam incident' firmly in the past. Tess wasn't sure what had been said, but she was happy that her status as Cherrywood's leading femme fatale had been short-lived. Let Bev and Peggy fight that one out between them.

'You're very early,' Candice said.

Tess laughed. 'Yes, I wanted to bring my contributions for the buffet over before anything happened to them. By which I mean before Raven ate them.' She nodded to the Tupperware container of iced buns she'd made that morning.

'Oi. I resent your accusations of bun thievery,' Raven said. 'You know, being forced to smell them while they baked was a form of torture akin to matchsticks under the fingernails. But did I ask for one? Nope.'

'You asked four times. I had to let you lick the spoon to keep you quiet. And the bowl. And the blender.'

'Unbaked bun doesn't count as bun. It's basically a drink.'

'What did you bring, then?' Tess asked her. 'You were still in your pyjamas half an hour ago.'

'That's because I got my contribution sorted in advance so I could treat myself to a lie-in, darling.'

'Lie-ins don't normally last all day.'

'Mine do.' Raven held up a carrier bag. 'See? Lemon drizzle cake.'

'What, you baked?'

'Don't be hilarious. We've had enough corpses around

here lately – I don't want to be adding any more to the body count. This is Morrison's finest.'

'You oughtn't to joke about that, Raven,' Gracie said disapprovingly. 'I still can't believe it. A skeleton, up there all this time! Right there in the garden while we were having our meetings.' She shuddered. 'That poor little girl.'

Marianne shook her head. 'Don't talk about it, Gracie. Tess was the one who found her. I'm sure she'd prefer not to be reminded of it.'

'Don't mind me,' Tess said. 'I'm fine. I mean, I'm not, it was pretty traumatic, but . . . well, I'm glad she's going to be buried properly at last.'

Candice nodded. 'She deserves a grave where we can mourn her.'

Tess had opened her Tupperware tub to examine her buns, but from the corner of her eye she kept a close watch on Marianne and Candice to see if their expressions would give anything away.

But there was nothing. Both looked sombre, and Marianne perhaps a little pale, but there was barely a twitch when Charity was mentioned. And yet they knew something, she was sure of it.

Secrets, all over the place. Even she had one, Tess reflected, thinking of the detective ex-boyfriend with the fake name currently mingling with villagers in the main hall. She'd been seeing far too much of him recently. What was worse, she'd started to enjoy it.

It was this murder business. It was bound to bring them closer, working together, finding themselves in emotional situations like the discovery of Charity's body last week. God, she'd been so close to staying the night at his! What could she have been thinking?

Bonding over a murder investigation was hardly a solid basis for letting him back into her life; making herself vulnerable a second time to feelings she'd worked hard to get free of. She needed to be stronger. After all, it wouldn't be long – she hoped – until the case was cracked and Liam would be gone.

'Can you believe Clemmie and Prue knew, all these years?' Gracie was saying when Tess tuned back in. 'And they never said a word – just let that horrible woman get away with it.' Her brow lowered. 'She should have been punished while she was alive. It simply isn't right, is it?'

'If you'd known Connie like Marianne and I did, you might understand,' Candice said. 'When you moved here, she was a frail old lady. But when she was younger . . .' She shivered. 'Let's just say I'm not surprised – not by any of it.'

'I don't know what I'm going to say when I see Prue.'

'It's not Prue's fault, Gracie,' Marianne said. 'She was a child. The way Connie treated her and Clemmie – we'd call it abuse, in this day and age.'

'Hmm.' Gracie's lips had pressed into a line. 'Yes, and so was the baby a child, wasn't she? Completely defenceless. If it was up to me – well, Prue's lucky I'm not the law.'

'So what did you make, Gracie?' Raven asked, obviously deciding a jollier subject was in order.

'Oh, this isn't mine,' Gracie said, looking down at the

large cake tin in her arms. 'Peggy asked if I could bring it in my car.'

'Come on then, let's see what Cherrywood's cake queen has come up with this time.'

Gracie removed the lid with a flourish.

'Um . . . wow,' Raven said, blinking. 'She's gone a bit retro for this one.'

Marianne glanced into the tin. 'It's Mr Darcy, isn't it?'

'Fresh out of the lake at Pemberley,' Raven said. 'I don't think she does cakes with their shirts on.'

Tess shook her head. 'We've created a monster.'

'Let's hope this one doesn't end up all over Bev's face,' Raven whispered to her.

Or all over Peggy's, Tess thought. It was amazing the woman could still find time for making cakes between multiple cleaning jobs, tarot readings and boiler room BDSM sessions.

Bev arrived next, along with a gaggle of her Players, who started getting into costume for the opening number. Pressed in by folk decked out in Seventies jumpsuits and sequins, Tess felt relieved that she hadn't let Bev press-gang her into doing a song. After a year of impersonating Cher (and occasionally Dolly) with Ian at the pub, she was sick of the sight of flares. Rhinestone brought her out in a cold sweat too.

Peggy arrived quite late with two carrier bags full of bread rolls, but the last of their little gang was still missing. Half an hour until showtime, and there was no Prue Ackroyd.

'Maybe she's not coming,' Tess whispered to Raven as they buttered rolls on the sandwich table. They were on food prep duty while the other ladies helped the cast with their make-up.

'Understandable, isn't it? You heard how Gracie was talking before. It's going to be that times a thousand once she starts showing her face around the village again.'

Tess sighed. 'Poor Miss Ackroyd. I can't help feeling she was one of the victims here. Marianne's right: it was child abuse, the way her and Clemmie were treated.'

'I know. Connie was the real villain, but she's dead, isn't she? People are angry – of course they are, a baby was murdered. They want someone to blame.'

'It just feels so unfair.' Tess flinched when she thought of the scar on Prue's cheek where her mother's wedding ring had cut the skin. How brutal must it have been, to still leave a mark nearly sixty years later? 'Connie hurt her too, Rave.'

'This is Cherrywood, darling,' Raven said. 'If it had been Aunty Clemmie – well, people liked her. But Miss Ackroyd was always seen as her mother's daughter, and now people know Connie was a killer . . .'

'Miss Ackroyd hated her mother. They didn't speak for fifty years.'

'People don't care about that. They just enjoy having their prejudices confirmed. Miss Ackroyd's done something wrong, they never liked her, and now they can justify why that was.'

'Shhh,' Tess whispered. 'Look.'

A hush fell on the crowded room as Prue Ackroyd finally made her appearance, hugging a plastic tub.

'Hello,' she said in a faltering voice. 'I . . . brought biscuits. Oatmeal.'

'Prudence.' Bev gave her a curt nod, then turned back to the cast member she was making up.

Gracie didn't even bother with a nod. She just turned, stared for a brief moment, then turned away again.

Marianne glanced at Candice, who nodded. Then she went to greet Prue, wrapping her in a warm hug.

'Prue, my darling,' Marianne said when she released her. 'We're so glad you're here at last. Now, will you come and give me the benefit of your expert eye over here? My poor Donna looks ill – too much foundation, I think. I never can seem to get it right.'

Miss Ackroyd summoned a weak smile. 'Of course.'

Peggy and Candice had joined them now, fussing and bustling around Miss Ackroyd. Peggy cooed over her homemade biscuits while Candice admired the way she'd done her hair. Miss Ackroyd looked pleased and flattered by the unprecedented attention, if a little dazed.

Tess turned to look at Raven, then blinked in surprise.

'Rave, are you crying?' she whispered.

Raven flicked away the stray tear. 'No. Shut up.'

'You are! What is it?'

'Well, it's that lot, isn't it? Going out of their way to show her they're still her friends, in spite of what happened. Girls together, supporting each other.' She shook her head. 'For so long I thought Grandmother was this cold, distant person,

302

but I understand her now. Really, when you break through her defences, she's rather lovely. Don't tell her I said that.'

'It is sweet, isn't it?' Tess said, watching the little gang as they guided Miss Ackroyd to the buffet table.

But in the back of her mind, a little voice was whispering, wondering – did one of them do it? Who, in this room, was a killer?

'I can't believe it took joining the Women's Guild to bring me and Grandmother together,' Raven was saying. 'I've never felt closer to her than I have these past two months. The things she's done, the stories she's got to tell: it's amazing.'

Tess squeezed her arm. 'I'm glad. Come on, let's go show Miss Ackroyd some support too. Gracie and Bev'll soon come round when they see the rest of us rallying.'

Chapter 28

Raven and Tess joined the little gang and said their good evenings to Miss Ackroyd.

'Do call me Prue,' she said to Tess. 'I'm not your teacher any more. Miss Ackroyd belongs in the past, with a lot of other things I'd like to leave there.'

Tess smiled. 'I'd like that.'

When they were sure Prue was feeling comfortable, the others gradually drifted back to what they'd been doing, leaving Tess alone with her.

'Did Oliver bring you down?' she asked.

'Yes. I was in two minds about coming, but he absolutely wouldn't take no for an answer.' She smiled. 'He's a good boy.'

'Why didn't you want to come?'

'I didn't know if people . . . if I'd still be welcome,' Miss Ackroyd said, breaking eye contact.

'Of course you are,' Tess said gently. 'You didn't do anything wrong.'

Miss Ackroyd cast a glance at Gracie. 'Not everyone seems to think so.'

'People are still in shock. They'll learn to understand.'

Tess remembered the diary in her pocket. It was rather delicate – Prue still didn't know who had taken it and why. But it had to be returned, sooner rather than later. Tess was about to broach the subject when Prue took her elbow to guide her a little way from the crowd.

'Teresa . . .' She looked around, as if worried they might be overheard. 'There's something I need to speak with you and Oliver about, when you have a moment. It's about that girl – that Nadia Harris.'

Tess was alert at once. 'You don't know where she is?'

'No. But I think . . . I think I might have worked it out. I was sitting with Nelson the other night, knitting bears for the shoeboxes, when it occurred to me.'

'What occurred to you?'

'The connection. Nadia Harris, and my sister. It may be nothing, but I can't help thinking . . .' She glanced furtively around, but everyone seemed engrossed in their tasks. 'You remember my Aunt Mercy, don't you?'

'Mercy Talbot? Yeah, I remember her working in the library when I was a kid. Was she your aunty?'

Miss Ackroyd nodded. 'My mother's sister. I was very close to Aunt Mercy, growing up – but that's neither here nor there.'

'Prue, I'm not sure I'm following,' Tess said. 'What does this have to do with Nadia?'

'You're a clever girl, Teresa. Don't you understand?'

Tess shook her head in puzzlement. 'No. No, I—'

They were interrupted by Marianne calling to them. 'Come on, you two. We don't have time for chitchat, it's curtain up soon. Prue, are you going to help me with this make-up?'

'We'll talk later, in private,' Miss Ackroyd murmured. 'Come and see me at the cottage with Oliver. I'd like to tell you together, since you've taken such an interest in the matter.' She gave Tess a conspiratorial nod and headed over to Marianne.

'What were you two whispering about?' Raven asked when Tess joined her at the food prep table.

'Dunno,' Tess said, feeling a little dazed. 'She was saying she had something to tell me about Nadia Harris.'

Raven looked up from the punch she was mixing. 'She's not heard from her?'

'No. She wasn't making much sense – said something about her Aunt Mercy. She wants to talk to me and Oliver later.' Tess nodded to the punch bowl. 'What's in that?'

'Oh, just fruit juice, lemonade, that type of thing. Dash of red wine. It's my own special sangria recipe.'

'Can I try it?'

Raven shrugged. 'Help yourself.'

Tess tasted a spoonful and coughed.

'Rave, this must be ninety per cent rum,' she gasped.

'Well, yeah. We want everyone to have a good time, don't we?'

'You can't serve that to the cast. They'll fall off the stage.'

'Relax. It's for the after-party, OK? I'm going to put it in the fridge to chill.' Raven frowned. 'What's up with her?'

Gracie was approaching, looking very green around the gills.

'Are you OK, Gracie?' Tess asked when she reached them.

'Girls, I'm so terribly sorry.' Gracie looked mortified, and not a little like she was about to throw up. 'I feel awful doing this after it was me who volunteered everyone, but I think . . . I really think I might have to go home.'

'What's wrong?' Raven asked. 'Are you sick?'

'Yes, all of a sudden I feel quite poorly. I am so, so sorry.'

'There has been something going around.' Tess patted Gracie's arm. 'Go on home, Gracie, and put yourself to bed. We can hold the fort here.'

'Do you want a lift?' Raven asked.

Gracie smiled weakly at her. 'Oh, could I? Thank you, dear. I'm sorry to give you the trouble, but I . . . I don't think I ought to drive.'

When Raven had gone, Tess helped herself to a plate of food and wandered over to where Marianne was applying make-up to the actor playing the young groom.

But there was no time for idle chat. Tess was grabbed right away by Candice and assigned an actor of her own to help with costuming and make-up. In the background, Bev got the chorus warmed up with a bit of 'Money, Money, Money'.

Tess winced. The am-dram group had been bad enough when all they'd had to do was act – the performance of *A Midsummer Night's Dream* on the bandstand in the park last summer was still spoken about with affectionate groans by the villagers. But now Bev had seized on musicals, the Players were expected to carry a tune too – the only thing they were even worse at than acting. Tess mentally congratulated herself on having volunteered for a role backstage, where she wouldn't have to sit through the caterwauling.

Liam would, though. She'd spotted him in the second row, where he'd get a good, clear sound. Ha! Every cloud . . .

An hour later, the performance was in full swing and Tess's sandwiches were still uneaten. After every scene, the actors piled in demanding help with costume changes and fresh make-up. Not until half-time did Tess get a chance to breathe.

As soon as the interval was called, the entire cast and crew packed into the backstage area and descended in a swarm on the buffet, where Peggy was serving. Tess just had time to grab herself a glass of punch from the fridge before the carnage began.

Filled with a need to escape the hot, sweaty bodies, Tess wove through the crowd and sneaked out on to a little balcony that overlooked the moorland swells surrounding the village. She breathed deeply, savouring the warm summer air.

'Hiding?' a voice behind her said a few minutes later.

'Liam.' She turned to smile at him, for once not bothering to suppress the stomach-jumping sensation she experienced whenever she saw him.

He joined her, leaning up against the balcony at her side.

'So shall we talk about the case or would you prefer some light flirting first?' he asked.

'Case, please.'

'I've got nothing,' he said, shrugging. 'Plenty of talk. Some people who think Prue got off lightly not getting charged as an accessory to murder, some who think this is further evidence she killed her sister. But it's just gossip; there's nothing we didn't know. You got anything?'

'I've been rushed off my feet, Lee. It's a hard graft, am-dram.'

'You didn't talk to Marianne?'

'I've barely had time to breathe, let alone sleuth,' Tess said. 'Oh!'

'Oh what?'

'I just remembered – Miss Ackroyd. She cornered me earlier and told me she'd worked something out – the connection between her sister and Nadia Harris.'

Liam straightened up. 'God, if she has I might just have to give her a big smacker on the lips. What is it?'

Tess pulled a face. 'I don't know, we got interrupted before she could tell me.'

'Tess, seriously? You let her get away from you with that under her bustle?'

'She didn't want to tell me until we were in private. Me and Ol are going to talk to her after the show.' Tess popped a ham sandwich into her mouth. 'She said it was something to do with her Aunt Mercy,' she mumbled through a mouthful of bread.

'Who was she?'

Tess put down her plate. 'Mercy Talbot. She was this old lady who worked in the library when I was a kid. She must've died twenty years ago. I'd totally forgotten her and the Ackroyds were related.'

'So she was, what, the mother's sister?'

'Yeah. I can't think what she's got to do with anything.'

'Nadia Harris . . .' Liam muttered. 'I wonder if this Mercy knew the Harrises.'

'Don't waste brainpower on it now, Lee. I'll grab Oliver as soon as the show's over and we'll get Miss Ackroyd to tell us the whole story.'

'We're getting closer, Tess. Aren't we?'

'I think so. Loose threads, but some of them are starting to ravel out at last.'

He turned to look at her. 'So what happens then, partner?'

'What happens when?'

'When we've solved the case. What happens next?'

'We tell the police, don't we? Justice is served and we can all sleep at night knowing our chances of being murdered in our beds have just dropped significantly.'

'That's not what I mean.' He paused. 'I'll be going home.'

'Oh. Yeah.' She looked out over the moorland, where a lone curlew was wailing plaintively to its mate. 'Where is home for you these days? Still London?'

'Yes.' He followed her gaze. 'Beautiful country here, isn't it? Bleak, but kind of hypnotic. If it had been my home, I don't think I'd ever have felt right living in a city.'

'No. I never did, although I tried to convince myself it was where I ought to be. You feel so hemmed in, when you've got the open spaces in your blood.'

'You don't miss it?'

'Some things. The excitement of it, being where there was always something going on. The career prospects, obviously.'

'Tess, I'm so sorry.' He moved closer. 'When I got assigned to the Porter case, I honestly never meant for anyone to get hurt. I never expected to . . .'

'To what?'

'Never mind.' He smiled as the off-key strains of 'Take A Chance on Me' drifted through from the hall. 'You remember this one?'

Tess suppressed a smile of her own. 'No.'

'Fibber.' He turned her to face him. 'Go on. Tell me you do.'

'OK, so I do,' she said, letting the smile escape. 'The house band were playing this our first night in Vegas.'

'That's right. I took you to Venice.'

She laughed. 'To fake Venice.'

'Well, it was still pretty magical.' He swept a soft fingernail down her cheek. 'I meant it, you know. When I joked about seeing if they could fit us in at the Chapel of Love. I'd have gone through with it if you would.'

'No you wouldn't,' Tess said, half in a dream.

'I would, you know. I promised to book us a honeymoon in the real Venice if you said yes. Do you remember?'

'Yes,' Tess whispered. 'I remember.'

And then they'd got back, and there'd barely been time to unpack before Tess had learnt the truth about the man she'd fallen in love with. For two weeks it had been just them in Las Vegas – two blissful, wonderful weeks of making love and being in love and believing it would last for ever. Then Tess's world had come crashing down. Supposing she had gone to the Chapel of Love with Liam that night. Where would that have left her?

311

He pulled her into his arms, and she didn't fight it. Strip away all the distrust and uncertainty, and the basic, simple truth was that Tess liked being there. She always had.

'I'll miss you when I'm gone,' Liam murmured, rocking her in time to the music just as he had that night in Vegas when, laughingly but with an earnestness in his eyes, he'd asked her to become his wife – and she'd come so, so close to saying yes.

'I've kind of got used to you being around too,' Tess admitted.

'You forgive me, then?'

'It's not that easy, is it? But we're . . . friends, I guess.'

He slid his hand into her hair, the other caressing her back in a way most un-friend-like. 'Let me take you to Venice,' he whispered in her ear.

'No, Lee. That gondola's sailed.'

'Then we'll launch a new one. We could start again, Tess.'

'Start again?' The words were sweet; tempting. Dangerous.

'You and me. Clean slate. Why not wipe it clean if we want?'

Tess was suddenly aware of his lips, brushing against her neck. She felt a shiver of excitement as they moved along her skin, although she knew that wasn't allowed.

'We shouldn't be doing this,' she whispered.

'Then tell me to stop.' Liam waited a second, then carried on nuzzling. 'Can't, can you?'

'We don't just get to kiss and make up, Lee. I'm a different person now.'

'You taste the same,' he murmured against her neck, and she could feel him trembling. 'Oh God, Tess . . .'

'I should get back inside.' But her own body proved her a liar, moulding to Liam's as his lips teased her skin.

'Tessie, come to Venice with me. I don't want to lose you again.'

And his mouth was on the skin under her ear, and then it was on her hot cheek. And then . . . then it was right there, on her lips, and his fingers burrowed deep into her hair, and she wrapped her arms around his neck . . .

A shrill scream filled the air. Tess pushed Liam away, snapping back to reality in an instant.

He looked at her, fear in his eyes. 'What now?'

'Come on.'

Tess ran inside, Liam hot on her heels. There was a crowd blocking her view of the buffet table, and impatiently she pushed her way through.

Then she saw what it was they'd all gathered to gawp at, and for a second she wondered if she might be about to pass out again.

It was Prue Ackroyd, stretched lifeless on the floor.

Chapter 29

For a moment, Tess wondered if for the second time in her life she was about to faint.

Miss Ackroyd . . .

Then her adrenaline kicked in. An emergency was occurring, and someone needed to act.

'Why is everyone standing around?' she demanded. 'Didn't anyone call an ambulance?'

Candice, who was kneeling by Prue's prone figure, looked up at her. 'I think it's too late,' she whispered. 'She's dead, Tess.'

'A doctor can be the judge of that. Get a bloody ambulance on its way here, right now. And get the police, and . . .' Tess paused. 'Nobody touch anything. This is a crime scene. I think.'

Liam finally fought his way through the crowd to join her.

'Right. Everyone calm down. Police. Er, ex-police.'

Peggy blinked. 'I thought you were a gardener.'

'Now I am. I used to be a copper.'

'What do we do?' Tess asked him.

'What you just said. Cordon off the area and request that

314

no one leaves until the police get here. I'll contact Della. And if someone could go ask the audience if there's a doctor in the house, that would be the most useful thing we could do right now.'

'I'll do it,' Marianne said.

'Everyone, if you have seats, please go out and take them,' Liam said. 'Try to rein in any panic. We don't know for sure that this woman's dead.'

'What happened?' Tess asked Bev, who was standing near her. But Bev just shook her head, looking dazed. The whole room seemed to be in a state of collective shock.

Liam exhaled when Marianne arrived back with an elderly gent, rather frail-looking. 'Please tell me you've got a medical degree.'

'I have,' the man said. 'Although it's been a while since I used it. Dr Lyon, retired GP. Where am I needed?'

The crowd parted to reveal Prue's prostrate form. The doctor knelt by her while Liam did his best to clear the crowd. Finally, only a handful of people remained.

'Someone's moved her,' the doctor said.

'I did,' Candice said. 'I put her in the recovery position. I . . . I'm first aider for our Women's Guild. Was that wrong?'

'No, it was good thinking.' He held his ear close to Prue's mouth, then took her wrist. 'But I'm afraid it's unlikely to do her any good now.'

'You mean she's . . .'

'No pulse. Not breathing. The paramedics will have the equipment to examine her more thoroughly, but it doesn't look good. I'm sorry.'

Instinctively Tess reached for Liam's hand.

Raven appeared at Tess's shoulder, as ashen as everyone else in the room. 'Ambulance will be here in ten minutes,' she said.

'Rave, what the hell happened?'

'Miss Ackroyd disappeared in the middle of a conversation. After ten minutes, Grandmother went to look for her and found her retching in the toilets. She helped her back out here, and Miss Ackroyd said she was feeling a little better when she suddenly started rambling nonsense and batting wildly at nothing, as if she could see things we couldn't. She kept repeating "Charity" over and over – it was scary to see. Then she . . . she . . . she grabbed at her chest and just . . . keeled over.'

'What had she been eating?' Liam asked.

'God, I couldn't tell you. Nothing the rest of us didn't have.'

Tess looked at Liam. 'Gracie went home ill too. She said she had a tummy bug.'

'Ring her,' Liam said. 'Someone needs to speak to her, right away.'

'Right.' Raven yanked out her mobile and pulled up Gracie's number.

Tess and Liam watched anxiously as she held the phone to her ear.

'No answer,' she said at last.

'How was she when you took her home?' Tess asked.

'I thought she was OK,' Raven said. 'But I mean, Miss Ackroyd seemed fine until . . . well, until she didn't.'

'Raven, can you go round and check on her?' Liam said.

Raven nodded. She was always a clear head in a crisis, very much her grandmother's granddaughter in that respect if nothing else. 'On it. I'll ring as soon as I know anything.'

She left, and minutes later the paramedics burst in.

But Dr Lyon had been right. It was too late. After five minutes of frantic activity by the professionals, Prudence Ackroyd was declared dead at the scene.

*

'Here.'

Gradually Tess became aware of Liam's arm, supporting her as he guided her out to the balcony.

'Where are we going?' she mumbled.

'To get some fresh air. You need to sit down for a minute.'

'Don't baby me.' She wriggled free of his arm. 'I'm fine, I'm not going to faint. I don't need you to look after me every time there's some bit of drama.'

'You just saw someone you've known your whole life dead on the floor, Tess. Stop trying to show me how tough you are and let yourself deal. It's allowed.'

She sagged back into his arm again, secretly relieved to have permission to feel as crappy as she did.

'She was so . . . happy,' she whispered as he guided her into a seat. 'Earlier, when everyone welcomed her. I think it was the first time she'd really felt part of a group who cared about her. Lee, it's so unfair.'

'It's murder, Tess. It's never fair.'

'You really think she was murdered?'

'That's the obvious answer, isn't it? But we'll see. She wasn't young; we can't rule out natural causes.'

'Oliver,' Tess whispered. 'It'll hurt him so much.'

She jumped as her phone buzzed in her back pocket.

'Raven?' Liam asked as she looked at the screen.

'Yeah.' She swiped to answer. 'Rave, is she OK?'

'She's fine,' Raven said, and Tess let out a low whistle of relief. 'Tucked up in bed. I almost felt guilty for dragging her out to answer the door, she looks so rough.'

'Thank God.' Tess turned to Liam. 'She's OK, Lee. Sick, but not unconscious or anything.'

'How's Miss Ackroyd?' Raven asked.

'Dead.'

There was silence for a moment as the word hung heavy in the air.

'Tell Raven to get Gracie to hospital,' Liam said. 'If whatever's made her ill is the same as what killed Miss Ackroyd, she needs checking over right away.'

'Rave, Liam says you need to get her to A&E soon as.' Tess paused. 'She didn't mention what she ate, did she?'

'That was the first thing I asked her.'

'Good thinking. Could she remember?'

'At first she said she hadn't had anything since lunch. Then she remembered she'd tasted some of the icing on Peggy's cake before bringing it over. That was all; she didn't have anything off the buffet.'

Tess looked at Liam. 'The Darcy cake. Gracie had a bit of the icing.'

'Right. I'll tell the crime scene guys; they're bagging up now.' He disappeared back into the hall.

'Thanks, Rave,' Tess said. 'Call me when you leave the hospital, let me know she's OK.' She hung up.

As the surge of adrenaline she'd experienced when action was needed died down, she slumped back into the chair. A sudden, overwhelming need to sleep hit her. But there was no time; there was still so much to . . . to . . .

She didn't know if she'd been asleep hours or minutes when Liam appeared again.

'There's nothing else we can do here.' He helped her up. 'The CSIs have bagged up samples of all the food to send for toxicology tests, and police will be asking for witness statements tomorrow.'

'Lee,' Tess mumbled, still half asleep. 'Mercy. Prue never told me about Mercy. And now she's . . . Is she really dead?'

'I'm sorry, Tess. Come on, I'll walk you home.'

Chapter 30

It was six days later when Liam heard from Tess again. He'd called her a couple of times to see how she was holding up after the events of the *Mamma Mia* performance, but she hadn't picked up. He got the distinct impression she was avoiding him.

He knew she'd respond to the text he'd sent today, though. If there was one thing guaranteed to bring Tess Feather scurrying back into his life, it was murder.

Liam glanced at the fresh printouts on his desk: the toxicology reports Della had summarised for him. What with those and the post-mortem results, there was no doubt Prue Ackroyd's death had been the result of a cold, premeditated murder. An arrest was about to be made. And this time, it was one he felt might actually result in a conviction.

Sure enough, quarter of an hour after he'd texted her, there was a knock at the door of the groundskeeper's cottage. When he opened it, there was Tess, her eyes glistening and cheeks pinkened by the exercise.

'Bloody hell, did you run all the way?' he asked.

'Pretty much. What do they say then, the reports?'

'Come in and I'll show you.'

She followed him upstairs and took a seat at his desk.

'So?' she said.

He almost laughed at her eagerness, but restrained himself, thinking it was hardly appropriate given the circumstances.

'Here,' he said, passing her the post-mortem summary.

She scanned it. 'Cardiac arrest brought on by . . . poisoning. So it was the food.'

'Mmm. Prue ate something that didn't agree with her.'

'Grayanotoxin, it says here. What's that?'

'A poison found in plants of the rhododendron family,' Liam said. 'Azalea, in this case.'

'And trace amounts of cannabis sativa.' She looked up. 'Cannabis?'

'Yep. But it was the azalea that killed her.'

'Azalea . . .' Tess muttered. 'Someone told me about azalea being poisonous. When?'

'Well remembered,' Liam said, nodding. 'It was me, at that first Women's Guild meeting. Your friend Raven wanted to grow it near your herb garden.'

'That's right. You said it'd give us a tummy ache if we muddled it with the rosemary.'

'And so it would, in small amounts. But when you're seventy-five and you've been given a large, concentrated dose, the effects can be rather more severe,' he said. 'Gracie Lister had a lucky escape. The toxicology reports confirm the Darcy cake was the source of the poison, but it was only in the chocolate icing used for the hair. The small amount she had was enough to make her ill but not to kill.'

'And you think it was put there by . . .'

'I was working in Peggy Bristow's garden for the best part of a week, and yes, I can confirm she has a thriving azalea bush.'

Tess shook her head. 'It can't have been Peggy.'

Liam sighed. 'Not this again. Tess, it had to be someone. Your faith in human nature's adorable and everything, but someone in this community is a killer and as upsetting as it is, it's probably someone you call a friend.'

'No, I mean it literally can't have been her. Not who killed Clemmie, anyway. You're thinking whoever did it hid in the house after the Women's Guild meeting broke up, right? Well, Miss Ackroyd drove Peggy home, so it couldn't have been her.'

'Yes, that's a pretty convenient alibi.' Liam looked grim. 'Too convenient, if you ask me.'

Tess frowned. 'You mean Peggy might have got Prue to take her home on purpose?'

'Maybe. There would've been plenty of time for her to go back to Ling Cottage after Prue Ackroyd dropped her off, wouldn't there? Prue told her she was going to the supermarket, so she knew Clemmie would be home alone. A pretty useful way of luring Prue out of the house too.'

'Yeah, but . . . Peggy? She hardly seems like a murderer.'

'You didn't think she seemed like someone who was into X-rated cosplay until recently either. People can surprise you, and not always in a good way.' Liam pushed the toxicology report over his desk. 'It was her cake – this confirms it – and I'd hazard a guess it was her azalea too. How else could it have got in there? Levels were way too high to have been accidental.'

'Death by Darcy, how very Women's Guild,' Tess muttered. 'Has she been arrested?'

'Not yet, but it'll happen over the next few days. I bet she didn't see that in her crystal ball.'

'Why, though? What's Peggy's motive? You said she couldn't be Nadia Harris.'

'I'm starting to wonder if I was too quick to dismiss that particular theory,' Liam said. 'She told me at the spa afternoon that her family had moved around a lot when she was young – doesn't that say army brat to you? She's about the right age too.'

'But you said she had her own paper trail.'

'Peggy Bristow has her own paper trail. Maybe the woman we know as Peggy Bristow isn't the original Peggy Bristow.'

Tess frowned. 'Identity theft, you mean?'

'Could be. If that's it there'll be a break in the chain somewhere. I just need to keep hunting until I find it.'

'If Peggy's our Nadia, that only gives her a motive to kill Clemmie. Why kill Miss Ackroyd too?' Tess demanded. 'And why now? Miss Ackroyd was staying with her for weeks – Peggy could've done it any time and made it look like an accident.'

'You said Prue had worked out the link between Nadia and her sister. If Peggy knew she was about to spill the beans to you and Oliver, she might've decided Prue needed silencing.'

'But how will she claim her inheritance, if she's living as someone else?'

'That I've yet to figure out,' Liam admitted.

Tess glanced at the post mortem report again. 'Cannabis. What was that for – just to make sure Miss Ackroyd would be feeling peckish?'

'The cannabis is from a different source.'

'Eh?'

He smiled. 'You ever wondered what makes those cupcakes of Bev's so popular around the village?'

Tess's eyes widened. 'No!'

'Mm-hmm. I've suspected it for a while, actually, ever since the show. Moreish, aren't they? Really seem to give you an appetite.'

'Bloody hell.' Tess stared at him for a moment. 'You know, I've lived most of my life alongside these people and I'm starting to wonder if I ever really knew any of them. So Peggy's now our chief suspect?'

'Yep. Still a lot of unanswered questions though. I'll keep digging into her history; you—'

'Keep my eyes and ears open, I know.'

'And see if you can find a chance to grill Marianne. She still knows something.'

'OK.' Tess scanned the report again. 'Are we sure Prue was the intended victim? Gracie had some poisoned icing too.'

'Only a small amount. Peggy gave her some to deflect any suspicion that she knew it was in there, maybe.'

'But anyone could have eaten it at the *Mamma Mia*

performance, couldn't they? How would she know it'd find its way to Prue?'

'Who was serving it?' Liam asked.

'Well, Peggy was, when I went up.'

'There you go, then. All she had to do was wait for the intended victim to turn up, then dish out a big chunk of the poisoned head section. Localised means easy to target.'

'Sin will out,' Tess muttered. 'I think Peggy knew what was in the Charity letters, Lee. "Sin will out," she said at the show.'

'Did she now?'

'Yeah. I thought it was coincidence, but it's quite an unusual phrase, isn't it?'

'It doesn't help her case, certainly.'

There was silence for a moment.

'Right,' Tess said at last, getting to her feet. 'I'd better go. I'll be in touch.'

'Wait.' Liam stood up too. 'I've got something to give you first.'

He took a gift-wrapped parcel from his drawer and handed it to her.

She frowned. 'What is it?'

'Nothing much. I saw it when I was out shopping and it made me think of you. Now we're close to cracking the case and I might be leaving soon . . . well, call it a souvenir.'

Tess looked at the gift for a moment, then peeled off the paper.

It was a snow globe, the kind they sell in holiday gift

shops. Inside was a tiny model of the Rialto bridge in Venice. Tess shook it and watched snow cascade over the arches.

'We can't go back, Lee,' she said quietly. 'Let's just stay friends and leave it at that.'

'I don't want to be just friends.' He stepped closer and laid a palm on her cheek. 'I don't think you really do either. Do you?'

'It's all I've got to offer.' She removed his hand from her face. 'I'm sorry, but . . . I really think it'd be better all round if we kept things strictly business.'

'You didn't think so when you kissed me at *Mamma Mia*.'

'You kissed me.'

'Yes, and then you kissed me back.'

'That was . . . I wasn't myself.'

'Tess—'

'Lee, I can't, really. Look, let me know if you find anything out, OK? I'll see you around.'

'Wait!' Liam said as she slung her bag over her shoulder. 'You forgot your present.'

'I can't take that.'

'Please. I got it for you.' He held it out to her. 'For old times' sake. It might've been fake Venice, but what I told you on the bridge that day was real. When I said . . . you know.'

When he'd said he loved her for the first time. When he'd asked her, half-jokingly and half in deadly earnest, to be his wife. She couldn't have forgotten that; he knew she couldn't.

Tess looked into his face. Liam didn't blink. She hesitated for a moment, then took the snow globe and left.

Chapter 31

Raven bounced into Tess's room the following Saturday when the church clock had just chimed six a.m. – or when the church clock would have chimed six a.m. if it didn't have considerably more manners than Raven Walton-Lord.

'Time to get up!' she yelled.

Tess groaned and pulled her pillow over her ears. 'Bugger off, Rave. I'm sleeping.'

'Come on, it's my birthday! It only happens once a year. You can sleep when you're dead.'

'One might have thought that at the ripe old age of thirty-one, the novelty of birthdays was starting to wear off a bit.'

'That'll never happen.' Raven prodded her. 'Get up and hang out with me. That's an order from your birthday queen.'

Tess removed the pillow to look at her friend. She was wearing the golden birthday crown, a plastic thing with big pink gemstones. Raven took birthdays and their associated privileges very seriously.

'Fine, I'll get up.' Tess swung her legs out of bed. 'Aren't you going round to see your nan?'

'We're having a family celebration tomorrow with Andrew. Taking him out for a meal. Today I'm all yours.'

'Until I have to go to work this afternoon.'

'All the more reason to enjoy ourselves now.' Raven's eye was caught by the snow globe that had appeared on Tess's bedside table. 'Where did that come from?'

'Liam gave it me a few days ago. It's Venice.'

'Why?'

'A souvenir of our time working on the case together, he said.' Tess shook it, hiding the Rialto in a blizzard. 'We went there together, me and him. I mean, not the real Venice – they had a mock-up at our hotel in Las Vegas. It was kind of magical.'

'Hmm.' Raven regarded her through one narrowed eye. 'You two seem to be getting close. You're not falling for him again, are you?'

'We're just friends.'

'Sure?'

'Totally sure.'

'Do you think you'll stay in touch, now you're crime-busting buddies?'

'Dunno,' Tess said, replacing the snow globe thoughtfully. 'If we're making a clean break, it feels like we should make a clean break, you know? I've spent nearly eighteen months trying to get over that man, and . . . well, I don't know if we can be just friends any more.'

'Because you fancy him too much.'

Tess shrugged. 'If you want to put it bluntly.'

'Think you could ever learn to trust him again?'

'Could you, if he'd done the same to you?'

'No.'

'There you go.' Tess pulled on her dressing gown. 'Come and get your present then, Birthday Queen. I got you chocolate for breakfast, according to custom.'

'Ooh, goody!'

In the living room Raven sat cross-legged on the sofa, as eager as any five-year-old, while Tess dug out her present.

'Arghh! Brilliant!' Raven said when she'd opened the package Tess handed her. It was the latest novel from her favourite author, Diana Skye. *The Centurion's Bride*. I've been dying to read it.'

'You're welcome.'

'God, Mum, I was just about to,' Raven said, rolling her eyes. 'Make us a cup of coffee to have with my breakfast chocolate, will you? You have to wait on me hand and foot today. Them's the rules.'

'So just a normal day then.' Tess went to put the kettle on.

When she came back in five minutes later, Raven was frowning at the back cover of her new Diana Skye. 'This sounds weirdly familiar.'

'You'll have read the blurb online, won't you?' Tess said, handing her a mug. 'I'm assuming you get her newsletter.'

'I suppose I must have.'

Tess sighed. 'Miss Ackroyd was a fan too, you know. I never would've pegged her for a romantic, but she did have a softer side.'

'I know,' Rave said soberly. 'Poor Ol's taken it hard. I think he was like the son she never had or something.'

'Let's get him over after I finish work, shall we? We can share a bottle of wine and watch a film. Birthday girl's choice.'

Raven didn't answer. She'd flicked to the middle of her book and was staring at it, her lips moving silently.

'What's up?' Tess asked. 'Don't tell me it's not up to her usual standard. I spent good Cher money on that.'

'Tessie, why is this giving me déjà vu? "His breath a feverish pant, Hunter pushed his body against Clara's throbbing maiden flesh."'

Tess looked puzzled for a moment. Then she met Raven's eye with a jolt of realisation.

'Gracie's notebook!'

'No.' Raven shook her head. 'No way. I've been reading Diana Skye for fifteen years. There's just . . . no way.'

'So what, Gracie copies Diana Skye passages into her notebook for handwriting practice?'

'She can't, can she? This one only came out three weeks ago.'

'Then Gracie must be . . . you know. *Her*,' Tess said.

Raven shook her head again. 'Bouncy, permy Gracie is Diana Skye? She always makes me think of a human Tigger.'

'She must be, mustn't she?' Tess nodded to the author's name on the cover. 'Is it a pen name?'

'No one knows,' Raven said. 'Diana's a complete recluse; never makes public appearances. There's a conspiracy theory that she's a secret alter ego of Barbara Taylor Bradford.'

'Or she's a secret alter ego of Gracie Lister.'

'But she was so angry – Gracie, at the spa day,' Raven said. 'You remember? She said Diana's books were a load of tosh.'

'Covering, maybe?'

'I don't think so. She sounded genuinely pissed off.'

They were interrupted by the landline phone in the hall, making them both jump. It almost never rang, except for occasional calls from family and telemarketers.

'I'll get it,' Raven said, getting up.

'Who was it?' Tess asked when she heard Raven come back in, not looking up from the Diana Skye book she was flicking through. 'Sales call?'

There was no answer. She glanced up, and blinked to see Raven's face streaked with tears.

'Oh my God! What's happened?' Tess jumped up and folded her friend in a hug.

'Tessie, I just got the worst birthday present ever.'

'What? Tell me, quick.'

Raven choked on a sob. 'I just inherited a fucking mansion.'

*

While Raven rang her grandmother, Tess phoned Bev to ask if someone else would be able to cover her shift that afternoon. She didn't want to leave Raven alone.

Tess knew Andrew's mental health had taken a turn for the worse lately, but no one had said anything about how he was physically. And Raven had been so sure it was just a rough patch – he'd had them before, and he always came through. The call from Rowan House to tell her that her uncle had gone in his sleep had come completely out of the blue.

'I just can't believe it,' Raven said. 'I knew he wouldn't be around for ever, but . . . it isn't fair, is it? I was going to see him tomorrow; the whole family were going to . . .' She gulped. 'Tess, it's my birthday.'

'I know,' Tess said gently, stroking her hair. 'Death's a bastard. It never plays fair, and it hardly ever gives us the chance to say goodbye.'

'Grandmother had her chance. The receptionist said she visited yesterday. She was the last person to see him alive.'

'Well, I'm glad she's got that comfort.' Tess drew back from the hug to look at her friend. 'Did they say what happened?'

'His liver. What else?' Raven reached for a glass of gin on the coffee table. 'It had done well to serve him this long, after everything he'd put it through. It failed in the night – painless, they promised me. He just went to sleep and then he . . . never woke up.'

'I'm glad he didn't suffer.' Tess shook her head. 'Clemmie, Prue and now Andrew. Charity too. Makes you want to punch something, doesn't it?'

'Makes me want to drink something,' Raven said, knocking back the rest of her gin and reaching for the bottle. 'I'm planning to be paralytic by midday, darling, if you wouldn't mind putting me to bed.'

'What happens now? About your uncle?'

'I'm heading over tomorrow with Grandmother and Mari to talk about funeral arrangements, what to do about his effects and all that stuff.' Raven blew her nose on the tissue Tess passed her. 'We were supposed to be going out for a family meal. Some birthday celebration, eh?'

'Want me to come? I can ask Bev to rearrange my shift.'

Raven patted her leg. 'No, you've done enough. Leave this for the family.'

'If that's what you want.' She paused. 'Rave . . . it was definitely natural causes, wasn't it? There couldn't have been any sort of, you know, foul play?'

'It was his liver, Tess; the doctor confirmed it. He drank himself unconscious nearly every day for years. He was eighty-six. It's not exactly a surprise.'

'No.' Tess pushed her fingers into her hair. 'You're right, I'm being ridiculous. It just seems a coincidence, that's all. Charity was his daughter, and whoever this killer is, they seem intent on bumping off everyone connected to her.'

'How could they have got to him? Rowan House wouldn't let in a stranger without checking it out with the family. I think this time it really is just a coincidence.'

'I guess so.' Tess shook her head. 'Ugh, I must have murder on the brain.'

'Does Liam still suspect Peggy?'

'Liam and the police. He reckons she could be arrested any time now.' Tess sighed. 'I know all the facts point that way, but . . . do you think she could have done it?'

'I wouldn't have said any of them could. But one of them must have.'

'Yeah, that's what Liam keeps telling me. I suppose I'm just in denial.' Tess reached for the bottle of gin and poured herself a half measure. 'Here's to Uncle Andrew, eh?'

'To my favourite uncle, who was worth more than fifty Cherrywood Halls. I hope he's at peace finally.' Raven bumped her tumbler with Tess's as they toasted the old man goodbye.

Chapter 32

'H ello, you,' Raven said when Tess rang her mobile the next day. 'Aren't you at work?'

'I just finished. Thought I'd call and see how you're holding up. Are you at Rowan House?'

'Yeah, we're just packing his stuff into boxes.' Raven sighed. 'It's horrible seeing his room get dismantled. Like we're taking him out of existence piece by piece.'

'I'm so sorry, love,' Tess said gently. 'Did you see him?'

'No. The undertaker took him before we arrived. I don't think I could've coped with that.'

'How are your nan and Marianne doing?'

'Grandmother's devastated, although she's stiff-upper-lipping it as ever. Marianne's her usual practical self, forcing the two of us to hold it together.'

'Is there much to go through?'

'Just his books, and some electronic bits and bobs he was in various stages of taking to pieces.' Raven coughed. 'And, er, there was some booze he'd managed to smuggle in somehow. Heavily watered down, thankfully.'

'You don't say,' Tess said, amused. She guessed there must be a member of staff listening.

'Anyway, the police took that, along with a bowl of peanuts and some other snacks.'

Tess's ears pricked up. 'The police were there?'

'Yes, yesterday. Nothing to be concerned about,' Raven said. 'They're just being extra cautious in the wake of Miss Ackroyd's death.'

'Right. So how did he seem two days ago when your nan saw him?'

'There seems to have been a mix-up about that. It was the holiday cover receptionist who rang yesterday, not the usual one – I think she must've muddled Grandmother with someone else's visitor. Anyway, no one from the family's been here for a week.'

'Oh. Well, call me when you're done.'

'OK.'

Tess put her phone away. She was heading for St Stephen's, where she'd arranged to meet Oliver.

He was waiting at the door, fresh from the morning service in gleaming surplice and the scarfy thing Tess had learnt was called a tippet.

'Hiya,' she said, standing on tiptoes to kiss his cheek.

'Hi Tessie.' He examined her face. 'How're you doing, love? You look tired.'

Tess rubbed her eyes. 'Exhausted. I didn't sleep a wink last night.'

'How's Raven holding up?'

'She's . . . rallying. She's at Rowan House, sorting through his things.' Tess glanced up at Oliver's purple-rimmed eyes. He didn't look like he'd been sleeping any too well himself. 'How about you, Ol?'

'I'm OK.'

'You're not, though, are you?'

He sighed. 'It's funny, isn't it? I have to deal with death all the time; it goes with the job. I've conducted dozens of funerals for people I would've called friends. But Miss Ackroyd . . . It really hit me hard. She was a nice old lady, you know, underneath the dragon act. Flawed, a product of the hand life dealt her, but . . . I couldn't help liking her.'

'I know. Me too.'

'I think it's the unfairness of it, partly. That she'd been taken just when she was finally facing up to the demons of her past. She was on the cusp of a whole new life – a kinder, happier one. Someone took that from her.' He cast his eyes down. 'Well, she's with God now. It isn't right for me to wish her back.'

'It's right to be angry.' Tess took his hand and gave it a squeeze. 'We'll catch whoever did this, Ol, I promise.'

'I hope so.'

'I've got something I want you to have, actually.' She took Prue's diary from her pocket. 'This was Miss Ackroyd's. The diary I told you about – the one Liam took from Ling Cottage the night we went there looking for clues. I'd planned to give it back to her after *Mamma Mia*, but . . . well, I think she'd want you to have it now she's gone.'

Oliver frowned. 'Me?'

'Who else did she have?' Tess said. 'I've been reading it. I thought there might be something there – a clue Liam had missed, maybe.'

'Was there?'

'No. It's just a teenage girl's diary – one who suffered a hell of a lot. But I think that if the village knew what was in it . . . There's another side to Prue Ackroyd in here, Ol. I understand her better now.'

'In what way?'

'I always thought she bullied her sister – babied her, you know, because Prue saw her as weak. But really, I think that was just Prue's way of looking after Clemmie. Prue might not have been able to prevent Charity's death, but she stood up to Connie on a hundred other occasions in order to protect her sister. Tried everything to get her away from Ling Cottage, out of reach of Connie's abuse. As much as Prue dominated over Clemmie, I believe she'd have done anything for her. I doubt Cherrywood gossip would be so hard on her, if they knew what she'd gone through.'

Oliver glanced at the leather notebook. 'It's rather private, Tess. I'm not sure how I feel about reading this.'

'Prue would want you to, I'm sure,' Tess said quietly. 'To know there was a reason she was the way she was, and to defend her memory. There's still a lot of bad feeling, even now she's dead. You can use this to clear her name to some extent – it really ought to be you, as the person closest to her at the end.'

'It is unfair, the way she's been judged,' Oliver murmured. 'People don't understand.'

'They might, if they knew. Keep it. Use it to help her the only way you can, now.'

Oliver hesitated, then nodded and tucked the book away.

'Is it true about Peggy?' he asked.

'That she's been arrested?' Tess nodded. 'I'm afraid so. Police took her in this morning.'

'You think she did it?'

'No. Yes. I don't know.' Tess gave her head an angsty shake. 'I mean, Liam thinks she might have, and he knows what he's talking about. I'm starting to think I'm just chronically naive. It's so hard to picture it being any of them, but Lee's right: someone did it.'

'I'm going to reserve judgement till they make a charge,' Oliver said. 'I might go visit her today, though, if I'm allowed. Be on hand with some spiritual guidance.'

'Ol . . . did Miss Ackroyd say anything to you, the day you drove her to *Mamma Mia*?'

'Like what?'

'Anything about her Aunt Mercy?'

He frowned. 'Mercy Talbot? No, why would she?'

'It's just that at the performance she said she had something to tell me and you – some connection she'd made between her sister and Nadia Harris. It involved her Aunt Mercy somehow. She wanted to talk to us in private, but . . . she never got the chance.'

'Sorry, Tess. She never mentioned Mercy to me.'

Tess sighed. 'Figures. So can I see her?'

'Yeah, come on. She's in the family plot.'

Oliver led her out into the churchyard, to a new grave

338

where a small patch of earth was still bare. A simple wooden cross with a brass plaque marked the spot, until a permanent memorial could be erected. The grave was swamped in flowers, wreathes and soft toys.

'Charity,' Tess murmured. 'When did you bury her?'

'The day before Miss Ackroyd died. Just a quiet little service: me and Miss Ackroyd. She didn't want anyone else. There's been so much hysteria about it, she felt it was best to keep the burial a private affair.'

Tess bent to examine the tags on the tributes. So many names she recognised. Gracie, Bev, Peggy, Tammy, Candice; even old Fred Braithwaite up at Black Moor Farm.

'Looks like nearly everyone in Cherrywood has been to pay their respects.'

'Yes. It's really touched a nerve for people.'

Tess fumbled in her handbag for her contribution: a little knitted bear she'd made. 'Well, this is for her too. I'm glad she's at rest now, poor lamb.'

'You want some time alone with her?' Oliver asked.

'I wouldn't mind.' She patted his arm. 'Thanks, Ol.'

When he'd gone, she knelt by the grave and laid her bear with the other tributes, making a little bed for him in the middle of Gracie's wreath.

'Well, kid, you never should've ended up here,' she muttered. 'Not like this. I'm sorry.'

She gazed at the writing on the plaque. Charity Ackroyd – Ackroyd and not Walton-Lord, she noticed. Not even an hour old when she died. Every one of the deaths recently had been linked to her: this little baby.

Perhaps this never had been about Clemmie's money. Prue's murder had been premeditated, but as Liam had observed, Clemmie's seemed very much like the action of a moment. Greed was a strong motivator, yes – but so was revenge.

'Who's fighting your battles for you, Charity?' Tess murmured. 'Who wants the people who wronged you dead?'

'Talking to yourself?'

She stood up. 'I'm talking to Charity. What're you doing here?'

'I spotted you outside the church with your friend,' Liam said. 'I guessed you might be coming to see her. I thought we were going to do it together.'

Tess flushed. 'Sorry. I just wanted some time alone with her.'

'Because you're avoiding me.'

'No I'm not.'

'Yes you are. I rang you three times after you texted me about Andrew.' He took her elbow and turned her to face him. 'What did I do wrong, Tessie? Is this about when we kissed?'

'Liam, please. We're in a graveyard.'

He dropped his arm from hers. 'You're right. Sorry.'

'I'm not avoiding you, OK?' Tess said. 'Well, I am, but it's nothing personal. There's been so much happening lately, I'm . . . drained. Emotionally and physically. I don't have the energy for undercover ex-boyfriends as well.'

'Just remember I'm here if you need someone, all right? If you need a friend, I mean.'

'Thanks.'

They were silent for a moment, looking down at the

grave. Clemmie's was to the right of it, with her mother Connie's next to hers. The marble looked clean and new after a recent scrubbing to remove some graffiti daubed on it by one angry Cherrywooder. Its fresh appearance felt inappropriate somehow.

'Doesn't seem right, does it?' Tess said. 'Connie sharing the same space as Charity.'

Liam glanced at Clemmie's grave. 'I'm glad mother and daughter were buried close to each other though.'

Tess blinked back a tear. 'And the last grave to be added will be Prue's. That's it, the whole family. None of them left.'

'When's the funeral?'

'Next Thursday. Candice and Marianne have taken charge of the arrangements.'

Tess moved along to Connie's headstone and read the inscription. *Constance Faith Ackroyd, née Armley. Dearly loved mother, 1927–2013.*

Dearly loved mother – the words seemed so hollow now. Clemmie would have chosen them – loyal daughter to the end even after all her mum had done.

'What was with the virtue naming?' Liam asked.

'It's a tradition with the women of their family,' Tess said. 'Wander around here and you'll find any number of Chastities, Mercies, Sobrieties and other horrors. All finished now, I suppose, with Prue being the last of them.'

Tess didn't look at him while she spoke. She was still staring at Connie Ackroyd's gravestone. Cogs were whirring in her brain: connections, clues, fragments of conversation, binding themselves together.

The last of them . . .

'Mercy Talbot'll be buried here somewhere,' she said.

'OK. And?'

'Let's find her. I might be having another of my famous humps.'

The cemetery at St Stephen's was small but crowded. Gravestones huddled together as if sheltering from the cold, the oldest almost worn away after hundreds of years battling the harsh moor-edge winds. It took them a full fifteen minutes to find Mercy Talbot's marker.

Tess was the one to discover it. Mercy was sharing a headstone with her husband Alf under an oak tree at the church's far end.

'Lee!' she called. 'I've got it. And I was right.'

He came to join her.

'Well? What were you looking for?'

'Read it.'

' "Here lies Alfred Talbot, cherished husband, 1919–1983",' Liam read. ' "Also his wife, Mercy Prudence Talbot, née Armley. After life's fitful fever, she sleeps well. 1927–2001." '

'Well?'

'Prue Ackroyd was named after her aunt, I guess. What of it?'

She shook her head. 'Come on, you're a detective. Look at the dates.'

'1927–2001.' He looked up, his eyes widening. 'Oh my God.'

'Same birth year as her sister. Connie and Mercy were twins, Lee. Non-identical twins.'

'And you're thinking—'

'It explains everything, doesn't it?' Tess's eyes glittered as she seized him by the wrist. 'They say they run in families. Charity Ackroyd could have been a twin too. That was what Miss Ackroyd was planning to tell me, the night she was murdered.'

'And Nadia Harris – she'd be, what, the elder twin?'

'Not impossible, is it? Sickly Betty Harris was expecting a baby. Supposing that baby miscarried? A grieving mother, a desperate father, a young girl pregnant outside marriage – there'd be no way Clemmie could know she was having twins without seeing a doctor. It makes perfect sense that she'd agree to hand her baby over to them in the hope of a better life for the child.'

'Clemency Ackroyd didn't know the Harrises though,' Liam said.

'But her best friend did.' Tess pressed his arm. 'Time to blow your cover, Lee. I think you need to talk to Marianne Priestley in a professional capacity.'

'Will she be at home?'

'No, she's at Rowan House, dealing with Andrew's affairs. We'll wait at your place till they get back.'

He nodded. 'Right.'

They were halfway to the gate when Liam's phone started jangling.

He scanned the screen. 'Della, my police contact. I'd better get this.'

Tess watched as he took the call. 'Del. What's the crack?'

'OK,' he said after a minute. 'Wow. No, I certainly didn't see it coming. Thanks, I'll be in touch.'

'What is it?' Tess asked.

'Well . . .' He seemed to be avoiding her eye. 'Two things. Neither good news.'

'What?'

'Andrew Walton-Lord. The cause of death might not be as natural as the doctor who first examined his body believed.'

'You mean it wasn't liver failure?'

'It was. But there are substances that can trigger liver failure, especially in people where that organ is damaged already.'

'What substances?'

'Rancid fat from rotting peanuts, for one. The police bagged up a bowlful of dry-roasted – the flavouring would've hidden the taste to an extent, but examination confirmed they were bad.'

Tess was silent for a moment while this sank in. 'What's the other thing?'

He grimaced. 'Tess, I don't know how to tell you this.'

'What? Lee, come on.'

'It's Raven. She's confessed to the murders of Andrew Walton-Lord and Prudence and Clemency Ackroyd.'

Chapter 33

'What? No!' Tess shook her head. 'That isn't possible.'

'I'm afraid so,' Liam said. 'Della told me Raven calmly walked into the station, told them she'd done it and demanded to be arrested.'

'But they can't think she's guilty.'

'No. They're holding her for questioning, though. People don't randomly confess to murders for no reason. She knows something, Tess.'

Tess sagged against a tree. 'This . . . Lee, none of this is right. I spoke to her less than an hour ago and she was fine – I mean, not fine, because her uncle had just died, but there was no hint she was about to confess to being a triple murderer.'

'Something must've happened to make her do it. Did she not say anything?'

'Nothing significant. Except – she did mention some mix-up about her grandmother not having visited Andrew two days ago after all. Yesterday the receptionist said she had.' Tess paused. 'And if she found out from staff afterwards that

345

Andrew might've been murdered . . . she's protecting Candice, Lee.'

'Oh God.' Liam groaned. 'Silly girl. Does she really think she's going to be able to get away with it?'

'She's grieving. She's not thinking straight.' She frowned at him. 'You remember our deal. You promised you'd make sure Raven was kept safe and out of this mess.'

'Well, yes, but I can't stop the woman randomly confessing to murders she didn't commit, can I?'

'You can get her out, though. You have to help her, Liam. Ring your contact and . . . I don't know, just do something. Please.'

'I'll do whatever I can.' He leaned against a gravestone. 'This is not helpful, Tess. It just felt like we were getting somewhere. Now we've got Peggy and Raven both under arrest, Candice possibly lying about where she's been and another potential murder on our hands, barely a week after the last one.'

'I need to talk to Raven,' Tess said. 'Can you get me to her?'

'I can try. Come on, let's drive to the station.'

'Hang on, let me grab Oliver first.'

Liam shook his head. 'Tess, we're not going to read her the last rites.'

'Ol's a vicar – people trust him. He might be able to get to Raven if we can't.'

Liam sighed. 'A priest, a barmaid and a gardener walk into a police station – I think I heard this one. All right, go on.'

*

When they arrived at the station, Candice and Marianne were already there. Candice was leaning over the desk in reception, looking daggers at the officer on duty.

'You will give me access to my granddaughter, young man, or I'll take this all the way to the top. The Chief Inspector is a personal friend –' she glanced at his badge – 'Constable Jeffries, and he could have a considerable influence on your fledgling career, I'm certain.'

'Madam, if I could make just two points. Firstly, I've told you that you'll be given an interview with your granddaughter just as soon as procedure allows. And secondly, I'm fifty-three, I've been a copper for over twenty years and my rank, if you'd like to examine my badge more closely, is sergeant.'

'Well . . . you should bloody well act your age then,' Candice retorted, her usual cool demeanour nowhere to be seen.

'Ouch,' Oliver whispered to Tess.

'Candy, now calm down,' Marianne murmured, guiding her away from the desk. 'We won't get anywhere with anger. Harsh words butter no turnips, you know.'

'Oh, sod turnips. As far as I'm concerned, Sergeant Jeffries can shove his turnips right up his—'

'Ahem,' Tess said.

'Tess,' Candice said, blinking. 'And Oliver, and . . . Sam. What are you all doing here?'

'You might as well call me Liam, Mrs Walton-Lord,' Liam said. 'Undercover's no good to me now. Anyway, Tess has already told half the village who I am.'

Tess shot him a look. 'Two people, come on.'

347

But Candice wasn't interested in that. There was only one thing on her mind.

'I'm assuming you've heard what's happened to my Raven,' she said to Liam.

'I have. I was with Tess at the time; she knows all about it.' He nodded to Oliver. 'And she insisted we bring the reverend here too.'

Candice turned triumphantly to Marianne. 'Excellent. They can help us.'

Marianne looked a little dazed. 'I'm sorry, but what on earth is going on?'

Candice sighed. 'Darling, there's . . . well, there's something I've been keeping from you. Mr Hanley here – he's not a gardener.'

'I am, actually,' Liam said. 'Your photinias have thrived since I've been on this case. You're welcome.'

'Case?' Marianne said.

'The letters,' Candice said in a hushed voice. 'I hired him to investigate. He's a private detective.'

'You daft old thing,' Marianne said, giving her a squeeze. 'You did that for me? Why?'

'After what happened to Clemmie, I was afraid you might be in danger.' She looked at Liam. 'I would ask if you'd made any progress, but at the moment I'm far more concerned about getting access to my foolish granddaughter.'

Liam nodded. 'Let me see what I can do.'

He approached the desk and smiled at Sergeant Jeffries. 'Ken. How's it going?'

Sergeant Jeffries looked up from some paperwork. 'All right, Liam? Sorry, but if you're after Della she's not in.'

'When will she be back, do you know? There's something important I need to talk to her about ASAP. The Ackroyd case.'

'She's out and about at the moment. Should be back in an hour.'

'Rowan House, right?'

Ken smiled. 'Now come on, you know I can't tell you.'

Liam grinned. 'Well, worth a shot. I'm in the Green Man for a pint later if you fancy joining me.'

'I might just do that.'

Liam went back to the others.

'OK, plan time,' he said in a low voice. 'Oliver, can you stay here and text Tess if Della turns up?'

'All right. What does she look like?'

'Thirty-two, very tall, Black, close-cropped hair, really stunning – you can't miss her.'

Oliver saluted. 'Roger, Captain.'

But Tess's thoughts were lingering somewhere else. So Liam thought Della was stunning, did he?

Tess had wondered why this police contact was so very cooperative when Liam needed information. Turned out he'd charmed his way into her good graces – and into God knew what else as well.

'The rest of you, come with me,' Liam said. 'We'll hole up in the caff across the road where we can talk in private.'

Tess, Marianne and Candice followed him out of the

station to a rundown-looking greasy spoon, where he ordered a couple of pots of tea.

'OK,' he said to Candice and Marianne. 'You two. If you want me to help the kid out of this mess then I need answers, now.'

Tess rested a hand on his arm. 'Lee.'

He looked at her, and his brow lifted. 'Right. Sorry, ill-judged bad-cop mode.' He turned back to the two old women. 'Er, in your own time. And I'm very sorry about your brother-in-law, by the way, Mrs Walton-Lord.'

Marianne was frowning. 'What did Tess just call you?'

'Lee. She calls me it on the rare occasions she forgets she can't stand me.'

'When did you two get so chummy?' Candice asked.

'Oh, ages ago. We nearly got married one time,' Liam said with a dismissive flick of his hand. 'Miss Priestley, I need to ask you some questions about your relationship with the Ackroyds.'

Marianne looked like she'd just stepped off a rollercoaster at full speed. 'Sorry, I think I misheard. Tess, did he just say you were married?'

'Nearly married,' Tess said. 'I met him down in London. We were in a relationship for a while. I don't like to talk about it.'

'Anyhow, that's not important right now,' Liam said. 'So, Miss Priestley, here's what we know. We know that Clemency Ackroyd became pregnant at the age of seventeen by Mrs Walton-Lord's future brother-in-law, Andrew. And we know that you knew all about it.' He put up a hand as she opened her mouth to speak. 'It's no good denying it.'

'I wasn't going to deny it,' Marianne said. 'I was going to say it was sixteen. She was seventeen when the pregnancy came to term, yes.'

'Oh. Right.'

'Don't mind him, he's always like this,' Tess said to Marianne. 'You're lucky he hasn't got a desk lamp in your face.'

Liam frowned at her. 'Tess, can you not undermine me in front of the witnesses?'

'I'm not undermining, I'm good-copping.' She looked at Marianne. 'When did Clemmie tell you she was pregnant?'

'As soon as she knew,' Marianne said. 'She skipped a monthly – we weren't savvy like girls today are, but we knew what that meant well enough.'

'Who else did she tell?'

'Me and Prue, that's all. She didn't know what to do, poor lamb. She loved Andrew, but . . . well, I think she realised he'd be too weak to go against his father. And she was right.'

'So she asked you to keep her secret.'

Marianne nodded. 'Right away she started making plans, plotting a future for the baby. Prue and I helped her conceal the pregnancy, even from their mother. It wasn't easy, but we did it.' She blinked hard. 'Right until the end, anyway.'

'Were you the only ones who knew she was expecting?' Liam asked.

'Andy did, of course. He was as much help as usual, Lord rest him. He'd usually passed out by midday. His father, Roland, was the only other one who was told. Clemmie did it herself – marched right in to have it out with him. She told me all about it.'

'Really?' Tess had never met Roland Walton-Lord, but she'd seen photos and he was a formidable old chap. She couldn't picture mild-mannered Clemmie Ackroyd confronting him.

Marianne nodded. 'She told him she wanted an abortion and if he didn't pay for it then she'd have the baby and tell everyone Andrew was the father. Drag the family name through the mud.'

'But she never really intended to have an abortion, did she?' Liam said.

'Of course not,' Marianne said. 'She just wanted the money – and he paid her well for silence: a lot more than the cost of the procedure. Clemmie put the lot into a building society account for the baby when it came of age. Swore she'd never touch a penny for her own sake.' Marianne shook her head. 'Prue loved her sister, but she never respected her. Called her weak. But in her own way, Clemmie was very strong indeed.'

'And meanwhile, Mrs Harris had lost her baby.'

Marianne blinked back a tear, and Tess saw Candice give her hand a squeeze of support under the table.

'Yes,' she whispered. 'A seven-month miscarriage. Poor Betty, she was devastated. The colonel was driven half mad with worry. He was convinced the grief might be the death of her – like I said, she was always sickly. So I told them . . . I said I knew where they could get a baby, if they just kept the miscarriage quiet. A friend of mine; a young girl in service who'd got herself in the family way. They could take the child and pass it off as their own.'

'And I'm guessing they jumped at the chance, right?' Tess said.

'Betty did. She was delighted with the suggestion. The colonel wasn't keen at first. He was a terrible snob, like I said, and a servant girl's bastard didn't satisfy his sense of self-importance. But when I told him who the baby's father was . . . he thought a lot of aristocratic blood. That and Betty's pleading soon won him over.'

'Tell us what happened the day the baby was born,' Liam said quietly.

Marianne flashed a look at Candice, who nodded.

'Go on,' she whispered. 'They're on our side.'

'We know there were two,' Tess said. 'That Charity was a twin.'

Marianne looked shocked. 'How could you know that? No one knew except . . . did Andy tell you?'

'Prue.'

'Prue? No. She didn't know.'

'She worked it out. Gave me a hint, right before she died.'

'Well, it's true,' Marianne murmured. 'There were two babies.'

'Tell us,' Tess said.

Marianne winced. This was obviously the most painful part of the memory for her.

'Of course, I didn't know it was twins the day Clemmie went into labour. I was sitting with her in her room at Ling Cottage. I sat with her most days – we knew she was getting close to her time, and my sister was a midwife. I'd raided her books, ready to do my bit when it happened. Like naive schoolgirls, we thought it would be that easy.'

'So when she went into labour . . .'

'Prue and Connie were both out when Clemmie's waters broke. I panicked, of course. I was only eighteen, and although I'd been with my sister when she'd delivered babies, I'd never done it myself.' Marianne smiled. 'Clemmie was a model patient, though. She really was quite Madonna-like, although I could tell it hurt like hell. You know what she said, when after four hours the baby finally crowned?'

'What?' Tess asked.

'She said, "Mari, my love, you must be exhausted." Four hours of labour with no drugs, no pain relief of any kind except her dad's old whisky decanter – I was ladling that into her pretty liberally, for what little good it did – and she was worried about me.' Marianne laughed, but it quickly turned into a sob. 'Sorry. I still remember it so clearly.'

'Take a moment if you need to,' Liam said gently.

'No, I . . . I'm fine, honestly.'

'What happened when you'd delivered the baby?' Tess asked.

'Clemmie started badgering me almost as soon as I'd cut the cord. I barely had time to give the little thing a wash. Clemmie didn't even hold her, although I could see she was longing to. She told me to wrap her up and get her out, before Connie came home.'

'You think she knew what her mother was capable of?'

Marianne shuddered. 'She knew there'd be trouble, at any rate. And her panic infected me – she looked so frightened.

So I wrapped the little girl in a towel and bundled her up in my big coat, and I took her to her new mum and dad. Oh, they were ecstatic. You should have seen Betty cooing over her. Beautiful little Nadia, with all her thick blonde hair. A few days later they registered her as their own child, with the intention she should never know the truth.' She sighed. 'Betty promised to write, let me know how the girl got on. But her letters dried up after a few years and I haven't heard a word about Nadia Harris since.'

'She seems to have gone completely off the radar,' Liam said. 'I can't find a trace of her since she was eighteen.'

'I've looked for her too. When Nadia turned twenty-one, around 1985 it must have been, Clemmie asked me to help find her. The little pot of money she'd put aside had grown quite considerably, collecting interest, and Clemmie wanted to get it to her somehow. But no one seemed to know where she'd disappeared to. I wondered then if she was still living.' Marianne took a sip of her tea with a trembling hand, then grimaced when she realised it had gone cold. 'I tried to convince Clemmie to spend the money herself, after that – to use it to break away from her mother. But she was adamant. It was Nadia's money and no one but Nadia would have it.'

'She must still have been in labour when you left to take Nadia to the Harrises,' Tess said.

'Yes. My sister would have been able to tell that, I suppose. But Clemmie and I, we didn't fully understand how these things worked. It must have scared her to death when she realised she was all alone and there was another baby coming.'

'Charity,' Tess murmured. 'Did you know, afterwards? That Connie killed her?'

Marianne shook her head. 'Clemmie told me she'd been dead at birth,' she whispered. 'Prue backed her up too – because her sister asked her to, I suppose. She'd never have done it for her mother's sake. Perhaps that was why Connie left her half of the cottage, even after so long with them not speaking. A reward for her silence.' She snorted. 'Oh, Prue would have hated that.'

'Do you know anything about the necklace?' Liam asked. 'The one Charity was buried with?'

'The Madonna and child? I know it was one of a pair. Clemmie bought two, one for each of them. She gave one to me to take to the Harrises for Nadia. I made sure Betty got it – the colonel never would have allowed it. He was determined to cut the biological mother out entirely. But Betty was soft-hearted, and she promised to keep it safe for the child when she was old enough. And Charity's we buried with her, of course, in the garden.'

'Do you know why Clemency wore a St Christopher?'

'She wore it for Nadia,' Marianne said, biting her lip as she fought tears. 'St Christopher, patron of travellers and of soldiers. Protecting her, wherever she and her army family travelled. Clemmie thought she could keep her safe by proxy.'

'How much did Prue know about all this?' Tess asked.

'She didn't know about Nadia, or the arrangement I'd made with the Harrises. Only Charity.'

'Clemmie didn't trust her?'

Marianne shook her head. 'Prue wasn't a bad person, but she could be avaricious, and she was a chronic meddler. Clemmie never told her about Nadia or the money. And Prue, for her part, was very hurt that Clemmie stayed with Connie after what she'd done. It did drive a wedge between them.'

Liam turned to Candice. 'Did you know all this?'

'Not all of it.' She glanced at Marianne. 'Much of it, yes.'

'You knew there were twin girls, that one was given up for adoption and one – you believed – was stillborn. You knew that child's name was Charity, and that the threatening letters you'd hired me to investigate had also been signed by a Charity. Why did you hold back information from me, Mrs Walton-Lord?'

'Because . . . because it wasn't my secret to share,' Candice said quietly. 'And because . . .'

'Because what?'

She looked at Marianne again. 'Because I knew it was against the law. Taking a baby, concealing a birth, giving it away without involving the authorities. That frightened me more than I liked to say.'

'You thought Marianne might go to prison?' Tess asked in a softer voice.

'Yes. Yes, I did.'

Marianne squeezed her hand. 'You soft old thing. You were worried about me, all this time?'

'Of course I was.' Candice smiled. 'You know, I'd miss you if they took you away from me. I hoped we could find whoever was writing the letters and put a stop to it, pay them off,

357

perhaps – make it all go away without having to involve the police. I felt sure it must be Prue sending them.'

'Will I go to jail?' Marianne asked Liam.

'It's a serious crime, certainly,' Liam said. 'But your age back then, and the time that's elapsed, and – no offence – your age now means you'd be very unlikely to get a custodial sentence. If you want my advice, you'll be as cooperative as possible from now on. Coppers look kindly on folk who are on their side.'

Tess's phone buzzed and she took it out to read the message. 'It's Ol. Lee, your girlfriend's back.'

'Tell him we'll be ten minutes. I've just got a few more things to get straightened out.'

'Do you know who's been writing me those letters?' Marianne asked.

'I'm . . . closing in, I think,' Liam said. 'What I can tell you is that I'm ninety-nine per cent sure that whoever wrote the letters also killed Prudence and Clemency Ackroyd, and perhaps Mr Walton-Lord too.'

'Who do you think that person is?'

'I don't know who they *are*, but I've got a good idea who they *were*. Nadia Harris.'

Chapter 34

Oliver was sitting in the reception area at the station, pretending to scroll Facebook on his phone, but in reality he was furtively looking at Liam's friend Della.

Liam was right: she was stunning – about six foot tall, with perfect bone structure. She looked like a model or something. Actually, the person she most reminded him of was Serena Williams, the tennis player, only with short hair. Were she and Liam seeing each other? Tess would be gutted if they were.

She'd say she wasn't, obviously, and then pretend to be fine and be extra, super fine with sugar on top just to prove it, but she'd be crying inside. No matter how much Tess tried to kid herself that she'd put Liam Hanley behind her when she left London, Oliver wasn't blind. He wasn't stupid either.

What was taking them so long? Were they having a round of crumpets?

'Um, excuse me,' he said to a passing police officer.

The man turned, then took a step back. Oliver hadn't had time to change and was still in his gear from the service earlier. It tended to disconcert people when they encountered vicars in full dress anywhere but inside a church.

'Can I help you, Father?' the man asked.

'Reverend. I was told that my fr—my parishioner was here being questioned in connection with a murder case and I thought I might be allowed in to . . . administer some spiritual comfort.'

The man's face was a mask of suspicion. Oliver tried not to take it personally. That was the man's job, after all, to be professionally suspicious.

'I can produce some ID if you like,' he said. 'And if you need to frisk the cassock for files or hacksaws, that's fine too. I just want to speak to her for ten minutes. Raven Walton-Lord.'

'Well . . . I don't know. Let me talk to the gaffer.'

Oliver watched him approach the woman, Della, and saw them whispering together, the male officer occasionally nodding in his direction. Then Della came towards him with a wide smile.

'Reverend,' she said. 'I understand you were asking about Miss Walton-Lord.'

'Yes, I believe she arrived here earlier. Is it possible to speak to her? I imagine she's feeling rather low right now.'

'Come with me.'

*

Marianne shook her head. 'No,' she whispered. 'Not that little baby. Not Clemmie's baby.'

'I'm sorry, but that's where all the evidence seems to point,' Liam said.

'But where is she?'

'I'm not sure yet, but I know where I need to look. In the meantime, be very cautious, OK?'

Candice looked worried. 'You're not saying Marianne could be in danger from this psychopath?'

'I certainly am. The twins, Nadia and Charity, are the link. Everyone who knew about them, who had a hand in this business, is dead – everyone except you, Miss Priestley. And with the letters, yes, I'd say the risk is very great that they will eventually target you.'

'Don't worry about me,' Marianne said stoutly. 'I can look after myself.'

'I'm sure the Ackroyd sisters would have said the same. Be extra vigilant, that's all. Try to avoid being alone.'

'I'll stay close to her,' Candice said.

'Meanwhile, what're we going to do about Raven?' Tess asked.

'What could your granddaughter have been thinking?' Liam asked Candice.

Candice shook her head. 'I can't understand what came over her. She was with us at Rowan House, helping to pack up Andrew's things. There was something she wanted to ask the receptionist about, so she went out to speak to her, and then . . . she never came back. When I went out to check on her, the receptionist said she'd bolted out of the door and driven off.'

'How did you know she was at the station?'

'The duty sergeant phoned me to say she'd waived her right to a lawyer, and to a phone call. She'd just asked him to call to tell us she was safe and that she didn't want to speak to either of us.'

'I don't get this,' Tess muttered. 'What could the receptionist have told her to make her do something so illogical?'

'We thought she might be protecting you,' Liam told Candice.

She blinked. 'You think Raven would do this for me?'

'Of course she would, if she thought you were in trouble,' Marianne said. She turned to Liam, her equilibrium recovered and her practical face on. 'You think she suspected Candice of having something to do with the murders so she turned herself in in her grandmother's place, do you?'

'It's the only explanation I can think of. It goes without saying that she couldn't have done it.'

'And when he says that, you know it must be true,' Tess said. 'He thinks everyone did it.'

'Why might she think you had a hand in it?' Liam asked Candice. 'Any reason you can think of?'

Candice shook her head. 'I have no idea.'

'Raven told me yesterday that you'd been to see Andrew the day before,' Tess said. 'But then when I spoke to her earlier, it seemed there'd been a mix-up.'

'That's right, I hadn't been for over a week. There are two receptionists – one only does occasional cover. I presumed she'd muddled me with someone else's visitor.'

'But suppose she didn't,' Tess said. 'Suppose that was what Raven found out.'

Candice frowned. 'What do you mean?'

362

'Andrew was killed by rotten peanuts. He always had peanuts when I went, in a little glass bowl on his bureau.'

'Yes, they were his favourite. I used to try to ration them, worried about his cholesterol, but he always had them from somewhere. Raven, I suppose – she spoiled him terribly.'

'Or from someone else,' Liam said. 'Do you have the number of Rowan House on you?'

'I have it by heart. Why?'

Liam passed her his notebook. 'Could you write it down for me?'

She did so, and Liam tapped it into his mobile.

'Hello, Rowan House?' he said, his voice dripping with charm. 'I wonder if you can help me. Detective Hanley, my colleagues were with you yesterday. Yes, Andrew Walton-Lord. Could I ask you to check an entry in your visitor book?' He paused. 'The fifteenth of June. I'm not sure what time. Mrs Walton-Lord – is there a signature?' He paused again, then glanced at Candice. 'There is. Would it have been you who was on duty? Your colleague. When could I catch her?' He nodded. 'Thank you, you've been very helpful.'

'How lax is security at that place?' Tess said when he'd hung up. 'They never even checked you were proper police.'

'Good thing too, since I'm not. Anyway, they didn't tell me anything confidential.' He glanced at Candice. 'You're sure you didn't visit?'

'I haven't quite lost my marbles yet, Mr Hanley,' Candice said coldly. 'Yes, I'm sure.'

'Then we've got an impostor. And by the sound of it, one

who's juggling her receptionists to make sure no one gets wise.'

'Andrew used to talk about his sister going to visit, whenever I went with Raven to see him,' Tess said.

Candice nodded. 'To us too. We never thought anything of it. Reality was so far out of his grasp, and he'd fixate on that little girl, Sarah. I assumed he was talking about Raven.'

'And Raven assumed he was talking about you. But it sounds like Andrew might've had another "sister" who came bearing deadly peanuts.'

Marianne shivered. 'How horrible. Poor Andy.'

'I suppose the right costume and mannerisms would have disguised the age difference between her and Candice adequately, if this Nadia was clever about juggling her receptionists,' Tess said. 'She must be quite an actress.'

'I still can't believe it,' Marianne murmured. 'Nadia Harris! After all this time, to have her come back into our lives like this.'

'Come on,' Liam said. 'Let's go see if we can talk Raven out of this nonsense. If we're lucky, we can get all this cleared up and take her home with us.'

*

'So you say Miss Walton-Lord is one of your parishioners?' Della said to Oliver as she led him to where they were holding Raven.

'Er, yes,' Oliver said, conveniently ignoring the fact that Raven had barely set foot in St Stephen's since she'd been expelled from Sunday school for making plasticine willies and sticking them all over the Noah's Ark. 'Her family have been in my congregation a long time.'

'Well, I hope you can talk some sense into her. She won't have a lawyer, and she's adamant she doesn't want to see her family. No one seems able to get through to her.'

'You don't think she did it, then?'

'I think she's about as likely a murderer as my elderly nana. But she wouldn't confess unless she knew something.'

'Like what?'

'Like the person she's covering for,' Della said. 'If she tells us who that is, she can go home now. But as long as she's insisting she did it, I don't know what I can do for her.'

Oliver wasn't sure what kind of room he'd been expecting to find Raven in. A dingy cell with bars on the windows, probably. In fact it was a comfortable interview room with a large glass door where Raven sat scowling at a desk, her arms folded.

Della unlocked the door and ushered him in. Raven looked up, then turned instantly away without making eye contact.

'What's he doing here?' she demanded of Della.

'I thought you might like to speak to your parish priest, if there was no one else we could call for you.'

'Well, you were wrong.'

'Rave, come on,' Oliver said. 'Just let me talk to you for ten minutes.'

'You can't talk me out of it, Ol. I confessed because I did it, that's all there is to it.'

Della shot him a look. 'You see? This is what she's like.'

'Can I have some time alone with her?'

Della looked at Raven. 'If that's OK with her.'

'Suppose,' she muttered.

Della nodded and went out, locking the door behind her.

'So I guess you must be worried about me if you put the vicar dress on especially to visit,' Raven said.

He smiled. 'Surplice, as you well know.'

'Was that how you got in? Did you threaten the duty sergeant with eternal damnation?'

'Worse. I told them you were one of my flock.'

'Ouch. I'll never live that down.'

He reached across the desk for her hands. 'Raven, what's this really about?'

'Ol, I did it, all right? Accept it.' He saw her eyes flick to the camera in one corner, then away.

'You know you didn't.'

'What makes you think it couldn't have been me?'

'OK, then it was you,' he said impatiently. 'So tell me why. Why would you kill Miss Ackroyd and Aunty Clemmie? The odd detention aside, they never did you any harm.'

'Because . . . because of that baby, obviously. They just stood by and watched that horrible woman kill her, didn't they? That needs to be punished. An eye for an eye, a tooth for a tooth, a life for a life – isn't that what the Bible says?'

'Jesus wasn't a fan of that bit. Neither am I.'

'For God's sake, Ol, spare me the sermon,' Raven muttered. 'They paid the price, and . . . and so they should have. I'm not sorry.'

'Yeah? How come you turned yourself in, then?'

'Because . . .' Raven looked like she was on the back foot for a moment. 'Because of Peggy. I couldn't see her take the rap.'

'Right. So why did Andrew have to die? You confessed to his murder too, right?'

Raven looked almost relieved, like this was going to be the easy bit. 'To get my inheritance, of course. I was next in line for the estate.'

'You never wanted the estate.'

'That's only what I told you. People lie.'

'They do. And some of them are a lot better at it than others,' Oliver said. 'You loved Andrew, didn't you?'

'No, I . . . not really. That was all just . . . pretend.'

'Raven, come on,' he said gently, squeezing her hands. 'It's clear you haven't thought this through. Tell me what this is really about. Are you covering for someone?'

She flinched. 'Of course I'm not. I'm confessing.'

'If you're protecting Marianne or your grandmother—'

'I'm not.' She snatched her hands away. 'Stop pretending you know me. You don't know me.'

'Yes I do.'

She snorted. 'Because you're guided by the Lord, right?'

'Because I've known you since we were three years old and you used to push the bigger boys into the sandpit for teasing me,' he said quietly. 'Because I've been with you through happiness and heartbreaks, hundreds of boyfriends who didn't deserve you, I've shared countless bottles of wine with you, and if I've never said this until now I'm sorry, but I love you, Raven. You're one of my best friends. Please don't lie to me.'

She buried her face in her hands.

'What's your best outcome here?' Oliver asked, sensing he was reaching her at last. 'You think the police just let you waltz in and confess to murders with no means, no opportunity, a very shaky motive and a story that doesn't stand up to even the most basic scrutiny? You can't just say, "I'm a murderer, lock me up." They will investigate, and whoever you're trying to protect will be found out. You're making things worse.'

Raven had disintegrated into gasping sobs now, all her grief, her fear, spilling out. Oliver stood up and went to rest his hands on her shoulders.

'I know you're hurting,' he said gently. 'I know you're going to miss him. That's OK. It's OK to hurt, Rave.'

'I will,' she whispered. 'I'll miss him so much. I know he barely knew me most of the time, always thought I was someone else, but I loved him, you know? I never had any family except the three of them. And you and Tess.'

'And your family want you home. Let me take you back there and we'll forget all this. You should never try to handle grief alone.'

She laughed through her tears. 'You know your problem, darling? You're too nice for your own good.'

He smiled. 'But you love me for it.'

'I bloody do as well.'

'Well? Are we going home?'

She paused to wipe her eyes with her sleeve. 'Yes. Yes, I think . . . I'd like to go home.'

Oliver nodded to the camera on the wall, and a minute later the door unlocked and Della came in.

'Um. I'd like to go home. Please,' Raven mumbled.

'You're withdrawing your confession?'

'Yes. I'm sorry for wasting your time.'

'Hmm,' Della said, pursing her perfectly sculpted lips. 'You know, I could charge you with that. But I won't, if you tell me who it was you were covering for.'

Raven shook her head. 'I . . . can't. I'm sorry, but if it comes to that you'll have to charge me.'

'Would it make a difference if I told you I just spoke with Liam Hanley? He's out in reception with your grandmother.'

Raven's head jerked up. 'Grandmother? What's she doing here?'

'She's being considerably more helpful than certain other members of her family, for a start.' Della claimed the seat Oliver had vacated. 'What if I told you we have reason to believe someone may have been masquerading as your grandmother to gain access to Rowan House?'

Raven blinked. 'What?'

'Did the receptionist there tell you that your grandmother had visited?'

'Well, yes. She said she was the last person to have seen Andrew alive – that she'd brought him a little hamper of food. Her signature was in the visitor book. But Grand-mother swore—' Raven stopped.

'Swore what?'

'Nothing.'

'Miss Walton-Lord, you're going to have to start working with me and not fighting me,' Della said. 'We're on the same

369

side, you know – assuming that, like me, you want to catch whoever killed your uncle.'

Oliver squeezed her shoulder. 'It's OK, Rave. They're trying to help.'

Raven hesitated. 'Well, she – my grandmother – she told me she never went to visit that day. So I thought . . .'

'You thought she was lying,' Della said. 'To cover her tracks.'

Raven winced. 'God, no, I didn't think that. Not really. I just thought it would look bad to the police – I mean, to you. She's seventy-nine. She just lost two old friends and a close family member. She doesn't have the strength to be the subject of a murder investigation.'

Della picked up a sheaf of papers and pretended to examine them. 'Miss Walton-Lord, I don't know what sort of cop shows you've been watching but I promise that at West Yorkshire Police we're not in the habit of hauling old ladies around and shining torches in their faces. And if your grandmother's story checks out – as I have every reason to believe it will – there's no reason she should find herself a suspect. Now, please, before I sign your release papers, is there anything else you'd like to tell me about why you came here today?'

Raven hesitated. Oliver gave her shoulder an encouraging press.

'Go on,' he said.

'Well, it was nothing, I guess,' Raven said. 'I never even thought of it, until the receptionist mentioned Grandmother visiting Andrew. It's Clemmie's missing St Christopher.'

'The one her sister claimed was switched for a Madonna,' Della said. 'Yes, Mr Hanley has made us aware. Continue.'

'It's just, there was one in this box of jewellery Grandmother donated to the village show. I'd forgotten until Tess reminded me about it. It had a broken chain. Probably not the same one, but . . .'

'. . . but you thought it might look bad for your grandmother if we were to find this out.'

Raven flushed. 'Yes.'

'And now I take this information and I go ask your grandmother about it. She in all likelihood gives me a perfectly reasonable explanation, and that's the end of that. You see how much easier life is when we all just communicate?'

'Yes. I'm sorry,' Raven mumbled.

'She did just lose her uncle,' Oliver said. 'You won't charge her with wasting police time, will you?'

Della broke into a smile. 'No. No, I'm going to discharge her and prescribe a restful evening with her family. Come on, Miss Walton-Lord. Let's take you back to the four anxious people cluttering up our reception.'

Oliver supported a still wobbly Raven as they followed Della to reception. As soon as they saw her, Marianne and Candice fell upon her with cries of delight and concern, one hugging her at each side until they were nearly in danger of smothering her between them. Tess, Liam and Oliver stood back, giving them their family moment.

'Ow,' Raven said, laughing. 'Guys, you're going to hug me to death.'

'You silly girl,' Candice said, her voice trembling. 'You,

silly, silly little girl. Raven, my darling, whatever were you thinking?'

'I didn't want you to get into trouble,' Raven mumbled.

'Well, of all the idiotic, half-cocked, nonsensical plans I ever . . .' Suddenly, Candice started to laugh. 'Oh, you really are the most wonderful idiot, Raven. You know, we're insanely proud of you.'

Oliver leant down to whisper in Tess's ear. 'You ever seen them hug before?'

'Nope,' Tess whispered back. 'Handshakes all round, usually. I think things are changing over at Cherrywood Hall.'

Candice pulled Marianne round to her and gave her a big kiss. 'And that's for you. I don't know where I'd be without the pair of you, I really don't. Certainly life would be a lot less interesting.'

Oliver smiled. 'Well, that answers one very old question,' he whispered to Tess.

Della cleared her throat. 'I hate to interrupt the reunion, but could I ask something before you all go?'

'Of course,' Candice said, reining in her joy for a moment.

'Mrs Walton-Lord, your granddaughter tells me you donated a jewellery box to the village show containing a St Christopher medal. Was this something you'd had for a while?'

'A St Christopher?' Candice said, blinking.

'It had a broken chain,' Raven said. 'It was in that box you gave me for the stall.'

'Oh yes, I remember. I found it lying in the mud, down near Black Moor Farm. I was going to have it repaired and advertise in the post office to see if anyone had lost it. You know, I'd completely forgotten I put it in there.'

'Oh!' Liam produced a couple of chain links from his jacket. 'I found these around Black Moor Farm too,' he said, holding them out. 'Susie was trying to eat them. Could they have come from the same chain?'

Candice squinted at them. 'Yes, I should think so. Very small, fine gold links, just like these.'

'That was what Prue was looking for, the night I found her going through Candice's jewellery.' Marianne sighed. 'She suspected us, I think, of Clemmie's murder. I suppose it was natural, with me the only other person who knew about Charity. I know that, but it still hurts. We were such old friends.'

'My colleague has the St Christopher now,' Tess told Della. 'She bought it at the show. She replaced the chain, but she might still have the original.'

'I guess the murderer dropped the necklace when they were fleeing Ling Cottage,' Liam said. 'It could easily have broken when they took it from the body.'

'Yes, there were some faint markings on the neck that would tally with that.' Della nodded to Raven. 'And there you go, Miss Walton-Lord. You see how easily these things can be cleared up when you just cooperate with the police?'

'I'm sorry,' Raven mumbled. 'I wasn't thinking straight, was I?'

Candice gave her granddaughter a squeeze. 'We've all had a difficult few days.'

'Putting it mildly.'

'But it's still your birthday weekend, Raven, and birthdays are a time for friends and family. You must all come back to Cherrywood Hall.' She held up a hand to silence any protests. 'No, I insist. Raven here will be shocked to learn the sorts of cocktails her grandmother can make with the ancient liquor cabinet of the Walton-Lords at her disposal. Let's go home.'

Chapter 35

'What do you think?' Tess asked two days later, when their usual routine had been re-established to an extent – although the funerals of Prue Ackroyd and Andrew Walton-Lord still hovered on the horizon, casting gloom over an otherwise idyllic country summer. She held up her latest knitted creation for Raven to look at. 'Getting better, aren't I?'

'Glorious, darling. Tell you what, I'll get us a pot to go with it if you like. How Women's Guild is that?'

Tess frowned. 'Pot?'

'It is a tea cosy, isn't it?'

Tess stuck out her bottom lip. 'How dare you. It's a hat, clearly.'

'Oh.' Raven looked worried. 'Er . . . it's not for me, is it?'

'No, it's for Lee. Just what he needs when it's twenty-five degrees out, right?'

'You knit for the man now?'

'It's a thank you for helping to get you out of the Big House.'

'One look at that and he might get me chucked straight

back in,' Raven muttered as she watched the hat disappear into Tess's handbag.

Tess's phone buzzed on the table.

'Speak of the devil.' She swiped the screen to take Liam's call.

'Tessie, you got your deer stalker handy?' he asked.

'Am I needed?'

'Always. I'm off to do some investigating. I could use my sidekick.'

'You're the sidekick. I'm—'

'Yeah, yeah, you're the talent. Are you busy or what?'

'Are you kidding? I'm bored stiff,' Tess said. 'I've been knitting you a hat; that's how bad things are.'

'Really? You made me something?' He sounded pleased.

She laughed. 'I wouldn't get too excited. Rave reckons it'll make you look like a teapot. Where're we going then?'

'First up, to see Peggy Bristow. Police released her yesterday morning.'

*

Tess met Liam outside the village hall half an hour later.

'Afternoon, partner,' he said, pecking her cheek.

'All right, no need to get carried away.' Tess rubbed her face where his lips had landed.

'OK. Today you don't like me. Good to know where I stand on the Tessometer.'

'I like you when you keep a nice, friendly distance. So did Della tell you about Peggy getting released?'

'Actually, I spotted her coming out of the post office.

Della's not around this week. She's on holiday with the family.'

'She's got family?'

'Yeah, husband and toddler. Even coppers have them sometimes, you know.'

So Della was married. Tess felt a wave of relief, then immediately tried to pretend she hadn't.

'I guess they couldn't find enough evidence to charge Peggy then,' she said.

Liam nodded. 'Which doesn't mean she didn't do it.'

'I knew you were going to say that. So what's the plan?'

'I thought we'd visit Peggy first, then after we'll see what we can find out from Bev and Gracie.'

'That's assuming Peggy's at home.' Tess jerked her head towards the village hall. 'For all you know she's down in the boiler room, giving Ian Stringer a celebratory post-release thrashing.'

He laughed. 'Well, I'm not going down there to check. We'll have to take our chances. Come on.'

'Did you speak to that receptionist at Rowan House?' Tess asked as they walked.

'Yeah. I asked her if she could describe the woman who'd been to visit Andrew Walton-Lord.'

'And?'

'Short, slightly hunched, grey curly hair . . .'

'Candice.'

'Yep. She identified her from a photo too.'

'But Candice said she didn't visit,' Tess said. 'Why tell such a stupid lie if it was her? She'd even signed the visitors' book.'

'I'm still thinking impostor,' Liam said. 'Ninety per cent of what people notice when they meet someone is hair colour, clothing and posture, and those are the easiest things to fake.'

'So you still suspect Peggy?'

'Unless she manages to talk me out of it. The fact she might have suspected she was about to be arrested makes the timing pretty suspicious too. Perhaps she was keen to bump Andrew off before she was locked up.'

'The police let her go though. That means they don't think she did it, right?'

'No, it only means they can't prove she did it. They have to let her go after twenty-four hours if they don't have enough evidence to charge her.'

'Oh. Here,' Tess said, producing the hat she'd made him. 'To say thank you for helping Raven.'

Liam blinked at it. 'Wow. Thanks, Tessie. That's really . . . something.'

'You're welcome.'

'It can double as a shopping bag as well. How big do you think my head is?'

'Roughly the same size as your ego.'

'It's going to cover my nose. Then how will I smell?'

'I'll resist the obvious joke and suggest you roll it up from the bottom.'

'Roll it up from my bottom. Yeah, I'll need to.'

They stopped outside Peggy's terrace house and Liam rapped the brass knocker.

'Who is it?' Peggy's voice called.

'Lieutenant Columbo and wife,' Liam called back.

They fixed on a pair of smiles as Peggy answered the door, looking puzzled.

'Oh. Sam. And . . . Tess too, how nice. What can I do for the two of you?'

'Can we come in, Ms Bristow?' Liam asked. 'We were hoping to talk to you about something.'

'I was about to head out, but yes, I suppose so.'

Reluctantly she beckoned them in and they followed her to the living room, where she gestured for them to take a seat. Nelson the cat, who Peggy had adopted following Prue's death, purred loudly on a crocheted throw.

It was a bare sort of place. No photos or pictures – the only ornament, if you could call it that, was a postcard showing some characterless hotel complex, which had been propped on the mantelpiece next to a pack of cards. And Peggy's cake rosettes, of course, the blue one taking pride of place at the head of a row of reds on the wall.

Did Ian and Peggy have grown-up kids? Grandkids? Had either of them been married before? Tess suddenly realised she had no idea.

'Will you want tea?' Peggy asked, from her expression evidently hopeful the answer was going to be no.

'Yes, please. Well-brewed, plenty of milk,' Liam said – just to be awkward, Tess suspected. Probably some sort of pre-interrogation detective mind game, like waterboarding but with PG Tips.

'Tess?' Peggy said.

'I will if he is. Thanks, Peg.'

379

'Right.' Peggy disappeared into the kitchen, looking not best pleased at the disruption.

When she'd gone Tess reached into her bag for a little iced cake wrapped in clingfilm.

'All right, bit over-cautious,' Liam said. 'I know the last person to eat one of her cakes died of poisoning, but I don't think you needed to bring your own.'

Tess tutted. 'It's a present for Peggy. Me and Raven made it. Well, I made it and Rave licked the bowl, which is about as good as it gets. I thought it might get us into our suspects' good books if we came bearing sweet things.'

'You bake as well as knit?'

She shrugged. 'I'm in the Women's Guild, aren't I?'

He shook his head. 'Only you would bring a triple murder suspect cake.'

'Well, there's no need to be rude. This is Cherrywood.'

'Here we go,' Peggy said when she'd bustled back in with the tea. 'Now, what can I do for the two of you?'

'I brought you this, from me and Raven,' Tess said, handing over her cake. 'Sorry, it won't be anywhere near your standard. I just thought you probably hadn't had much time to bake this weekend, what with being . . . you know.'

Peggy smiled dryly. 'Banged up?'

'Er, yeah.'

'So is that why you came? That was very kind.'

'Well, one reason. We wanted to ask you about something too.'

Peggy picked up a sugar cube with a pair of silver tongs and plopped it in her tea. 'Anyone else? Sam?'

380

'Ms Bristow – no, no sugar, thank you – I need to straighten something out,' Liam said. 'My name isn't Sam.'

She frowned. 'Of course it is. I was calling you Sam the whole time you were sorting out my shrubbery.'

'Yeah, sorry about that. I'm not really a gardener either – at least, not all the time. My name's Liam Hanley. I'm a detective.'

'What? Don't be ridiculous.'

'It's true, I'm afraid. I've been undercover.'

Peggy shook her head, dazed. She looked at Tess. 'Did you know about this?'

'I did,' Tess said with an apologetic grimace. 'I was sworn to secrecy. I'm sorry, Peg.'

'Tess has been helping me with my investigation,' Liam said.

'Into the murder?' Peggy winced. 'Sorry, I mean murders, don't I? Plural now, of course. I still haven't quite got my head around Prue being gone.'

Liam nodded. 'I was hoping you'd be able to answer some questions.'

Peggy visibly stiffened, and a mask of suspicion spread over her features.

'I already told you people everything I know,' she said. 'You turned my house upside down, you held me for a day and night, there can't possibly be anything else. You can tell your boss—'

'I am the boss,' Liam said. 'Ms Bristow, I'm not sure you quite understand. I'm a private detective, I'm not police.'

'You can talk to him,' Tess said in her most reassuring

381

tone. 'He's not interested in catching you out. He just wants to work out who killed Prue and Clemmie.'

Peggy still looked wary. 'The police released me. That means they don't think I did anything wrong.'

'No, it means they don't have enough evidence to charge you. Yet,' Liam said as he stirred his tea.

'Young man, just what do you think you're suggesting?'

Tess shot him a look. 'He's not suggesting anything. He's just a clodhopping pillock who doesn't know how to talk to people.'

Liam nodded. 'She's right, it's not one of my skills.'

'No one suspects you of anything,' Tess said soothingly. 'Your cake was the means of carrying out a murder, which means you can help us get to the truth. That's all.'

Tess leaned back against the sofa, stroking the cat that had made its home in her lap as she did her best to project vibes of trust and reassurance.

'Like I told the police, I've no idea how that azalea got into my cake,' Peggy said, relaxing a little.

'Can you tell us how you baked it?' Liam asked.

'Well, I got the ingredients from Plumholme Morrison's.' Peggy looked thoughtful. 'Then . . . let's see, I started by sieving the flour into my big Pyrex. Then it was twelve ounces of caster sugar creamed with the same amount of softened butter – well, I'd forgotten to leave that out so it was a microwave job, but I don't think it suffered for it. Then—'

'We don't need the recipe, Ms Bristow,' Liam said, struggling to keep the impatience out of his tone. 'I just want to know if you did anything different to usual.'

382

'Not a thing.'

'The azalea was in the chocolate icing used for the hair. You've got no idea at what point it got in there?'

'I haven't a clue,' Peggy said. 'It wasn't in any of the ingredients – they were all tested.'

'Did anyone else have access to the cake?' Tess asked.

'The only other person who handled it was Gracie when she took it down to the hall in her car.'

Tess looked at Liam. 'You think the poison could've been added on Gracie's watch?'

'I don't see how,' Liam said. 'Unless Gracie left the thing long enough for the head section to be stripped down and re-iced, or switched it for an identical cake, then it must have been poisoned before she touched it.'

Peggy had drawn herself up at the suggestion that it might have been swapped for an identical cake.

'And who else could have iced it so well, I'd like to know?' she demanded. 'I can promise you that what was served at the performance was my original, unaltered cake. I'd know it anywhere.'

'Anyway, Gracie got a dose of the poison too,' Tess reminded Liam.

Peggy nodded. 'She asked to taste the icing when she picked up the cake. Gracie has a weakness for chocolate buttercream.'

'That doesn't mean she's in the clear,' Liam said. 'She might have done that deliberately to deflect suspicion.'

'Yes, but it means the azalea must have been added to the icing in this house, while it was being prepared,' Tess pointed

383

out. 'She couldn't have added it while she was taking it to the hall.'

'Did you leave the cake unattended at any point?' Liam asked Peggy.

Peggy shook her head. 'I was working on it solidly all morning.'

'OK.' Liam put his tea down. 'Thanks for your time, Ms Bristow.'

Tess frowned at him. 'What, we're done?'

'Well, there's no point pursuing this, is there? If Ms Bristow says she didn't leave the cake unattended, then there can only have been one source of the poison.'

Peggy glared at him. 'Are you suggesting I added it, young man?'

'If you didn't turn your back on the thing and there was no one else in the house, what other explanation can there be?'

'How dare you,' Peggy said in a low voice, getting to her feet. 'Prudence Ackroyd was a very dear friend of mine.'

'Really,' Liam said flatly. 'I understand you've expended a lot of energy trying to convince the village that your very dear friend murdered her sister. To cover for your own guilt, I presume.'

'You've got not a shred of evidence for any of these accusations. I could sue you for slander.'

Liam didn't flinch. 'Or you could tell me what it is you're not telling me.'

'Just what are you implying?'

'I'm implying you did leave the kitchen. I'm implying you

384

left your half-prepared cake for a significant period while you were elsewhere in the house. And I'm implying there's another person who could give you an alibi, if I promised not to say anything to his wife – I mean to his current wife, of course.'

Peggy stared at him. Then slowly she sank back into her chair.

'How did you find out?' she whispered.

'I can't tell you that. Suffice to say someone saw you.'

'Oliver caught you giving Ian a good seeing to in the village hall boiler room,' Tess supplied helpfully.

Liam glared at her. 'Yes, thanks, Tess.'

'Good God. The vicar?' Peggy said, her eyes widening. 'How?'

'He's a trustee. He's got a key,' Tess said. 'It took him two double gins and a bag of smoky bacon crisps to recover.'

'He never said anything to me.'

'What was he going to do, ask you where you bought your fetish gear over communion?'

'So are we all on the same page now?' Liam asked. 'Ms Bristow?'

Peggy sighed. 'All right, it's true. I did leave the cake while we were – while I was entertaining.'

'How long for?'

'I don't know, an hour perhaps?'

'And was the front door locked while you were with Ian?'

'Goodness, I can't . . . maybe. I don't always lock it when I'm in.'

'Did you tell all this to the police?'

'A version of it,' she said cautiously. 'I told them Ian had called to discuss the sale of our old house.'

'You'd be better off telling them the truth,' Tess said. 'Who are you trying to protect anyway? Surely not Bev?'

Peggy laughed. 'Lord, no. I'll be honest, the thought of getting my own back on that woman was the main reason I didn't tell Ian to shove his anal beads where the sun doesn't shine.'

'Isn't that the whole – you know what, never mind,' Liam said.

Peggy smiled. 'It's funny, isn't it? At the spring show, Beverley said he left me because he was getting something from her he couldn't get at home. But when he realised he couldn't get what he really wanted, he soon came running back.'

'So who are you protecting?' Tess asked.

'Myself. I've rather got a taste for playing the wronged woman, having everyone on my side.' She paused. 'And Ian, I suppose. I can't imagine he'd want his tastes in that area getting out. As much as he did me wrong and all, we were married for twenty years.'

'How long has your affair been going on?' Tess asked. That wasn't really relevant; she was just being nosy.

'Around two months. Ian's always had his little peccadillo. I did wonder when he left me how he'd get along with Beverley.'

Tess pictured Ian, with his flares and Sonny moustache, and shook her head. 'Just goes to show, you never can tell.'

'Everyone likes their bit of slap and tickle, don't they? Some just prefer the slap to the tickle.' Peggy sipped her tea

386

calmly. 'Ian always said I'd rather a talent for it. Nice to be good at something, eh?'

'Thank you, Ms Bristow, that's been very, er . . . enlightening,' Liam said. 'Just one last thing. At the show, you used a specific phrase.' He nodded to Tess.

'Sin will out,' Tess said. 'You used it when you were talking about Bev and Ian.'

'Perhaps I did. What of it?'

'It's quite an odd phrase, isn't it? Sort of formal and old-fashioned. What put it into your head?'

'Well, I don't know,' Peggy said, frowning. 'I suppose it just occurred to me. Why?'

'It's occurred somewhere else recently, that's all. We wondered if there was a connection.'

'Where did it occur?'

'In some threatening letters received by Prue Ackroyd before her death,' Liam said. 'That phrase was used in every letter. I believe the person who wrote them is also our killer.'

Peggy sat up straight. The idea she might just have incriminated herself was written all over her face.

'Oh, well. That'll be my gift, I suppose – I mean my second sight.'

'Mmm. Any more earthbound explanation?'

'Well . . . I suppose Prue might have said it while she was staying with me and put it into my head,' Peggy said.

'That's possible, I suppose. OK, I think that's all.' Gesturing to Tess to follow, Liam stood up.

'Oh! One last thing,' he said when he reached the door.

'Ms Bristow, does the name Nadia Harris mean anything to you?'

Peggy shook her head. 'Never heard it before. Why?'

'Prue Ackroyd never said anything to you about a Nadia Harris?'

'No, she didn't.'

'What about her aunt, Mercy Talbot? Could she have mentioned her to you in the period leading up to her death?'

'Not a word, no. Is that relevant?'

'I'm not sure yet. Goodbye, Ms Bristow.'

Chapter 36

'Ooh, you Columboed her,' Tess said when they got outside. 'That's sneaky.'

Liam shrugged. 'I learnt from the greats.'

He took out his pad and started scribbling notes.

'You still think she did it?' Tess asked.

'Let's just say I'm far from convinced she didn't.'

'So what next?'

'We split up. You take Gracie, I'll do Bev.'

'You don't think we should do them together? I thought Peggy relaxed a bit more with me there.'

'You're not coming to the pub,' he said firmly. 'I'm about to confront Bev Stringer with her husband's infidelity, the very illegal secret ingredient in her bestselling buns and the suggestion she might be a triple murderer. I don't think you want me losing you another job, do you?'

'Fair point.' Tess squeezed his arm. 'Good luck.'

He patted his pocket. 'Don't worry. Got my lucky hat right here.'

Tess left him and turned up cobbled Royal Row towards the Old School House, Gracie's place, easily identifiable from the white wooden beehives dotting the front lawn.

'Tess,' Gracie said when she opened the door. 'What a lovely surprise. Is Raven not with you?'

'No, just me today. But I do come bearing gifts from the two of us.' Tess dipped into her bag for another miniature cake. The poor thing had got a bit squashed on the walk over, but Gracie regarded it with delight.

'My dear, did you make this?'

Tess laughed. 'Why does everyone say it in such a tone of surprise? Yes, I made it. Well, Raven stuck the glace cherry on top, which she assured me was also an important job.'

'How is Raven? I heard about that unpleasantness at the police station.'

Of course she had. Nothing stayed secret in Cherrywood.

'She's OK,' Tess said. 'At least, she will be.'

'Whyever did she do it? Confess to the murders like that?'

'Oh, grief, I think,' Tess said vaguely, unwilling to go into Raven's suspicions about Candice. 'You know what bereavement can do to people.'

'I do, sadly,' Gracie said, bowing her head for a moment. 'Now, will you come in and have a little piece of this cake?'

'That would be lovely, thank you.'

Gracie bustled inside. Tess followed her to a cluttered, homely living room.

'I am sorry about the mess,' Gracie said. 'I wasn't expecting company.'

'Please don't worry about it. My fault for not calling ahead.'

Gracie removed a large scrapbook from the armchair so Tess could sit down. There was a pile of *Guild Life* magazines on the table, with various cuttings piled up waiting to be stuck in Gracie's album.

'I've been compiling a little history,' she said. 'Anything that appears in the magazine about groups in the local area, I cut it out and stick it in my book. Eventually I'm hoping to write a volume on the role the Women's Guild has played in our county over the years. Something to keep me busy while my girls – I mean my bees, you know – are in their quiet period.'

'That's a good idea,' Tess said politely. 'You can certainly put my name down for a copy.'

'Thank you, dear. Now. Tea with your cake?'

'Yes, please.'

While Gracie was out serving up the cake, Tess examined the cluster of photographs on the mantelpiece. There were loads – a young woman graduating from university, babies and toddlers, children in school uniform. She was guessing the man in the centre, dressed in top hat and tails on his wedding day, was the late Mr Gracie.

There was a photo of the Women's Guild ladies too, Gracie smiling happily between Clemmie and Bev on what looked like a trip to the seaside. Even stern Prue, standing beside her sister, looked happy for once. Tess turned away.

'Your grandchildren?' Tess asked when Gracie came back in with a tray, nodding to the photos.

'Yes,' Gracie said. 'Well, step-grandchildren, technically. Stephen was a widower when I met him, with a daughter already in her teens.' She gestured to the photo of the girl in mortar board and gown. 'Veronica lives in Australia now with her husband. And here's Hattie, Laurie, Chelle and little Corrie,' she said, indicating the children. 'He's the only boy – a real monkey.'

'They certainly have quite a brood. Are you close?'

'Rather, yes. Veronica calls about once a month. I love to hear news of the children.'

'It must be tough with them so far away. Did you never have any of your own?'

Gracie was silent as she handed over the cake and tea.

'Sorry,' Tess said, biting her lip. 'That was rather personal. None of my business.'

'Oh, you weren't to know. We couldn't have our own, as it turned out. But I grew very fond of Veronica.' She took a seat. 'So what brings you here other than cake? I've never been honoured by a home visit before.'

OK. This was it. She had to be gentle, not like Liam and his galumphingly insensitive detective size twelves.

'Well, I just wondered . . .' Tess reached into her bag for the copy of *The Centurion's Bride* she'd bought Raven for her birthday. 'I wondered if you could sign this for Raven.'

Gracie stared at it. 'I'm not sure I understand.'

'I hope you don't mind. I know you shun publicity, and sorry if I'm overstepping the mark, but it would just mean the world to Rave. She's read everything you've ever written. That's why she's not here,' Tess fabricated wildly. 'She was too starstruck, once she realised it was you. I think we might have a swooning fit from her at the next Women's Guild meeting, if she doesn't throw her knickers at you.'

'But dear, you're not saying . . . you can't think I'm this

Diana Skye woman?' Gracie laughed. 'Honestly, how terribly funny.'

'But you must be,' Tess said, frowning. 'I mean, your notebook – there were sections of this book written in it, verbatim. Long before it was published.'

Gracie had picked up her tea from the table. She put it down again without taking a sip.

'You said you didn't read it,' she said quietly.

'I didn't. But Raven did. I'm sorry.'

'That notebook contains my most intimate, private . . . she had no right.'

'She didn't mean anything by it, Gracie,' Tess said, keeping her voice gentle. 'She was just looking to see if she could find out who it belonged to.'

Gracie had picked up the copy of *The Centurion's Bride* and was regarding it with undisguised disgust. 'Absolute rubbish. I wonder how Raven can read it.'

'Are you honestly saying you didn't write it? It was right there in your notebook.'

'Oh yes, I wrote it all right,' Gracie said, still sneering at the book. 'Foolish schoolgirl fantasies. Wish fulfilment for idiots and dreamers.'

Tess blinked. 'Gracie, I don't understand. It's your book.'

'That doesn't mean I have to be proud of it.'

'Why wouldn't you be? These books are on all kinds of bestseller lists. I'd be proud as anything if it were me.'

'I used to be,' Gracie said quietly, putting the book down. 'That was back when I believed in my stories. When I thought there really was some strong, handsome stranger

393

who could make it all go away – whisk me off to a better life. But that's a dream I abandoned long, long ago.'

'But you still write them.'

'For the money. That's all.'

The money. Yes, Diana Skye must make good money – she'd written enough bestsellers in the past thirty or so years. And yet Gracie lived a modest life, Tess thought, glancing round the cottage with its few luxuries. What did she do with her earnings? Send them to her stepdaughter in Australia, perhaps?

Tess's gaze fell on the photo of Stephen Lister, Gracie's late husband, on the fireplace. He was skinny, with an awful Eighties mullet, large square glasses and a wide, friendly grin. He looked pleasant enough, although Tess knew that didn't prove anything.

'Were you happy with your husband, Gracie?' she asked softly.

'Hmm?'

'Stephen. Did you love him?'

'Stephen?' Gracie's gaze followed Tess's to the photo. 'No. No, I don't suppose I ever did.'

'I'm sorry.'

'Spilt milk,' Gracie muttered. 'Spilt milk, that's all.'

'You're not upset with me, are you?' Tess asked. 'I thought you'd be proud. I didn't realise it was . . . complicated.'

Gracie tore her gaze away from the photo and summoned her usual bright smile. 'It's nothing. It doesn't matter.'

'Are you feeling OK now? In yourself, I mean.' Tess glanced at the uneaten cake in Gracie's hand. 'That was a nasty scare you got at *Mamma Mia*.'

'Yes, it was very unpleasant,' Gracie said, shuddering. 'I felt like my guts were inside out, and my head was spinning. I can't bear to imagine what poor Prue must have gone through.'

'You think it was Prue the cake was meant for?'

Gracie looked surprised. 'Well, of course. You can't believe I'd be the target? I'm far too uninteresting to be murdered, dear.'

'But why would anyone want to poison Prue?'

'She wasn't the most popular person after what was found in her garden, was she?' Gracie looked down. 'I feel dreadful that my last words to her were hard ones. That little girl, you know, Charity – well, I couldn't help being angry. A lot of people were, not only me, but still, I feel bad about it.'

'You don't think it really was Peggy who poisoned Miss Ackroyd, do you?'

'Oh, no,' Gracie said, looking shocked. 'Peggy couldn't do anything like that; I've known her for years. I wonder if the most likely explanation isn't that it was all a terrible accident after all. Lots of people grow azaleas, don't they? I do myself.'

'It couldn't have been an accident.' Tess sipped her tea, trying to look like she was making casual conversation rather than interrogating a witness. 'At least, the police say not. The dose was too big for it to have got in by mistake.'

'Who told you so?'

'Bev, probably, or some other village gossip. These things always seem to find a way into circulation, don't they? Sin will out, as they say.'

Tess watched Gracie's face to see if the phrase caused a flicker, but her features were already twitching so much with emotion as she thought about Prue and Peggy, it was hard to tell if it had registered.

'I'm sure it wasn't Peggy,' Gracie said. 'Positive.'

'Well, someone killed Prue, and we know what happened to Clemmie wasn't an accident. Who do you think it was if not her?'

'I really have no idea. No one we know. Perhaps it was this girl, this Nadia Harris, if she was going to inherit their money.'

Tess stiffened. 'You know about Nadia Harris?'

'Of course. She was Clemmie's heir, wasn't she? I thought everyone knew that.'

'The fact Clemmie had an heir was common knowledge, but not her name. Who told you about her?'

'Well . . . let's see, somebody must have,' Gracie said, frowning. 'Possibly Prue did. Or it might have been Peggy.'

'Peggy?'

'Yes, I'm sure she was talking to me about Nadia Harris at *Mamma Mia*. Or perhaps I overheard – yes, that was it, she was talking to Prue. You know, with all the drama afterwards I'd completely forgotten about it.'

'Right,' Tess said, feeling dazed. Hadn't Peggy just denied any knowledge of Nadia Harris? And yet here was Gracie saying Peggy knew all about her.

That definitely pointed the finger of suspicion firmly back in Peggy's direction. Tess wondered how Liam was getting on talking to Bev.

Chapter 37

Liam banged at the door again with his fist.

'Mrs Stringer! Come on, let me in. I just want to talk.'

If Bev had been pleased to see him when he'd sought her out in her living quarters over the pub, that feeling had been very short-lived. She hadn't taken the revelation of Sam the gardener's true identity well at all. No sooner had the word 'detective' passed his lips than he'd found himself deep in conversation with the door.

'Sod off, copper,' Bev called back. 'I know your kind. You put our Sally's boy inside with your tricks, for nothing but a bit of recreational. Entrapment, they call that.'

'I'm not the police and I'm not trying to entrap anyone. You were a witness to a murder and I want to know what you saw, that's all.'

'What part of "sod off" are you not getting, my lad?'

'Right. You're making me do this, Mrs Stringer.' Liam patted his pocket to make sure his lucky hat was still there. 'If you don't open up, I might have to have words with my contact at West Yorkshire Police about your own little bit of recreational, if you know what I mean. And I know you do.'

There was silence for a moment. Then the door opened a crack and a narrowed eye peeped out.

'Ten minutes,' the voice behind it said.

The door opened and he followed Bev to a grubby living room with nicotine stains on the ceiling. There was no offer of tea here, no friendly invitation to take a seat, but he helped himself to one anyway.

'Them buns are perfectly legitimate,' Bev said, perching on the edge of a chair as if ready to do a runner. 'Ask around the village – anyone'll tell you how popular they are. They've raised a fortune for things round here. The church roof, nursery's new playground—'

'Popular is not the same as legitimate, Mrs Stringer, as I'm sure your Sally's lad can tell you. Those buns contained cannabis, didn't they? And I don't think you need me to tell you that supplying a controlled substance constitutes a criminal offence.'

Bev met his gaze defiantly. 'They were a good turn. I only started making them to help out old Clemmie.'

He frowned. 'Clemmie Ackroyd?'

'Her arthritis. It gave her terrible pain, and they wouldn't give her nothing for it. You can't tell me that's right, making something illegal that could take an old lady's pain away.'

'It's not my job to decide right and wrong,' Liam said. 'That's why we have the law.'

'The law isn't always right. Look at all those poor boys who were arrested before the Sixties just because they liked to stick with their own. All the young lasses who died getting back-street abortions. That was the law then, wasn't it?'

Liam frowned, thinking back to what Tess had told him about the night she and Oliver had confronted Prue. 'Back-street abortion. You know, you're the second person around here to mention that recently.'

'So?'

'Just a coincidence. Detectives never ignore a coincidence – not in a murder case.'

'Are you going to tell the real police about my buns, then?' Bev demanded.

'They already know; they found it in the ones they took from *Mamma Mia*. I imagine they'll pull you in for question-ing quite soon. Might be a slap on the wrist, if you're very lucky.'

'What, they know? Then why the hell am I talking to you?'

He grinned. 'Had to get in, didn't I?'

Bev shook her head. 'Entrapment,' she muttered. 'My old dad was right. Never trust a copper, self-employed or otherwise.'

'Come on, you've been selling them all over the village. You can't have thought you'd get away with it for ever,' Liam said. 'Look, before I go, can you just tell me if the name Nadia Harris means anything to you?'

'Not a thing.'

'Are you sure?'

'Are you deaf? Not a thing, I said.'

Right. So that was the way she wanted to play it. Liam hated the belligerent ones. Once they closed up, there was nothing you could do with them.

Well, he had one more ace up his sleeve.

'Mrs Stringer, are you aware your husband's having an affair?'

It worked. Bev's petulant expression morphed into one of shock.

'And how would you know?' she demanded.

'I'm a detective. There's a clue in the name.'

'Well, doesn't surprise me, I suppose. He's been off at all hours lately. I should've known there was something going on.'

'Aren't you angry?'

She shrugged. 'What's the point? Boys will be boys and men will be men. Ian's my third husband, Sam or Liam or whatever your name is. I learnt to stop expecting much of them about quarter of an hour into my first marriage.'

'Do you know the identity of Mr Stringer's lover?'

'Some young slapper, I suppose. More fool her. She'll not be getting much for her money.'

'Suppose I told you it was Peggy Bristow?'

She blinked. 'Peggy?'

'Apparently your other half has a taste for masochism,' Liam said. 'I assume you knew that.'

She smiled grimly. 'Married me, didn't he?'

Bev was doing her best to appear unconcerned, but her fingers were moving constantly, picking at the dry skin around one cracked nail. She was either nervous, lying or both.

'Mrs Stringer, I'm going to put my cards on the table,' Liam said. 'I think you did know about your husband's affair.'

'What, you think I'm mug enough to stay with a man

who's playing around on me? I might not be a spring chicken but I can still take my choice, lad.'

'I think you knew, and to save your own face you kept it quiet. Didn't you?'

'Rubbish.'

'It must be humiliating to see your husband back in the arms of the woman you thought you'd so completely enticed him away from.' He took in Bev's platform cleavage and peroxide curls. 'Especially when that woman looks like Peggy Bristow. I suppose you'd rather live a lie with Ian than have to admit to everyone in Cherrywood that you were cuckolded by your husband's frumpy ex-wife. You've still got your pride, right?'

There was a distinct flinch this time. 'That's not true.'

'But there were other ways you could get your revenge, weren't there, Mrs Stringer? Ways like . . . oh, I don't know, framing your old friend for murder?'

'What?'

'You knew about your husband's affair with Peggy Bristow, didn't you? Come on, I'm not stupid.'

Bev hesitated.

'OK, fine,' she said at last. 'All right, so I did know. And what's more, I gave it my blessing – what do you think of that? Ian wasn't going to get what he wanted from me, I can tell you that for nothing – I mean, do you know what he wanted me to do? Gags and riding crops and all sorts; it was disgusting. So as far as I'm concerned, he can just bloody well keep getting it from Peggy. Stops him pestering me for it.'

'Did you really give your blessing? Or did you concoct

a plan to frame your love rival for Prudence Ackroyd's murder?'

Bev folded her arms. 'Utter nonsense. You've got no proof of any such thing.'

'Ms Bristow tells us she left her cake unattended while she was in bed with your husband,' Liam said. 'She also tells us she doesn't remember locking the door after her lover arrived. That would give you plenty of time to sneak in and stir enough azalea into the pre-prepared hair icing to kill, wouldn't it, Beverley? Or should I say, Nadia?'

'What drivel are you talking now?' She stood up. 'I don't have time for this. I've told you everything I know. Now get out, and until you have some solid evidence, I'd advise you to keep your filthy accusations to yourself.'

★

'So which one of them is lying?' Tess asked when they were sitting on the swings in the children's playground, comparing notes.

'Hmm. I wouldn't trust Bev further than I could chuck her, but she didn't flinch when I dropped the name Nadia,' Liam said. 'But Peggy . . . You say Gracie heard Prue telling her about Nadia Harris?'

'Yep. And if that's true, it means Peggy lied to us. Very coolly, I might add.'

'Another thing. You ever think it's strange she chose the village hall for most of these liaisons with her ex-husband? She's got a perfectly good house.'

'The first time I saw her sneaking in was when Miss

Ackroyd was staying with her,' Tess said. 'Same when Oliver spotted her first.'

'But not the night he caught her with Ian. That was after Prue was back at Ling Cottage. Why risk losing her job by using the hall as a shag pad when they could be alone at her place?'

'Ol wondered if her and Ian liked the thrill of potentially getting caught.'

'Or maybe Peggy wanted to get caught.'

Tess frowned. 'Why would she want that?'

'So that when pesky detectives and police officers turn up asking where she was while her icing was being poisoned, she could have a believable alibi to hand,' Liam said. He held up his hands. ' "Wasn't me, Officer, I was boffing the ex-husband. Don't believe me? Ask the vicar." '

'Ooh. That's devious, that is.' Tess frowned. 'But what if she wasn't boffing him at the time? Then Ian would rat her out.'

'Course he wouldn't. He knows what she does to boys who've been bad.'

'You really think it's her?'

'She's still my lead suspect,' Liam said. 'Don't you think she gave in a bit too easily when we pressed her on the affair? Barely even made the effort to deny it – almost as if she wanted us to know.'

'Hmm. I guess.'

'Wine gum?' He offered her one from a packet he had in his pocket.

'Cheers.' She selected a black one and sucked it thoughtfully while she rocked her swing.

'What about Gracie? Anything?'

'Well, she was really weird about this Diana Skye business,' Tess told him. 'I almost blew my chance of getting anything else out of her; she closed up like a clam. Luckily I managed to talk her back round to get this juicy clue about Peggy and Nadia Harris.'

Liam smiled. 'I bet you never thought in terms of juicy clues till I turned up, did you?'

'It's certainly expanded my vocabulary.'

'So what we know is either Peggy's lying or Gracie is.'

'Or she's misremembered. She was quite shaky on the details – couldn't recall at first where she'd heard about Nadia. There's a strong possibility she overheard Prue talking to someone else entirely.'

'This is it, Tess.' Liam's eyes were sparkling. 'One more breakthrough and we'll have this thing nailed.'

'Let's just hope we can nail it before anyone else gets hurt.'

Chapter 38

It was raining the day of Prue Ackroyd's funeral, which seemed to fit.

As a queue of mourners, huddled under umbrellas, waited to get into St Stephen's, Tess reflected that she'd been getting far too much wear out of her black trouser suit lately. She wouldn't even have time to wash it before it was pressed into service again for Andrew Walton-Lord.

Raven was ahead of her, and Oliver was holding hands with Tammy behind. He'd felt unable to take the service himself, so Tammy's mum Alison had been asked to lay Miss Ackroyd to rest.

'You OK?' Tess whispered to him as they made their way into the church.

'I'm OK.' He blinked the rain out of his eyes. 'See enough of these things, don't I?'

'That doesn't make it easier, I guess.'

'In a way, it does. You do start to accept that death is a part of life, and if you have faith that it's not the end, you know you'll see the person again. But this . . .' His eyes were drawn to the hearse, and the coffin visible through its windows. 'This feels different. This makes me angry.'

'Because this wasn't a part of life,' Tammy muttered. 'It was murder.'

They claimed a pew inside and waited for Alison to start the service.

It was a sombre affair, even for a funeral. Tess had been to services before that had been vibrant and full of joy – truly a celebration of someone's life, like the one she'd attended for Archie Maynard, Oliver's big brother. Archie's friends had been asked to wear their football strips to commemorate the life of the soccer-mad lad, and the church had been filled with colour, warmth and laughter. It had been the happiest kind of sadness.

But this wasn't like that. The church was barely filled – only twenty or so people there. Tess knew Prue hadn't been popular, but it still made her sad – and a little angry – to think that the old lady should have so few mourners. At Clemmie's funeral, it had been standing room only. As gorgon-like as she might have seemed to the kids in her classes, Miss Ackroyd had been a good teacher. She must have taught half the village how to read and write, and she'd awoken a love of knowledge in Tess herself that had sent her down a very different path to her three brothers.

She felt particularly hurt at slights from people Prue would have considered friends. From the Women's Guild there was Candice and Peggy, but no Bev or Gracie. The village's attitude to Prue had softened a little since the full scale of the abuse she'd suffered and the efforts she'd made to protect her sister had become known – Oliver had done sterling work in posthumously defending his friend from her critics.

Tess suspected it was only thanks to him that the mourners today were in double figures at all. But Prue's two old friends from the Guild apparently still stood firm in their condemnation, which made Tess sad.

There was no Marianne either, although that was due to illness rather than neglect. As the person who'd known Prue the longest, Marianne had penned a eulogy for Candice to read on her behalf.

It made for a gloomy scene as rain battered at the stained glass. Tess could see Oliver crying silently, the tears dripping from his cheeks mirroring the downpour outside.

It was a traditional service, as the staunchly high church Miss Ackroyd would no doubt have wanted. The thin congregation chanted their responses to the vicar in a dirge-like monotone.

'Father, we commit our sister Prudence to your care and to her everlasting life,' Alison said.

'And also with you,' Tess mumbled.

Oliver nudged her and pointed to the order of service card she was holding. On autopilot, she'd turned over two pages and was giving the wrong responses.

'Sorry,' she mouthed. 'Er, thanks be to God.'

'Grace and mercy be with you all,' Alison said a few minutes later.

Oliver, seeing she'd drifted into a daydream, nudged her again before she missed the response.

'Oh, right. And also with you.'

Ugh, she must be half asleep. She was going to be in trouble with Ol afterwards, when they headed to the Star for

407

the wake. At least now there was a hymn to wake her up a bit: one she knew the words to as well. 'Jerusalem', chosen by Prue's friends to mark her many decades in the Women's Guild.

When the singing was over, they sat back down for the last part of the service.

Grace and mercy be with you . . .

The words of the last prayer whirled around Tess's brain as she tried to concentrate on what Alison was saying.

'Mercy Talbot,' she muttered.

Oliver shot her a look. 'Tess, shh,' he whispered.

'Sorry.'

Grace and mercy . . .

A familiar klaxon had started blaring in Tess's head, demanding to be heard.

*

'Guys, I need to dash off,' she said to Raven and Oliver as soon as the service was done.

'You're coming to the wake, aren't you?' Raven asked.

'I might come later. There's something urgent I need to do.'

'What?'

'I'd better not say until I've done it. Could be nothing. See you in a bit, all right?'

She rushed home and fired up the laptop.

*

Marianne tutted as she picked a mouldy onion out of the fridge and threw it in the dustbin.

She did hate waste. How had that one got away from her? It had rolled to the back and made a nest for itself behind a box of eggs when by rights it should have been in last week's beef stew.

She stopped tidying the kitchen to blow her nose. She felt awful, leaving Candice to go to Prue's funeral alone, but she hadn't wanted to pass on her germs to the rest of the mourners. Some of them would be quite elderly.

She hoped there'd been a good turnout. Raven would have been there, of course. And Tess and young Oliver, and the Women's Guild ladies.

Thinking about Raven made her smile. She was proud of her, lately more than ever. For decades Marianne had been trying to forge a better understanding between the last of the Walton-Lords and her grandmother, and if there had been one good thing about these miserable last few months, it was seeing the pair of them finally grow closer. Now, since the incident at the police station when Raven had offered herself in her grandmother's place – foolish, wonderful child that she was – it felt like their funny little family was more tightly knit than ever before.

Marianne stopped for a moment and leaned against the worktop, feeling dizzy. She ought really to be in bed, where Candy had left her with a hot water bottle and a Lemsip before heading out to the funeral. But Marianne was an active body, always had been, and she couldn't abide doing nothing. She'd been working since she'd left school at fifteen, and a day in bed felt like too much of an indulgence to be allowed.

Still, she was getting old. Cherrywood Hall, which not so far in the past would have required a whole staff of servants to keep it running, now only had her and Candice, with Peggy Bristow coming a couple of times a week to clean. But Marianne was seventy-seven, and Candice would be eighty next month. Perhaps it was time to look at getting some residential help – a housekeeper, maybe.

She straightened up when there was a knock at the door. Who could that be? Surely everyone was at the wake, unless it was the young gardener from the cottage – no, not gardener. Detective. Liam, wasn't it? She was still struggling to adjust to the fact that he'd secretly been working for Candice all this time.

'Oh. Hello,' she said when she answered the door.

On the step was Gracie Lister, beaming as always and clutching a pot of homemade jam to her chest.

Chapter 39

Liam groaned and dropped his head to the desk. It was covered in enough paper to clear a rainforest, and his whiteboard had been scribbled over so many times it was unreadable. None of it was helping him find what he needed – the missing link that would confirm his suspicion that Peggy Bristow was in fact Nadia Harris.

He was sure she must be the killer. There were just too many odd details in her story to add up. If you're having kinky sex with your married lover and you don't want people to find out, you don't do it in one of the most frequented public buildings in the village. And if you're doing it at home surely the first thing you think to do is lock the door. It did sit right with him. No, she'd poisoned her own cake, has set herself up with an alibi so embarrassing that would ever doubt it was true.

Identity theft was a tricky business, though. If y to start a new life, leaving your real identity b needed some serious documentation. Without a b cate, without a passport, without a national number, things like getting a job or renting a hou very difficult indeed.

Taking the identity of a dead person was one common way to do it. He'd investigated fraud cases where that had happened. But once you started pulling at the loose threads, their back stories quickly started to unravel. There'd be a break in the chain somewhere – something missing.

Yet search as he might, there was no break in Peggy Bristow's chain. Liam had found her birth certificate, national insurance number, even some wedding photos. If she was Nadia Harris, she'd covered her tracks well.

'Is it nap time?'

He looked up from his desk. Tess had barged in without knocking in typical Tess fashion and was standing over him, tapping her foot.

'Tess.' He rubbed his eyes. 'I thought you'd be at Prue's wake.'

'I skipped the wake so I could do your job for you.' She chucked a sheet of A4 down on the desk. It was a computer printout of a young woman's passport photo, blown up to full size. 'I've been looking into Nadia Harris. There was a new angle I wanted to explore.'

Liam squinted at the photo. The woman was about twenty, with curly brown hair in a style that would've been fashionable in the Eighties.

'This is Nadia Harris?'

'No. This is Grace Lister.'

He stared at her. 'You what?'

'Lee, you look knackered,' she said gently. 'Let me make a coffee.'

'Oh, no. You don't just get to spring something like that on me then break off to do a tea round. Explain.'

'You were right – it was identity theft. The only problem was you were looking in the wrong place.'

'So are you trying to tell me . . .'

Tess nodded. 'The woman we know as Gracie Lister isn't Gracie Lister. Correct.'

'So she might be Nadia.'

'Yep. In fact, I'm certain she is.'

'How do you know all this?'

Tess took a seat at his desk. 'It was the funeral that started me thinking. The virtue naming. All the women in that family follow the pattern, don't they? Constance, Mercy, Clemency, Prudence, Charity. Supposing our Nadia Harris had been hiding in plain sight, all this time?'

'You mean Gracie?'

'Exactly. Might she not choose the identity of someone with her own real name? "By the grace of God I hope you keep it safe for her", the Felix letter said. Sounds like a riddle to us but not to Clemmie – not if she was keeping her secret fortune safe for a child she'd named Grace.'

Liam picked up the photo. 'Who was the real Grace, then? How did you find her?'

'Always a break in the chain, right?' Tess said. 'Fake Gracie's family gave me the clue. Her stepdaughter Veronica and the four grandchildren – she's got photos of them all over her house.'

'Right. And?'

413

'And they don't exist. I don't know where she got the photos, but there are no such kids.'

He frowned. 'I don't understand.'

'I had a lovely chat with Veronica Lister on Facebook earlier,' Tess said. 'She was very surprised to be told that her stepmother was alive and in frequent contact with her, given that the real Grace died in 1989. Veronica was also shocked to learn she lived in Australia with her husband and four kids when she lives in Chiswick with her wife and labradoodle.'

'Bloody hell,' Liam muttered. 'Is it definitely the right Veronica Lister?'

'Yep. She sent me some family photos over Messenger, including one of her dad Stephen, identical to the one on Gracie's mantelpiece. Only she sent me the full photo, where he's got his wife – his real wife – beside him.' Tess shook her head. 'That should've been a clue, shouldn't it? Who has a wedding photo showing the groom but not the bride? I'm an idiot.'

'So is our Gracie a liar or a fantasist? That's a lot of unnecessary effort for a cover story.'

'I know. She'd given names to all the kids – sounded one hundred per cent genuine when she was telling me about them. I think you're right; it is some sort of fantasy for her.' Tess passed him a Diana Skye book from her handbag. 'Speaking of which, I skimmed the blurbs for a few of these too. They're quite telling.'

'The Major's Mistress,' Liam read. 'Wish fulfilment for army brats, right?'

414

'Yep. A lot of them are on that theme – young girls, isolated and lonely in military encampments, find love with handsome men in uniform who offer them a better life.'

'You said her own books made her angry.'

'Not just angry. Bitter. Bitter that the dream never became a reality, I suppose.'

'Diana Skye . . . Nadia Harris.' He bashed his forehead with his palm. 'Oh my God! I can't believe I didn't see that before. The first name's an anagram, isn't it?'

'I noticed that today too. And Scottish islands for the surnames.'

'So she wrote the Charity letters,' Liam muttered. 'You think that's what this was all about – revenge for her sister?'

'I guess so,' Tess said. 'But how would she even know she had a sister? That's what I don't get.'

Liam thought for a moment. 'The Felix letters. The one that looked like it had been opened recently. That talked about mourning Charity, and a life having been taken.'

'And if she read that while she was at Ling Cottage for the Women's Guild meeting . . .'

'It might have made her angry enough to kill.'

Tess nodded. 'Not so difficult, is it? Pretend to leave, conceal yourself somewhere until Clemmie's alone and . . . well, we know the rest.'

'And she had access to Andrew Walton-Lord too, assuming she was the one impersonating Candice. He'd have been able to tell her about Charity.'

'So one by one, she got her revenge on everyone involved in covering up her sister's murder. Including her own parents.' Tess stood up. 'Come on. We should take all this to the police.'

'Right.' Liam put the photo of the real Grace Lister and the Diana Skye book into a satchel. 'Where's Marianne Priestley? At the wake?'

'No, she wasn't at the funeral. Bad cold, so she gave her eulogy to Candice to read.'

Liam spun to face her. 'Tess, for God's sake! I said she wasn't to be left alone, didn't I? Why didn't you tell me this earlier?'

'I know, but . . .' Tess grimaced. 'Sorry, Lee, I didn't think. She won't be in any danger now, will she?'

'Please tell me Gracie's down at the Star eating ham sandwiches with the rest of them.'

Tess's eyes widened. 'No. She didn't go either.'

'Right. Change of plan. We need to get up to Cherrywood Hall, right away.'

*

'Well, dear, how nice to see you,' Marianne said when she'd shown Gracie into the library and made them a cup of tea each. 'I thought you'd be at the wake.'

'I didn't feel right going, after Prue and I had cross words right before she . . . well, you know.' Gracie bowed her head. 'I thought perhaps I wouldn't be welcome.'

'Oh, nonsense. Of course you would.' Marianne paused to blow her nose. 'I'm so sorry. You've caught me in rather a weakened state today.'

'I know, you poor thing. I bumped into Candice earlier

and she told me you were feeling too poorly to go to the funeral.' Gracie put the jam she'd brought down on the table. 'I made this for you. It's spiced plum – ideal for clearing the sinuses.'

'Thank you, that's very thoughtful.'

Gracie's gaze fell on a Diana Skye book lying on the coffee table. 'I didn't know you were a fan of hers.'

'It's actually my first one,' Marianne said, laughing. 'Raven's always singing her praises so I thought I'd see what all the fuss was about.'

'What do you think?'

Marianne picked up *The Major's Mistress* and examined the cover. 'They're rather better written than I expected. I think I'm a little too unromantic to appreciate the plots, unfortunately.'

Gracie nodded. 'I'm the same, these days. I believed in it all once though.'

'We do when we're young, don't we? Although I never had much time for boys, even then.'

Gracie took the book from Marianne. 'I had the idea for this one when I was sixteen. There was a young officer I was enamoured of – you might say he was the inspiration. Although of course, it was many years until I had the skill to actually write it.'

Marianne blinked. '*You* had the idea for it?'

'Well, yes,' Gracie said. 'Didn't Raven tell you? I'm the author. I assumed it would be all over the village by now, Cherrywood being Cherrywood.'

'You? You're Diana Skye?'

'Certainly.'

'No. I don't believe it.'

'It's true, I promise you. Diana Skye is my pen name. An anagram, you know, of my real one. Clever, isn't it?'

'That's not an anagram of . . .' Marianne's heavy, cold-filled brain slowly caught up. 'You mean Gracie isn't your real name?'

'Well, my birth name is Grace, of course. But you know that, don't you, Marianne, as a very old friend of the family?' Gracie said sweetly. 'Such a good friend to my mother that you helped her sell me off to the highest bidder.'

'What?' Marianne whispered. 'You're her? You're Nadia Harris?'

'It's nothing personal, dear. Out of all my ladies you were always rather a favourite. But sin will out, you know, and in the end it has to be punished. I do hope you understand.'

'Gracie, good God! You can't be planning to—'

Gracie raised a hand. 'Now, Marianne, there really is no point arguing with me,' she said in the condescending tone a mother might use to reprimand a child. 'This is for your own good. I'm afraid I must insist that you have a spoonful or two of my jam.'

Chapter 40

'Any luck?' Liam said as he and Tess strode through the Italian garden towards the hall. Tess had her phone to her ear as she tried to get hold of Raven at the wake.

'No answer,' she said, hanging up. 'I guess she put her phone on silent while she was in church.'

'Damn it!'

'We're probably worrying over nothing. I'm sure Marianne's fine, Lee.'

'Yeah?' He nodded to a yellow Clio parked outside the hall. 'Whose car is that then?'

'Oh God,' Tess said, her eyes widening. 'Gracie's.'

'She's getting sloppy, parking up in plain view like that. She knows she's nearly out of time.' His brisk walk sped up into a run.

When they reached the house, Liam banged at the front door with the flat of his palm.

'Maybe she went out,' Tess said.

'Then why is Gracie's car here? We need to get in, Tess. God knows what's going on in there.'

She took her phone from her ear. 'No answer from Oliver either.'

'Right.' He turned to her. 'We'll never break that door down; it's solid oak. I'm going to drive to the pub and get Raven and Candice back here with the key, quick as I can. You call Della – I'll give you her number – and ask her to get all the coppers she can spare over here as soon as possible. We need to get into that house.'

*

The knock sounded again: loud, urgent, reverberating through the old oak and stone of Cherrywood Hall.

'I really ought to get that, Gracie,' Marianne whispered.

'I'm sorry, dear, but I can't let you do that.'

Marianne was in the armchair, her hands bound behind her with a length of rope. Weakened by her head cold, it hadn't been too difficult for the younger woman to overpower her. The knots were tight, burning into her wrists. Under her chair, Susie the Pomeranian whimpered in her sleep.

'What happened to you?' Marianne said, trying not to look at the jam as Gracie unscrewed the lid. 'Why would you kill your own mother? Surely not for the sake of two hundred thousand pounds?'

'Oh, no,' Gracie said, curling her lip as if the idea was beyond vulgar. 'No, this was never about the money. What would I do with it? I make plenty as Diana Skye, and I send nearly all of it to the charity for displaced children. Well, I was sort of a displaced child myself, wasn't I?'

'Then why did you kill Clemmie?'

'I would have thought that would have been obvious,' Gracie said, looking genuinely surprised. 'Didn't I tell you sin must be punished? It's been a long time since I stopped believing in a God who could do that for me.'

'You're unhinged. You must be.'

'Perhaps I am. And I think perhaps you would be too, in my circumstances.'

'I thought I was giving you away to a better life,' Marianne whispered. 'Didn't your adoptive parents treat you well?'

Gracie looked up from the jam and gave a bitter laugh. 'Oh yes, very. I had every luxury a little girl could want, until my mother died.'

'Betty died?'

'When I was nine. After that I still had every luxury a little girl could want. Except love, of course – that was a luxury too far. The colonel didn't think such things were important.'

'Did you know he wasn't your real father?'

Gracie nodded, and Marianne thought she detected a sheen of tears.

'Mother told me,' she said in a low voice. 'On her deathbed. I was illegitimate, my real parents a teenage servant girl and a debauched playboy lush. The Harrises had taken me to replace a dead child of their own.'

'That must have hurt.'

'Actually, I was rather carried away by the idea,' Gracie said dreamily. 'It sounded very romantic to a child with an overactive imagination. Mother even gave me a necklace, a Madonna and child medallion, that she said my real mother had wanted me to have. Well, that was the icing on the cake, so to speak. It was such a perfect little story that I stored it away in my heart. For a long time it was all that kept me going.'

'That's right. Clemmie bought the necklace to show that even though she'd had to give you away, she still thought of herself as your mum. Keeping a little part of herself close to you.' Marianne tried to catch Gracie's eye. 'She did love you, you know.'

'I thought so too,' Gracie muttered, speaking half to herself. 'I was starved of love, after Mother died. For years I wore that medallion, dreaming of the real mother I'd never known. I made an idol of her in my mind; bestowed every perfection I could think of on her. And I swore that one day, when I got free of the colonel, I'd find her.'

'Did the colonel mistreat you?' Marianne asked in a soft voice. 'He never struck me as a cruel man.'

Gracie gave another harsh laugh. 'He wouldn't have said so. I'm sure he thought he spoiled me. But he didn't want me – not after his wife was gone. He didn't abuse me, but he never showed me an ounce of love.'

'Poor little girl. You must have been so lonely.'

'Yes,' Gracie whispered. 'Yes, it was a lonely life, moving from place to place with a father who couldn't or wouldn't love me. Every time I made a friend, we'd move on and that would be that. I'd be on my own again.'

Gracie's eyes were hazy, far away in the past. Marianne rubbed her bound wrists against the chair, trying to loosen the knots, but she was too weak to budge them.

'I used to wish I had a sibling; someone to share that life with,' Gracie continued. 'Then when I got older, the dreams changed. I began to fantasise that someone would appear to give me all the love I couldn't find anywhere else – some handsome man who'd fall in love with me and whisk me away.'

Marianne glanced at her Diana Skye book. 'And those fantasies became your books.'

'Yes. But they were just stories; they never came true. I was a foolish child to think anything so happy, so convenient, could happen to someone like me.' Gracie reached up to touch her neck, where her Madonna would have been, then dropped her hand as if remembering. 'And all the time I clung tighter to the idea of my mother, my real mother, determined that one day I'd find her.'

'What happened next?' Marianne asked, interested in spite of her fear.

'When I was eighteen, my father died. Well, I made sure of it. He was getting frail and I couldn't bear the idea of having to care for him.'

'You mean you killed him too?'

Gracie nodded. 'We were living in Turkey. In the local language it was called *deli bal* – mad honey. It was a hallucinogen, very dangerous if taken in excess. Concentrated nectar of the rhododendron family, produced by honey bees. My father was old, with a weak heart, and he succumbed to it easily.'

'Oh my God,' Marianne muttered. 'The same poison you used on Prue.'

'Yes, the girls did me proud,' Gracie said with a fond smile. 'The honey they produced when I started gorging them on my azaleas was deadly in sufficient amounts. Mixed in with the chocolate icing for the cake, dear Aunt Prue never would have tasted it.'

'What did you do after you'd killed the colonel?'

'Well, I was finally free. That's when I started my search. It didn't take long to track down my real father, although it was many years later that I finally summoned the courage to confront him. For a long time I just watched from a distance, learning about him and his family, biding my time.'

'Andrew. How did you find him?'

'I knew where I'd been born: a little Yorkshire village called Cherrywood. Betty told me my father had been a wealthy drunk from an old family there. It wasn't too hard.'

'And then you went to see him.'

'Yes,' Gracie whispered. 'There was a woman – a little, stern-looking person – who visited him. I learnt her name, her routine. One day a new receptionist started. It wasn't hard to pass myself off as Candice.'

'Did Andrew know you?'

'I told him who I was the first day. On some visits he knew me; others he muddled me with different people – a sister who'd died, his brother's wife.' She sighed. 'He was very sweet. You know, I visited him for years; we became quite close. It was such a pity I had to kill him.'

Marianne stifled a shudder. 'So he told you everything, did he?' she asked.

'Over the years, yes, he came to trust me. In bits and pieces

I learnt it all – at least, nearly all. He told me about this girl he'd loved but been too cowardly to marry. About the twins she'd borne him, Grace and Charity, and how the elder had been saved while the frailer one was left to die. The guilt I felt, knowing that, was unbearable for a time.'

'I never knew Clemmie had named you,' Marianne murmured.

Gracie nodded. 'Grace. Such a pretty name; so much nicer than Nadia. After Nadia I was Penelope for a time – a baby whose identity I borrowed. But when I started searching graveyards for someone I could use to begin a new life in Cherrywood, I knew it would have to be a fellow Grace.'

'So it was Andrew who told you about your sister.'

'That's right. The sister I'd always dreamed of when I was being dragged from camp to camp. In my gut, I'd always felt I did have a sister. Do twins know on some level, do you think, that they are twins? After all, we shared a womb.'

Gracie stopped, waiting for a response – needing one, it seemed. Her eyes were wide, flashing with strange fire.

'I think perhaps they might do,' Marianne said, and Gracie gave her a grateful smile.

'But it wasn't Andrew who told me the whole truth – what happened to Charity, I mean,' she said. 'I think even on his bad days, something at the back of his mind reminded him it was secret. He told me she'd died, that Constance had let her die, and until the night I killed my mother I honestly believed the cause of her death was natural.'

'How did you find out the truth?'

'You remember the meeting?' Gracie asked. 'We were

425

filling the shoeboxes, Clemmie and Prue cool with each other as usual. And on top of it all, they'd gone and forgotten the friendship horseshoe again.' Gracie paused, frowning, as if this among all things still rankled. 'I left to use the bathroom. That raggedy kitty of Clemmie's was scratching at the sideboard in the study, a mahogany thing full of little lockable drawers, and suddenly I was curious. What secrets did she keep in there?'

'How did you get the key?'

'I didn't need it; the top two drawers were unlocked. There was nothing in the top one but old receipts. But the middle one . . . I thought it might be locked at first, but it opened easily with a little wiggle. I opened the letter on top and read it. It was signed Felix – that was Andrew's first name, which I suppose my mother called him by as a pet. It was written like a riddle, but I knew right away what it meant. Andrew had told me enough for me to put two and two together. "To take a life is a terrible sin," he wrote, and that he'd never be able to forgive Constance. I knew then that Charity had been murdered.'

'So you killed her. You killed your own mother.'

Gracie nodded. 'Once I knew about Charity, the idol fell. The perfect mother I'd dreamed of didn't exist. Clemency Ackroyd was a coward: weak – too weak to save my sister from that child-murdering bitch. That's when it hit me – all the anger, all hurt at what Clemmie had done to my sister and to me. I had to make sure she paid the price, for both of us.'

'She was a child, Gracie,' Marianne said, wincing at the

pain in her raw wrists. 'Seventeen. And yes, she was weak – physically weak. She'd just given birth to two babies. She saved your life when she asked me to smuggle you out.'

Gracie scoffed. 'Smuggle me out to what? A loveless life, no roots, no friends, no real family. And then to let her mother get away with it – to care for her, give her a life of ease and comfort with no consequences for what she'd done! Clemmie betrayed me, just like she betrayed Charity. You all did – Connie, Prue, Clemmie, Andrew. You. Did you really believe that could go unpunished?'

'We were trying to help you.' Marianne shuffled in her seat, feeling blood where the ropes dug into her flesh. 'Was this always your plan? To kill us?'

'Not at first. When I moved here, all I wanted was to get to know my relations. I planned, one day, to reveal who I was – still naive, still dreaming of the loving family I'd never had. It was only that night, when I finally understood what had been done to my sister, that I realised I had to avenge her.'

'Why did you write me the letters?'

'Oh, I didn't, dear,' Gracie said, looking puzzled. 'Charity wrote the letters. I merely transcribed them.'

Marianne shook her head. 'You're really quite insane, aren't you?'

'I don't think there's any need to get personal, do you? There's no reason we can't keep things civil.' Gracie picked up the jam. 'And now I think it's time to take your medicine.'

'Gracie, please,' Marianne said, watching in horror as she inserted a teaspoon into the jam and scooped out a generous spoonful. 'You don't need to do this.'

'But of course I do, my love. I can hardly let you live after I killed the others, now, can I?'

'Will it hurt?' Marianne whispered.

'Just a little, that's all. This jar contains a generous amount of hyoscine, a medicine that will cause respiratory failure when taken in overdose. It's made from deadly nightshade, you know. I fancied a change from azalea.'

'How do you know about all that?'

'Plumholme Women's Guild hosted a talk,' Gracie said. ' "Dr Crippen, His Life and Crimes" – he was a hyoscine devotee too. The regional federation have put on a fabulous programme this season, don't you think?'

'Yes, they've excelled themselves.'

'Now come on, don't make this any harder than it needs to be. Open wide.'

Marianne clenched her teeth and turned her face away as Gracie brought the spoon to her mouth, like a mother feeding a reluctant infant. But before Gracie could force her victim's mouth open to administer the poison, the door burst open and Liam and Tess came running in, with Candice, Raven and Oliver hot on their heels.

'Oh no you don't,' Liam panted as he pinioned Gracie's arms behind her back, the spoon of jam falling to the carpet. 'Say goodnight, Gracie. The show's over.'

Chapter 41

'"Say goodnight, Gracie"?' Tess said later when the fireworks were all over and she, Liam, Oliver and Raven were sitting round a table at the Star. 'Is there a special module on one-liners you have to take at Police Academy?'

'Punning and snark is actually most of the first year.'

Oliver took a long draw on his pint. 'It's certainly been an action-packed few months. I reckon I'll be good for drama for the next fifty years or so.'

'It's sad, isn't it?' Raven said. 'I mean about Gracie, or Nadia or whatever she was called. She couldn't have been in her right mind. I suppose the loneliness drove her a bit loopy.'

'Grace. Divine favour.' Oliver sighed. 'Ironic really. She got a tough lot in life.'

The whole thing had been quite surreal. Gracie, her murderous plan foiled, had greeted them as calmly and politely as if she'd been welcoming them to a tea party. Meek as a child, she'd gone along with Marianne and Candice when they'd insisted they should be the ones to accompany her to the station, and they'd supported her with a strange sort of tenderness to the police car.

'I suppose she'll get life for it,' Tess said. 'It's weird to think of Gracie Lister in prison, knitting those little floppy bears in her cell.'

'I suspect it might be a psychiatric facility for that one,' Liam said. 'Raven's right. She can't have been in her right mind.'

'So she's family,' Raven said. 'I'll have to visit her.'

'You'd do that?' Liam asked. 'She killed four people. Your uncle among them.'

'I know. Still, it's hard not to pity her.' Raven shuddered. 'The way she smiled at us. It's all so gruesome.'

'Hey, do you still own a mansion?' Oliver asked her.

She frowned. 'Good point. I suppose Gracie might have been Andrew's heir, mightn't she? He was her dad.'

'Her parents weren't married, though,' Tess said. 'In books that always means you get bugger all. Not to mention that it was her who killed him.'

'Yeah, I don't know how all that works.' Raven brightened. 'So there's a chance I might not own Cherrywood Hall after all.'

Tess laughed. 'The reluctant heiress. Now there's a Diana Skye title.'

'Will Marianne be OK?' Liam asked.

'I think so,' Raven said. 'She was pretty shaken up but she's a tough old thing. Grandmother knows how to look after her.'

Tess nudged her. 'Hey. There'll be a vacancy for Women's Guild president now. What do you reckon?'

Raven laughed. 'Oh no, darling, not me.'

'You could schedule spa days and gin-tasting every month.'

'Hmm, that's true. I'll think it over.'

'So Gracie attacked her mother with the clock after she worked out how Charity died,' Oliver said. 'Why did she switch the necklaces?'

'She told Marianne she wore the Madonna that Clemmie gave her for years,' Raven said. 'Saw it as representing the perfect mother she'd imagined Clemmie must be. I suppose when that dream was shattered, she felt as a symbol it was rather hollow.'

'So she replaced the St Christopher Clemmie wore to keep her absent daughter safe with her own Madonna,' Tess said. 'It was a sneer, I think – a last cocked snook to the woman she felt had betrayed her. Then I guess she dropped the St Christopher in the mud when she was fleeing the house, where Candice found it.'

'And for Prue she used azalea honey produced by her own bees,' Oliver said. 'Colonel Harris too. Ghoulish, really.'

Liam nodded. 'I'm guessing she'd found out about Peggy's affair with Ian – let's face it, they were hardly discreet. I can't imagine it was difficult to watch from a concealed place until she saw Ian arrive at Peggy's before *Mamma Mia*, then wait until they were doing the deed to sneak in and mix her honey with the chocolate icing for the hair. She must have realised Prue was on the cusp of working out she was Nadia Harris. Although I suspect murder had always been her plan – knowing Prue was on to her just speeded things up.'

'Gracie even ate a bit of the Darcy icing herself to deflect suspicion,' Tess said. 'Just enough to make her sick, of course, not to kill. I imagine she spat most of it into a bush on her way out. And she made sure she was first on buffet duty before she went home, where she could dish out the poisoned section of cake to Prue.'

'Azalea poisoning sounds like a nasty way to go,' Raven said. 'I hope poor Uncle Andrew didn't suffer like that.'

'Mmm. The rotten peanuts,' Liam said. 'The fat in them can be fatal to someone whose liver is already diseased. Gracie snuck them in inside a hamper, disguised as Candice. Police found the wig she must've worn hidden in her attic, along with the typewriter used to write the Charity letters.'

There was a sombre silence as the four of them sipped their drinks, reflecting on the grisly events of the last few months.

'So what happens now?' Tess said.

Oliver shrugged. 'I guess everything goes back to normal. And may I be the first to say, hurrah and thank the Lord.'

'Not too normal, though,' Raven said, smiling. 'You've still got a girlfriend.'

'All right, that is pretty unusual.' He waved to Tammy, who was serving behind the bar. She blushed a little as she waved back.

Liam nudged Tess. 'Disappointed?'

'What, that justice has been served? Course I'm not.'

'That things are about to go back to normal. You've enjoyed sleuthing with me, haven't you? You're addicted to solving puzzles, admit it.'

'True. But in future I think I'll stick to Sudoku, which is

for the most part non-lethal.' She grinned at him. 'I did solve it though.'

'Sorry?'

'I solved the case for you. I was the one who worked out Gracie was Nadia Harris. You're welcome.'

'Don't get smug. You know I'd have got there eventually.'

'Yeah, and by the time you did Marianne would've been dead. So again I say, you're welcome.'

He smiled. 'You certainly earned your fee; I'll admit that much. Well done, partner.'

'When will you be going home to London?' Tess asked. 'Will you wait until after the trial?'

'Actually, no.'

'What, you're going back right away?' Tess was so weary after the events of the day, she didn't even bother to check the stab of disappointment her treacherous body had the temerity to feel.

'Yes. I've got a few things to sort out down there. But I'll be back in a week or so.'

'Back? What for?'

'Well, you know that empty office above the chip shop next door to your flat?'

'Yeah?'

'It's about to be not so empty.' Liam grinned. 'Meet your new neighbour, Tessie. Cherrywood Investigations is opening for business.'

Acknowledgements

I'm very grateful to the team at Headline, and in particular my editor Bea Grabowska, for helping make this book the best that it can be. I'd also like to thank my former agent Laura Longrigg, who worked with me on this book before her retirement, and to my current agent Hannah Todd for her advice and support.

Also, a special thanks to my writer friend Marie Laval, who has probably forgotten the anecdote she once told me over tea and cake in Hebden Bridge that helped to inspire a scene in this book!

Acknowledgements